THE ABERRATION

BY

AL GIANNINI

JAMES PAUL PUBLISHING COMPANY
4888 Davis Boulevard Box 110
Naples, Florida 34104

With the exception of John Licciardi, my lawyer and my friend, who appears in this yarn under his own name, all of the characters in this book are fictitious contrivances of the author's imagination, and any resemblance to actual persons, living or dead, is purely coincidental.

Book and dust jacket designed by
POON & GIANNINI ADVERTISING, INC.
Providence, RI

Published by
JAMES PAUL PUBLISHING COMPANY
Naples, Florida

Printed in the United States of America
May 2000
First Edition

ISBN 0-9679457-0-4

Acknowledgments

To Nick and Paula Shirghio, and
to Helmut and Marlies Lange.
They were there for me when I needed them most.

To Cheryl Deering and Dr. Nancy J. Carini for their blind and unquestioned faith in me.

To Annemarie, my lovely wife, for her patience and forbearance. Without her unfailing encouragement and her unwavering support, the writing of this book would have been impossible.

To Rose and Pierino, my father and mother, for their undying devotion to each other and to us, their children. They have passed from this earth but they are not gone. The values they instilled in us by their living example could only have been drawn from the strength of their rock-solid faith in God. These pages explore the clash of those values with those of the title character, *The Aberration*.

ONE

Providence, Rhode Island
1927

THE UNDERTONE of their voices rebounded off the marble floor and walls from across the cavernous bank lobby but Giuseppe couldn't make out their words. It didn't matter. He wasn't interested in what they were saying. Giuseppe pretended to be occupied by noisily rubber-stamping meaningless scraps of paper that he would immediately discard, but his focus was on Mr. Downey, the office manager. Downey was engaged in obsequious conversation with a plump, ostentatiously dressed matron who looked down her nose at him while she briskly cooled herself with an accordion-fold fan.

He had been avoiding Giuseppe for more than a week.

The bell of the trolley clanging outside the bank's front window drew Giuseppe's attention from behind the brass bars of his teller's station. He turned to see the conductor gesturing angrily at the LaSalle touring car that partially blocked the trolley tracks, and the liveried chauffeur who leaned against it smoking a cigarette while totally ignoring the trolley conductor's angry demands.

Giuseppe was relieved when, finally, the matron offered her limp-wristed hand to Downey. He took it and led her to the door where, bowing and scraping in obeisance, he bid her good day. The chauffeur saw them coming. He quickly flipped his cigarette into the street, turned to open the car door for his employer, and with his back to her, he smiled at the trolley man and gave him the finger.

Mr. Downey scurried back to his desk, mopping his brow with his handkerchief. Giuseppe saw his chance. He placed the NEXT TELLER sign in his window—though it struck him as an empty gesture, since, with the departure of the matron, there was not a single customer in the bank—and headed across the lobby to intercept Mr. Downey.

"Mr. Downey, excuse me, please," Giuseppe called as he hurriedly approached his boss.

Downey turned. At the sight of Giuseppe's tall, broad-shouldered shape bearing down on him, he flinched. Giuseppe dwarfed Downey whose eyes widened in alarm behind his gold-rimmed glasses. Giuseppe, recognizing Mr. Downey's apprehension, slowed to a stop and came the rest of the way slowly.

"Excuse me, Mr. Downey. Did you talk to him yet?" Giuseppe spoke in a subdued, deferential tone.

"Oh good heavens!" Mr. Downey's high-pitched voice was tight with lingering anxiety. "Must we do this again?"

"But Mr. Downey, it's been almost two months."

"I told you! I'll talk with him when the time is right."

Giuseppe hesitated, not wanting to defeat his purpose by appearing too pushy, then continued, "But surely, there must have been some … "

"When the time is right and not before! Mr. Bishop is president of this bank! He can't be bothered with every wild-eyed idea that's bandied about by one of you guin… ," Mr. Downey's face flushed as his faux pas resonated in the silence.

" … by one of your kind," he stammered. "Now please return to your window." His forehead grew clammy. He patted it nervously with his handkerchief.

Giuseppe bristled over the near insult but recovered quickly.

"My kind, Mr. Downey?" Giuseppe asked with a smile. "I'm not sure what you mean. Could you be more specific? Were you going to say guinea? Perhaps wop or dago might have been more definitive?"

Still patting his brow, Mr. Downey glanced furtively around the lobby.

"Never mind! I've said all I'm going to say. Go back to your window."

"My window, Mr. Downey?" Giuseppe turned and gestured with a broad sweep of his arm as he continued, "Look at my window. Look at the other windows. There's nobody waiting. I don't know as much about banking as you, Mr. Downey, but I know one thing. You've got to have customers. Putting money in. Taking money out. Borrowing money. Paying back loans. You've got to have money going both ways all the time at those windows."

Giuseppe paused, turning slowly, scanning the entire bank from where they stood in the middle of the lobby. The other employees feigned disinterest in them.

"My idea is a good one," said Giuseppe. His passion grew as he continued. "A lot of, excuse me—*my kind*—would be good customers. They work hard. They put away for the future. But they don't have time to come down-city. When this bank is open, my people are working. When they get off from work, the bank is closed. Do you think they are going to take time off from work just for the pleasure of doing business with you?"

"You are bordering on insolence, Mr. Parisi. I order you back to your window at once!" His voice became louder, higher-pitched.

Giuseppe disregarded the command. He looked for a long time into Mr. Downey's eyes, searching for any sign of understanding. He found nothing there.

"Excuse me, but I don't think so," said Giuseppe. His voice was sad but resolute. "I don't have to follow your orders."

"How dare you?! You will do as I say! I am your superior!" Spittle foamed at the corners of his mouth.

"No, Mr. Downey. You were my boss, but you were *never* my superior. And now, I no longer work here."

He had saved most of what he earned since the day he started with the bank as an errand boy. He withdrew his savings, and with his money bulging against his chest in the inside pocket of his jacket, he left the bank for good.

GIUSEPPE WALKED BRISKLY from downtown Providence to Federal Hill. He wore a look of determination on his face as he maneuvered through the clusters of housewives who crowded the sidewalks picking over the fresh fruit and vegetables while they haggled about the prices with the pushcart peddlers. Shoppers and storekeepers alike, all neighbors, nodded hello to Giuseppe or called out greetings to him. He didn't see or hear them.

He was focused and intense but when he caught sight of the barber pole at Lorenzo Lanieri's shop a short distance ahead, his resolve crumbled. His pace slowed. Without thinking, he came to a stop. He had been so sure of himself just a half hour earlier when he quit his job but now he hesitated. He stared at the hypnotically spiraling barber pole, summoning his courage.

TWO

THERE WAS ONLY one customer in the shop and Giuseppe was glad it was Jack O'Hearn. Jack and his family were the only non-Italians in the entire district. They had lived there since long before Giuseppe was born. He was like a Dutch uncle to Giuseppe and to all the other kids that grew up with him. Everyone had a deep respect for Jack O'Hearn, a clean-living family man who went to Mass every day, and Jack returned it in kind.

Jack had risen through the ranks from rookie fireman to Battalion Chief. In the course of their growing up, he had taken every kid in the neighborhood, boys and girls alike, for a ride on Ladder 11. When any kid did something special, like make the honor roll or achieve some athletic honor, that kid would get to ride with Mr. O'Hearn at the tiller, the steering wheel that's located at the very rear end of the truck. The kids idolized him. They would rather have been beaten by their parents than to have earned a rebuke from Mr. O'Hearn.

Lorenzo Lanieri was stropping his razor with O'Hearn tilted back in the chair, his face lathered up, when Giuseppe entered.

"Hey Giuseppe, w'at da hell you doin' here?" Lorenzo's natural tendency was to speak Italian but, though O'Hearn spoke fluent Italian, Lorenzo considered it impolite to initiate it himself. He continued in his version of English, "You sucha big shot now at Industrial

Trusta Bank," at those words he crossed himself with elaborate mock ceremony drawing a chuckle from O'Hearn, "they let you take the day off?"

"Hello Giuseppe," said O'Hearn. He gave Giuseppe an approving once-over as he continued in his soft, Irish brogue, "It's clear you don't need a haircut. Yet, here you are looking fine and dapper, all dressed up in your handsome business duds, when you're supposed to be down-city foreclosing on some poor, defenseless widow." His smile was warm as always but his eyes asked for an explanation.

"Hello, Mr. O'Hearn." Giuseppe smiled back bravely, but he was so nervous he missed the joke. His level of confidence was far less than what he felt a half hour earlier when he quit his job.

Unable to remember the opening lines of the speech he had prepared, he simply blurted out, "Mr. Lanieri, I'd like to borrow your back room. I've decided to go into the banking business. I just quit my job so I can get started right away."

Lorenzo stopped stropping in mid-stroke, "You w'at?! You quitta you job? W'at kinda dumb summinabitchin' thing you do you quitta you job?!"

Jack O'Hearn reached over the side of the chair for the handle, pumped the chair upright and wiped the lather from his face with Lorenzo looking from one to the other in bewilderment.

"I had to do it, Mr. Lanieri," said Giuseppe. "I've wanted to do it for some time but I was afraid. Now, they made the decision for me."

"They've let you go, have they?" asked O'Hearn. "Is that what you're tryin' to tell us, lad?"

"No sir, Mr. O'Hearn. It wasn't like that at all. It's just that I decided there's no future for me there, so I quit, just like I said."

For a moment, Lorenzo was dumbstruck.

"You jus' t'ree months married wit' a wife an' you quitta you fuckinna job?! *Stunate!* W'atta you thinka that Mr. O'Hearn? He quitsa the steady job an' now he wanna open up a summinabitchin' bank! Inna fuckinna barber shop! *Che cazzo* Giuseppe, w'at th' hella you thinkin' about?"

"I know it might sound crazy to y... "

"Mighta sound crazy?! No! No mighta! Its for sure! You crazy!" Lorenzo continued. "An' you wife, w'atta she gonna say? Soon maybe you getta bambino an' you no gotta job an' you sit all day in back-a-da-shop play wit' youself an' den … "

"Excuse me, Mr. Lanieri," Giuseppe shot back, instantly regretting the heat that sounded in his own voice, "but what I say to my wife and what she says to me is between her and m… "

"*I* no wait a minute, *you* wait a minute … ," Lorenzo was silenced by the touch of O'Hearn's hand on his arm.

O'Hearn hadn't taken his eyes off Giuseppe during their heated exchange. Turning to Lorenzo, he said gently, "Lorenzo, old friend, it's clear that whatever is happening here isn't easy for the lad. Why don't we just let him say what he has to say in his own way and in his own time. Go on Giuseppe, we'll try to stay out of your way."

"Thank you, Mr. O'Hearn." Giuseppe turned to Lorenzo, gently took his shoulders in his hands and looked him squarely in the eyes as he continued softly, "Mr. Lanieri, I apologize if I've offended you. You've honored me with your friendship for as long as I can remember and I don't want anything to change that. I would never intentionally do anything to upset you but it's obvious that I did and I'm sorry."

Giuseppe turned to O'Hearn as he continued, "You too, Mr. O'Hearn. I'll always remember when I won a spelling bee in school and you let me ride with you in the tiller seat at the back of the fire truck. That's a memory a ten-year-old will never forget. You both mean a lot to me. I think you know that. Please try to understand."

Giuseppe paused to collect his thoughts, then continued, "This isn't something that fell on my head this morning like Newton's apple." The analogy was lost on Lorenzo but its gist was not. "When I try to convince my bosses at Industrial that my idea is a good one, they almost laugh at me. I've thought it through and I've dwelled on it for a long time."

"You've thought what through? What is it you have in mind, lad?" asked O'Hearn.

Giuseppe was, at first, tentative, but as he looked from one to the other, his energy grew. He stepped briskly to the cash register. Looking to Lorenzo, his expression asked permission to open it. Lorenzo nodded his OK. Giuseppe took two bills from the register, handed one to Lorenzo and the other to O'Hearn.

"Smell them," said Giuseppe.

"W'at did you say? Smella them?"

"Smell, lad? Smell the money?"

"That's right. Humor me! Just close your eyes and smell them." Giuseppe was bursting with anticipation as Lorenzo and O'Hearn self-consciously sniffed the bills.

"Well? What do you smell?"

"Coffee?" asked O'Hearn. "Do I smell coffee?"

"Me too. That'sa what this one smells like too," said Lorenzo.

Giuseppe collected the bills and returned them to the register. He bent over and put his nose to the open cash drawer.

"And your cash drawer smells like a coffee can," Giuseppe announced with enthusiasm.

"Has the lad suddenly gone daft, Mr. Lanieri?" asked O'Hearn.

Lorenzo shook his head, chuckling softly as he began to see where Giuseppe was going.

"Excuse me, Mr. O'Hearn. I hope you don't mind my asking, but where do you keep your money?"

"I don't mind at all. I keep it in the bank. The very bank where you work … where you *used* to work."

"And how far is the bank from your office at headquarters?"

"Why, it's one block over. You know that, Giuseppe."

"And how about you, Mr. Lanieri? Where do you keep … ?"

Lorenzo, alternately shaking and nodding his head, saw it coming. "In a coffee can, Giuseppe. Just'a like mosta my customers."

"I'm astonished," exclaimed O'Hearn. "Why in the world … ?"

Giuseppe answered for Lanieri, "Because Mr. Lanieri's office is *not* one block over from the bank. It's right here … a thirty minute walk to the bank. I know. I just came from there."

O'Hearn sent a questioning look to Lorenzo. Lorenzo shrugged and replied, "When I canna go to the bank? Durin' lunch? Afta people get offa work? That'sa the only time they can come for a haircut. The bank'sa no open when I'ma not workin'."

"Exactly!" said Giuseppe. "That's what I tried to tell my bosses at the bank. I told them there's a lot of money sitting in a lot of coffee cans. Money that the bank could use for investment and growth. I told them they have to make it easy for people to take it out of their coffee cans and put it in the bank. How? They have to open small offices. Right in the neighborhoods where the people live. And they have to stay open late so people can go to the bank after they get home from work."

As he spoke, Giuseppe reached into his jacket, pulled out a bulky envelope and tossed it gently to O'Hearn. O'Hearn saw it was loaded with cash. He looked up questioningly at Giuseppe who nodded his approval. With raised eyebrows, O'Hearn thumbed through the bills as Giuseppe continued.

"My bosses are not interested in my idea. There's no future for me at Industrial so I decided to make my own future. I've saved almost every dime I ever earned and now it's time. I'm confident I can make it work. And so is my wife, Mr. Lanieri."

Lorenzo responded with a sheepish grin, a shrug of his shoulders and a gentle, dismissive backhand wave of his hand as though he were brushing away his own earlier allusion.

"I know it won't be easy to get started," Giuseppe continued. "I can't pay rent, but I'll give you a percentage of my profits. And it won't be fancy, but my first customers won't mind doing business from your back room. They'll be people who already know me, and if they know me, they know they can trust me."

O'Hearn handed the envelope to Lorenzo, motioning with his eyes for Lorenzo to look inside. Lorenzo riffled through the cash as Giuseppe continued.

"They will, in turn, send others to me. That, of course, is what I'm counting on."

Lorenzo and O'Hearn exchanged glances.

"That is a great sum of money, lad," said O'Hearn. "I'm proud of you, as I am sure Mr. Lanieri is."

"Giuseppe, *figlio mi'!*" Lorenzo softly exclaimed. Then, with quick movements, he slipped the envelope into Giuseppe's inside jacket pocket and patted it down. With that he went to the door, hung the BACK IN THIRTY MINUTES sign, glanced furtively both ways out the windows, drew down the window shades, locked the door and turned off the lights.

There, in a darkened barbershop, with two old friends conspiring to help their young and determined friend get started, Providence Savings & Loan was born.

THREE

Providence
1972

"IS HE IN?" It was a perfunctory question. Luco Parisi wasn't interested in an answer. He didn't even glance at his father's secretary as he bullied his way past her desk. He was twenty-four, handsome in a slick way, and full of himself.

Helen Franklin had been Giuseppe's private secretary since long before Luco graduated from Brown and joined the firm. She was devoted to Giuseppe, but whenever his son, Luco, came near, she had to repress an involuntary shudder of contempt.

"I'll ask him if he can see you," she began but Luco continued straight for Giuseppe's door. She chased after him as he ignored both her words and her presence. With Helen close on his heels, he pushed through the closed door without so much as a polite knock.

Giuseppe Parisi was standing behind his desk, gazing out the window as he talked on the phone. He spun in surprise when they entered.

"I'm sorry Mr. Parisi," Helen protested, "I tried to … " She cut herself off and drew her hand apologetically to her lips when she saw he was on the phone.

Giuseppe gave her an understanding nod before his eyes fell upon Luco in a long, withering look. Then he turned his back and spoke quietly into the phone.

"Something has come up, Martin," said Giuseppe. "Can we finish this at another time? Yes. Thank you. Goodbye."

Giuseppe turned away from the windows, placed the phone into its cradle and continued to stare at it. After a long time, he went to Helen, took her by the arm and guided her to the door.

"It's all right, Helen," he said softly. "I understand. Don't give it another thought." Ignoring Luco, he, ushered her out and closed the door quietly behind her. For a long moment, he stood facing the door, his back to Luco. When he turned, Luco was leaning back in Giuseppe's chair behind the desk, hands clasped behind his head, half-turned to the windows, enjoying the view with his feet up on Giuseppe's desk.

Luco didn't hear his father approach, the thick carpet having silenced his footfalls. Sensing his presence, Luco looked up to see his father standing at his feet, glaring at him. Luco responded with an insolent grin.

"Lighten up, Pop. You're what, sixty-eight?" said Luco in a light, throwaway manner, "It's gonna be my chair before long anyway. I'm just breaking it in."

Giuseppe was not amused. He continued to glare at Luco.

Luco recognized the finality in his father's gaze. With forced casualness and a condescending snicker, he got out from behind the desk. He looked up into his father's eyes with barely concealed scorn, adjusted his lapels and shot his cuffs, then waited for his father to step aside. Giuseppe remained in place. Luco had no choice but to detour around him.

"What is so important that you had to behave like an overbearing, unrefined oaf?!" asked Giuseppe. His voice was tight with disgust. Luco paid scant attention to him. He wandered around the office as though taking inventory and assessing the value of the furnishings and decorations.

"Aw gee, Pop. I'm sorry if I embarrassed you," said Luco. He wandered back to face his father who stood eight inches taller. Tilting his head back to look up into his face, Luco continued with obviously feigned awe, "It's just that I get all quivery with goose-bumps whenever I come anywhere near this office."

For a long time, Giuseppe looked silently at his son. When, finally, he spoke, his voice was low but intense.

"Your mother never could see past your manipulative smile. God rest her soul, what could she possibly have been thinking when she left you all her stock? Until the day I die, I'll never understand it."

Luco's grin faded.

Giuseppe walked slowly to the door. As he reached for the doorknob, he continued, "And, yes, Luco, you're right. I'm sixty-eight, but neither you nor I know what the good Lord has in store for me."

He opened the door and, turning to face Luco, he said, "So, in the meantime, unless I specifically invite you in, you will stay *out of that chair* and *out of this office*. Now, get out!"

Luco, though burning inside, willed an air of nonchalance upon himself. He ambled to the door where he paused and said in a matter-of-fact tone, "By the way. You're on your own for lunch today. I have an appointment and it might run a little late."

"A *business* appointment?"

Luco stopped short and hesitated.

"Sure, Pop," he said with a patronizing smile. "Of course. What else?"

Luco gave his father a wink and a flippant, two-fingered salute, then turned and left the office without another word.

For a long, painful moment, Giuseppe stared in silent gloom at the door.

FOUR

GIUSEPPE DIDN'T DELUDE HIMSELF about the kind of appointment Luco was rushing off to keep. He had never lost sight of the fact that Luco had been chasing girls ever since junior high school. In spite of the all-to-frequent phone calls from angry parents who demanded that Luco stay away from their daughters, Luco's mother continued to shower him with extravagant gifts, effectively nullifying Giuseppe's efforts to exercise control over their son's behavior. He was nonetheless devoted to his wife and to her memory, but Giuseppe was unforgiving of himself for having allowed her to so greatly influence the formulation of Luco's values.

HIGH SCHOOL FOR Luco Parisi had been a three-year party. He was intelligent enough to manage a B average without putting any effort into it. He also made the starting lineup on the varsity baseball team in spite of dodging every practice and workout that he could get away with. He could have been a standout had he approached his studies and baseball with the same dedicated fervor that he applied to his pursuit of excellence in the art of fornication, to which he had been initiated, albeit in rudimentary fashion, in the eighth grade. Aiding him in his quest were the very generous spending allowance slipped to him each week by his doting mother and the new, red '64 Camaro she gave him on his sixteenth birthday.

Luco was soon very much in demand by the ardent, though heretofore-sexually-deprived, post-pubescent, female population of Hope High School. He had earned deserved renown as one who was abundantly talented and generously equipped to render the services for which they lusted. Luco made no attempt to discourage the propagation of his legend.

Tales of his licentious crusade preceded him to Brown University where he made his offerings available to all. The scope of his generosity extended beyond the all-female student body of neighboring Pembroke College to the singularly lithe and supple body of Brown's Dean of Psychology, Dr. Hannah Job. Hannah had long ago come to terms with the unfortunate appellation evoked by her name. She was thirty-eight and though she concealed it with loose-fitting and dowdy clothing, she took narcissistic pride in her exquisite body. She harbored a growing resentment toward her husband, the varsity soccer coach. He was spending more and more time at the British Club with his chums, throwing darts, drinking beer and nurturing the growth of a world-class belly.

At first Hannah had discounted the magnitude if not the essence of the awe-struck accounts of Luco Parisi's performance. Accounts that had found their way to her through the grapevine, having originated from grateful and gratified beneficiaries of Luco's libidinous largess. After he signed up for one of Dr. Job's courses, she conceded to herself that he did indeed emit a magnetic and strangely erotic force-field. The thought struck her that it might be a good idea to look into it more closely. Perhaps she might even do a paper on his type. She decided to do a clinical case study of him.

One misty afternoon, with the ECAC soccer quarterfinals being played a mere two blocks away at Brown Stadium, Hannah summoned Luco to her second floor flat under the pretext of discussing a recent paper Luco had turned in. She greeted him at the door wearing a soccer team jersey that stopped a little below mid-thigh.

"Well hel-*lo*, Doctor Job." Deliberately, slowly, he surveyed her entire body from top to bottom and back, his eyes coming to rest on the imprint of her nipples. Luco was stunned, but in an instant, he recovered, with the delightful speculation that she might be wearing nothing under it. With a leer, he said, "How good to see you."

Hannah waved him in, closing the door behind him. She said, "Let's not stand on ceremony here in my home. Why don't I call you Luco and you can call me Hann."

"Hann?" he asked, disbelieving. She was setting him up according to plan.

"Yes, Hann. Come now, Luco, you're not going to pretend that you've never heard my full nickname are you? After all, we're adults and we can speak freely, can't we?" she replied with a gesture consisting of a loosely closed fist, palm facing the ceiling, moving back and forth in front of her the way a crap player shakes the dice before a roll. She smiled inwardly at the incredulous look on his face as he silently completed the thought that she had planted, 'Doctor Job. Hannah Job. Hann Job. Hand-Job Hannah!' She had shaken him. This was going exactly as she had planned.

Hannah sat him in a soft sofa and took a seat opposite him in a hard, straight-backed chair that placed her knees almost at his eye level. She put on a pair of glasses with oversized, circular lenses. While pretending to examine his paper, she crossed and uncrossed her legs several times, each time awarding him tantalizing confirmation that she, indeed, wore nothing under her jersey. Peering undetected over the top of the paper, she concealed her satisfaction.

When she thought he had simmered long enough, she stood up and faced him, saying, "Luco, would you mind very much assisting me in a clinical experiment? I feel you would make a marvelous case study." She didn't wait for an answer.

Slowly and deliberately, inch by tantalizing inch, she raised her jersey over her head and let it fall to the floor, hanging from one of her fingers. She turned and with the jersey trailing along behind her from her finger, she walked languidly down the hall to the bedroom door where she paused, turned to him and said, "Come now, Luco. In case you haven't noticed, you're alone with a naked woman who would like very much to get laid. I'll be waiting in here."

When Luco burst into the room seconds later, it was immediately clear that he was armed and ready. Hannah, wearing only her glasses, lay half reclining against the over-stuffed pillows she had propped up for that purpose. Though she was still intent on conducting this endeavor as an academic exercise, she heard her own involuntary intake of breath as she caught sight of Luco's nakedness.

Luco addressed himself without delay to the assignment at hand. Hannah, in response to certain of his more exploitive techniques, found herself at cross purposes. On the one hand, her plan had been to remain detached so as to make mental notes for later recording. On the other hand, she had never before been laid like this. She tried to resist the temptation to join in with abandon.

"Mmm, I see," she said in a tone as though she were examining a student's paper. Then, though still fighting to keep her case study idea from slipping out of focus, she said with an emphasis she had not intended to reveal, "Yes, I see. I do see! I do! I do! Yes!"

Responding to her awakened enthusiasm, Luco shifted into four-wheel drive. He became the personification of eroticism in perpetual motion. Without conscious thought, Hannah discontinued the delusion that she was conducting a clinical experiment. The pretense over, she released herself to Luco's extraordinary talents.

"It's becoming clear. Yes. Clear! YES!" she began with a choked whisper that rose to a shriek. "I understand! Oh, GOD, I underSTAND!"

AN INTERESTED OBSERVER, had there been one, might have noticed that Hannah's recurring need for Luco to come to her home for 'academic review' coincided with dart tournaments at the British Club or with soccer games—preferably away games.

She suffered no delusions that she had exclusive rights to Luco's services. Nevertheless, though she couldn't avoid the sting of jealousy when observing his never-ending mating ritual with others, Hannah contrived other ways to be in his company. She and her husband would, from time to time, invite several Brown and Pembroke upperclassmen for wine and cheese discussion group sessions.

It was at one of those in his junior year that Luco zeroed in on a tiny, dark-haired Pembroke sophomore named Marla. He cut her out of the herd, but try as he might for much of the evening, he couldn't make any headway with her. She tried to convince him that she was waiting for her boyfriend to get off work and meet her there. Luco would have none of it, even as she insistently refused him, explaining that she really did have a boyfriend and his name was Phil Peters. At the mention of his name, he flew into a blind rage, insulted her, and stormed away from her.

WITHIN MINUTES OF the graduation ceremony, Marla became Mrs. Phil Peters and Phil was signed by the New York Yankees. For three years he made a name for himself with their minor league club, had gotten a lot of good press, and was a sure bet to be called up to the majors in time for the next spring training.

During those same three years, Luco Parisi had risen to a middle-level executive position at Greater Providence Bank & Trust. However, he enjoyed a level of authority and influence that far exceeded his official position, largely as a result of his instinctive ability, and shameless willingness, to manipulate to his personal advantage the fact that he was Giuseppe Parisi's son.

Also during those three years, although Luco had enjoyed the favors of countless women, many whose names he had long since forgotten and some whose names he had never learned, there was one name that had been indelibly etched into his memory.

When Luco heard Marla was in town, he needed only a few phone calls to learn she was staying at the Downtown Marriott. Seizing the opportunity, he contrived to 'accidentally' run into her while Phil was at pre-game practice. Luco had never forgotten about his last encounter with Marla.

Nor had Marla. At the sight of Luco approaching her in the hotel lobby, the memory flooded back to her.

Though she was pleased about coming home, she was painfully aware that the few days she would spend in Rhode Island would do little to diminish the bleakness of the interminable road trips she felt forced to take with Phil and the team. So when Luco invited her for lunch, she fought back the welling surge of disgust that lodged in her throat, telling herself that, perhaps, spending a little time with Luco would make her life with Phil seem brighter by comparison.

During lunch, her distaste for Luco simmered beneath the surface of her placid smile as she looked across the table at him, only half-listening to his idle chatter. Luco paused while the waiter delivered a fresh cocktail to Marla and cleared the table.

"Thank you, Luco," she said after taking a sip of her drink. "I wasn't looking forward to another solitary lunch. This was a nice surprise."

"Yeah. I couldn't believe my eyes when I saw you step out of the elevator. But then … "

Luco's voice trailed off. There was something in the way Marla peered at him over the rim of her glass that he was unable to read. Was she coming on to him? Was she challenging him? Was she simply feeling the effects of the alcohol?

"Then, what?" she asked.

"It's just that … well … that last time … at Professor Job's party? I thought you might still be holding it against me. I wouldn't blame you if you did."

"We were in college. College kids do dumb things."

"Maybe so," he said, "but I did come on pretty strong."

"Strong?" Marla asked. She took a long pull from her drink, placed it on the table, and slouched back in her chair. A humorless grin slowly formed on her lips but never made it to her eyes. In a mocking tone, mimicking his voice, she said, *"Awright! Have it your way, bitch! But someday you're gonna come crawling to me with your legs open, and when I'm finished with you, I'm gonna dump you!"*

Luco glanced self-consciously around the room.

"Yeah … some people might think that was a bit strong," she said with a trace of bitterness. Then she sat up and continued in an off-handed manner. "Look. You were feeling your hormones. As I recall, your hormones had earned you quite a reputation. I'll admit to you now … I might have been tempted … ," she let her last words hang in the air while she drained her glass, caught the waiter's eye, and signaled for a refill, then said, " … but I was spoken for."

Luco went on full alert. She admitted that she was interested, he realized, and her speech was becoming slurred. Another drink or two and she'd be putty in his hands. Yet, there was a glint of hardness in her eyes that left him unsettled.

"So … how *is* Phil?" he asked, tentatively.

"We're married, you know."

Luco nodded. He was unsure of his position and how he should proceed. He remained silent as Marla continued.

"He was signed by the Columbus Clippers—the Yankees?—right after commencement. They're in town for a three-game series against Pawtucket."

She took a hard pull from her drink. Her smile vanished.

"Phil's out there right now, as we speak, at pre-game practice, having the time of his life," she added, staring glumly into her drink.

"You make every road trip with Phil?" asked Luco.

Her head snapped up. She continued bitterly, "Not any more! I've had enough of living out of a suitcase in one dreary hotel after another. Hanging out with a bunch of women I don't want to know, whose conversation can't get beyond ERAs and RBIs and BOBs and Ks and … God, I hate it. From now on, when the Clippers go on the road, I'm heading for Providence."

"How did Phil handle it when you told him?" he asked, his confidence building.

"I didn't. Not yet. After today's game, when he gets to about the fourth inning of his play-by-play recap, I'll be bored to tears. That's when I'll tell him."

She took another long drink and slouched back in her chair. She gave no sign of discomfort as Luco openly surveyed her body.

"Well, now," he crooned, "things are looking up. Maybe you'll let me prove to you that one thing I'm *not* … is boring."

Marla studied Luco for a long time, looking past his lurid grin. Her speech was getting thick but her mind was clear. She had no trouble reading the look in his eyes. It was the same look he wore when he swarmed all over her at *Handjob Hannah's* party. She simmered in resentment at her husband for having fun at the ballpark while the only entertainment she could find had to do with this conceited, arrogant pig. If Phil's out there enjoying himself without me, she thought, it'll serve him right if I enjoy myself without him!

She fought back the wave of revulsion that threatened to sweep over her, and manufactured what she hoped was a coquettish grin.

"Now, that sounds like you're comin' on to me," she said. "*Are* you comin' on to me, Luco? 'Cause if you're comin' on to me, that would make it twice in five years. Don't you think that's pushing it?"

Then, through a sudden burst of playful giggling, she gushed, "*Someday you're gonna come crawling to me with your legs open!* Isn't that hilarious?" Just as suddenly, she grew serious. She leaned forward on her elbows. Her arms squeezed her breasts together, creating a bulge that drew Luco's attention.

"You're not still pissed at me, are you, Luco?"

When he looked up, she gazed at him with droopy eyelids.

"I'm very tired, Luco," she said, licking her lips. "Please see me to my room."

Luco's veneer of savoir-faire gave way to lust and anticipation. Without a word, he leaped to his feet, almost knocking over a passing busboy, tossed some money on the table, took Marla's arm, and herded her to the elevator.

LUCO OPENED THE door and ogled her swinging hips as she led the way to the bed where she sprawled out on her back.

"Luco, honey, come sit here by me," she said thickly, patting her hand on the bed. Luco didn't notice that beneath her drooping lids, her eyes were clear and sharp. He noticed only that they were focused on the region below his belt. His reaction was instantaneous and clearly unmistakable. He sat beside her and rubbed his hand up her belly.

"Lunch was so nice, Luco. How can I thank you for such a lovely day?" she asked with a tiny giggle. She pushed his hand gently to one side but allowed it to brush against the outer perimeter of her breast.

Luco had been transformed from pursuer to pursuee and didn't know it. He continued to think this was all his idea but he was totally off-balance. His voice was unable to construct words. He had been rendered silent but for intermittent, involuntary, guttural emissions. He bent to kiss her. In the instant before their lips met, she turned away, deflecting his kiss. She rolled out from under him and stood up at the far side of the bed, facing him.

"I ... want to have it, Luco," she moaned softly as she reached behind her and began to lower the back zipper of her dress. When her zipper reached waist high, her dress slipped from her shoulders. She held it up with her other hand and, still facing him, she implored, "Please, Luco ... give it to me *now!*"

Luco clawed wildly at his shirt buttons with one hand and his Sansabelt waist clasps with the other, grunting and behaving altogether like a wild boar rooting about under a dead and decaying tree trunk.

"What the hell do you think you're doing?" she asked sharply. Her voice was crisp and hard. She was clear-eyed, steady, and very sober.

Her imperious tone stopped Luco dead in his tracks. His zipper was half-opened with its pull handle firmly between the thumb and first finger of one hand. The other hand was frozen in mid-tug at his shirt.

"Wha ... what do you mean?" he croaked. "You just said you wanted it! You told me to give it to you!" He remained in his half crouch, unable to decide whether or not he should continue to undress.

Marla removed all uncertainty from his mind.

"The *key*, you dildo!" She continued in a searing tone. "I wanted you to give me *this!*" Pulling her zipper back up, she stepped to the dresser and snatched up the key that Luco had laid there. Swiftly, she went to the door and flung it wide open.

"And now, you arrogant, detestable, conceited pig, you can haul your slimy ass out of this room before I call security. And take your hard-on with you!"

She had enjoyed that every bit as much as she thought she might, even taking pleasure in the unexpected stirrings of arousal that she felt within her as she was setting Luco up. She would take equal pleasure in telling Phil about it, and even greater pleasure knowing Phil would be seething with anger and doubt through every practice and every game, not knowing for sure where she is and what she's doing. It would serve him right. She hated the life he had inflicted upon her.

FIVE

THE LONG, PAR-THREE SIXTH HOLE at The Alpine Country Club points directly at the clubhouse. A manicured berm with sculptured plantings separates its huge, rolling green from the members' parking area where a golf cart with a single rider and no golf clubs headed toward the sixth tee. It came to a halt alongside the green, its driver respectfully waiting for the group on the green to hole out.

On the tee, some 205 yards away, Luco Parisi's foursome saw the group ahead clear the green. As Luco was setting up to hit his tee shot, the others in his foursome cautioned him about the cart that was then coming toward them straight down the middle of the fairway.

The cart ran up directly onto the tee box, much against club rules. The animated gestures and decidedly profane admonitions from the players on the tee dwindled to ineffectual murmurs when they saw the expression on the face of the cart's driver.

Phil Peters stepped from the cart, walked up and stood face to face with Luco who, an instant too late, grasped what was happening. Phil fired off a single, textbook, left hook, catching Luco flush on the jaw. He went down without a sound, ending up flat on his back in the soft, cool grass.

Phil glanced warily at each of the other three, one of whom was Luco's father-in-law, Mario "Papa Cheech" Ciacchone. The other two came out of their daze and moved menacingly toward Phil, their intentions unmistakable.

Papa Cheech embodied the classic pose of a golfer waiting to take his turn. He stood with his feet apart, cigar stub in his mouth, his three-wood supporting his beefy hands that were draped over the butt end of the club. He hadn't changed position since Phil began his run down the fairway, moving only his head to follow the action that unfolded before him.

He knew Phil since Phil was the thirteen-year-old second baseman sensation for Ciacchone Plumbing & Supply in the Tim O'Neil Amateur League. He liked Phil. He thought of him as a real man. A man of honor. Not like this worm of a son-in-law that lay sprawled on the ground at his feet.

Papa Cheech raised the fingers of one hand in a half wave-off and made an almost indiscernible movement of his head. The other two stopped their advance.

"Nice game in Pawtucket last night, Philip," said Papa Cheech turning to Phil.

"Thanks, Papa Cheech."

"Two for three, three RBI. Eleven chances, no errors. Good relay to the plate cuts off the tying run."

"Thanks again, Papa Cheech." Phil was humbly touched that Papa Cheech, after all the years, still followed his career.

"By the way, Philip," Papa continued after a slight pause, motioning with his head toward the prostrate Luco, "can I assume you have a reason for this?"

"I have a reason, Papa Cheech."

Papa didn't alter his pose. He looked into Phil's eyes, nodding thoughtfully. When it became clear that Phil was not going to volunteer the reason, Papa took the cigar stub out of his mouth between his thumb and first finger, wiped his lips with the back of his hand, and returned the cigar to his mouth before finishing with, "It's good to see you, Philip. You should come around more often. Now go get some rest before tonight's game. I'll clean this up."

THE VOICE WAS MUFFLED FROM behind the thick door of the steam room but by leaning his chair back, with his head pressed against the door, and with his eyes closed in concentration, Artie, the locker room steward, could make out the words.

He didn't see three, fifty-something-year-old golfers get up from the card table where they had been sitting naked, playing hi-lo-jack and drinking. They were all poured from the same mold—medium height, broad and squat, deep-chested and powerfully built, and hairy all over, except on their heads. With cigars clamped in their mouths, they approached the steam room in a boisterous, playful mood, snapping towels at each other's bare asses and legs, and carrying fresh drinks that sloshed all over themselves and the floor.

They came to where Artie was sitting and planted themselves right in front of him. Artie flopped his chair forward and sat upright. Uneasiness hung over him as he looked up at Ponzi, Pasco and Paulie DiCarlo, and they looked balefully down at him. When Artie failed to speak or to move, Ponzi the Elder spoke. As always, he spoke for all of them.

"So awright, Artie, wudd'ya say?" asked Ponzi, motioning with a pull of his head toward his shoulder.

"I dunno, Mr. DiCarlo. Wudd'ya mean?" Artie knew what Ponzi meant. But he also knew what his orders were.

"Wudd'ya mean, wudd'oo I mean?! Me and my bruddas wanna get in there. That's wudd I mean! But, you gotcha self parked in the way," said Ponzi with equal measures of incredulity and impatience.

"I'm sorry, Mr. DiCarlo. You can't go in. Luco Parisi's in there."

"Fuck him! Now get outta the way before my brudda Pasco kicks your ass out onto the first tee and my brudda Paulie stuffs it into a ball washer!"

Artie realized he was walking on thin ice. This was The Alpine Country Club. While its membership was liberally sprinkled with community leaders and was substantially represented by the professions, it also consisted of a large contingent of successful businessmen and tradesmen, hard working guys who made it up from the streets, fighting their way to affluence with no handouts from anyone. They were generous and outgoing to a fault … and volatile in their temperaments. You just didn't want to go around pissing them off. In that regard, Artie sensed he might be slipping.

"I can't, Mr. DiCarlo." Artie tried to choke back the whimper that he felt welling up in his voice. "Mr. Ciacchone told me not to let nobody else in."

"Papa Cheech?!" Paulie the Younger blurted without thinking, then shrugged his shoulders in apology to his two brothers who gave him a look of reproach for his breach of protocol.

"Papa Cheech is in there too?" said Ponzi the Elder in a calmer tone. He stepped around Artie and put his face to the tiny window but was able to see only a surreal suggestion of forms through the steam.

"Awright, Artie," he continued, "if that's the way Papa Cheech wants it, me and my bruddas can wait. But wha' the fuck they doin' in there he don't want no one else in there?"

"Aw jeez, I dunno, Mr. DiCarlo," Artie lied unconvincingly.

Ponzi the Elder glanced at his brothers then looked down at Artie with a conspiratorial grin.

"C'mon, Artie. We seen ya wit' your ear stuck against the door. We don't need no details. Jus' give us a hint."

"Well ... awright ... I couldn't hear everything with you guys makin' such a ruckus out here ... but it's got somethin' to do with Luco's ... aw shit," Artie squirmed, " ... with Luco's pecker!"

THEY SAT ASTRIDE THE BENCH, nose-to-nose, with towels draped over their heads and their spread-eagled knees touching. Papa Cheech growled through clenched jaws, spraying Luco's face with sticky splatter from the ever-present cigar stub that was clamped between his teeth. Luco wanted desperately to back away from his father-in-law but it was impossible. Papa Cheech had a death grip on Luco's painfully throbbing dick.

"You think just 'cause I let my baby daughter marry you, I like you? You think I don't know what kinda worm you are? You think I can't figure out what you done that Phil Peters hadda come out there and drop you? You think I'm some kinda moron?!"

As he continued, Papa Cheech's powerful grip gave Luco repeated, agonizing, squeezing yanks to add emphasis to his words, "Because I know one thing for *sure*. It's about *you* ... and *him* ... so it must be about his *wife*, and if it's about his *wife*, it must be about your *pecker!*"

With each crushing yank, Luco recoiled in pain. His eyes were wild with fear. With his free hand, Papa Cheech removed the cigar stub, wiped the back of his hand across his lips and returned the cigar to his mouth. Then, as he spoke, he reached behind himself, feeling for an object that he had placed there.

"So now you listen. I swear this on my soul and on the soul of my dear, departed wife, Amelia. If you *ever*, in *any* way, bring *shame* or *sadness* to my baby daughter," Papa Cheech jerked mightily on Luco's dick with one hand and whipped his other hand up, waving a straight razor in front of Luco's terrified eyes as he hissed, "that will be the *end* of your *pecker!*"

SIX

Providence
1983

AFTER THE MERGER with First Great Bank of Providence in '64, Giuseppe became CEO of the new entity, Greater Providence Bank & Trust. Except for the horrendous, seven day blackout of his life following the sudden death of his wife, he had never missed a day at the office. Years later, upon reaching his 80th birthday, he reluctantly reduced his ten-hour workday to six hours.

Giuseppe didn't do business lunches anymore. Not since his wife died and he spent several sleepless days and nights manipulating his conscience, searching his soul, trying, without success, within the tenets of his Roman Catholic faith, to create a justifying rationale for suicide. He was theologically forbidden to end his life, yet he felt he had no reason to continue it. Faced with the ultimate quandary, he would have been unable to function at all had it not been for his oldest and dearest friends Lorenzo and Pierino.

Their friendship began when they were toddlers in Rochetta al Volturno, a tiny village at the foot of the Apennines in southern Italy. Giuseppe and Lorenzo came over on the same boat at the age of nine with their parents. Pierino was eleven when his father sent for him two years later. His father had come to America before Pierino was born and they had never seen each other.

Lorenzo and Pierino also had lost their wives in recent years. They too had felt the soul-crushing desolation that would have devoured their friend Giuseppe if they had left him to deal with it on his own. They packed overnight bags, moved into his home and inserted themselves into his life, overriding Giuseppe's pitiable protestations. Bonded by the force of their lifetime friendship, they were able to pull Giuseppe out of himself, to come to grips with the loss of his wife as a devastating but unalterable fact of life, and to go on with the business of living the rest of his own life.

LORENZO AND PIERINO WERE already seated at their regular table by the front window overlooking Atwells Avenue when they saw Giuseppe's car turn into the small parking lot next to the restaurant. The waiter had just delivered their customary bottle of Chianti to the table and poured a sample. Pierino approved the wine and nodded his head for the waiter to pour. After several minutes of making jokes to each other about what could be keeping Giuseppe, their attention was drawn outside by the sudden movement of the car-valet running full tilt from the parking lot. He burst through the front door of the restaurant and ran directly into the owner, Joe Martella, a broad rock of a man. Martella grasped the young man's shoulders, stopping him in mid flight.

"What is it, Louis?" demanded Martella. "What's wrong?!"

The small dining room, normally animated with the movement of waiters, busboys and patrons, and filled with the sounds of conversation and levity, fell to stillness.

"It's Mr. Parisi, Mr. Martella. I think ... I think ... "

"What Louis?! You think what, dammit?!" Martella didn't even realize that he had lifted the boy off the floor.

The realization of what Louis was trying to tell him suddenly struck him—an instant after it had struck Lorenzo and Pierino. They were on their feet sprinting for the door. Martella was right behind them as he dropped Louis and barked over his shoulder to his maitre d', "Vito! It's Giuseppe! Get the rescue truck here fast! Then call Luco."

Vito had already dialed 911 the minute he saw the look on the face of the car valet. Now he silently crossed himself after giving them directions.

GIUSEPPE HAD PULLED INTO the lot and come to a stop in front of the attendant's kiosk. He remained in the car as he did every day, waiting for Louis to come over and open the car door.

Louis pulled on the door handle but the door was locked. He knocked on the window but Giuseppe simply sat there with his eyes closed, wearing a contented, peaceful expression on his face. Louis called out to him but there was no response. He pounded hard and long on the driver's window. Still no reaction at all. It was clear that Giuseppe needed help. He ran to the other side of the car. That door was also locked. The motor was running. The gearshift was in park.

He raced into the restaurant.

LORENZO AND PIERINO got there first. Seconds later, when Martella arrived, they were on opposite sides of the car, shouting Giuseppe's name and vainly struggling with the door handles. Martella shouted, "Stand back!" and with a single blow of his fist, he smashed in the right front door window. Reaching in with his bloodied hand, he found the button for the locks and unlocked all the doors.

Lorenzo tried to rouse Giuseppe but succeeded only in causing him to topple forward against the horn pad on the steering wheel. Pierino climbed in the passenger side, reached over and turned off the ignition, stopping the motor and silencing the blaring horn.

The small lot was soon cluttered with patrons who had followed the action from inside, some of them still wearing their napkins the old fashioned way, tucked into their shirt collars. As the Rescue Squad siren drew near, Martella looked around for Louis. The car valet was by himself, apart from the crowd, with his head bowed against the side of the building. Martella quietly approached him.

"I couldn't wake him up, Mr. Martella." Louis was distraught and openly sobbing. "He looked so … so peaceful … but I knew he needed help. I wanted to help him … but I couldn't open the doors. He needed me! And I couldn't do anything to help him!"

Martella took Louis gently into his arms.

"It's all right," Martella said softly. "It's all right. There's nothing you could have done to change anything."

"But I ... I should have ... "

"No, Louis. You did everything anyone could have done. Our friend was probably gone a second or two after he put the gearshift in park. God rest his soul."

"Oh God, Mr. Martella, how I'll miss him." Louis was struggling to regain control. "He's ... he was ... such a good man. He did so much for us. My mother and my sisters. When my father died ... without his help ... we ... I don't know what we would have done."

Martella released Louis from his hug, held him at arm's length and examined him until he was convinced that Louis was okay.

"There were many like you, Louis. We'll never know how many people ... how many families ... Giuseppe helped. He was truly a great man." He put an arm around Louis' shoulder and continued, "Come. Let's go back inside. There's nothing more for us here."

Martella turned and started back toward the restaurant with his arm around Louis' shoulders. They stopped in their tracks as the Rescue Squad rolled a gurney carrying Giuseppe's body into the back of the wagon. Nearby, Pierino was talking with a medic and pointing in Martella's direction. As Martella drew near, she stepped in front of him.

"Just a moment, sir," she said, taking his bloodied hand. "Your friend said I should have a look at this."

Martella cast a glaring look at Pierino who, with Lorenzo, escorted Louis back into the restaurant.

"It's no big deal, lady. A couple of scratches," he replied.

He tried to pull his hand away but she held on. Martella winced in pain and stopped resisting.

"Yeah, right," said the medic, shaking her head in wonder.

"What is it with you big guys?" she continued as she probed his hand. "Figure your manhood's on the line if you show pain?"

She continued to probe, looking into his eyes for reactions.

"Doesn't look like you broke anything but you're cut up pretty bad. Sure to need stitches. Better ride in with us. Let the doctor have a look."

"I'm not going anywhere!" he replied gruffly. "Just clean it up and put a couple of Bandaids on it!"

He regretted the tone of his own voice and having brought the hurt look to the medic's face.

"Please," he added softly, with a warm smile and an apology evident in his dark eyes.

INSIDE THE RESTAURANT, customers and the other employees clustered around Louis, offering him comfort. Lorenzo and Pierino returned to their table where the three glasses of Chianti remained untouched. Suddenly feeling the weight of their years, they lifted their glasses to each other, bringing them together in a crystalline clink, then gently touched their glasses to the third glass, the one that was to have been Giuseppe's, in a silent farewell to their old friend.

SEVEN

AS WAS THE custom following a burial, family and close friends assembled at the home of the deceased's next of kin for refreshments, small talk and reminiscences, some laughter, some tears. Luco's wife, Celia, though saddened by the passing of her father-in-law, nevertheless had made the arrangements for the wake, the Mass of Christian Burial, the funeral and had even given the caterer specific and detailed instructions for the reception.

In contrast, Luco did a lot of hand-shaking, back-patting, waving and smiling across the room to new arrivals, and ordering drinks for himself and whomever he happened to be with whenever a server came within range.

Giuseppe had been buried less than two hours earlier but Luco had no qualms about using the post-burial reception to bring up business matters with some of the bank's customers and employees who had come to pay their respects. Confronted with his unseemly behavior, visitors grew uneasy in his presence and quickly excused themselves from him as soon as protocol would allow.

Soon, finding he had no one to talk to, Luco drifted to the bar that the caterer had set up in the sun room overlooking the terraced gardens in the back yard. His niece Gloria observed the others breaking away from him. Pointing with her thumb over her shoulder, she said to her husband, Mickey, "My uncle is all by himself over there. People are dodging him. Go on over and see if you can keep him from acting like a horse's patoot. I want to go sit with Mama. She was Grandpa's little girl and she's taking it so hard."

"Yeah, you go ahead, darlin'," Mickey replied, kissing her lightly on the cheek, "you see to Mama. I'll take care of your uncle Luco."

Luco, using a skewer of olives to stir his martini on-the-rocks, saw Mickey coming, turned to the bartender and ordered Mickey's usual selection, Fernet Branca straight up, with a Bass Ale chaser. As Mickey drew near, Luco, without conscious thought, stood up taller. He was only of medium height but he was an inch taller than Mickey and he took pleasure in lording it over him.

It was a wasted exercise. Mickey Hoban was never aware of the difference in their heights. He had let himself go somewhat since the days when he was starting catcher on the Brown University baseball team. For the past several years, he had assiduously avoided any activity that required physical exertion. That, combined with his penchant for Fernet Branca and Bass Ale, had instigated a pronounced increase in his waistline. Mickey became conscious of it only when, in the presence of an attractive woman, he found it increasingly difficult to suck it in.

Even so, there was something about Mickey. Maybe it was his impish face. Or the laugh wrinkles next to his light blue eyes that began his smile before his lips did. Whatever it was, it brought out the warm fuzzies in every red-blooded female who set eyes on him. His wife Gloria, beginning to show signs of wear, no longer regarded that as cute.

Mickey took the Fernet, clinked Luco's glass with it, downed it in a single gulp and followed it with a deep draft of ale.

Luco was entranced by the ritual. He returned the silent toast by taking a measured sip of his martini before saying, "For crisake Mickey how can you do that? The beer, OK. But that other crap ... Jesus! My father knew you were drinking that at his funeral he'd turn over in his grave just so he could puke!"

"Not a chance of that, lad," said Mickey with a chuckle, easing into his Irish brogue. "When your ma died, you were still in the army in Germany. Gloria and I moved in with your papa, don't y' remember. He and I shared many a glass of that marvelous potion he used to brew in the cellar. He tried to pass that stuff off as Chianti. 'We drank this when we were children,' he would say."

Mickey paused in bitter-sweet reflection before continuing. " 'We grew up on this,' he would say. Many's the time that red lightning knocked me on my Irish ass, but it never affected Giuseppe. Then, without fail, before calling it a night, he'd pour us a Fernet and raise it in a toast. 'Death to the stomach fleas,' he would say, and we'd slug it down. There must be something to it because I never got sick after a night of drinking with your papa. No, lad, it was your papa that taught me about the miracle of Fernet Branca. The ale is my own idea."

Mickey was brought starkly back to the present by Luco. With no concession to the solemnity of the occasion, Luco replied, "Yeah, yeah. Miracle my ass. Listen, Mickey," he continued, eager to change the subject. He put his arm around Mickey's shoulders, and guided him through the sun room into the garden, saying, "I want to run something by you. This guy I know could use a little help from my bank."

Mickey was astonished. Here they were, before the ink was dry on the death certificate, and Luco Parisi was wanting to talk business. And he was referring to the bank as *my* bank.

"Luco, for crisake! Can't this wait until tomorrow?!" Mickey's exasperation would have been apparent to most anyone, but to Luco, it went unnoticed.

"This guy's from the old neighborhood. He has to raise some cash real bad so he came in to see me looking to refi his house. I offered him a 90 percent loan-to-value. So he thinks about it a minute, then he says, 'After paying off the first, that leaves me about 60K short.' I say, 'Short of what?' He says, 'Short of what I need to make a very serious problem go away.' "

Luco paused, took a long swallow from his drink and remained silent. He waited, biding his time, pretending to take in the beauty of the gardens. He knew that Mickey couldn't resist talking numbers.

After a slow beat or two, Mickey said, "What problem? To some folks, $60,000 is chump change. To others, it might as well be the national budget. Where does your friend fit in? What kind of numbers is he talking? And why are you telling me about this? How is it any of my business? It's *your* bank."

Luco missed the sarcasm in the emphasis Mickey placed on *your*, taking it instead as a compliment. Abandoning coyness, he stepped in front of Mickey, faced him squarely and launched right into it, "So a thought struck me as he was telling me about his problem."

He paused again, taking a sip of his drink while holding eye-contact with Mickey. His eyes were intense under brows hooded against the brilliant sunlight as he continued, "The thought that struck me was this. Suppose this guy's house gets a solid appraisal with a lot of meat in it. Enough meat to justify a loan that will net him what he needs after paying off the first mortgage? You've been the chief outside appraiser for Greater Providence Bank ever since the new mayor got elected. With *your* name on the appraisal, I could run a loan package like that past the board with no tough questions." He paused again, creating a dead spot that Mickey would instinctively feel he had to fill, as would most people. He did.

"Numbers, Luco," Mickey said. "Numbers! Most appraisers can finagle their work a bit in their clients' favor, and they usually do. To a degree. But you're not giving me any numbers. How much finagling does your guy need?"

"At 90 percent LTV, he needs to bump his appraised value by 67K to net out 60."

"So what's his house worth? 700? 750? No big deal. So the appraiser bumps the value up to 770 - 820K. You don't need me for that."

"200K, Mickey. It's worth 200,000 dollars."

"200?!" Mickey was incredulous. The arithmetic presented itself to him instantaneously and automatically. He continued, "You want me to write up a 200K house at 267K and make it so believable that nobody questions it?! Gimme a fuckin' break, Luco!"

Luco stood motionless with his arms half folded, one hand holding his drink, his eye-contact intense and unyielding. When he spoke, his tone was in direct contrast to Mickey's. It was little more than a whisper but it commanded Mickey's full attention.

"Without our special help, here's what the guy's looking at. At 90 percent LTV the most I can loan him is 180. He pays off his first and he's left with 70K. That's 60K short of what he needs real bad. $60,000 worth of multiple fractures, a lot of pain and a long stay at Fatima Hospital. During which the vigorish on the 60 keeps growing at 25 percent per week."

Luco neglected to mention that his 'client' needed only $40,000 to retire his debt, not $60,000, and that the other $20,000 was to be Luco's fee.

"But why?" asked Mickey. "You want to bail this guy out, that's your business. Why should I stick *my* neck out? Do I even know the guy for crisake?"

Luco at last broke eye-contact. He unfolded his arms and took a sip of his drink. With a casualness that belied the essence of where their conversation was going, he strode the few steps to the stone bench alongside the brick walkway. He sat back languorously, draping an arm over the back of the bench. He drained the rest of his drink and, without looking, flipped the empty glass over his shoulder into the shrubbery where it landed without a sound.

Then he held up his hand with his fingers spread, his palm facing Mickey, and said, "Five, Mickey. Count them. Five thousand in your pocket. Tax free. On top of your regular fee. And five thousand in mine. My bank picks up a solid loan … and the gentleman in question saves a bundle on pain killers. How about that?" he continued with a broad grin. "You figure that's enough reason to hold out a helping hand to a fellow in need?"

EIGHT

Providence
1990

HE SANG mostly in the privacy of his car, being painfully aware that he had neither a voice nor a sense of pitch. Nevertheless, he belted it out, *"I've Got You Under My Skin,"* in unison with Sinatra's every vocal pause and delayed slur into a chord change. He was as familiar with the score as Nelson Riddle and he devotedly mimicked Sinatra, gesture for gesture, including every subtle shoulder shrug and lip twitch.

As he and Sinatra were tacit while Riddle vamped his big band into a key change, the electronic chirp of the car phone muted the music. He angrily pressed the SEND button, "This better be goddamm important it couldn't wait another ten minutes I'm in the fuckin' office!"

"Where are you right now, Uncle Luco?" came the reply after a momentary hesitation. Howard Pastore never used profanity of any kind, and considering his uncle Luco's response, he was glad he hadn't asked one of the women in the office to make the call.

"Oh. It's you," said Luco. His sister's son, Howard, was not given to idle chatter or casual acts. There would be some valid reason for his call. "I'm on I-95 just north of Elmwood. Why?"

"You'd better get off the interstate at the next exit, Uncle Luco. The TV says the entire highway at the downtown interchange has been shut down by an accident. In a few minutes, I-95 will be a gigantic parking lot."

"OK. Tell Rochelle I might be a little late." He pressed the END button. Luco does not use the words *thank you* easily.

ENTERING THE CITY FROM the south on I-95 is not for the faint of heart. Especially at 8:15AM on a weekday. Coming out of a gentle turn to the left, the unwary driver is deceived by five northbound lanes that look as though they will all sweep to the west of downtown Providence. In reality, the two rightmost lanes are sucker traps.

The traffic streams under an overhead rack of freeway signs. The sign at the far right points its arrows straight down to the two rightmost lanes declaring, I-195 EAST CAPE COD EXIT 1/2 MILE. There's nothing to warn that two lanes of traffic from the Allen's Avenue access ramp will intrude into the flow of the two rightmost lanes of the freeway.

THE SUN HAD CLIMBED ABOVE its own shimmering reflection in the Providence River and had ignited the few remaining April clouds to a blazing whiteness. The early morning rain shower had stopped only moments earlier.

Wilma Hutchings, in lane 1, the far left lane of I-95 northbound, was seeing the Providence skyline for the first time. She was in a state of heightened anticipation, having agreed to a long weekend on the Cape with a USAir captain. A married captain she had met only two weeks earlier. A man whose copulative exploits were spoken of in awestruck whispers by her sister flight attendants, many having preceded her in partaking of his carnal ministrations. Wilma's reverie was marred only by the stubborn road-splatter on the windshield of her Alamo Rent-A-Car, white Mustang convertible … and by the highway sign that flashed by overhead, telling her that if her plans included going to the Cape, she'd better find a way real quick to traverse five lanes of tailgating, lane-changing, horn-blowing, frenetic, finger-throwing neurotics.

"Ooooh, bullshit!" she shrieked as she yanked the wheel to the right. The thought of glancing into her rear view mirror never entered her mind.

The maroon Grand Marquis in lane 2 that had been keeping pace abeam the Mustang's right rear quarter nose-dived as its driver jammed on the brakes and swerved madly to the right. The Grand Marq smartly backhanded the left rear of a silver Camry station wagon in lane 3, sending it into a counterclockwise spin. The left-to-right impact slowed the Camry's forward motion just enough that Wilma, by then securely in lane 2 with her attention focused ahead of her, didn't see any of what had taken place.

What she did see was the opening in lane 3 that the pirouetting Camry had provided for her. She didn't hesitate. With another sharp cut to the right she was in lane 3. Then, like a cheetah seeking out the weakest prey in a herd of gazelle, Wilma scanned the stream of traffic pouring into lanes 4 and 5 from the Allen's Avenue on-ramp. She focused not on the cars but on the drivers, looking for the slightest hint of weakness or indecision that would prompt her to move in, forcing an opening where there was none. This would put her in lane 4, on track for Cape Cod.

THE ALLEN'S AVENUE ON-RAMP makes a climbing approach to the freeway. Upon reaching the crest, it curves slightly to the left then lets down, so that where it joins I-95, it matches the freeway's gently down-sloping, left-curving shape. On paper the merging traffic flow thus envisioned by the designers would be smooth, safe and expeditious. In reality, the traffic on the freeway remains out of the view of drivers on the access ramp until they reach its crest, which is, at least in this case, too late.

In the left lane of the two-lane on-ramp, chockablock full of diesel it had just taken on at the Sunoco dock not five minutes behind him, a tanker roared its determination to attain highway speed by the time it entered I-95. Nearing the top of the on-ramp, the driver, craning his neck, peered over the top of the divider to plan his attack. His objective was twofold. His first priority was to find the first available opening. Failing that, he would create one through boldness and intimidation. He would then brazen his way across to lane 1 or lane 2, either of which would grant him unimpeded bypass of Providence as he made his way north to Pawtucket. He was wholly unprepared for the scene that unfolded before his eyes.

Way over on the left, in lane 1, a white Mustang convertible had just cut off a maroon Grand Marquis that swerved to the right, knocking the hind legs out from under a silver Camry station wagon. The Grand Marq then over-corrected to the left and jumped the curb. It slammed into the concrete retaining wall that separated the northbound from the southbound lanes, went into a spin and came to rest at ninety degrees to the traffic flow. It effectively blocked off lanes 1 and 2, while the spinning Camry blocked lane 3. All following traffic successfully came to a stop, having endured numerous cases of front end and rear end damage, a plethora of epithets hurled in several languages, and an abundance of erect middle fingers in an assortment of colors.

The Camry wagon in lane 3 had stopped rotating but its engine was still running wide open. Its driver sat at the wheel in a daze with the accelerator floored, the drive wheels spinning on the wet pavement. When the tires finally made traction, it shot out at a forty-five degree angle, streaking from left to right toward that spot in lane 4 that in mere seconds would be occupied by one very heavy and very fast tank truck.

Instinct and experience told the tanker to stay off his air brakes on the wet pavement. Timing it for the instant when the body of his truck passed clear of the stalled traffic in lane 3, he cut hard to the left, trying to pass behind the Camry. He felt that he had it made. And he would have. Except, at that precise instant, the Camry driver came out of his dazed state, saw what was in front of him and slammed on his brakes. Without the slightest clue of what had happened, nor of what was coming next, the Camry skidded to a stop directly in the path of the tanker.

The tanker was out of options. He swiftly downshifted and floored it. The moment he felt the wheels grab, he spun the steering wheel viciously to the right. At the same instant, he hit first the brakes then the accelerator hoping to start a jackknife to the left, away from the Camry. It looked like it was going to work, and it might have, except for Murphy's Law.

As the tank body swung like a wiper blade across the highway, its rear wheels slid onto a dry spot and dug in. The tank body separated from the tractor, toppled and ruptured, spewing its load of diesel across the entire highway.

Free of its load, the tractor shot forward and plowed into the rear of the Camry. The Camry's driver, having exited it the moment he came to a stop, stood a few feet away on the highway watching in detached confusion as his beautiful new Camry wagon was slammed into the concrete retaining wall and totally demolished by a lunatic in a truck tractor cab.

Miraculously no one was seriously hurt. Nonetheless in the days ahead, the number and magnitude of insurance claims for whiplash injuries in a single event would soar to a new record.

Wilma made the turnoff to I-195 East to Cape Cod without the slightest hint as to what she had left behind. Her thoughts had already drifted back to Captain Awesome, her heart a-twitter.

In minutes the jammed traffic would extend all the way to Jefferson Boulevard, seven miles south.

AS LUCO STARTED AROUND the Thurbers Avenue curve, the brake lights of the thickening mass of vehicles filled every lane all the way to downtown. After Howard's call, he was able to work his way to the right breakdown lane and make it to the exit. He was smugly euphoric, thinking of all those poor saps who would be trapped on 95, perhaps for several hours. His pleasure soon faded. Nearing the end of the exit ramp, the disagreeable prospect of beginning his day by taking Allens Avenue into the city jolted him back to reality.

Tractor trailers, tank trucks and delivery vehicles of every size and type duke it out every day in a no-holds-barred free-for-all. They dart and swerve in a frenzied scat-dance to avoid the infamous Allens Avenue potholes and ruts, while diesel locomotives push freight cars with arrogant impunity along the railroad tracks that run down the center of the avenue. To the right, where deep-water docks protrude into the Providence River, oil and gas terminals lie sprawled behind disfigured chain link fences, sucking the cargo out of rust-ridden, ocean-going tankers.

Buildings of indeterminate architectural origin border the roadway. They have been patched-up and added-to for years without the slightest concession to aesthetics, without a single tree or planting of any kind whose seed hadn't been blown there by some long-ago wind with a warped sense of humor.

LUCO PARISI'S RELATIONSHIP WITH his beloved, cream-colored Rolls-Royce was deeply personal. Almost man and woman. As salvo after salvo of filthy, pothole water assaulted his Rolls, Luco felt defiled and in need of a bath. Yet he had no choice but to continue. There was no better route. The short drive to the city was at once slow and frantic. Everyone cut everyone else off at will. Tanker trucks and freighters pulled from their loading terminals and transfer stations into the stream of traffic without so much as a glance. Luco gripped the wheel tightly. Perspiration rolled from his forehead into his eyes.

Soon he had passed through the worst of it. The old Davol Rubber plant slipped by on the right. Now a trendy shoppers' mall, in its former life it was the home of one of the country's leading manufacturers of enema bottles, urinary drains and a mind-boggling assortment of other ingenious yet inglorious syringe-type devices for males and females in need of urinary tract assistance.

Luco began to relax a bit as the road curved to the right around the Narragansett Electric Company power plant. It then swept back to the left, passing within feet of the riprap bank of the river where it flowed under I-195. The same I-195 on which Wilma Hutchings, only minutes earlier, raced in quivering passion toward her rendezvous.

LUCO PULLED INTO THE PARKING GARAGE at the rear of the building. Horace, the attendant, took one look, and as he opened the door for Luco, said, "Shee-it, Mr. P! You been doin' eights in the Cranston landfill wit' dat Rolls?"

Ignoring the question, Luco handed him a twenty and said, "Horace, when I come back down in about two hours, what am I going to find parked in my spot?"

"Mr. P, you gonna find the spiffiest Rolls in this buildin'. Of course, it's the *onliest* Rolls in this buildin'." Horace deftly palmed the twenty and doubled over laughing in appreciation of his own wit, notwithstanding that virtually identical dialogue had taken place at least twice a week for the last two years. Luco's reserved space included plumbing, along with all the other necessities for washing and grooming a car. He wouldn't even think about subjecting his Rolls to the indignity of an automatic carwash.

Luco started for the entrance. Before he got there, Horace scrambled ahead of him to open the brass-framed, glass door with gold-leaf lettering that read GREATER PROVIDENCE BANK & TRUST.

NINE

THE DIRECT ENTRANCE TO GPB&T from the parking garage opens to a foyer with a staircase and two elevators on the left and two rest rooms on the right. Mirrored elevator doors reflect the sculpted, oiled teak walls of the foyer. At the far end of the foyer, full-width stairs with a brass handrail at each end and another in the middle ascend three steps to the main lobby. To the left, four tellers work behind a long counter that faces the front of the building. Against the wall at the far left end of the lobby are the brochure racks and standup writing gondolas with their racks of various forms and applications, and ballpoint pens secured by beadchains that are—it must be a rule in bank design—too short by about three inches.

Everything else, except security central, is located on floors 9, 10 and 11: administrative offices, board room, trusts, investments, marketing, commercial loan, conference rooms, cafeteria, and clean room for the mainframe computer. Security central occupies a two room suite on the second floor opposite the stairwell and elevators. One room is divided into a lavatory and kitchenette. The other room contains a bank of monitors arranged in an arc around a master control console.

SHEILA MCCUSKER, VIEWING THE monitors from the captain's chair at the control console, had picked up the Rolls when it entered the garage. As she watched Luco examining himself in the foyer mirrors, she punched in a number on the speakerphone. A female voice answered in a single word, "Rochelle."

Sheila said, "He's on his way up."

Luco continued to appraise himself in the full-length mirrors as the elevator slowed to a stop on the 11th floor. His double-breasted charcoal blazer was cut to broaden his shoulders and accentuate the slimness of his hips. He absently toyed with its antiqued onyx buttons while he admired himself. His shirt had bold vertical stripes of maroon on white with a solid white collar. It provided the perfect background for his necktie with its random pattern of black and maroon geometric shapes on light gray silk. His front-pleated trousers of black on black flared ever-so-inconspicuously to a solid break on the instep of his tasseled, Bally loafers. His entire ensemble was hand-fitted and hand-sewn by Patsy Alifanio.

A boyhood friend of Luco's father since the old country, Patsy, at the age of eighty-six, still had the eyes and hands of a surgeon and the heart of a Stradivari. He was every bit as good as Armani and his price was lower by a half. Luco always liked very much what he saw when he looked in a mirror. Even if he was bare-ass. *Especially* if he was bare-ass. However, dressed in Patsy's work, Luco's admiration for himself was unabashed.

"In your face, Armani." he said aloud as he thumbed his lapels. "Who needs you and the rest of those overpriced, faggot assholes!"

In security central, Sheila and her assistant, Claude, burst into laughter just as Sheila took a bite of doughnut and a sip of coffee. She coughed wildly to clear her windpipe.

"That man so caught up with hisself he forget he's on candid camera," said Claude through his laughter. Then, turning to Sheila, he asked, "You all right, Miss McCusker?"

Laughing and coughing, she nodded OK. It was curious, she thought, that someone could so completely forget about the presence of cameras and microphones that he himself had ordered installed.

"GOOD MORNING MR. PARISI. Mr. Hoban is waiting in your office." Rochelle always addressed Luco as Mr. Parisi, unless they were assured of absolute privacy. She handed him his call slips, letting the touch of her fingers linger on his.

"In *my* office?" asked Luco. He didn't break contact with her touch. She moved closer to him and tilted her face up to his.

"I was unable to convince him that waiting for you out here would be more in keeping with your desires and practices," she said. Her closeness and the scent of her fragrance created a stir in the recesses of Luco's libido.

He replied, "I'll talk to Mr. Hoban about that," then, making no attempt to conceal his gaze into the top of her scoop neck dress, he added with a lascivious grin, "but I hope you didn't tell him *too* much about my ... *desires* and *practices*." She returned his grin in kind and didn't flinch when he brushed his arm against her breast as he stepped around her to enter his office.

MICKEY HOBAN WAS SITTING AT the conference table in the alcove to the right of Luco's desk. He looked up from the table on which were strewn his open briefcase, scattered papers and a calculator. Smiling a greeting to his wife's uncle, he said, "Top o' the marnin' laddie," with the charming Irish lilt that he affected so easily. Luco didn't return the greeting, didn't smile, didn't even make eye-contact. He didn't acknowledge Mickey's presence in any way. He closed the door behind him without a sound and crossed the room, not to where Mickey sat waiting for him but to his own desk. Luco placed the call slips on his desk, busied himself for a few seconds arranging them in some kind of order, then pressed the intercom button for Rochelle.

Her response was instantaneous, "Yes, Mr. Parisi?"

He spoke toward the intercom, "I'm expecting Mr. Hoban. When he arrives, make him comfortable and ask him to wait."

"Yes, Mr. Parisi."

Mickey looked questioningly at Luco. "Is this some kind of grand joke you're playin' Luco? Sure I'm sittin' right here not fifteen feet from you in this glorious office," he continued, though his smile and his Irish charm had diminished by a half.

Luco took a file folder from the corner of his desk, opened it and studied its contents for a long moment, appearing to make notes in the margins. His eyes never once met Mickey's. Mickey, on the other hand, had his eyes riveted on Luco as though trying to will Luco to look up and declare the whole thing a joke. Luco didn't.

"Luco!" Mickey said with the urgency he would have used if he had his hand on Luco's shoulder and was trying to shake him from a sleep. No reaction.

"Hey Luco! C'mon! Let's cut the bullshit, OK?" Mickey had lost any trace of blarney in his speech.

Unhurriedly, Luco laid down his pen, jogged the papers neatly together, placed them into the file folder and returned the folder to the spot on the corner of his desk from which he had taken it. Once again he buzzed for Rochelle.

"Yes, Mr. Parisi?"

"I'm ready for Mr. Hoban now. Please show him in."

Mickey, thoroughly confounded, ping-ponged his gaze back and forth from Luco to the door.

Rochelle came in, walked up to Mickey and said, "Mr. Parisi can see you now, Mr. Hoban. Please come in."

"I'm already in," Mickey blurted out, about an octave higher than normal.

Turning to Luco, acting it out on instinct but as convincingly as though they had rehearsed it, Rochelle politely said, "Mr. Hoban is here to see you, Mr. Parisi." She turned and left the room, gently closing the door behind her. Mickey, in his baffled state, forgot to look at her round little ass, for which he had the greatest admiration.

"Mickey, good to see you. I hope I didn't keep you waiting too long," Luco said, finally looking at Mickey but making no effort to rise or to offer his hand.

Mickey, his smile completely gone, looked at Luco, then at the door as if to be sure Rochelle had left, then back at Luco.

"Awright. What the hell was that all about? Who do you think you're jerking around here?" Mickey wasn't sure whether he should be angry or nervous, so he was unable to put real conviction into his words.

Luco remained motionless, staring silently into Mickey's eyes for several long moments. Moments that were calculated to increase

Mickey's discomfort. When he finally spoke, it began quietly but without a hint of warmth in his voice or in his facial expression.

"You can save your top o' the marnin' blarney Mick bullshit for your beer-swilling chums at the Players' Pub. This is *my* office." His voice gained a little steam. "My *private* office. When Rochelle tells you to wait out there," he said, pointing to the door, his voice well on the rise, "you park your ass out there and you stay out there or you get the fuck out of the building. If you don't, Rochelle is going to get that feisty little Irish lass down in security to come up here and slap you cross-eyed. And believe me she can do it without even breaking a sweat!"

Then, abruptly, Luco's face relaxed into a pleasant, familial grin and the tightness went out of his voice. "Now, do those papers you're playing with have anything to do with the Pearsons loan?" he asked as he took a seat across from Mickey at the conference table.

Mickey's blood had risen to the back of his neck. He normally wouldn't take that kind of talk from anyone but he felt his position might be less than solid. He was, after all, in the wrong for having made himself at home in Luco's office. Besides, he thought, Luco had gotten it off his chest in private and was now back to his old self. Moreover, he reminded himself that he and Luco had a good thing going. He stalled for a couple of beats while he told himself to stay cool.

"OK, Luco," he said, finally, with exaggerated calm. "OK. We got a lot of good stuff going for us ... we gotta stay focused ... no harm done ... OK."

Mickey turned the papers around, arranging them for Luco's view as he launched into his presentation.

"Yeah," he said, getting to Luco's question, "these are my roughs for the Pearsons appraisal. I just ran a tape to double check my figures. They look good. I dug up three good comparables that changed hands in the last 24 months," Mickey said, pointing them out with his finger as he spoke. "I checked them out," he continued, beginning to regain a little enthusiasm and spirit. "They're real solid. None of them will go back on the market for a long time. Even if there's a death in the ownership, the way I've doctored their addresses and the property ID numbers, not even Perry fucking Mason will be able to make the connection."

Luco heard and sucked up every word as Mickey spoke. He never glanced at the papers spread before him. He didn't have to. He had learned over the past seven years that Mickey knew the appraisal business inside out.

Mickey was formerly the Tax Assessor for the City of Providence. He had won the job as a political handout for the Herculean effort he had put out in getting the mayor elected in his first try for public office. In short order, Mickey had moved his cronies into the more sensitive middle and upper level positions they now still held in the Assessor's Office. Then, partly through sleight of hand but mainly through an in-depth knowledge of personnel law as it pertained to standards, practices and requirements, he arranged for his cronies to receive civil service status, along with the entitlements and protections that go with it. Their loyalty to Mickey bordered on the suicidal.

Two terms later, the mayor lost his bid for reelection. Mickey found himself out of a job, but the loyalty of his staff continued to burn, with even greater intensity than before. With willing and eager complicity, and with no questions asked, they gave Mickey full and immediate access to the department's entire data base of records.

TEN

"BASED ON WHAT you have just told me, Mr. Peters, let me try to encapsulate your situation. According to the terms of your credit line, your balance must be reduced to zero for thirty consecutive days at least once in every twelve month period. The last time your account showed a zero balance was eleven months ago, ergo, before the first of next month, you will be required to make a payment in the amount of $480,000. You have advised us that you will be unable to make such a payment and have asked Miss Aiello to devise an alternative so as to preclude what appears to be your imminent default."

Howard Pastore remained motionless as he spoke. He sat in one of two overstuffed chairs at a rectangular coffee table. His legs were crossed, not the way most men would cross their legs, with one ankle resting on top of the other knee, but more the way women did it, with one entire thigh draped over the other. Phil Peters sat in the other chair facing him. A matching sofa completed the grouping.

Howard's unblinking eyes held unwaveringly on Phil's from behind gray-tinted, steel-rimmed glasses. Upon concluding his summary, he turned abruptly to Jeanne Aiello who had remained at her desk. "Is that essentially accurate, Miss Aiello?" he asked.

The mention of her name and his sudden movement took her by surprise, jolting her attention back to Howard. She had been gazing dreamily at Phil out of the corners of her eyes, only half listening to Howard's remarks.

"Yes, Howard," she replied, recovering quickly. She came around from behind her desk to join them.

"That's why I asked you to come in," she continued. "Since I'll need your approval on anything I come up with, and with only a month or so to work something out, I wanted you to hear Philip's story in his own words."

Her straight, black hair was pulled back in a long, loose ponytail. Her brown eyes were set far apart and her mouth was a little lopsided, with its left side preceding the right side into a smile. She looked younger than her 38 years.

She wore a silk blouse and a linen skirt that stopped at mid-knee with an eight-inch slit on each side. She would rather be dead than wear a shirt and tie or the other mannish fashions that so many of her contemporaries had embraced.

Phil couldn't take his eyes off her. He was fascinated by her proud carriage and her smooth, fluid movements as she crossed the room and lowered herself into the sofa. He became self-conscious wondering if Howard had caught him staring at her.

Howard hadn't noticed.

Jeanne had.

So preoccupied was he with his imagined visions of Jeanne, his awareness of the present hadn't yet caught up with what she had just said. The break in conversation lasted too long. Jeanne covertly signaled Phil that Howard was waiting for him to speak. Phil awakened to reality.

"Mr. Pastore, thanks for hearing me out. I suppose you're aware that my company and your bank have had a solid relationship since long before I bought it from Vince Bonetta."

"You suppose correctly, Mr. Peters," said Howard. "The relationship between Production House Graphix and this bank predates my entering the banking business.

"And perhaps *you* are aware that the founder of this bank was my grandfather. He spoke glowingly and often of Vincent Bonetta, the former owner of your company, both as a businessman and as a person. Though I have never met Mr. Bonetta, I admire him.

"Even before you told us in your opening remarks, I knew that five years ago, Mr. Bonetta offered Production House Graphix to you at terms so incredibly favorable to you, you would have been a fool had you not bought the company. To your credit, under your ownership, Production House Graphix has not only continued its growth, its rate of growth has been greatly accelerated.

"Also to your credit, and more to the point at hand, you have been open and pragmatic in your detailed portrayal of the circumstances that led to your present condition."

Suddenly, Howard closed his eyes and tilted his head back as though in deep contemplation. Phil shot questioning glances at Jeanne. She answered him with an almost imperceptible shake of her head, and eyes that said, "Don't say a word. Don't add a thing."

After a long, silent moment, Howard opened his eyes and turned his gaze to Jeanne, but he continued to direct his comments to Phil. "Miss Aiello will draw up a proposal that will enable you to properly address your present indebtedness, taking into account your current cash flow condition and a cash flow projection covering a suitable period of time."

Turning back to Phil, he concluded by saying, "Since time is short, a thirty day extension of the credit line is advised. Miss Aiello will draft a letter to that effect. Now, if there's nothing further … "

Howard got up, followed by Phil and Jeanne. As Howard and Phil shook hands, a trace of a smile appeared behind Howard's close-cropped, jet-black, full-face beard. His dark eyes were eloquent with understanding as he said to Phil, "Mr. Peters, you can count on our help." Without another word, he left the room.

For a long moment, Phil looked at the door in puzzlement. When he turned back to Jeanne, he found her bubbling over with a broad smile.

"Did I just hear what I think I heard?" he asked, barely able to contain himself.

"Yes! Yes! Yes!" she cried in a whispered shout, pumping her fists in triumph. She did a double pirouette and flopped into the sofa. Phil slumped into the sofa next to her, limp with post-crisis relief.

"He did it!" said Phil. "He came through, just like you said he would."

"Oh, Phil, I'm so happy for you. I know how important this is to you," said Jeanne. "Howard's hand in this makes it a fait accompli. Mr. Parisi will have to approve the final agreement but he has never rejected a proposal after Howard has put his stamp of approval on it."

"Strange guy, though, isn't he?" said Phil. "Nothing against him," he added quickly, "he's high on my list of heroes right now. But his eyes. They burn holes in you when he talks."

"And the *way* he talks!" Jeanne exclaimed. With wonderment in her voice, she continued, "He never says 'uh' or 'you know?' or stumble over a word. And that double-breasted suit. Did you ever see a suit fit anyone so darn perfectly? Talk about straight-laced. I bet if we looked in the glove compartment of his car, we'd actually find gloves."

Jeanne hesitated. A quizzical smile grew on her face. Finally she asked, "Well? What do you think of him?"

"He seems to grasp the picture completely," said Phil. He pondered a moment then added, "but there's more to him than that. He seems to be a lot older than his years. He allows his decisions to be influenced by ... no ... it's more like he actually *bases* his decisions on a set of values that were so prevalent during the younger years of our parents but are so rare today."

From Jeanne's reaction, Phil sensed that the question he answered was not the question that Jeanne had asked. She quickly confirmed it.

"That isn't what I meant and you know it," she said with a teasing grin. As she spoke, she slipped out of her shoes, drew her legs up and folded them under her. Phil couldn't avoid noticing that the slits in her skirt performed magnificently.

"No, I *don't* know, Jeanne."

"Come on, Phil. He's so perfect! His manner, his speech, the way he dresses. How many real men do you know like that? Nobody here has ever seen him in shirtsleeves. Or with his necktie loosened. Even last year when the air conditioning went down for a week in August, he never removed his jacket. And he never broke out in a sweat!

"And the way he crosses his legs! Do men cross their legs like that?!"

"Wait a minute, Jeanne," it finally hit him, "are you asking me if Howard's a ... if he's a ... wow! Just because a guy crosses his legs a little dainty makes him queer?! A guy's reputation can be ruined just by questions like that even if he isn't queer?"

"Now calm down, Phil," she said with a note of apology in her tone, "it's not as though it were a subject of open conversation. Some of the girls and I are just dying of curiosity. It doesn't matter to us one way or the other. We just thought it would be a hilarious irony if Howard Pastore, the nephew of the great Luco Parisi who is recognized throughout the civilized world as a womanizer of the first order, turned out to be gay."

"Yeah," he chuckled after reflecting on that thought. "Wouldn't that be a riot? I don't think Luco could handle something like that."

Suddenly, without warning, the present became irrelevant. There wasn't a single word either of them wanted to utter, or to hear. In the resounding hush that befell them, they knew, with certainty, what the other was thinking. Simultaneously, both their thoughts had slipped back to six weeks earlier.

HIS WIFE, MARLA, DIDN'T make the trip. Her lingering distaste for Southwest Florida dated back to when she was "forced" to endure the oppressive heat and the maddening no-see-um gnats while she sat in the stands watching her husband have the time of his life on the baseball diamond. Phil's feelings on the subject were ambivalent. He was happy that she didn't come—if she had, he knew she would spend her entire day in the hotel's lounge—yet, remorseful for feeling good that she stayed home.

Phil's company had a booth at NEPGA, the Northeast Printers & Graphic Arts Expo. It was being hosted for the first time by the Registry Resort in Naples, Florida.

Jeanne Aiello was also attending NEPGA, working the Greater Providence Bank & Trust booth, promoting their multi-layered financing package to potential purchasers of equipment. When, on the final day of the show, Phil stumbled upon her at the end of a long Friday, both he and she were delighted. Neither knew the other had been there, just three aisles away, the entire week.

They decided to unwind by relaxing over a casual dinner and flying out the next day. Their window table at the Brass Pelican overlooked the Registry's pool one story below and the mangrove forest that stretched to the Gulf of Mexico a quarter mile distant to the West. They were seated in time to enjoy the sunset with a cocktail before dinner.

Jeanne and Phil had enjoyed many a business lunch together over the last several years. They had become friends and over time had found themselves, in an easy and intimate way, sharing knowledge of each other's personal lives.

Jeanne had dated, a few times seriously, but never so seriously that she considered making a lifetime commitment, and until she could make that commitment, she refused to fall to the temptation to become a live-in lover. In later years, when flashes of the two or three men that she liked the most entered her thoughts, she would sometimes ponder the question of whether, perhaps, she had been hoping for too much, though her ponderings would be short-lived and unencumbered by regrets.

Phil had been making a name for himself in baseball with the Yankee organization when his wife Marla began to drift away. She stopped going on his road trips, preferring to remain at home with her ever-more-frequent companion, Absolut on-the-rocks.

He was devoted equally to Marla and to his deeply-ingrained, Roman Catholic view of the measureless bonds of marriage. She made it clear that the travel demands of professional baseball and the lack of a place to call home were more than she wanted to bear. Though it had been his lifelong dream to play in the majors, he gave it all up for his marriage. He quit baseball and began a new career working for Vince Bonetta at Production House Graphix.

At first, Marla showed some improvement. She continued to drink but appeared to have it under control. However, as Phil progressed, his responsibilities grew. Like most of his associates, he often worked late into the night and frequently on weekends.

That proved to be too much for Marla. It wasn't that she became a flaming drunk. It's just that she drank all the time. It was as though she had determined precisely her penultimate blood-alcohol level. The level at which both her interpersonal consciousness and her sexual appetite became numbed, yet at which she retained her primary psychomotor functions. It seemed she also had determined, through months of trial and error, the rate of intake of Absolut that would accurately maintain that level. She had reached her nirvana.

Jeanne and Phil both knew with certainty that their feelings for each other had gone far beyond platonic quite some time ago. Despite their knowing, they had never put it into words. Except for the longing caresses unconsciously lavished on each other with their eyes, they had never made contact. They had never kissed, never embraced, never even held hands.

FOLLOWING THE LONG DAY ON THE FLOOR, the flaming sunset, the cocktails, the dinner and the wine, their conversation faltered. They talked of everything and nothing, diligently avoiding that which mattered most. Over another bottle of wine, they retreated to the shadows of silence but they looked deeply into each other's soul with a clarity beyond the capability of words. In the unspoken sharing of their thoughts, their silence was rendered by the silent cries of their need.

Reaching for their wine glasses, his fingers brushed against hers. Unable to contain their yearning for each other any longer, they reached desperately across the table, groping for each other's hands.

"Philip, we've got to *do* something," she said in a choking plea that underscored their passion, "and we've got to do it *now!*"

Still gripping his hands, she rose, tugging him to his feet. Everything else and everyone else in the Brass Pelican sank into oblivion. Somehow, never once breaking physical contact after having at long last experienced each other's touch, they made their way through the boardwalk maze over the tropical pools to the elevator and to Phil's room. Once inside, their lips met and bound them together while their hands frantically explored each other's body as though they were sightless lovers bent on "seeing" every inch of the other. They were naked before they got to the bed.

Their hungry kisses and groping caresses were like a mad, scrambling, uncontrolled dash through the undergrowth of their passion. It was over quickly, an explosive release from the years of suppressed desire. Though spent, they clung to each other with their arms, their legs, their lips, trying to maintain total body contact. Their kisses and their touch became soft, tender, almost contemplative. Soon their needs were reawakened. Savoring every nuance, whispering exclamations of carnal ecstasy through their joined lips, they subconsciously measured their pace of escalation, pausing to fully explore each new level of rapture before elevating themselves to the next. When it was done, they slept in each other's arms.

PHIL DIDN'T KNOW HOW LONG his mind had been replaying that weekend in Naples, or even if, in his absence, Jeanne had spoken to him.

Her arms hugged herself under her breasts with her hands caressing her upper arms. Since that weekend in Naples, they had not uttered a word referring to it and they had not been alone together outside Jeanne's office. Now, it was impossible to ignore the stirrings of its memories.

Unable to contain himself any longer, Phil said, "Jeanne, we've been friends ... much *more* than friends ... for years ... and I ... I ... "

"It's all right, Phil," she said with a sad smile when he faltered.

Slowly she unfolded her legs, reached down and put her shoes back on as she continued, "I understand. You feel it would be wrong for you to tell me what I *know* you're feeling. Well, I'm under no such constraints so I'll say it for both of us. Philip, I love you. And I know you love me. We've probably been in love for years but we've been such close friends we never noticed. Our glorious weekend in Naples changed all that. But I know too well that neither you nor I will let it happen again, not so long as you're married.

"I don't know Marla well enough to hate her but I do hate what your being married to her has done to you ... *is* doing to you ... is doing to *us*," as she rose to her feet.

"Jeanne, for God's sake ... ," Phil stood up, reaching out to her.

"No, Philip, there's nothing more to say," she interrupted him. There was kindness in her voice. And anguish.

She said, "It's time for you to go. I'll walk you to the elevator."

ELEVEN

LUCO PICKED UP THE PAPERS Mickey had spread on the conference table before him, jogged them into a neat stack and handed them back to Mickey.

"What's the bottom line?" Luco asked.

"A good solid 540K. I'll have the formal package on your desk the day after tomorrow."

"OK, I'll set up a closing date for next week."

Soon after his father died, Luco had deftly maneuvered himself into a position of absolute power at GPB&T. The loan board met every Tuesday morning to review loan proposals that the bank's loan officers had prepared. Ostensibly, the board's authority also included reviewing loan proposals brought in by its CEO, Luco Parisi. In reality, whatever Luco put on the table was considered a done deal. Approval was automatic.

Mickey was still feeling good about the manner in which he had manipulated this appraisal. Luco's less-than-enthusiastic response left Mickey somewhat off balance.

"That's it?" he asked. "Luco, this one was a tour-de-force. Why don't you look happy?"

Luco leaned back in his chair before answering.

"The Goyette Building. You recall the Goyette Building?" Luco asked, referring to one of their more recent deals. Of course, Luco knew full well there was no way this one could possibly have slipped from Mickey's memory.

"Yeah, sure." This brought Mickey down abruptly from his high. "The commercial office building in North Providence. Never had better than a fifty-two percent occupancy rate since the day it was built. A white elephant if I ever saw one. I get stomach pains whenever I think about it."

Mickey hadn't wanted to do the Goyette deal in the first place but Luco persuaded him with an extra bonus if he could meet the target figure of 1.2 million.

"I still can't believe I went along with it. I bumped a 950K building up to a million two," Mickey continued, "and when you took Goyette's house in Narragansett as added security, I bumped up that musty old dump too, clear out of the market."

He fidgeted, nervously packing his papers and his calculator into his briefcase and glancing repeatedly at Luco as he did so. He noisily snapped his briefcase shut and stared at Luco, waiting, but Luco remained silent.

"Talk to me Luco," Mickey's tone was taut. "I'm getting stomach pains. Why did you bring up the Goyette case?"

Luco sat up straight.

"Goyette missed his last three payments … "

"He what?!" Mickey gasped, springing to his feet.

" … but I covered them."

"I told you we shouldn't do that deal! I told you it was too weak but you really put the pressure on me. You gave me your sworn fucking word Goyette could make good on it!"

"Take it easy, Mickey," Luco replied. His voice was quiet but tight as he continued, "I told you I covered it but … if it goes on much longer, I'll have to figure some other way to handle it."

"Covered it my ass! You can't cover it!" Mickey had completely lost his composure and didn't realize he was skating close to very thin ice. "You're the banker! You know that! The only way you can cover it is to make the payments yourself and I know goddamm well you're not gonna do that, you greasy fuckin' guin… !"

Mickey went silent. He heard his own words come flooding back to him as though they had been spoken by someone else. In slow motion, he sank into his chair, groping without success for something to say that would undo his last words.

For what seemed like a painful eternity to Mickey, Luco returned his silence. When finally Luco spoke, it was in a guttural whisper that resonated with fury and dripped with venom. His use of the English language could range from intelligent, articulate and polite through locker room raunch all the way down to in-your-face street.

"Guinea?! You call me a guinea?! You don't even know what the word means you shanty-Irish prick! But *whatever* guinea means, you're married to one. And that guinea you're married to happens to be my niece."

With no change in his menacing tone, Luco continued, "There's one thing about guineas that if you don't already know you goddamm well better learn. They're big on respect. They give respect, they expect it in return. When they are treated with *dis*respect," Luco slammed his open palm down on the table with such force that Mickey was visibly startled and his briefcase bounced into the air, "it is taken as an unforgivable blow to their honor."

"Come on, Luco," Mickey was contrite, "you know I didn't mean anything. How could I mean anything like that, the way I loved your old man? He made me feel like I was his own son. For crisake we're like brothers, you and I, we call each other names, we don't mean anything. Why do you want to make me feel like shit?"

Though it was clear that Mickey was truly sorry he had stepped out of bounds, Luco didn't back down at all. Moving to sit at his own desk, he buzzed for Rochelle. When she entered, Luco told her with a dismissive wave of his hand in Mickey's direction, "Mr. Hoban was just leaving." Mickey knew it was useless to make any further attempt to undo what he had said. He rose to leave.

Rochelle led him to the door and waited until Mickey was out of earshot then said, "I was just going to buzz you. René Goyette is on hold. I told him you were in a meeting. He said he would wait." With that, she retreated to the outer office, closing Luco's door behind her.

"I WAS SUPPOSED TO HEAR FROM YOU two days ago, Goyette." Luco made no attempt at cordiality. The tension of his conversation with Mickey was still in his voice. "You better have good news for me."

"I wish I did, believe me, but I don't. I couldn't raise it. I can't raise it."

"What are you telling me?!"

"What I'm saying is that I have exhausted every resource, called every favor and groveled at the feet of everyone I know who might have access to that kind of money. It is clear, Luco, that they are exercising far better business sense than I did when I bought the building. There is no way to sugar-coat this. I'm out of options. There is no hope of my raising any money. I apologize for any inconvenience this might create for you."

"Inconvenience?! You're behind over 30 Gs on your payments! I cooked the fuckin' books to cover you! They can plant my ass in federal prison and this might create an inconvenience?!"

"That isn't what I had in mind, Luco," Goyette continued in a calm tone that Luco found disconcerting. "Though certainly it might inconvenience you, I thought you might prefer to make those back payments out of your own funds, as well as any subsequent payments I am unable to make. That is, until I have sufficiently recovered and am in a position to reimburse you. You could then re-cook the books to make them audit proof, the account would be up to date and no one would be the wiser."

The implications were unmistakable. The alternative would lead to audit, investigation, disclosure, disgrace and prison.

"Listen you slimeball son-of-a-bitch," Luco was livid, he kept his voice down but his fury was clearly evident, "you sat right here in my office with tears running down your flabby cheeks when nobody else would refi that drafty old mausoleum-with-a-view that you live in. When nobody else would even consider your loan application for the fucking Goyette Building. You came to me and I came through for you. Now you've got the balls to tell me I should shell out thirty big ones plus ten more each month and by the way, ha-ha, sorry to inconvenience you, old chum?

"Not a chance, you miserable bastard! Before I do that, I'll … "

"Please, Luco," Goyette interrupted with exaggerated calmness and patience, "I needn't be reminded of all that you did for me. You did, in fact, come through when all others had turned their backs on me and I was grateful to you.

"On the other hand, as I remember it specifically, I expressed my gratitude with an undisclosed cash payment to you in the amount of $250,000. Therefore I'm somewhat dismayed by how you are reacting to my suggestion. After all, you did, at the time, justify that payment as risk insurance?"

"Yeah. That was risk insurance and as of now, you fat, candy-assed slimeball, the risk is all yours!" Luco had lost control. "Have you got any idea what kind of services I can buy for 30 grand? There's some guys I know that enjoy snapping somebody's bones only because they like the sound of it. For a lousy grand, they would do anyth ... "

"Excuse me for interrupting, Luco," Goyette's tone and manner were as though he were regretfully turning down an invitation to tea, "but I do have to run. Oh, by the way. I almost forgot to mention. I have recorded this entire conversation on tape that I will seal in an envelope and turn over to my attorney. My directions shall instruct him to play the tape should any untoward event befall me. Do have a nice day."

ROCHELLE ENTERED HIS OFFICE and closed the door behind her. Luco sat fuming at his desk. She walked behind him and began to massage the muscles of his neck where it joins the shoulders.

"You are really up tight, baby," she cooed, "that must have been some phone call."

"Mmm, nice try, Shel," he said, "but not now. OK?" He stood up and gave her a peck on the cheek and started to leave.

"This day has gotten off to a lousy start. I'm going to the club for a workout and a sauna," he said as he neared the door.

"Call me when you're finished?" She called to him. She took a step toward him then stopped, with legs slightly parted, her hands caressing the fronts of her thighs.

"Yeah ... we'll see," he mumbled as his eyes traced a detailed course from her lips to her hands. "Maybe I will."

JUST THE SIGHT of Phil Peters left a bitter taste in Luco's mouth. Waiting for the elevator, Luco noticed Jeanne and Phil coming his way. They appeared to be engrossed in conversation and hadn't noticed him. Luco impatiently pressed the button again while he kept looking at Phil who, thankfully, didn't take his eyes off Jeanne. As the elevator arrived and the door opened, Luco quickly entered and pressed the garage button. The door closed before Phil saw him.

They had known each other since sandlot baseball days. Luco was good, better than most, but from the beginning, he played in the shadow of Phil. All the kids played in Phil's shadow, but except for Luco, they all idolized him as a baseball player. Phil was a natural.

Luco was jealous not so much of Phil's superior talent as he was of the recognition and accolades that were bestowed on Phil, and the genuine friendship that developed so naturally between Phil and the other kids. Luco had no one with whom to share that jealousy of Phil. He could never express it without risking censure by the others.

Luco and Phil played together at Hope High School. During that time, their life patterns began to take shape. While Phil was proving himself to be a scholar as well as a standout on the baseball diamond, Luco was proving to himself that there was no end to the supply of girls who were ready, willing and able to indulge him. He had looks, money, a sharp car, and experience.

Phil, on the other hand, to save money for college, worked part time, resulting in a social life that was severely limited. However, with his straight A scholastic record and his consistently outstanding achievements on the baseball diamond, Phil's admittance to Brown University was never in doubt.

AS PHIL STEPPED INTO THE elevator, Jeanne offered her hand. Without a word, their eyes spoke tender phrases. They released their grip in a slow caress. The elevator door closed.

'Philip, I love you. And I know you love me. We've probably been in love for years ... '

Hearing Jeanne's words out loud had awakened him. She was right. He did love her and he had loved her for years. Her words echoed in his mind. He was absorbed by what she had said, what they had talked about. His thoughts were 1300 miles away, savoring that magical weekend in Naples, as he stepped from the bank into the garage.

He caught a peripheral glimpse of the car bearing down on him, driving too fast down the exit ramp. Phil spun and jumped. One foot slipped out from under him on the still wet pavement, launching him into a twisting back-flip. He landed safely off to one side, bruising one knee and destroying his trousers. He caught only a glimpse of the car, a cream-colored Rolls, but was unable to see the driver.

Luco Parisi's attention had been diverted to inside his car. He was oblivious to the acrobatic evasive maneuver that had taken place and to the grim event that had been narrowly averted while he thumb-dialed his cell phone.

TWELVE

"MR. PARISI'S OFFICE," ROCHELLE answered on Luco's private line.

"It's me," said Luco. "I'll be finished at the gym by eleven. How about meeting me at the apartment? Some of my ... desires and practices ... might need your attention."

"Yes, Mr. Parisi," she replied formally and after a slight hesitation, continued, "eleven-thirty will be fine." She then dismissed the filing clerk who had been standing before her desk.

Luco pressed the END button on his cellular phone without so much as a 'see you later.' Rochelle looked at the ornate grandfather's clock in the lushly appointed sitting area outside Luco's office and said to herself, "Two hours! My God, I'll be wringing wet by then."

SHE LET HERSELF IN WITHOUT knocking and heard the shower running in the bathroom. Passing through the living room into the bedroom, she found Luco's workout clothes and gym shoes strewn on the floor. Through the open bathroom door, Luco's naked figure was visible behind the steam-fogged glass of the shower stall. Though his image was ghosted, what she was able to see of him caused her to gasp reflexively, the sound masked by the shower noise.

She backed away undiscovered. Unable to take her eyes off him, she removed her clothes with trembling fingers, draped them carefully over the backs of chairs and drew back the bed covers. She lay down on her back with pillows propping up her head to give her a view over her breasts and along her flat tummy with its pubic fur cap at the far end. She looked down the length of her legs, parting them so her feet would not obstruct her view through the bathroom door into the shower. Nor would they obstruct Luco's view when he entered the room.

When the shower stopped she felt the room resonate with the sound of her own breathing and the timpanic pounding of her heartbeat. Unaware that she had arrived, Luco stepped from the bathroom glistening wet, both hands overhead briskly toweling his hair dry. The physical movement carried through his body causing his member to dance like a double-jointed puppet on a string. Rochelle focused on it as though hypnotized.

Surprised by the sight of Rochelle, the first thing Luco saw was the dark, inviting apex that she so openly presented to him. The pace of his toweling slowed involuntarily to a deliberate, sensual massage as he dried himself. Everywhere. The dancing puppet slowed, assuming a more resolute and assertive persona. A tiny moan escaped Rochelle. Her entire body trembled in anticipation.

NORMALLY, HIS WORKOUTS ACTED as an aphrodisiac. Not this time. His mind was elsewhere. During his session at the gym, he couldn't shake off the effects of what had taken place earlier in the office—Mickey's outburst upon learning the Goyette deal might go bad; his own telephone argument with René Goyette; the specter of foreclosure. His scam was coming unglued.

Now with Rochelle under him, Luco was performing on autopilot, and when he's on autopilot, his puppet takes on a life of its own, sustaining its attention span indefinitely.

"Oh LOUUU-co, DAAAR-ling," she whimpered, "I think … it's … it's … gonna happen … again!"

If they had been counting, they would have known that it had already happened three times for her. In the beginning, Rochelle had been like a dynamo, thrashing wildly, matching Luco move for move and, at times, whipping about like an unrestrained high-pressure hose. After the third time, she lay in absolute submission with both arms fully extended on the pillows while Luco continued without interruption. Her eyeballs rolled back and her head rocked from side to side in metronomic rhythm with Luco's unrelenting and undiminished movements. Her earlier cries and screeches had become a low, almost hypnotic moan of primordial, erotic pleasure.

There are those who do their best thinking while jogging, or swimming laps, or punching a light bag. For Luco, it was sex. It was possible for him to sort out and analyze business matters of the highest magnitude while at the same time performing up to the most hopeful expectations of his partner of the moment.

"Don't wait for me, baby," Luco feigned sincerity as he whispered with his lips brushing her ear, "you go for it."

He thought about the lucrative thing he and Mickey had going. There was no shortage, it seemed, of big spenders who got themselves bent over the table. Their appetites drove them beyond their means. Unable to manage and regulate their rising success, they succumbed to excesses that they rationalized as their rightful due.

"Oh, nOooo!" she moaned in helpless protest. "I ... wanna ... wait ... for you."

"It's OK, baby," he said while kissing her eyes, an act he had always felt worked rather well in conveying the impression that he cared, "this one is just for you."

He viewed his 'clients' as assholes who got what they deserved. They bought and spent their way into the company of the real heavy hitters, forgetting Mark Twain's admonition that the surest way to the poorhouse is to have rich friends. Along the way, they would be confronted with the need to make substantial and undisclosed cash payments. The inevitable girlfriends. Girlfriends' babies. Girlfriends' abortions. Girlfriends who want to become wives where wives already exist. Girlfriends who are bribed with lush apartments, flashy cars and expensive trinkets to never again utter the words divorce and marriage.

Rochelle's breathing became labored as her body again grew animated. She attempted to say something but whatever it was came out as a high-pitched "Unh! ... Unh! ... Unh! ... " in cadence with the rhythm of Luco's movements.

To encourage her enthusiasm, Luco replied, "Yes!" to each of her utterances creating a combined dialogue that said, "Unh! Yes! Unh! Yes! Unh! Yes! Unh! Yes!" Though Luco had to suppress a laugh, it had the desired effect on Rochelle. She threw her arms around his back with a renewed strength that took him by surprise, momentarily forcing the wind out of him.

And gambling. Why is it, Luco thought, that so many of those people, after undergoing years of sacrifice, countless hours of work and untold financial risk to build a successful business would turn to gambling? Were they too stupid to realize that the well was not bottomless? Or did they in fact realize it, perhaps too late, and resort to gambling in a desperate bid to refill the well?

Ultimately, when they ended up owing money to people who charged vigorish—interest—at the rate of 25 percent per week and who had no sense of humor about late payments, they turned to Luco for salvation. They would mortgage all their property to Greater Providence with Mickey inflating his appraisal to whatever figure Luco gave him. A figure that would be enough to pay off the outstanding loans against the property plus the amount the client needed to satisfy his personal problems. Plus Luco's fee. In cash. Unrecorded.

With both of her hands, Rochelle grasped Luco's black, wavy hair at the back of his head and pulled his head back. She stuck her tongue deep into his mouth, found his tongue, and while sucking it into her own mouth, cried, "Turn over! I want to get on top!" With his tongue in her mouth it sounded like a string of grunts. No matter. When she threw him off her and scrambled wildly into position, he understood. Rochelle was beginning to get Luco's attention.

Luco reflected on the seven years that began the day they buried his father and he struck his first deal with Mickey over a drink in the garden. They had skimmed over $8 million, but he told Mickey it was only two. Mickey, deceived by Luco into believing that he was a full partner in the venture, received one million.

"C'mon Luco ... c'mon ... c'mon ... c'mon ... Luco ... PLEASE," Rochelle implored. She rode him like a jockey with her feet high in the stirrups.

Luco regretted having jeopardized their entire operation by taking on the Goyette deal. He hated to admit it but Mickey had been right.

"Luco ... PLEASE ... make it with ME ... PLEASE darling!"

He remembered all too vividly how Mickey had pegged Goyette as a phony. Goyette hadn't shown any signs of the panic or urgency that had been so evident in all the others. He had been too easy. Too cool. Goyette didn't flinch and he didn't even try to bargain when Luco told him the "fee" would be $250,000.

"Luco, BAAAby! ... Let it happen! ... It's ... it's gonna HAPPEN! ... I can't hold it BACK!"

After the foreclosure auction, there'll surely be an audit. The investigators will discover and expose the entire scam. They could force him to make restitution or could put him behind bars for bank fraud, or both. Luco had known from the start that something like this could someday happen. He realized the end was near.

His thoughts drifted to Germany and to Erika. With her help, he had prepared for it. He wanted to be with Erika.

"Oh ... YES ... we CAN, Luco ... we CAN!" Rochelle didn't realize that she was beating Luco's chest with her tiny fists. He never felt it.

His focus was completely on Erika. His eyes looked at Rochelle but in her place he saw Erika. Rochelle's voice became Erika's voice. His breathing grew erratic and he increased his speed to match Rochelle's frantic, abandoned pace.

With her hands pressed flat upon his chest and her head thrown back, she cried out in a low, wailing moan through lips drawn tightly down at the corners. Then she fell forward on him, kissing his lips, his cheeks, his eyes and his neck, through the final glorious seconds of his conclusion.

HE STOOD PEERING THROUGH the curtains, looking down into the service alley two floors below. Shortly, a cab pulled to a stop. A figure darted from the house into the back seat. With her dark, oversized sunglasses and her head shawl obscuring most of her face, it would be impossible for anyone to identify that figure as Rochelle.

She would be a little late getting back to the office but no one would notice. Office business often called her out of the building.

Luco took another shower, threw his sweats into a gym bag and dressed in his business clothes. His Rolls was in the garage below that is entered from the service alley. Luco had selected this apartment mainly because he was able to come and go without being noticed. He hadn't forgotten the dire promise Papa Cheech had made to him in the steam room.

He waited another minute or two to be certain the cab was gone, then he picked up the phone and dialed a fourteen-digit number. It was almost 8:00PM in Nürnberg, Germany. There was no answer at Erika's shop. He dialed her home number. Again there was no answer.

'Where the hell is she?' he thought. 'Her shop closes at seven. It isn't that long a drive to her home. Her driver has made the trip so many times he could do it in his sleep for crisake. Why isn't she at home? She's with someone, isn't she? Who, goddammit? Who's she with? She's beautiful. Sexy. Divorced. Who did she take home with her from some big shot's cocktail party? She can be had, you know. You know she can be had. Didn't she take you home, asshole?!'

He slammed the phone into its cradle so hard a piece of the plastic broke off and skittered across the room. He sat down heavily on the edge of the bed with his elbows on his knees and his head in his hands.

'Put it out of your mind,' he scolded himself. 'She runs a business. She's got commitments. She's got clients to entertain. Social events to attend. Important people to meet. She's got a life to live. You expect her to live like a freakin' nun?'

ERIKA'S DIVORCE SETTLEMENT had endowed her with a mansion but, when she and Luco became lovers, she was struggling with an income that was barely sufficient to cover the expense of its upkeep. Confident in her talent, she knew that Mode-Erika could be successful if she could elevate her image. When the space next door to her shop became available, Luco told her to take it. He paid the lease in advance. He also poured in large sums of money for remodeling and redecorating and then even more when Erika tentatively suggested that a grand opening event might be a good idea.

Luco told her to go all out but in a selective way. To make her grand opening elegant, sparing no expense, but to keep it private, by invitation only, and to combine it with a showing of her original designs. With the help of a young and eager public relations firm, her opening event was a smashing success, receiving flattering coverage in the papers and on the TV news. Soon her creations became *de rigueur* at the highest levels of Nürnberg society and ultimately commanded such exorbitant prices that only the most affluent could afford to wear them. Before long, she found herself regularly included in their social functions.

Of all the women he had—that's the way Luco thought of women. He didn't know them, or date them, or love them, he had them—Erika was the only one who could exercise dominion over their relationship. He wanted her. He needed her. But he hated wanting her and he hated needing her. Most of all, he hated admitting to himself that he didn't have the *coglione* to try to change it.

Erika's passions ran deep and hot but he had yet to discover which buttons to push to arouse them. There had been times in their lovemaking when he found that her fires had been ignited and were burning furiously before he had any idea what had caused it. He discovered that aspect of her sensuality a few months after they met in Nürnberg.

It had already become clear to Luco that this woman was not subordinate to his sexual initiatives. It was midday and they were in a taxi returning from lunch at Steigerle's. In a moment of uncertainty, having been unable to establish himself as the controlling force, Luco made a desperate attempt to elevate his stature. He imagined that by bragging about his loan-skimming side business and his laundering of mob money, thus implying a measure of mob status and power to himself, he might shock Erika into a more submissive role. He could not have been more astonished by her reaction.

Instead, she had soared instantly to the summit of arousal. She spun in the seat and mounted him, fully clothed, crying, "Ach, mein Gott! Mein Gott! Mein Gott!" There was no time to remove any garments. She kissed him deeply with wet, sucking sounds while holding onto his ears with both her hands and crushing him under her wild pounding. It was over in seconds, before Luco could even react to what was happening, but not before the driver had to swerve in desperation to avoid the tram that was bearing down on them. By the time the cab pulled up to the door of her shop, mere minutes later, Erika was again fully composed.

Days later, when Luco asked if she would consider carrying some money for him, she jumped at the chance. Subsequently, she made many trips. She didn't know whose money she was carrying. It didn't matter to her. Just knowing it was mob money and that there was the risk of getting caught was sufficient for her. Her arousal would begin the minute Luco would call her and tell her to get ready for another trip. When she arrived in Providence, she and Luco would have a day or two together at his hideaway apartment. During such courier trips, she could not restrain herself and she wantonly used Luco to fulfill her rampant physiological requirements. At all other times, she held her sexual needs and desires in check in accordance with her master plan for sustaining a lasting relationship.

LUCO WAS ALMOST RELIEVED that the game had ended. His uncertainty about Erika's activities in his absence was maddening. Things will be better when he gets to Germany.

Soon after they foreclose on Goyette, he thought, Luco's loan-boosting scam will be exposed. Before that happens, he will have to leave town. He has put away a sum of money that he could only have dreamed of a few short years earlier. In addition to the seven million from his loan-boosting scam, he made another million-and-a-half by laundering illegal money for a Federal Hill wiseguy, with Erika's willing participation.

There were no phone calls and no meetings. The trickiest part was getting the wiseguy's cash out of the country. A courier would hand-carry a sealed envelope containing a key to a bus station locker where Luco would find a suitcase filled with several hundred thousand dollars in small bills. After hours, in a locked vault, Luco would exchange the small bills for large bills that he could easily conceal in luggage that he would then carry to Switzerland. There he would deposit the cash into his private numbered account.

Later, Erika made most of the trips, taking the money into Nürnberg. From there, her driver, Reiner, would drive the suitcase to Basel. He wasn't told what was in the suitcase. He would simply place it in a train station locker, removing from the locker an identical suitcase filled with clothing in Reiner's size. His instructions would be to take the night off, have a good dinner and a pleasant evening, and to return in the morning.

Before the end of the next business day, the contents of Reiner's suitcase would have found their way into Luco's numbered account in Die Schweizer National Bank.

THIRTEEN

THE LOUNGE IN JOE MARTELLA'S restaurant is not a big room. There are no sitting areas except at the bar that is formed in the shape of an expanded letter U. Mostly the patrons stand elbow-to-elbow and back-to-back. Given the decibel level of thirty or more simultaneous conversations, and all the unavoidable jostling, it would be a pickpocket's paradise were it not that this was Martella's-On-the-Hill.

On any given day, the dinner crowd might include a mix of judges, lawyers, prosecutors, physicians, heavy-hitter business people, politicians, high-level police officials, and even a smattering of wise guys. All of them, likely, grew up together and regularly broke bread together on The Hill. A pickpocket would have to be certifiably insane to even consider plying his craft in Martella's place on Federal Hill in Providence, Rhode Island. It was probably the safest haven from crime on the entire continent.

Around 5:30, many of the after-work regulars show up for a drink or two before heading home. Not infrequently, some of them change their minds and settle in for an early dinner at the bar before the place fills up.

Mickey Hoban got there around 5:15 and by the time he reached the far end of the bar, his drink was waiting for him. He took a stool between two empty ones, threw down the Fernet Branca and sipped his Bass Ale in quiet, pretty much keeping to himself. Moments later, Howard Pastore came in. Catching his eye, Mickey beckoned him to take the stool next to him.

Until then Mickey had been feeling somewhat glum so he looked on in grateful amusement as Howard gave detailed instructions to Gino, the bartender. He ordered a Southern Comfort old-fashioned, touch of bitters, no sugar, a splash of cherry juice, muddle the fruit and top it off with two undamaged cherries on a skewer. Gino, leaning heavily with both hands on the bar, listened in resigned silence then said, "Excuse me, Mr. Pastore, was there something wrong with the drinks I made for you the last time you were in?"

"Not at all, Gino," said Howard after a moment's thought, "they were very good."

"And how about the time before that, Mr. Pastore? How were the drinks that time?"

"As I recall, Gino, they too were flawlessly prepared. I would recommend them without reservation."

"And the time before that?" Though he spoke softly and with proper deference as he muddled the fruit for Howard's drink, it was impossible for Gino to totally conceal his annoyance.

"Yes. Those too. But is there, perhaps, a point to your questions?"

Mickey had been listening intently, his head turning to follow the dialogue as though he were watching a tennis match from a midcourt seat.

"As a matter of fact, Mr. Pastore, can you tell me when was the last time I booted one?" said Gino, ignoring Howard's question.

"If 'booted one' means serving me a wrong drink or an improperly prepared drink," Howard folded his arms across his chest, tilted his head back with his eyes closed in thought for a long moment, then continued, " … I cannot recall a single instance in which you, as you say, 'booted one.' "

Finished preparing the drink, Gino placed it before Howard and asked pleadingly, in a low voice so as not to be overheard by others at the bar, "Then, with all due respect Mr. Pastore, why do you have to keep giving me the whole freakin' nine yards every freakin' time you order this same freakin' drink?"

Howard delayed a beat or two before replying.

"Well, Gino, we have just established that you have not once 'booted one' while using that method," said Howard. Then, unable to maintain his deadpan expression a second longer, he broke into a beaming smile as he delivered the Q.E.D., "and since reciting 'the whole nine yards' each time I place my order has had such good results, it would be illogical to tamper with such a proven formula." Mickey had seen it coming and had already broken into laughter.

Gino was open-mouthed and speechless for a second. When finally it dawned on him that he had been had, he said, "I don't believe it!" as he slapped his forehead with his open palm.

"Neither do I!" said Mickey, still laughing. "You've been ordering that same drink using the same spiel for how many months now? Just to set Gino up for this gag?!" Raising his glass in toast to Howard, he said, "Touché!"

"Mr. Pastore, this one's on me," said Gino with a friendly smile as he placed the drink before Howard, "you've earned it." Then turning to Mickey, "How about you, Mr. Hoban? Ready for another Fernet and Bass? Next one's on me."

Mickey nodded yes to the drink as the humor of the moment faded away. Without realizing it, he had again turned serious. Remnants of his 'Goyette' confrontation with Luco haunted him.

"You surprise me, old pal," said Mickey. "Fun and frivolity are not among the traits you banker types are widely known for."

" 'Fun? Frivolity?' A curious choice of words, Michael," Howard replied, "since neither could be applied to you at the moment."

Mickey had already retreated into his thoughts. His meeting with Luco Parisi that morning had left him unsettled and preoccupied the entire day. Not so much for his unfortunate *guinea* comment. Luco would never let him off the hook by admitting it but he knew Mickey didn't mean anything by it and Mickey knew Luco would soon forget about it. But the Goyette loan was another matter. If that loan were to fold, and it looked like it was heading in that direction, Greater Providence would foreclose on the loan and put Goyette's building up for auction. Mickey knew, of course, that it would sell for far less than the inflated appraisal value he had placed on it and that the proceeds of the sale would be insufficient to pay off Goyette's remaining loan. That would then force the bank to do the same with Goyette's house in Narragansett. The sale of the house would produce similar results and the bank would surely begin an internal investigation.

Mickey couldn't shake off the sense of impending doom. Howard's solicitous remark hadn't yet registered on Mickey. When he didn't respond, Howard continued, "You seem to be uncharacteristically morose. It troubles me to see you this way. Is there some way I can help?"

There was not one thing about that meeting that Mickey could talk about. Howard was unrelentingly ethical and honest. And he was totally in the dark about the scam that Mickey and Luco had been running. Mickey had long ago come to terms not only with the illegality but also with the immorality of what he and Luco were doing. It was only when he and Howard were together, just being buddies, that pangs of conscience nagged at him.

Emerging from his reverie, Mickey knew he must change the subject. He took a long pull from his Bass Ale and put on his friendly, "twinkling-Irish-eyes" face. Affecting his lilting accent, he said, "Can it be that lurking behind your cold facade one might possibly find a beating heart?" asked Mickey, sidestepping away from the direction of Howard's comment. Mickey loved to needle Howard in fun about cold, dispassionate bankers having computer chips in place of hearts. Warming to his subject, he said, "Saints in Heaven! If they find a heart, what would come next, a trace of compassion?! Word of this were to get out, lad, you'll be drummed out of the Bankers' Hall of Gloom!"

They had a strange, almost "odd couple" relationship. There was nothing at all similar about them. Mickey was one of the few who liked Howard and wouldn't take part in the behind-the-hand comments others made suggesting that Howard was a closet homosexual. They first met a few weeks before the marriage of Mickey to Howard's sister, Gloria. Howard admired Mickey's natural Irish affability and he welcomed Mickey's unabashed friendship, which asked for nothing but friendship in return. Howard didn't get very much of it from others.

Mickey had succeeded not only in sidetracking their conversation but in elevating his own mood as well. They small talked, covering the same ground they always covered with Mickey deriding bankers in general, including Howard. He described them as heartless creatures who are immune to and cloistered from the vagaries and hazards with which the real business world must contend on a daily basis. Howard was losing ground as Mickey continued about bankers' stress-free lives. About their never having experienced first hand the magnitude of the commitment that is required of the budding entrepreneur nor the depth of the loss with which he is faced every day. Though Mickey was dead serious about everything he said, he delivered it all in the form of good natured, drinking-buddy banter.

By then, Howard was well into his third old-fashioned, exceeding his usual limit of two. "While a grain of truth might possibly exist in some of what you say," said Howard in an effort to retaliate, "your generalization is far too broad. Only last month, a customer came to us in dire straits. The man was in default on a sizable loan, though admittedly as a result of bizarre circumstances over which he had little if any influence."

Howard went on to assert that if Mickey's characterization of bankers was indeed accurate, then as a result of the default, GPB&T should very well have called that customer's other loans and foreclosed on his business, his building and his home. They had all been pledged as security. Instead, Howard related how an alert and sensitive loan officer, who had some ideas about setting up a new loan package that might save the customer from ruin, had asked Howard to intercede.

Noting that he had gained Mickey's rapt attention, Howard warmed to his task. He pointed out that in addition to saving the customer, the bank's response had the added effect of protecting the jobs and economic security of the employees of his printing business.

"Our customer's employees—those were very real people, Michael—are now far more secure because of the action we took," Howard proudly continued in a thoroughly serious vein. "The man struck me as a solid individual. A throwback to years past when honor and a man's word were the only necessary ingredients to a contract. I later learned that he had even sacrificed a promising baseball career, the fulfillment of a lifelong dream, to hold his faltering marriage together."

Howard stopped abruptly, struck with the realization that he had inadvertently revealed the identity of the customer he had been describing; an unforgivable breach of confidentiality. He wondered in the awkwardly silent moment that followed whether Mickey had picked up on it.

"Don't sweat it, Howard," said Mickey with a kind smile, "I didn't hear a word you said." He had correctly read the mortified expression on Howard's face. "But, yes," he continued, "I know Phil Peters well. He and I and your uncle Luco played baseball together. And you're absolutely right. Phil is a truly honorable man." Then, attempting to restore a lightness to their conversation, he finished with, "One of the very few remaining in western civilization ... if you'll pardon my cynicism."

Mickey always liked Phil, ever since they were kids playing on the Ciacchone Plumbing & Supply baseball team. Though he followed Phil's career in the sports pages, they went their separate ways after college, running into each other only at wakes and weddings of mutual friends and relatives. He told Howard he was proud of him and happy that they were going to help Phil.

Howard was put at ease by Mickey's deft and sensitive handling of the gaffe. Relieved and encouraged, he went on to confide that he had already approved the outline of a proposal that Jeanne Aiello had prepared. At a meeting set for next week, Phil, his lawyer and his accountant will review the final draft of the package. If Phil accepts the plan, and there's every reason to expect that he will, it will require nothing more than Uncle Luco's official stamp of approval.

" ... and that, my dear Michael," said Howard with exaggerated pomposity, "should urge you to rethink your unfounded notion that all bankers are heartless and cold."

THE BAR WAS BEGINNING TO fill up with early arrivals for dinner. All the stools were taken and standees were beginning to form into clusters.

Had Mickey or Howard noticed him when he entered through the side entrance from Barker Street, they would not have recognized him. Nor did any of the other patrons as he jostled his way through the crowd and took up a standing position behind and between Mickey and Howard. He was a large man in his mid-thirties, wearing a slightly rumpled, light gray suit. The knot in his blue- and white-striped tie hung an inch below his undone collar button. His short blond hair, receding along both temples, was slightly longer than a brush cut and fell limply in random directions.

This wasn't his first stop of the evening. Though he didn't yet show it, he had already had just enough to make him belligerent. The first inkling Mickey and Howard had of his presence was when he got Gino's attention and ordered his drink.

"Gimme one o' these faggot drinks this guy's havin'," he said, pointing with his thumb almost in Howard's face. He didn't say it loud enough for anyone other than Mickey, Howard and Gino to hear him. Gino immediately recognized this man in the gray suit as a type. He was a man to be watched closely. Mickey too had been in enough barroom situations that he knew this customer could be trouble. Only Howard seemed oblivious to the possibilities.

Gino placed the drink on the bar between Mickey and Howard. As Gray-Suit reached for it, he intentionally jostled Howard, forcing Howard to make eye-contact. Gray-Suit's lips were turned up at the corners but there was no smile in his cold, blue eyes.

" 'scuse me, pal," he said, raising his glass to Howard and ignoring Mickey completely, "here's to ya."

"No harm done, my friend," Howard quietly replied. He looked directly into Gray-Suit's eyes. Mickey observed that although Howard hadn't changed position, his face, no, his entire being, had taken on a new stance. As though alertness and readiness oozed from every pore and a confident energy field emanated from him. Mickey had seen this transformation once before, in the gym where Howard took part in a martial arts tournament.

"So how's about drinkin' with me, then?" That was a bit louder, causing a few heads to turn.

"It is not my wish to offend you, my friend, but we are enjoying a drink and a private conversation."

"Don't gimme that shit! You called me your friend so you can goddamm well drink with me!" That was louder still. Most everyone in the bar stopped talking and turned their attention to what was developing.

Gino made a move as if to intercede but was dissuaded by Mickey. Quietly, so that Gray-Suit couldn't hear, Mickey said, "Relax and enjoy the show. Trust me, Gino." Then Mickey got up, shuffled his stool away from the bar creating a space next to Howard and sat back down. Gray-suit observed the move with puzzlement. Nonetheless, he stepped forward to occupy the space vacated by Mickey, placing himself to the right of Howard who continued to sit facing the bar.

Without turning to face Gray-Suit, Howard said, "We seem to have gotten off to an unfortunate start. If you will permit me to clarify my position, perhaps we will be able to avoid any further misunderstanding." Howard spoke quietly, but as he spoke, he removed his steel-rimmed glasses with slow, deliberate movements, folded them and inserted them into his breast pocket.

"Yeah, awright, so go ahead an' esplain, y' goddamm pansy." As he spoke, Gray-Suit turned sideways to the bar so that he faced Howard squarely. He planted his feet apart and put his glass on the bar.

"Thank you," said Howard. He spoke slowly, looking straight ahead. "My position is this. I was having a quiet drink and pleasant conversation with my friend. You disrupted that conversation in a decidedly boorish and offensive fashion. To ameliorate the effects of your appalling manners, or perhaps to amplify them—it remains unclear to me which was your intended course—you invited me to be your drinking buddy."

"W' th' fuck you talkin' about? What kinda bullshit ... ?"

"One moment, please," Howard cut him off, turning only his head to look directly into Gray-Suit's eyes. "I have no desire to drink with you. Given the choice, I would prefer instead to share a convivial libation with a camel whose odor and whose manners, no doubt, would be infinitely less offensive than yours."

Howard moved his glass forward and motioned for Gino to clear it. Then with both hands resting lightly on the bar, he continued, "Nor have I the slightest desire to look at you or even to be in the same room with you. You, sir, may take pride in having achieved success at something. You have reached the pinnacle of repulsiveness and repugnance. Therefore, I have no wish to talk any further with you."

Gray-suit hesitated a long moment, perhaps waiting for the meaning of everything Howard had said to fall into place, before exclaiming, "Awright, asshole!" He grabbed Howard's shoulder with his left hand and spun him into position for a right cross. He never knew what happened next.

Howard correctly anticipated Gray-Suit's move and head-slipped the right cross so that it passed harmlessly over his right shoulder. Howard used his slipping motion to the left to spring-load the muscles and sinews of his upper body. Before Gray-Suit could bring his right hand back into position, Howard delivered a devastating left-to-right chop to Gray-Suit's neck. Clearly hurt and stunned, Gray-Suit's defenses went down. In a lightning-quick move, Howard twisted to the right, drawing his right elbow back with his arm bent like a gunfighter's pulling from a high holster. With fingers tightly extended, he speared them deep into Gray-Suit's chest right under the sternum. Gray-Suit's sharp exhalation of breath was short and pained. Quickly drawing his right arm and hand back to the same position, Howard drove the heel of his hand up at a forty-five degree angle. There was a distinct crunching sound when his blow caught Gray-Suit on the bridge of the nose as he was doubling over from the effects of the spear to the chest. Gray-Suit was out cold. Before he crumpled to the floor, Mickey caught him under the arms and lowered him onto his bar stool.

The whole thing took place in less than ten seconds and the only sounds were those of Gray-Suit's air escaping him from the blow to his chest, and the crunch of his nose being broken.

Howard, embarrassed, turned to the other bar patrons and said with heartfelt sincerity, "I truly apologize to all of you. I hope this will not cast a pall on your evening."

In response, the entire bar crowd broke into applause, men and women alike, giving Howard a standing O.

JOE MARTELLA DOES NOT PERMIT boisterous behavior, the kind of behavior one would expect in a sports bar. When he heard the applause, he stormed into the bar from the dining room. Anticipating his arrival, Gino had left his station and intercepted Martella as he entered the bar. Watching from the other end, Howard and Mickey saw Gino draw Martella off to the side and whisper at length into Martella's ear, all the while gesticulating in the general direction of Howard, Mickey, and Gray-Suit who remained propped up and unconscious on a bar stool. There was nothing about Howard's dress or his grooming that would suggest that he had just rendered unconscious a lout who outweighed him by about eighty pounds, without ever leaving his seat.

Still feeling very self-conscious about the whole thing, Howard put his glasses back on and saw Martella approaching. He stood while Martella made his way through the crowd to his end of the bar. Shaking his head in penitence, Howard said, "Mr. Martella, I'm sorry that I let this happen in your place. It was inexcusable."

Martella simply nodded in acknowledgment then turned to face Gray-Suit. Speaking over his shoulder to Gino who had resumed his station behind the bar, he asked, "Gino. Is this the gentleman you told me about? The one who was so uncomplimentary to one of our respected patrons?"

"Yes, Mr. Martella, he's the one."

Gray-Suit was beginning to come out of it. Mickey helped to steady him as he struggled to his feet. Martella gave him a long, appraising, top-to-bottom once-over, then did the same to Howard. He shook his head in wonderment as he looked from one to the other. Finally he said to Howard with a smile of admiration, "*Che cazzo*, Mr. Pastore! Look at him. He's twice your size. He looks like he got run over by a truck and you look like you stepped out of a catalog. Please, sit down and enjoy.

"Sir, don't worry about your bar bill. It's on me," Martella said to Gray-Suit in a kind manner. "Let me help you to the door."

When they reached the street, Martella positioned himself and Gray-Suit so that Gray-Suit's back was to the restaurant and Martella stood facing the restaurant, face-to-face with Gray-Suit. Several faces peered out at them through the glass door and the window. He grasped both of Gray-Suit's shoulders in his hands in a gesture that looked friendly and warm.

There was still a lot of black in Martella's hair, giving the lie to his seventy-three years. His thick eyebrows intensified the glint of menace that shone from his black eyes, sending a shudder up Gray-Suit's spine. Glaring directly into Gray-Suit's eyes, but wearing a broad smile that made lip reading unlikely, he said, "There are people inside who are looking at us through the window and the door. They see me smiling at you. They think I am inquiring about your well-being and that all is now good between us. It is not." Gray-Suit winced with pain from Martella's death grip on his shoulders.

Still smiling for the benefit of the audience, Martella continued, "They think I am telling you to come back another time when you are feeling better. I am not."

He released his grip momentarily to clap him on the shoulders in what would purport to be a friendly, fatherly gesture. Then, clamping them shut again, still smiling, he finished, "Don't come back. Ever. Not to Martella's. Not to Federal Hill. Now turn and walk to your car. Wave to me and smile until you are out of view of my friends inside."

Gray-Suit did as he was instructed.

FOURTEEN

PHIL HAD NO SOONER launched his tee-shot from the seventh tee than it entered a screeching, diving turn to the left, duck-hooking into a thicket of pines from which an escape shot would be impossible. Even as the ball was in flight, and its destination certain, he broke into hearty laughter.

Such a reaction to a bad shot was beyond the imagination of anyone who had ever played golf with Phil. He was a fierce competitor on the golf course, demanding the best from himself and harshly berating himself for any shot that was less than perfect. However, as a sixteen handicap player, it was a given that he would hit about a dozen truly bad shots even on his best days. Accordingly, he spent much of every round of golf hating himself. The reason Phil could laugh at himself on this very special day was clearly understood by his playing companions.

A COLD FRONT HAD SWEPT through Rhode Island two days earlier leaving a cloudless sky, temperatures in the low eighties, and a soft, gentle breeze. It was a day for picnic coolers, hot dogs and Frisbees at Goddard State Park. A day for soaking up the sun's rays or romping in the surf at Narragansett Pier or Scarborough State Beach.

Boats of every size made their way through the pass at Galilee, fighting its awesome current while their occupants blithely waved to the spectators who lined the sea wall in front of George's Restaurant. Inexperienced first time boaters were easily deceived into smugness by the comfortable ride on the smooth, gentle waters inside the Harbor of Refuge. However, they would become wide-eyed and apprehensive upon leaving its protective, rip-rap walls and entering the open, rarely calm waters of Rhode Island Sound.

It was as beautiful a day as could be imagined but, for Phil Peters on this day, there was even more to celebrate.

That very morning, Phil, his lawyer John Licciardi, his accountant Dino DiBenardo and Vince Bonetta studied the loan package that Jeanne Aiello had presented. Greater Providence would rewrite Phil's credit line and his existing loans into a single new loan in the amount of $837,000, and would extend the length of the term to twenty years. The net effect on Phil's cash flow would be a reduction of almost $12,500 per month in debt service. It was everything that the four of them had hoped it would be. Howard Pastore, Executive Assistant to the President, had already studied the proposal and given his approval. It remained only for Luco Parisi to initial it and for GPB&T's legal department to draw up the contract.

Phil was ecstatic with relief.

JOHN AND DINO HAD BEEN Vince Bonetta's lawyer and accountant, as well as friends and golfing pals since long before Phil quit baseball and signed on with Vince at Production House Graphix. Soon after that, the four became a regular foursome, changing partners with each round of golf. They didn't play for a lot of money, usually a five dollar Nassau. The most that had ever changed hands in their foursome was thirty-five dollars and the winnings always went on the table against the bar tab. No matter. On the course they competed as though the Ryder Cup were at stake. Today Vince and Phil were playing partners and they were getting creamed. Phil, giddy with relief over the outcome of their meeting with the bank that morning, couldn't do anything right. As a result, they were two down after six holes and had just pressed their bet when Phil duck-hooked his tee shot into never-never land.

"Sorry, Partner," said Phil, still laughing.

"You don't look sorry," Vince replied. "You leave me by myself to fight off these two barracudas and you think it's a riot? I think I liked you more as the miserable, pain-in-the-ass that we all know so well."

As the four walked off the tee toward their carts, Dino stage-whispered to John for the others to hear, "What's this? Do I hear rumblings of dissent in the ranks of our worthy opponents?" To which John replied, beating his fist against his chest in a theatrical display of anguish, "Alas! It grieves my sensitive soul to bear witness to such petulance and acrimony!"

The first row of cars in the club parking lot was separated from the seventh tee by the cart path and a flower bed, with the tee box running parallel to the edge of the parking lot. The lot was filled with cars of every type, size and color. There were Corvettes, Town Cars, Marks, and Cadillacs, as well as a smattering of Q45s, Jags and Ferraris. And one cream-colored Rolls-Royce. It was parked in the slot directly opposite the seventh tee.

It caught their eyes and became the subject of their comments as they approached their carts.

"Will you look at that?" said Dino, shaking his head in wonderment. "Isn't he a classic jerk? He parks it right there where it will be admired by anyone who happens to pass this point."

"Happens past?! You can't play the course without passing this point," said John with a laugh.

Both carts left the seventh tee. In the trailing cart, with Vince chuckling over their repartee, Phil mused idly over their comments. Since he was the only one of the group who was not a member of The Alpine, the significance of their remarks had eluded him. Besides, a lingering fragment of a memory nagged at him. He turned in his seat to take another look at the Rolls as they drove away from the tee. When it came to him he said to Vince, "A car a lot like that one damn near ran me down a couple of months ago."

"What happened?" asked Vince. "Did the guy stop?"

"No, but it doesn't matter. It was my own fault. My mind was elsewhere and I stepped in front of it. I saw it at the last second and had to do some fancy footwork to get out of the way. I don't think the guy ever saw me."

Vince and Phil lost the front side three and two and went one down on the close-out press as Licciardi drained a forty foot no-brainer for birdie on seven. Then Vince, playing like a man possessed, single-handedly won the press with birdies on eight and nine. He reached the par-five eighth after hitting a gorilla tee shot and a four-iron into the green. On the par three ninth, his eight-iron tee shot flew into the hole and spun out, leaving himself a six-inch putt for birdie.

This spurt had the effect of bringing Phil back into the game but it also awakened John and Dino. The back nine turned into a dog-fight with the lead changing hands three times. John and Dino were one down going into the long, uphill, par-four eighteenth but Dino made the only par in the group to halve the side.

John and Dino won five dollars. And the bragging rights.

THE NOISE LEVEL IN the men's grill room rose steadily as four-some after foursome straggled in. Before long, any attempt to have a quiet conversation became virtually impossible so they adjourned to the hushed comfort of the dining room. Leaving the brightness of the grill room, where the late afternoon sun streams through the wall of windows that overlook the ninth green, it took several seconds for their eyes to adjust to the subdued lighting of the dining room. As they groped their way to their table, neither Vince nor any of the others in his group noticed the two men seated at a table across the room near the draperied windows.

Luco Parisi and Mickey Hoban were deep in discussion and oblivious to the rest of the room.

"I heard you came through for our old friend, Phil Peters," said Mickey.

"Yeah?" asked Luco. "Just what is it you heard?"

"I heard he got a tit caught in the wringer. Needed big time money to get healthy again and you came to his rescue," said Mickey as he raised his glass in a commendatory toast to Luco.

"That's private bank business," said Luco. His lips curled into a smile that was pure fake.

"C'mon, Luco, you have made one very happy customer who has some very happy people working for him who enjoy spreading the good word," Mickey replied in an upbeat tone. He chose his words so as to lead Luco to an indistinct conclusion as to how the story got out.

"So there's people out there got a case of diarrhea of the mouth. So what're they sayin' about this private business between Phil and me?" He began to slip into his street dialect, a sure sign to Mickey that Luco was starting a slow burn.

"Luco, relax for crisake!" Puzzled by the way Luco was handling this, Mickey tried to lighten it up. "Far as I know, Tom Brokaw hasn't picked up on the story yet so it'll be a while before it makes national TV."

"You didn't answer my question." Even his fake smile was gone. "Answer my fuckin' question." His low, guttural whisper was like a shout.

Mickey felt his own heat rise and fought to restrain himself. His smile vanished as did any further attempt at pleasantry. Being talked to in this manner by his uncle-in-law was beginning to happen all too frequently. Just last week in Luco's office, Luco had humiliated Mickey and Mickey had to fight off the urge to pound him. Taking a slow pull from his Bass Ale, he delayed for a long moment before speaking. When he did, his eyes locked on Luco's like tractor beams.

"Whatever your problem is, I'm getting tired of your bullshit. You want an answer? OK, here it is. The word is that Phil got screwed big time. By one of your *compare* right here at The Alpine no less. It put Phil behind the eight-ball with his credit line. You could have defaulted him, taken over his company and foreclosed on his building. Instead, you bailed his ass out with a cushy new package."

"That's what you heard?" asked Luco. He offered no apology to Mickey but both his face and his tone of voice had softened perceptibly.

"Yeah. That's what I heard. Now you tell me if I heard right."

"You heard right," said Luco. He sat back in his chair and took a sip of his martini. "Except for one minor detail," he continued. Then he went silent, looking over the rim of his glass at Mickey, stalling, waiting for Mickey to ask what that minor detail was.

"Kiss my ass, Luco," said Mickey. He wasn't going to bite. "I told you, I've had enough of your games. You want to tell me, go ahead. Otherwise, let's change the subject."

"The one minor detail is, none of what you described was done by me," said Luco retreating from his street dialect. "I pay people who are very good at what they do to do that sort of thing for me. They assemble the facts, analyze the figures, come to an agreement with the client, then they present their final proposal to me for my stamp of approval. Since I regard my people as having the highest level of insight and competence, rare indeed is the occasion when I would overrule them and turn down one of their proposals."

"So it's a done deal then?" asked Mickey, brightening.

"Done," said Luco, while chuckling through a mirthless smile. He skipped a beat then continued, "and *un*done. This is going to be one of those rare occasions."

"What the hell does that mean?" asked Mickey with some uneasiness.

"What does it mean? Let me explain what it means. What it means is their proposal, Phil's proposal, is out on its feet. One tiny push from me and he's gonna fall flat on his ass and stay down for the count."

Mickey was stunned. After a moment he recovered enough to ask, "Luco, what the hell are you saying? Phil's an old friend for crisake. He needs help and your people have told him he's going to get it! You can't be serious!"

Luco didn't hear a word. He looked at Mickey but he didn't see him. It was as though Mickey wasn't even there. Luco's eyes had lost their focus, but distant images from his life shone clearly from the recesses of his memory—Phil's girlfriend, Marla, turning him down in college; Phil's wife, Marla, scornfully throwing him out of her hotel room; Phil, the avenging angel, attacking him on the golf course—images that stoked the fires of his hatred.

Everywhere he looked, he saw Phil. He hissed, "I'm not only gonna reject your loan, I'm gonna call your credit line. Then when you can't come up with $480,000, and there's no way in hell that you can, I'm gonna call your other loans and foreclose on you, you sorry son-of-a-bitch. You don't know it yet, Mister Great and Wonderful, but you're fucked. I couldn't do your dipso wife but I'm gonna do you and this is even better."

For a long time Mickey sat in silent disbelief looking at Luco as though seeing him for the first time. Though he had never deluded himself into thinking of Luco as a man of high moral and ethical fiber, he saw this vicious and calculated attack on a boyhood chum as a new low in Luco's behavior. He felt a sudden onset of remorse for his own complicity in the fraud he and Luco were running. He was devastated with overwhelming emptiness as he looked into the face of his own flawed character. His thoughts churned in a maelstrom as he grappled with the implications of Luco's unflinching ability and willingness to betray. Suddenly, the Goyette loan materialized in Mickey's thoughts as the reality of his own vulnerability swept over him.

"What's happening with the Goyette loan?" said Mickey, making no attempt to sugar coat his tone. "Has he made his payments?"

"Goyette?" asked Luco. The abruptness of the change of subject had thrown him off balance. He needed a moment to scramble back to the present.

"Yeah, Goyette!" said Mickey. He was clearly agitated and his tone was commanding. "Now *you* answer *my* question! What's happening with Goyette's loan?!"

"PHIL, I DON'T KNOW ABOUT the Rolls that almost ran you down but the one that was parked next to the seventh tee belongs to him," Vince said, motioning with his eyes to the other table. "I'm sure you know Luco Parisi."

Phil and the others turned discreetly and saw Mickey and Luco in what was clearly an intense conversation.

"Yeah, I know him," said Phil. The unmistakable bitterness in his voice ended their light-hearted, après-golf banter.

After a short, awkward pause, Dino spoke. "Maybe you ought to rethink the bad blood that exists between you and Luco," he said. "Need I remind you that his bank did just give you one helluva loan package."

"What's between Luco and me is personal," Phil said seriously, but not unkindly, "and it's ancient history. It hasn't affected my business relationship with Greater Providence. PHG *is* one of their better clients, and they value my business.

"Matter of fact," he continued, turning to Vince, "they've valued my business since long before it *became* my business. I've never lost sight of the fact that my relationship with Greater Providence got one hell of a jump-start from the twenty years that you owned PHG and did business with them."

"You're not the first person who ever got a jump-start," said Vince, "but you made yours *work* for you. That's what matters."

"Just as you did, Vince," said John. "Remember when you were trying to get PHG started and you needed bank financing?"

"How could I forget," Vince chuckled. "I had no assets, no bank account and no credit history. Good thing my father and Luco's father were lifelong friends. Any other banker would have laughed me out of his office. Not Giuseppe."

Vince paused in reflection, then he continued.

"I'll never forget his exact words. He said, 'Vincenzo, you are the son of my dearest and oldest friend. You have learned your sense of honor from Pierino Bonetta. There is no collateral that could be of greater value than that. So now, let's talk about what it will take to give you a good start.'

"They were two of a kind, my father and Giuseppe. They not only believed that a man's word was his bond, they conducted their lives by it."

"Yes, Vince, they did," said John. "I never knew two men whose principles and values so closely paralleled each other's throughout their lives as your father and Giuseppe."

"Or whose results were so radically different," said Dino.

"Ah, yes!" said John. "And then there's Luco."

"And then, there's Luco," Vince repeated, turning to look at Luco as he spoke. "As a banker, he's a natural. He's good at it. Real good. The way he's engineered acquisitions and merged their resources has given Greater Providence a record of growth that even Giuseppe never imagined possible.

"In the process, he's learned how to speak and act with dignity and sophistication, and how to wield authority. But, we've all known him since we were kids. And we know that just beneath the surface, he doesn't have even a trace of character. He's a slimeball. A very rich slimeball. But a slimeball.

"What a pity that a son like Luco could be born to such a great man. It must have been a burden for Giuseppe to carry. I'm sure he was proud of Luco's business achievements, but from the standpoint of morality, the only value that truly mattered to Giuseppe, the reality that his own son had slipped through the cracks must have been devastating."

"How do you account for something like that?" asked John, not really expecting an answer. "Luco is the absolute antithesis of everything his father stood for."

They paused, immersed in their thoughts.

"Wait a minute!" said Dino, breaking the mood. "We're supposed to be celebrating. Lest we forget, something even more important than Phil's new loan took place today. I kicked ass on the golf course and John Licciardi's five bucks are burning a hole in my pocket. Next round is on me."

"DIDN'T I TELL YOU I'm handling it?" Luco answered Mickey's question with a question, vamping for time to decide what and how much to tell him. He had long savored plots of revenge against Phil. Now it had grown to be the only bright spot in his immediate future, a future that was growing gloomier by the day because of the Goyette loan. Luco didn't know how much longer he could conceal the failure of that loan from the Board. He knew he would have to disappear very soon but before he did, he looked forward to the pleasure of ruining Phil and letting Phil know he did it.

"Handling it? Handling it?!" Mickey was close to losing it. "What's that supposed to mean?! That his back payments have all been made? That his loan has been fully paid?! Because if it means anything else, we're looking at doing time!"

"Hold it down," Luco said with forced calm.

"Hold your ass down! Answer my question!" Mickey's voice was on the rise, his face beet red.

Luco had not leveled with Mickey. Neither Goyette nor Luco had made any further payments. The loan was headed for default and Luco knew he would be unable to prevent it. For a single, brief, uncharacteristic moment, he considered the effects all this would have on Mickey. He decided to reveal the full truth.

"No."

"No?" Mickey didn't know what to make of Luco's terse answer. "No what? For crisake make sense!"

"No, his account is not paid to date and no, his loan has not been fully paid."

"You bastard. You lying bastard! You told me three months ago you'd cover for it." Mickey was still angry, but recognizing the hopelessness of their predicament, he had lost some of his steam.

The tension between them, they realized too late, had become apparent to others in the room. It was at that moment that Luco noticed the other table and saw Vincent Bonetta looking at them. Luco sent a big smile and a nodded greeting to Vince, muttering to Mickey through unmoving lips, "There's your pal, Phil Peters. Look happy. Smile."

Vince nodded back. The others at his table didn't observe the exchange.

Turning back to Mickey, Luco said, "Face reality, Mickey. We had a good run, but it's over. We can't change anything by fighting about it." As he spoke the words, a strange feeling of resolute calm came over him.

From the corner of his eye he could see that Vince was still watching. Luco put on what he hoped was a placid expression and a contented smile to portray to the other table that all was normal. He continued, "There's a board meeting in two days and Goyette's loan will be on the table. My nephew has prepared the case file and I'm sure, knowing Howard, it'll be perfect. I'll do what I can to derail it but if he recommends foreclosure, I'll have no choice but to concur."

"Goddamm, Luco!" Mickey was sinking. He ran a hand through his hair using his arm to shield his face from the other table. "How can you be so calm? What are we gonna do? Goyette's building will go on the block and it won't pull near enough to cover the debt. Then they'll put his house up and the same goddamm thing will happen. Then they'll pull an audit and they'll see my name on both appraisals. Damn!"

"Come on, Mickey, get a grip! Something like this was bound to happen. You had to know at the start that it couldn't last forever. As far as doing time? Forget it. There's no trace of any money going to you. Your lawyer will argue that all you're guilty of is sloppy work. You might have to find another line of work but they can't put you away just for being a lousy appraiser.

"Besides, you've got a cool mil buried somewhere that I assume your lawyer doesn't know anything about. That ought to take some of the sting out of going into early retirement.

"For me it's a different ballgame. If they start leaning on some of my clients, like that weasel Goyette, they'll have no trouble proving collusion and fraud. They can put me away for a long time.

"But you know how these things go. With paperwork, legal notices and all, we have a few weeks until the foreclosure auction. The shit won't hit the fan until then. For right now we're still in the clear, but if you have a contingency plan, Mickey old chum, it's time to put it in gear." Luco had made his escape plans a long time ago and assumed Mickey had done the same.

Mickey looked over and saw that Vince and the others were in a festive mood, having a great time and enjoying one another's company. After a moment, the connection between their joviality and Phil's new loan package struck him. He fell into a murky silence in the realization that their joy would soon turn to gloom at the treacherous and vengeful hands of the man sitting across the table from him.

"Let's beat it, Luco," said Mickey. "Phil's over there celebrating the very thing that you're gonna use to stick it to him, and with all the other shit that's coming down on me, I just need to get outta here, and right now."

"Okay, stay cool," said Luco. He stood, straightened his tie and shot his cuffs. "Let's just go over and pay our respects on the way out."

"No way!" Mickey leapt to his feet. His legs shot his chair backwards, upsetting a tray stand, creating a clatter that brought the attention of the entire room. He ignored it. His hand shot out, grabbed Luco's sleeve and pulled him nose-to-nose. Through clenched teeth he said, "You want to get your kicks playing Mr. Nice Guy all the while you're salivating about how you're gonna stick a knife in Phil's back, you do it without me! I'm outta here." With that, Mickey left without so much as a glance at the other table.

"NOW WHAT THE HELL WAS that all about?" said Vince. "For a second it looked like Mickey was going to slug him."

"Mickey's an old friend of yours, Phil," asked Dino, "but it sure looked like he was avoiding you."

"Yeah, it did, and I wish I knew why but ... damn ... don't look now. We're about to get company," said Phil. Luco approached their table wearing a broad smile, holding his arms extended as though in greeting to dear, long-lost relatives.

"Hey guys, good to see you," said Luco. He gave a cursory nod to Dino and John and virtually ignored Phil. Turning to Vince, he asked, "How's the real estate business in Florida treating you, Bonetta?" Without waiting for a response, he continued, "You're looking good. Staying in shape? Watching out for the old ticker?" Again leaving no space for anyone to say anything, he pressed on as he gestured for the waiter, "Mickey asked me to give his regrets. He suddenly remembered he was late for another appointment and had to hotfoot it out of here."

The waiter arrived at tableside immediately.

Still smiling broadly, Luco patronizingly put an arm around the waiter's shoulders and with a magnanimous sweep of his hand told him, "Bring my friends here a bottle of our finest red and a bottle of our finest white to complement their dinner selections."

Then he turned to the table and said, "Enjoy it with my best wishes, my friends. Now I, too, must run."

"Hey, that's a bummer, Luco baby," said Vince through a fake smile, trying for all the world to sound like a Hollywood press agent brushing off a minor talent, "but nice gig rappin' with you, sweetheart. We'll do lunch."

Luco gave no sign that he recognized the sarcasm. His smile remained unbroken as he made eye-contact with each of them, except Phil, and with a courtly bow, turned and left the room.

FIFTEEN

SLEEP WOULDN'T COME TO VINCE. Because he would be flying back to Naples in the morning, and he wanted to spend his last evening with his father, he had left The Alpine before the others. Now, with his eyes wide open, gazing without focus at the ceiling while his father slept peacefully in a downstairs bedroom, his father's words resonated in his thoughts.

VINCE HAD DRIVEN DIRECTLY to Cappie's Tap where he found the saloon almost deserted. Cappie was stationed on a barstool at the rear door that opened to the lighted bocce courts in the back yard. From that position, he was able to keep one eye on the front entrance and the other on the hotly contested match that was underway. It was drawing to a close, much to the boisterous urgings of the gallery that would soon swoop in for another round or two of refreshment between games.

Cappie turned and his face brightened as Vince came in and approached him. In a single, seamless move, he retrieved his polished ebony cane from where he had leaned it against the wall within easy reach and spun off the stool onto his good right leg. He propelled himself by twisting his hips to sling his withered left leg forward in unison with the cane, letting his powerful left arm and shoulder take his weight. He reached out with his right hand to take Vince's but instead, Vince brushed it aside and they man-hugged.

"Cenzo, old friend," said Cappie with that special warmth that is known only to lifelong friends. "I heard you was up here. I'm glad you didn't skip town without coming to see me."

"I would never do that, Rico," said Vince. To most everyone else, Enrico Caputo was known as Cappie, but to Vince, he was still Rico. And to Rico, Vincenzo was Cenzo. Rico and Cenzo. Those were the names they had used with each other since pre-school days, almost fifty years ago.

"How's the leg treating you." Everyone else pointedly ignored Cappie's bad leg. Vince couldn't.

"Not bad, Cenzo," Rico said lightly as he rapped his cane against his bad leg. "The Yankees took another look at me but for some dumb reason they think I might be a step too slow gettin' down to first."

Then without leaving any space for Vince to jump in and press for a straight answer, he continued, "Anyhow, your father's outside with Mr. Lanieri, watchin' the matches. He told me to let them know when you showed up. Grab yourself a table and I'll go get them." Without waiting for a response, Rico spun on his cane and was out the door.

AT THE AGE OF THIRTEEN, it was clear that Rico was born to be an athlete. Not only was he in superb physical condition, he was gifted in those qualities that are found only in the finest athletes—superior eyesight and hand-eye coordination; quick-start speed as well as sustained speed; total body and limbs dexterity; smoothness and economy of motion; situational awareness. And courage.

When he was fifteen and working in a candy manufacturing plant, Rico's hopes and dreams of playing major league ball came to an excruciating end when a fifty-five gallon drum of syrup fell on him from the top of a fifteen foot stack. His co-workers found him, crushed, battered and mercifully unconscious, on the concrete floor of the warehouse.

A team of surgeons operated on him throughout the night and into the next day. They saved his life but they knew Rico would be almost totally paralyzed. He would be able to speak and would have control of his eyes but would not be able to turn his head. He would have the ability to grasp feebly with his right hand and to raise it an inch or two from the bed, but his left arm and hand, as well as the rest of his body, would be immobile. Later, after he had come out of it and they felt he was strong enough to face the reality of their prognosis, they told him that he would be bedridden for the rest of his life. Expecting an outpouring of anguish and self pity and despair, they were wholly unprepared for his reaction.

His face became a mask of determination and rage. Unable to shake his head, he shook his eyes wildly from side to side and said with all the force he could muster, "That's bullshit!" His voice croaked from oxygen-induced dryness as he continued, "I'm not gonna spend my life in a bed. I won't! Don't never say that again!"

Eighteen months later, with the aid of parallel bars in the hospital's rehab clinic, to the pleading and urging and shouts of joy from his best friend Cenzo, he took his first step.

The candy company agreed to pay all of Rico's medical expenses and awarded him a generous lifetime pension. Years passed before Rico learned the reason for their extraordinary largess. It had been inspired by Vince's uncle, a well known lawyer, the mere mention of whose name struck dread into the hearts of his coutroom opponents. Before a suit had even been filed on Rico's behalf, Vince's uncle had pointedly described to the company's executives the magnitude of their culpability if it were to become known that Rico had suffered his devastating injuries while they knowingly employed him as an underaged worker.

"HOW DO YOU EXPLAIN it, pa?" Vince had asked as he and Lorenzo Lanieri clinked their Sambuca glasses and sipped. He had just described the scene he witnessed in the club dining room earlier that evening and was echoing the question John Licciardi had asked. Vince's father, Pierino, stirred his espresso in silence and waited for Vince to continue.

"You pa, and you, Mr. Lanieri, and Giuseppe, God rest his soul—you were like peas from the same pod. All three of you set the highest standards of morality and principles for yourselves and you never compromised them." Vince looked squarely into his father's eyes and continued, "You and ma raised six kids and every one of us tries every day to live up to the example you've set for us."

"What the hell is this? Did I die and nobody told me and now I have to listen to my own eulogy?" said Pierino as he refilled the Sambuca glasses from the bottle Rico had left on the table.

"Sorry, Pa," said Vince continuing in earnest, "I didn't mean to get sappy." Then he turned to Lorenzo and continued, "Giuseppe himself told me the story of how he started his bank in the back room of a barber shop. Your father's barber shop. And how your father made it his mission in life to see that Giuseppe got off on a solid footing. For whatever His reasons were, God never sent any children to you and Mrs. Lanieri but my point is, you are the son of your father. His values became your values, just as my father's values became mine."

"Thank you, Cenzo," said Lanieri, "but what is it you're trying to say?"

"It's just that Luco turned out to be such a waste. He's the opposite of everything his father stood for. There's no depth to his character. He's a lowlife with a glossy finish."

Pierino didn't like this kind of talk. When Giuseppe was alive, in his later years, he would confide his innermost feelings of despair about his son to Pierino and Lorenzo, asking nothing more than the understanding ear and heart of his oldest and dearest friends. It was quite another thing to talk about it in his absence. It struck him somehow as a betrayal of Giuseppe's confidence and trust.

"I hope none of what you feel about Luco will ever change your respect for Giuseppe's memory," Pierino said solemnly.

"Not a chance, Pa," said Vince, "you know how I felt about him. Nothing can change that. But that old rule about an acorn falling not far from the tree sure didn't apply in this case. Luco is a violation of everything Giuseppe believed. If this acorn really did fall from Giuseppe's tree, it must have rolled down the hill before its seed was planted."

Pierino sat motionless and silent. With no movement of their heads, Pierino's eyes met Lorenzo's, and for a long moment, something passed between them. It didn't escape Vince's notice but he was unable to fathom the significance of what took place.

"There's an exception to every rule, Cenzo," Pierino finally answered, his eyes downcast and fixed, "but it's not always easy to recognize one when you see it."

"I don't think I know what you mean, pa."

"I do," said Lanieri when Pierino didn't respond right away. "Tell him, Pierino." There was a slight edge to his tone.

"Tell me what? What's going on here? Did I miss something?"

Pierino gave Lanieri a look of annoyance before continuing, "Sometimes, when a rule is defiled, it's possible to mistake the exception for the imperative."

"Now I'm sure I don't know what you mean."

Vince was in awe of his father. Here was a man who never went to school yet he had educated himself to a level far above that of many university scholars. As a young man, he had immersed himself in one subject at a time until he mastered it. He began with the English language since to write it, to speak it, to read it, and to comprehend it were essential to his success in all other pursuits. He followed that with the study of architectural and structural engineering, coupled synergistically with the study of applied mathematics and physics. And simply because he was fascinated by them, he was a lifelong student of history and geography.

Pierino hesitated for a long, serious moment. He looked deeply into his son's eyes, searching for something. To Vince, it was clear his father was wrestling with himself. During that silent exchange, Vince observed that Lorenzo remained focused on Pierino.

"He has a right to know, Pierino," Lanieri said with intensity.

"Pa, what is it?" Vince asked, suddenly concerned, "Are you all right?"

"It's OK, Cenzo, I'm fine," said Pierino. "I was just considering your metaphor. The acorn vis-à-vis the tree. Mr. Lanieri vis-à-vis his father. Giuseppe vis-à-vis his father. My sons and daughters vis-à-vis me. All are acorns that fell close to the tree."

"Yeah, same as you vis-à-vis your father and your father's father I suppose," Lanieri interrupted, clearly agitated. He didn't know what a metaphor was nor did he know the definition of vis-à-vis but he instinctively knew it worked in this case. "Goddammit, Pierino, you've considered long enough. Either you set the record straight or I will."

When Pierino wasn't forthcoming, Lanieri turned to Vince and said, "OK! Your father swore me to secrecy more than seventy years ago and I have honored it," then turning to Pierino, "but now we have one foot in the grave and there's no one after us to pass this on."

Pierino placed his hand on Lanieri's shoulder and said in submissive resignation, "OK, old friend, you're right. But it's for me to do."

Vince waited, looking from one to the other, then said, "I don't know what's going on but we were talking about genetic traits. About heritage. About exceptions to rules."

"Yes," said Pierino, "exceptions." He exchanged a private look with Lanieri before continuing. "What about my father, Cenzo? What memories do you have of him?"

"Not many, pa. I was just a little kid when he died. Mostly I remember you always shined your shoes and dressed up in a suit and tie when we went to visit them."

Vince grew pensive as his memories stirred to life. "I remember him as being distant." He paused in thoughtful recall, then continued, "No. It wasn't distance, pa. It was more like … coldness. Now that I think about it, I don't have the slightest memory of Grandpa ever hugging any one of us, or being playful with us in any way. We never enjoyed going to their house. It wasn't a place for kids. But, you treated him always with respect and demanded that your kids do the same. We grew up regarding him as a good man."

"So as you grew older," said Pierino, "you came to believe that I was a chip off the old block. That my values, my principles, my character were shaped by my father's."

"Ha!" Lanieri barked reflexively, drawing a puzzled glance from Vince.

"Yes, pa. Just as mine were shaped by yours."

"And I thank God every day that you and your brothers and sisters are what you are. I'm proud of every one of you. But, to continue your metaphor, was I the acorn from my father's tree?" Pierino asked. It was a rhetorical question that begged no answer.

Again he became silent. Without realizing that he did it, he slowly shook his head, not as an act of saying no, more as a gesture of acknowledging the long-ago reality of what he was about to relate.

"In the old country, Lorenzo, Giuseppe and I were friends from birth. They saw with their own eyes some of what you're going to hear. Except for them, there are things about my life that your mother and I never revealed to anyone for reasons we thought at the time were important. As Lorenzo has just reminded me, those reasons no longer exist.

"Giuseppe is seven years dead. Your mother's been gone over twenty years. Now I'm eighty-seven years old. I can be called at any time. Lorenzo is right. Suddenly, it's important to me that my history be remembered accurately by my family."

Lorenzo patted Pierino's forearm and smiled at him in encouragement. Pierino nodded to him in return.

"You were right Cenzo. Yes, my father did influence my values and my principles, but not in any way that you might imagine.

"The day I married your mother, God rest her soul, was the last event in my life that was of any significance to my father. Why? Because it signaled the end of my weekly wages going into his pocket."

Vince could not disguise the look of astonishment on his face. He had never before heard his father say anything even remotely disrespectful about any one of his family.

"I know this shocks you, Cenzo, but you will understand in a moment. He was my father and according to God's law, I treated him with respect all my life. Even though he and his wife—she was never my mother—regarded me as nothing more than an indentured servant since the day I arrived in this country."

Lorenzo again rested his hand on Pierino's forearm and in a soft voice said, "You have to go all the way back, Pierino. To Italy. To your father's father."

Pierino's eyes lost their focus. His voice sounded remote as though emanating from deep within a distant dream as he continued.

"My father came to America leaving my mother behind. She was in her seventh month carrying me. She died bringing me into this world. My grandmother took care of me, but soon, when I was two years old, she too died. My father sent a letter leaving me in the care of his father, a warped, child-hating, sadistic, wheelchair-bound old man. That miserable bastard used to beat me any time he could get his hands on me. He didn't need a reason. Beating me was his recreation. His favorite trick was to reach a hand out to me, dangling ripe figs or grapes or a piece of bread to tempt me to come close.

"The first time he did it I fell for it. From then on I knew it was a trap but I was always so hungry I would try anyway. Sometimes I was too fast for him and I was able to snatch them before he could grab me. But sometimes I wasn't and then there was no escape from his powerful grip. He would reach under the blanket that covered his legs, pull out a piece of lead pipe that he had concealed there for this very purpose and he would club me with it. Not once, but many times. On my arms, on my back, on my legs, on my head. Most times he didn't stop until the old ladies of the village came screaming out of their cottages to rescue me and he would tell them he caught me stealing his figs while he slept."

Pierino lapsed into silence as his narrative awakened long ago memories that were filled with sadness and pain.

"Cenzo," said Lorenzo, continuing for Pierino, "we seen it with our own eyes, me and Giuseppe. We were six years old and he was a mean, crazy old man. We cried and ran for the old ladies to come. And all the time, when it was over, we cried some more because we couldn't do nothing to help our friend. It happened over and over. One time I got too close trying to pull your father away and the old bastard caught me too. Mother of God that pipe hurt so bad. And I was so scared I pissed my pants. He swore if I told my parents about the beating he gave me he would kill your father. I told them I fell down a ravine chasing a rabbit."

"My God, Pa," said Vince in anguish, "how did you get through it? How did your father deal with it?"

"He didn't. About a year after I got here, I tried to tell him about it. He cut me short. He told me to never mention it again. I'll never know how much he knew about it. Two years later, we learned that the crazy old man died. The subject was never again raised."

"Pierino, tell him about when you got here," Lanieri prompted.

"I was overjoyed when my father sent for me to come over. He loved me, I thought, and he wanted me to be here with him and his new wife.

"I was half right. He wanted me all right. I found out *why* he wanted me the day after I got here. That's when he took me to the county seat. He slipped some money to a certain clerk and the clerk handed over counterfeit work papers that showed my age as sixteen.

"Then my father took me straight to the Wanskuck Mills. He showed the papers to the floor-boss and flashed some money to him. The man looked back and forth from me to my father—I was just eleven years old, a child, and I looked it—then he looked around, nodded his head, and took the money. My father left me there to start my new job. Twelve hours a day. Six days a week.

"My father was well off. He didn't need my money to run the house. Nevertheless, I never saw a penny of my wages. My stepmother insisted that I turn my pay over to her. My father, my hero," his voice now tight with bitterness, "backed her up and made me do it. He didn't have the *coglione* to stand up to her. Every payday he would be waiting for me when I walked in the door. He would hold out his hand. Never even said hello. Just held out his hand, impatiently snapping his fingers until I handed him my pay envelope. Then this man, my father, would make me wait while he counted my pay money to be sure I hadn't spent any of it on the way home."

"Pa," said Vince, his eyes welling with tears, "you don't have to say another word." He looked to Lorenzo for support but saw his eyes too were filled as he wagged a finger and shook his head at Vince, signaling him to let his father continue.

"Yes I do, Cenzo. It's best I finish this for once and always." The bitterness had disappeared from his voice. In its place, his tone betrayed a plaintive mourning for that bond between father and son that was forever missing in his life. "All those years ... those barren years ... I drew my strength from the hope that my father had plans for me. That he had a secret, grand design to make it right with me. Maybe when I got married, I dreamed. Maybe then he would somehow find a way to show his love for me.

"Well, God blessed me with your beautiful mother and I got married." There was a long pause during which Pierino seemed to make himself over into a new mood, the kaleidoscope of his life flashing through his recall. Gazing squarely into the eyes of his son, the somberness of his expression dissolved into a rueful grin.

"Even after all that ... if he had just put his arms around me and told me he loved me ... "

He paused, slowly shaking his head. Then he continued, "My father's wedding gift to me, his first born son, was ... unique. Perhaps in some grotesque way that I will never understand, it was a symbol of our relationship. His wedding gift to me consisted of ... are you prepared for this? ... socks."

"Excuse me, pa. What? What did you say?" asked Vince.

"I said, socks, Cenzo," Pierino continued. "Three pairs of socks. After thirteen years of working twelve-hour days, six-day weeks and never seeing a penny of my wages, my father, the man who would 'mold my values' and 'shape my character,' finally demonstrated his love for me with a gift of *socks* to start off my married life."

Then Pierino fell into hollow laughter. Vince and Lorenzo did not join in. It was clear to them that the tears in Pierino's eyes were not tears of joy. His laughter ended as abruptly as it had begun.

"Don't you see Cenzo?" said Pierino after regaining control. "We were talking about genetics. About the passing down of traits and characteristics and perhaps even of values. About rules and exceptions. About acorns that fall from trees.

"To continue your metaphor, my father *was* the acorn that fell from *his* demented father's tree. But I have to believe that they were the *exception*, not the rule, and it was only by God's merciful grace that He used me to restore the imperative to the rule.

"So you see, Cenzo, Luco does not render the rule invalid. He, too, is the tragic exception to the rule, the aberration in his genetic lineage."

SIXTEEN

IN THE DARKENED OFFICE, the light from his computer monitor etched Howard's face in bas relief. He was compiling support data for the report that he would present to the board in the morning. The specter of foreclosure, as always, had left him with a hollow feeling. In most cases, he knew, no one really wins. For the bank, properties sold at auction rarely bring market value. For the principals, foreclosure is frequently a precursor to financial devastation.

He was unaware that daylight had given way to the night. After everyone else left for the day, he had entered the Goyette loan file to get a feel for what the bank could expect to recover from a sale of Goyette's assets. He already knew that his uncle Luco had written the loan but he was pleased when he saw that Mickey had done the property appraisals. Mickey was the best in the business, he thought, as he entered search data into the computer. An appraisal report bearing Mickey's signature was considered to have been intensively researched. A comparative market analysis prepared by him in support of an appraisal report cited only properties that bore a direct relationship to the property under appraisal. There were no surprises with his work. A property was worth what Mickey Hoban said it was worth.

Howard split his screen. On the left half of the screen, the outline of the loan file showed that the appraised value of Goyette's properties far exceeded the outstanding loan balance. If this case did go to foreclosure and if they did have to sell off the Goyette Building, they should have no trouble getting enough to pay off the remaining loan in its entirety. He began to feel a little better. On the right side of the screen, he called up the tax records of the City of North Providence. He keyed in the PIN (Property Identification Number) of the first property Mickey had used as a comparable for Goyette's office building.

Mickey's appraisal narrative had described it as similar in most important respects to Goyette's building—location, type of construction, age, general condition, number and size of rental spaces, occupancy rate, parking and other amenities. Instead, the tax record that scrolled onto the screen was for a two-family tenement house in a residential neighborhood, miles from the location given in Mickey's report. There was nothing about that property that related in any way to the Goyette building.

By itself, that didn't mean a lot to Howard. It is not rare for the clerk in the Tax Assessor's office to misread a handwritten form and to punch in a wrong PIN. Howard keyed in the address of the property as shown in Mickey's report on the left side of the screen. The message that appeared read, NO RECORD FOUND. PRESS ENTER TO REVISE SEARCH CRITERIA. PRESS ESCAPE TO EXIT.

Howard sat motionless, staring at the screen. The first shadows of doubt crossed his imaginings. He again cleared the search criteria. This time he keyed in only the owner's name. In a few seconds, a list of four properties appeared—the owner's principal residence, two plots of unimproved land on the Smithfield line and a condo in a new community under development adjacent to Louisquisset Golf Club. None of those resembled in any way the property Mickey had designated as a comparable. Howard called up the second comparable. The results were similar to the first. It too, Howard found, was what he reluctantly defined in his thoughts as a phantom property.

Quickly, Howard switched to Goyette's oceanfront home in Narragansett. A search and analysis of the comparables yielded similar results. The conclusion was inescapable. Mickey had grossly and intentionally overstated the appraised values of Goyette's properties. It was clear that he did so for the sole purpose of inflating the loan values. The term bank fraud crept into Howard's thoughts.

He found himself unable to focus. If it had involved only his uncle Luco, he might have been able to grasp it, but Mickey's apparent complicity dealt him a heavy blow. He was torn. Mickey was Howard's brother-in-law and his only true friend. In spite of the hard evidence he saw before him, Howard berated himself for thinking that Mickey could in any way be involved in something like this. Yet, in the cold light of reality, he knew he was thinking like a fool. What other possible explanation could there be? Professionally, he was secure in his own competence to deal with it. On a personal level, he felt betrayed and violated.

HE ROSE FROM HIS desk and went to the windows. Howard could discern a flurry of foot traffic on the Westminster pedestrian mall ten stories below his corner office as shoppers and employees made their way to parking lots and garages for their cars. It was dark and the shops were in the process of closing for the day.

One block to the right, the massive, dingy-gray city hall stood sentinel at the head of Exchange Place. It was still too early but Howard knew that in a couple of hours, the broad steps of city hall would surrender to the occupation forces—the street people. In keeping with the historical multiculturalism of the city of Providence, they'll come in all colors. They will speak many tongues and profess several genders, the two that emerged from the Garden of Eden and those that have evolved, or have been contrived, since then.

Their diversity, he mused, resolves to a single common denominator. Squalor. It seeps into every crevice of their existence, sounding a mute rallying cry to others similarly denuded of life's foliage. Having long ago abandoned any pretense at the practice of personal hygiene, they are united in kinship by their stench. It emanates from their flesh to penetrate garments that are permanently soiled with the excrement and secretions of their foul and abused bodies.

Revulsion welled within him as the image continued independently of his will. They will remain the night through, sprawled on the concrete steps, pulling from bottles in brown paper bags, bumming cigarettes from each other and from passing strangers, coughing up phlegm and noisily spitting out disgusting spumes of virulence. They will leave their positions only to retrieve cigarette butts discarded by passers-by or to step around the corner for the elimination of body waste. Even hyenas take care not to foul the place where they sleep, Howard thought, making the subliminal jump that it would be unforgivable for his uncle Luco to foul the place Howard's grandfather had built.

HE RETURNED TO HIS computer, exited the program and shut it down. He still resisted the scenario that fought to take shape in his thoughts. His mind was in a whirl as he strode slowly to the elevator. He walked past the aging Mrs. Masters as she whirled her vacuum cleaner out of his path. He never heard the vac nor did he hear her say, "G'night, Mr. Pastore," nor did he even see her.

He walked past her, head down, to the elevator, turned and faced its door, waiting for it to open. Mrs. Masters, watching him in puzzlement, saw that he had not pressed a call button. Slowly, not wishing to meddle but concerned by his unusual behavior, she approached him. It wasn't until she gently touched his forearm that he became aware of her presence. Turning to her, looking into the beautiful and sincere smile that beamed from her exquisite, cocoa-brown face, he suddenly felt better.

"Good evening, Mrs. Masters," he said, placing his hand over hers. His smile was a warm rebound of hers. "I didn't see you come in."

"Evenin', Mr. Pastore," she said, "I been here a while, doin' the other end so's not to disturb you. You was in there messin' with that computer an' all."

At the mention of the computer, a cloud crossed his thoughts and it showed in his eyes.

"You all right, Mr. Pastore?" she asked. "Anythin' I can do for you?"

Her concern was open and sincere. He was touched.

"Thank you, Mrs. Masters, but I'm fine. I'll be out of your way in just a minute, as soon as the elevator gets here."

"Here now, let me push that down button again for you. Sometimes it don't catch on with the first push."

In a few seconds, the elevator door opened. Howard said good night and stepped in. As the door started to close, he reached out and stopped it by pressing his hand against the rubber bumper. He said, "I'm all right, Mrs. Masters. Really. Please don't be concerned. I just want to say, thank you." He released the door and it glided silently to a close.

THOUGH HOWARD HAD BEEN sleepless through the night, he appeared fresh and rested. His presentation to the board was dynamic and flawless. It was a thorough and uncolored recitation of the facts. For his summation, he reduced it to its barest essentials. Goyette had missed the last four payments and had conceded that he would be unable to make the next one. Howard's examination of the file showed that, almost from the start, Goyette had abandoned both the business plan and the cash flow projection that he had submitted as part of his original loan application.

A new business plan as well as a new cash flow projection were presented by Goyette at the request of the bank. The former was described by Howard as " ... a document that is abundant of fancy but wholly absent of validity." The latter, this time prepared under the watchful eye of a GPB&T auditor, was " ... woefully inadequate to service the debt."

Everyone at the table knew the Goyette loan was one of Luco's. They looked on in disbelief while Howard, with his unblinking eyes locked on Luco's, defined the use of those documents as " ... underwriting irregularities without which the loan application would certainly have been rejected." They perceived Howard's condemnation of the writing of the loan as a finger pointed directly at Luco. The board members were discomfited and entirely unprepared to deal with what was unfolding before them.

Howard closed with, "My recommendation therefore is foreclosure," and asked, "Does anyone wish to add anything that might alter my conclusion?" Only then did he release Luco's eyes and return his gaze to the other board members. Luco saw it as a thinly veiled challenge to his judgment, if not his authority.

In apprehension, the board members turned in unison to Luco, expecting his scathing rebuttal. Instead, for a long, precipitous moment, Luco remained silent. He had been skewered by his nephew Howard and there was no way out. Howard's facts, logic and ordered presentation defied contradiction. Luco was seething with rage. Nevertheless, he put on a contemplative face and adopted an air of fatherly benevolence as he made one final attempt to overcome Howard's argument.

"Aren't we being hasty, gentlemen? Ms. Aiello? Need I remind you that by helping Goyette ride this out, we would stand to profit by his recovery and growth. We hold in our hands the fate of not only his business but his home as well. Can't we look at this simply as a case of a man needing a little support over a rough spot? Is there anyone in this room who has never been up against the wall and in need of help?"

The question reverberated in the silence that followed it.

Howard couldn't believe his ears. "A rough spot?!" he exclaimed. Echoing Luco's words, he continued, "Is there anyone in this room who owes the bank almost a million dollars, is five months in arrears and whose financial outlook is at best poor and at worst dismal? If so, his only hope is to enlist the aid of a venture capitalist and the last time I looked, the term venture capital is not to be found in our charter.

"I insist we maintain our focus," he continued. Again, Howard's gaze locked on Luco's. "It is the Goyette loan and only the Goyette loan we are discussing and, since we are, there is one further point I would make. It is likely that a case could be made to show that Mr. Goyette's original loan application was patently fraudulent, given the irrelevant postulations of his business plan and the ludicrous fantasy hypothesized by his cash flow projection, both of which, lest we forget, were legally a part of his loan application.

"As a practical matter, no useful purpose will be served were we to seek legal redress for that act of fraud. It is more to the point for us to re-examine our lending criteria in general and specifically to make a determined effort to ferret out the kind of duplicitous information that adorned Mr. Goyette's loan application ... *and that was so willfully accepted at face value by this bank.*"

There was no mistaking the emphasis Howard placed on his final words. For a fleeting instant, it appeared that Luco was going to erupt. Everyone in the room sensed that something more than a board meeting was happening but they had no idea what it was. With the exception of Luco and Jeanne Aiello, they hadn't even fully understood the meaning of every word that Howard had spoken. Nonetheless, the essence of his narrative was unmistakable, as was the specter, raised by the insinuations of his final statement, of the bank's culpability.

Before Luco could utter a word, Howard leaned toward him, imposing his face as close as he could to Luco's without leaving his seat. Radiating with intensity, he fairly hissed, "Let me be candid. The Goyette loan is dead and needs to be buried! Its ghost needs to be exorcised! Foreclosure is our only option. Are we in agreement?"

'He knows!' Luco thought. *'He's got to know or he wouldn't be in my goddamm face in front of these people!'* He fought to keep a placid face but his eyes twitched under the strain of trying to think his way through this. *'But he can't know.'* His mind raced wildly. *'How much could he know? Not everything. Not anything. Mickey! He's tight with Mickey. Mickey got drunk. The asshole got drunk and spilled everything! Wrong! Howard would have jumped me right away. Why would he wait until now? What the fuck's going on here? Here? Yeah. Why's everyone here? What the hell are we here for? Oh yeah, Goyette. What do we do about Goyette? No choice. No way out. You're fucked. Be cool. You can't win this fight. Be cool.'*

Incredibly, from the bowels of his distress, he raised what passed as a congenial smile. He wrenched his eyes away from Howard's. As only he could do it, he was able to avoid direct eye-contact with the others while in fact glancing at each of them in turn. When finally he was able to speak, he decided on a self-effacing 'aw shucks' manner.

"I hope you will all excuse my moment of irrelevant introspection. Of course you're absolutely correct, Howard. You have, as always, been thorough and objective. Please excuse me if it seemed I was questioning your conclusions. If there is no objection from the other members, I support your recommendation." With that he excused himself and left.

Howard's grim and unbroken stare had never left Luco's face. Jeanne, except for an occasional fleeting glance at Luco, focused only on Howard. She and Howard remained seated and pensive as the others, clearly relieved that the confrontation had been averted, poured coffee and made small talk.

SEVENTEEN

A CONE OF THUNDERSTRUCK silence trailed behind in her wake. Conversations halted in mid-sentence. Keyboards stopped clacking. Movements became frozen and all eyes followed her. Her footfalls were silent on the carpeted floor. The only sound came from the rattling of the paper that she clutched in her hand. Her arms swung wildly as she stormed from the elevator through the partitionless general office area toward the office of the president.

Jeanne Aiello pushed through the double doors of Luco's outer office. Rochelle was not at her desk. Jeanne then burst through the closed door into Luco's private office. There was no one at Luco's desk either. For a fleeting instant, thinking that he was out, she wanted to scream in exasperation. Then her attention was caught by a slight rustling sound and a glimpse of movement in the corner of her eye.

She spun to see Luco scrambling to his feet from the couch. Rochelle was all arms, hips and flailing legs, struggling to rise to a sitting position while trying desperately to pull her dress down from around her waist. Luco couldn't miss the smirk of contempt on Jeanne's face as she took notice of the flagrant protuberance in Luco's pants. Quickly thrusting his hands into his pockets to camouflage the evidence, he said to Rochelle with stilted business formality, "Would you excuse us for a moment, please?"

Having fully rearranged herself with a final smoothing of her dress at her hips and thighs, Rochelle stepped unsteadily into her high heels as she haughtily responded, "Of course, Mr. Parisi." However, her equanimity suffered a visible jolt when Jeanne stepped forward, hooked the toe of her shoe under Rochelle's panties that lay forgotten at their feet and kicked them high into the air saying, "You forgot your résumé!"

As they wafted down directly in front of Luco, he pulled his gaze from the panties to Rochelle and froze in trepidation when he envisioned what was about to take place. He found himself transfixed, as though he were hypnotically constrained from taking any action. Rochelle locked her eyes on her floating panties. She drew her arm back, gauging their flight. Finally, in a reflexive attempt to retrieve her panties and terminate her embarrassment, she lunged for them with a wild, roundhouse swing of her arm.

To Luco's horror, she snared the panties in mid-flight, at the precise moment that they floated past Luco's still-bulging fly. Under the full force of its own wild impetus, her hand slammed into him, catching not only the panties in her frantic grasp but the contents of his fly as well.

"UNGHHH!" he gasped in a sharp, exhalation of breath, doubling over from the below-the-belt impact.

For a long moment, the tableau was frozen in time. Rochelle, mortified and disoriented, was unable to release her firm and no doubt painful grasp of Luco's panty-draped bulge. Both she and Luco, in unison, looked first at her hand, then at each other, then at Jeanne, then back at her hand. Luco grasped her wrist and tried to pry her hand free.

It wasn't until Jeanne, seething with fury and not at all entertained, exclaimed sharply, "Hey you! With the dick in your hand! Get the hell out!" that Rochelle was able to recover sufficiently to release her grip. She marched unsteadily from the room with Jeanne's eyes following her all the way, while Luco stole to his desk. Once seated, he attempted to regain his dignity and to reestablish his authority.

"Just who do you think you are, Ms. Aiello?" asked Luco. "How dare you barge in through closed doors?"

Jeanne stepped to his desk, planted her feet apart and stood with her tightly bunched fists on her hips. Completely ignoring his question, she asked, "Do you think for one minute I give a single damn what you do with your bimbo in your office? Or anyplace else for that matter?" Her voice dripped with scorn.

"Need I remind you, Ms. Aiello, that you are talking to the president of this bank. Your employer. The person who pays your salary. You would be well advised to modify your tone." Given the circumstances, he was unable to portray any real conviction.

"Tell me this is some kind of sick, perverted, practical joke," she said. In her hand she clutched a paper that she rattled in his face as she spoke. The incredulity in her voice made it clear she believed otherwise.

"Perhaps you might care to tell me what you're referring to," he replied with a condescending smile. He had no doubt what Jeanne was worked up about. He had fully expected a visit from her but had to admit to himself that he was surprised by the vehemence of her reaction.

Jeanne flung the paper toward him causing him to flinch. "Just tell me the original of this letter has not gone out in the mail," she said through clenched teeth, though she knew full well that it had.

Luco picked up the paper knowing what it was before he looked at it. He had dictated it to Rochelle, fine-tuning the wording each time she printed it out. After the sixth revision he was satisfied enough to sign it.

July 16, 1990

Production House Graphix, Inc.
57 Kilvert Street
Warwick, RI 02886

ATTENTION: Mr. W. Philip Peters, President

Dear Mr. Peters:

I hereby deny your request for renewal of your line of credit #5203-10-383008. Be advised that this loan and other affiliated Greater Providence Bank & Trust debt must be paid in full within sixty (60) days of this letter.

Note #5203-10-383008	Present balance: $481,967.84
#5203-464167	Present balance: 153,342.35
#5203-464769	Present balance: 201,594.09

Very truly yours,

GREATER PROVIDENCE
BANK & TRUST

Luco Parisi
President

cc: Jeanne Aiello, *V.P. Commercial Lending*
Howard Pastore, *Executive Assistant to the President*

P.S. Please convey my warmest and most personal regards to your lovely Marla.

He knew every word by heart. He pretended to read it, then laid it squarely before him on his desk before asking with theatrical calm, "Ah, yes. My letter to Mr. Peters denying his loan. May I surmise by your erratic behavior that you are not in agreement?"

"You know damn well I'm not in agreement! The man has collateral out the gazoo and a perfect payment record. He's known throughout the community as a man of unblemished character." Jeanne was building up a head of steam. She bent forward over Luco's desk, imposing her face as far as she could into Luco's. Leaning with both hands on his desk for support, she continued in a voice that trembled with anger, "The only thing he's short on is cash flow and that's only because he got screwed by one of your four-flushing country club buddies. This loan is about as low risk as you can get. And your nephew Howard agrees with me! He put his OK on it without reservation. You have never overruled Howard before. Why this time, damn you?!"

Luco sat back with his elbows on the arms of his chair, his hands together with widespread, steepled fingers. He leaned his head back against the headrest so that his eyes looked down the slope of his nose at Jeanne.

When he offered no response, she pressed on with ill-concealed anger, "You saw the package I put together. It's been sitting on your desk for three weeks! What part didn't you like?"

Still he said nothing.

A depraved grin slowly took shape on his lips and his eyes lost their focus into the distance. They filled with something intense and burning. Puzzled, Jeanne asked herself, 'What am I seeing here? It isn't anger. Can it be hate? Yes, there's no question. It's hate. But what, or whom, does he hate? It can't be me. He doesn't know me well enough to hate me. And it certainly isn't his nephew Howard. That leaves ... Phil?! Yes!'

Through some kind of telepathic symbiosis, no doubt energized by their mutual though opposing passions, Luco was able to read her thought process. As she drew to the correct conclusion, Luco broke into a broad, evil grin. It suddenly fell into place for her.

"You sick bastard!" she hissed as she snatched the letter up from his desk. "You never intended to approve it, did you? Phil Peters never stood a chance! It didn't matter what I wrote, did it?"

Without waiting for a reply, she took a few steps toward the door that Rochelle had neglected to close. She spun to face Luco then continued in a blistering tone, "You used me you gutless weasel, and you used Howard, your own nephew. You didn't have the backbone to confront Phil yourself. You used us to set him up for you."

Jeanne stormed through the door in a rage, pointed her finger at Rochelle and said, "You! Did you get your panties back on yet?" With an abrupt motion of her thumb toward Luco's office and her voice on the rise, she finished with, "Well you might as well take them off again and get back on the couch. But don't expect to find anything resembling balls under that thing you were hanging onto a little while ago!"

As Jeanne neared the elevator, its door opened and a very grim Howard strode swiftly out. Seeing her approach he came to a stop and waited, waving his copy of the letter for her to see. "Have you seen this?" he asked, his black eyes flashing in anger.

"Yes, Howard, I did," she answered trying to affect a softer tone than she had used moments ago. "I just had a nice little chat with your uncle about it and I made no effort to sugar-coat my position. Matter of fact, I'm not sure if I still work here. Expect him to be in a foul mood."

"Thank you, Miss Aiello," he said, "but that bastard is about to learn what the term foul mood means."

Jeanne stared in wide-eyed wonder at Howard as he briskly advanced in attack mode toward Luco's office. It was the first time ever that Howard had uttered an expletive in her presence.

HORACE PULLED UP IN her car just as Jeanne stepped out into the garage. Burning rubber, she drove two blocks east on Orange, turned right on Pine then left on Dorrance to the I-95 on-ramp. She cut with total abandon across three lanes of the interstate to avoid being trapped in the two exit lanes that quickly veer off to the right for Pawtucket and points north.

Heading south, she put the spurs to her Corvette and quickly shot up to eighty-five. It was only eight miles from downtown to the Post Road turnoff and only two more miles from there to Phil's office, where, in just a matter of minutes, Jeanne bounded from her car almost before it came to a screeching stop. Her noisy arrival drew the attention of the entire Production House Graphix clerical staff from inside the smoked-glass-walled office.

"Please tell Mr. Peters that Jeanne Aiello is here and I'd like to see him," said Jeanne while restraining herself from dashing through to Phil's office.

"Did you have an appointment, Ms. Aiello?" the receptionist replied.

"No, Felicia," said Jeanne with a glance at the receptionist's desk nameplate, "but if you'll let him know I'm here, I'm sure he … "

"You're from the *bank*, aren't you?" Felicia interrupted coolly, with emphasis and a liberal coating of distaste on the word *bank*.

"Yes, but … "

Felicia ignored Jeanne, picked up her phone and punched in a three-digit number. "Ms. Jeanne Aiello is here. From the *bank*," she spoke into the phone, again treating the word with disdain. In mere seconds, a man entered through a door on the far wall, letting in the muffled sounds of the pressroom. As he approached Felicia's desk, the door swung silently to a close behind him, restoring quiet serenity to the front office.

He wore a shirt and tie under a dark blue, denim shop apron which he removed, carefully so as not to disturb his neatly-coifed gray hair, and draped it over an empty chair as he came near. His shirt sleeves were rolled up two turns to below his elbows but his tie remained snug and trim against his buttoned collar. He was not a big man, perhaps an inch shorter than Jeanne, with sloped shoulders and a trim build, notwithstanding a hint of a belly. He carried himself with a casual looseness and walked with a slight shuffle. As he drew near, Jeanne could see that his nose had been rearranged more than once, perhaps in the ring, but it in no way detracted from the man's good looks in spite of his sixty-plus years of age.

His hazel eyes locked on hers as he introduced himself, "Frank D'Uva. Plant Manager. We'll use the conference room. Follow me."

His tone was non-committal and distant. He didn't offer his hand nor did he wait for a response as he turned and led the way.

"Excuse me, Mr. D'Uva," said Jeanne impatiently as she followed him, "but I want to see Mr. Peters, not you. No offense intended."

He reached the door to the conference room, looked inside to be sure it was unoccupied, ushered Jeanne in and closed the door behind them. He motioned for her to take a seat at the Corian marble table and took the seat opposite her.

"No offense taken," he replied with a measured chill, "but what do you say we do without the sparring and get to the point. Just what the hell are you doing here, anyway?"

"I told you!" she fired back, "I came here to see Phil Peters. Your boss! Not you! Now suppose you just tell Miss Warmth out there to fetch him and you can go back to whatever you were doing."

"Let's get this straight right off, lady. There's only one person in this building tells me what to do and that's not you." His tone remained constant but his eyes had turned to ice. "You think you can come in here like a storm trooper and start giving orders, you got another think coming."

She took a slow, deep breath, realizing she was handling this badly.

"You're right, Mr. D'Uva, and I do apologize," she said contritely. "It's just that I really do need to see him. Something has gone terribly wrong and I want to prepare him for it. Please, will you tell him I'm here."

"I can't do that. Besides, you're too late. He tore out of here right after he read this. I got no idea where he is," he said as he pulled a folded paper from his shirt pocket and tossed it on the table in front of her. "This came this morning by special courier."

It was the letter. Though it was now neatly folded, it was obvious that someone had earlier crumpled it into a ball.

"Phil read it, swore, threw it on the floor and took off," he continued. "Felicia picked it up. After she read it, she called me in. I told her not to tell anybody else, but knowing her, I'm giving long odds that everyone in the building already knows that Phil's loan got shot down."

"Oh dear Lord, no," Jeanne groaned.

"Phil doesn't keep secrets from us. He told us how he got stiffed big time by Continental Chain. He also told us just how bad he needed that loan to pull us through," said D'Uva. He was a little puzzled by what appeared to be genuine concern on Jeanne's part as he continued, "Last month, Phil told us that you approved his loan. Now this!"

"Mr. D'Uva, I *did* approve the loan and so did my boss, Mr. Pastore. As far as we knew, it was a done deal. I learned about this only thirty minutes ago," she waved the letter as she spoke, "and so did Mr. Pastore. Please believe me."

D'Uva looked for a long time into her eyes and became convinced Jeanne was on the level. "What the hell's going on here, lady?" he asked.

"I wish I knew, Mr. D'Uva, but right now I just want to find Philip. Do you have any idea where he might be?" she asked. A measure of desperation showed through in her voice and on her face.

Again he studied her deeply for several seconds without saying a word. He then started scribbling on one of the yellow legal pads that were arranged around the table in front of each seat. When he finished writing, he buzzed for Felicia. He handed her the paper and said, "Start at the top and put me on with the person I wrote down. As soon as I finish a call, unless I tell you different, do the same with the next one and the ones after it."

The phone on the conference table chirped briefly. Through the glass wall, Felicia nodded for D'Uva to pick up.

"Hey Roger, how's the boy? ... Yeah, great! ... No, not today, Roger. Is he there? There's something I want him to take a look at before we run it. ... Not there? ... Naw, no sweat. ... Veal steak? Love to but I havta pass. I'll be in later in the week though. ... Yeah. See ya."

Except for the luncheon specials that were being offered, the next two calls were much of the same. Jeanne, who had slumped in her chair feeling helpless sat up fully alert when, during the next call, she heard D'Uva say, "He is? ... He what?!"

"Is he there?" Jeanne interrupted but D'Uva gave no sign that he heard her.

"Where is he now? ... Is he OK? ... ," he asked intently.

"What's going on?" Jeanne sprang to her feet.

"The police?!" he exclaimed. "You called the police?! Why the hell would y ... ? Oh! Tommy's there? That's a break."

Jeanne snatched the phone from his hand, said, "Please hold," into it, stabbed the hold button, pushed her face into D'Uva's and hissed, "Tell me where he is! Right now!"

He had been nose-to-nose with some very tough people, in the ring and out of it, and he was impressed by this lady. He cancelled the hold button as he gently pulled the phone from her grasp and spoke into it, "Hang on a second, Liu." He turned the mouthpiece against his chest and said, "The Cathay Terrace. It's down Post Road about a mile past the ... "

She was out the door before she finished saying, "I know where it is."

JEANNE SWUNG HER CORVETTE into the Cathay Terrace parking lot and screeched to a stop. She leaped from the car and started to run toward the restaurant. At that moment, she saw Phil and brought her hands up over her face to stifle a scream. One of his arms hung limply over the shoulder of a big, well-dressed man without whose help, it was clear, Phil would have been unable to stand. A lovely woman with olive skin and loosely styled, black hair, held onto Phil's other arm. When Jeanne ran up to them, the man said, "My name is Tommy. This is my wife Laura. We're friends of Phil. We just happened to be here when this happened."

THEY DECIDED TO TAKE Phil to Jeanne's house. The three of them eased Phil into the back seat of his own car and Tommy got behind the wheel. With Jeanne leading in her Corvette and Laura bringing up the rear, the motorcade made its way south on Post Road. They turned left on Main Avenue, passed under the final approach path of T. F. Greene Airport's runway 5-R, then took a right on Button-woods. Soon the scent of salt water, carried ashore on a cooling zephyr, told them Greenwich Bay was near.

With the sun high over the bay, the vista was spectacular. Following the flocks of diving, screeching, feeding seagulls, sportfishermen dashed wildly about in pursuit of bluefish, their wakes tracing erratic paths through the choppy surface. Sailboats out of East Greenwich, Cowesett and Apponaug ran before a fresh westerly breeze toward upper Narragansett Bay and the midbay islands of Patience and Prudence. Some would circle around the northern tip of Prudence, lower the hook in the sheltered waters of Potters Cove and hoist the party-time pennant.

Boat traffic around Warwick Light was heavy. Power boats of all sizes steamed toward and out of Warwick Cove. They gave wide passage to the barely submerged wharf pilings off Warwick Country Club and the lethal Flat Rock that lurked mere inches beneath the surface between the light and Sandy Point at the tip of Potowomut.

HELPING PHIL FROM THE CAR and negotiating the three steps up to Jeanne's bayfront veranda took the combined efforts of Tommy and Jeanne while Laura ran ahead to hold the doors open. Though the view from Jeanne's home on the north shore of Greenwich Bay was captivating, it went unnoticed. Their focus was more immediate.

Together, they stripped Phil down to his jockey briefs and put him down on the bed in the guest room where he immediately fell into a fitful sleep. They hadn't intended to strip him but, each time they removed a garment, they found more scratches and cuts. None were serious but they set about cleaning and dressing those that needed it. Tommy kept his distance while Laura and Jeanne ministered to Phil. When they were finished, they went out to the kitchen. The unspoken question, palpable in the awkward silence, nagged for an explanation.

"I want to thank you both for all your help," Jeanne said. She glanced toward the bedroom, then continued, "I suppose I should explain about … "

"It's not necessary, Jeanne," Laura interrupted. "We really don't know Phil all that well. He's just a friend of Tommy's brother. And we've never met his wife. Whatever you and Phil have … "

"But I want to, Laura. Somehow I … need to." Jeanne turned and looked again for a long moment toward the bedroom where Phil lay asleep. When she turned back, she sensed Laura's empathy.

"We've known each other for about ten years. We met through business but we were drawn to each other. We became friends. Soon, we found ourselves confiding personal things about our lives to each other. We told ourselves we were just good friends. For a long time we pretended that's all it was.

Jeanne looked away. Laura recaptured her eyes.

"And now?" asked Laura.

"And now we know that we have something that's so very special ... and so very beautiful ... and so very hopeless."

Laura looked at Jeanne, waiting for her to continue. When she didn't, Laura asked, "Jeanne, what happened today?"

Jeanne looked out at the bay for a long time, collecting herself. When she turned back to Laura, she was moist-eyed but matter-of-fact.

"A few months ago, Phil's company completed a very large project. His client refused to pay. I won't burden you with the details. The bottom line is, Phil's cash flow suffered terribly. As a result of it, he saw he wouldn't be able to make a payment that was coming due against his credit line. He came to us, explained the circumstances, and we drew up a new loan package. My boss, Howard Pastore, approved it. The only thing left was getting the president to sign off on it. Normally that's a mere formality. Luco Parisi has never overruled his nephew Howard on a loan package. Today, out of the blue, he sent Phil a letter by special courier. He not only denied the loan but he's demanding full payment of all his other debt as well. That could destroy Phil. There's no way he can raise that kind of money."

Tommy became especially interested at the mention of Luco.

"Excuse me, Jeanne. Did you say Luco Parisi?" he asked.

Jeanne nodded a yes.

"Parisi vetoed the whole plan?"

"Yes ... and that's what must have sent Phil over the edge," said Jeanne. "After Howard and I had assured Phil that his loan was approved, getting that letter must have been too much for him to handle."

"It occurs to me that with all that's happened, I never mentioned my last name. It's Bonetta," said Tommy.

"Bonetta." Jeanne thought a moment. "Phil used to work for a Vincent Bonetta. He bought PHGraphix from him. Are you related to him?"

"Vince and I are brothers," Tommy replied with some grimness.

As named executor to Vince's estate, he held intimate knowledge of all of Vince's assets. Moreover, he was familiar with every financial detail of Phil's buyout of PHGraphix from Vince. It was immediately apparent to Tommy that GPB&T's action could bring Phil to financial ruin. If that happened, it would be virtually impossible for Phil to repay Vince the $600,000 he still owed him.

Tommy pulled out his cell phone and headed for the veranda. As he punched in an eleven-digit number, he said, "I'm not at liberty to tell you the details, but my brother Vince needs to know about this."

EIGHTEEN

"ROGER FIVE-FOUR-NINER, approved. Report back on frequency before reaching SHERL."

Vince playfully lip-synched the controller's words that came through with perfect, static-free clarity in his headset, then acknowledged with two clicks of his yoke-mounted mike button. He had made the same request many times—to leave the frequency for a few minutes to check destination weather—and he knew what the controller's response would be. He also knew that five nautical miles past SHERL, a radio fix out over the Atlantic some 38 miles southeast of JFK, he would be leaving New York Center's airspace. New York would soon hand him off to a new controller before Vince entered that new controller's sector of airspace.

Vince didn't need to get a weather update. He knew he would be on the ground at Quonset State Airport in less than an hour. Providence, only eight miles north of Quonset, was reporting ceiling and visibility unlimited and was forecasting it to remain that way at least until noon the next day.

He was five-and-a-half hours out of Naples, Florida and he had no idea why. The first message on his answering machine had said, "Something's come up. How soon can you get here?" The second message, time-stamped only a minute later, said, "Sorry … should have mentioned ... it's not about pa. He's fine." Both voices belonged to his younger brother Tommy.

Vince tried to call back but was unable to reach his brother either at Warwick Police Headquarters or at home. He left word on Tommy's voice-mail for him to check with the guys at Quonset Approach Control to learn his ETA. Puzzled, and with his adrenaline level rising, Vince had quickly scrawled a note to Gabriele saying, "Didn't want to interrupt your showing. Had to launch right away. Message from Tommy sounded urgent. Sorry about dinner. Good luck with the Scheelens. Call you tonight." His wife was then showing a pricey beachfront high-rise condo to a German couple who had gobs of money to spend for a vacation home.

Vince removed his headset, turned off the cabin speaker and welcomed the solitude. He disconnected the autopilot and executed a series of slow, coordinated rolls, fanning the florid face of the low, western sun with his left wingtip. The sun joined in the game by firing a kaleidoscope of flashing colors off the polished metal surface of his rocking wings. He felt the soft, almost whispered caress of the two, geared Continental engines, soothingly smooth in perfect synch with each other, and with his mood.

That was the true reason for his going off frequency. He wanted to again drink in the awesome spectacle of the setting sun retreating below his left wingtip, glowing red with the exertion of its fatal struggle against the night. To view one more time the ocean below, sparkling orange and gold in its unique symbiosis with the sun, shedding its light to join the sun in blackness as it merged into the earth.

God, how he loved this.

About twenty years earlier, he and his brothers John, Tommy and Ben were having dinner after a day of fishing off the southeast light at Block Island. Their mother, Rose, had prepared what a normal person, that is, someone who was not Italian and had not grown up eating at Rose's table, might aptly describe as a banquet. The brothers had not lived at home for several years, "at home" being Rose and Pierino's house, since they were married and living at their own "homes." They grew up looking upon Rose's table presentations as normal and they assumed that everyone else dined the same way. Later, the fallacy of that assumption came to be impressed upon Vince's oldest brother.

John made his home in the midwest after his discharge from the USMC at the end of WWII. He had met, fallen in love with, and married an *american* girl. That is, a non-Italian. It didn't matter that she was of German descent. To Rose and Pierino, there were only Italians and *americans*. If you were not Italian, it followed that you were, by definition, *american*. You could be an O'Donnell, a Burnstingle, a Berman, a Smythe, a Koski, no matter, you were *american*. This had everything to do with ethnicity, even though the word had not yet come into fashion and neither Rose nor Pierino, as young parents, had ever heard the word, and nothing whatever to do with nationality or patriotism. They were fiercely patriotic Americans. Therefore, when they used the word *american* in the above context, it was as if they were speaking it with a small *a*. They intended no inference other than to define whether or not one was of Italian descent.

John's wife didn't know a *braciole* from a bagel nor, it seemed to him, did anyone else west of Chicago. For years, the only time he received Italian cooking of any kind, let alone Rose's one-of-a-kind presentations, was when he visited "home."

On this occasion, whereas Vince, Tommy and Ben enjoyed their dinner, John became emotionally immersed in his. He relished the sight, the fragrance, the touch and the soul of each morsel before consigning it to his palate. Every few moments, with his face glowing in total rapture, his eyes closed and his head swaying gently from side to side, he would utter a soft moan of pleasure. If Rose were not so inherently naive and innocent and flattered, it might have been embarrassing for all. Ben finally felt compelled to say, "John, take it easy! Control yourself! You look like you want to rub the food all over your entire body!"

Savoring the memory, Vince had to laugh at the parallel it drew with his own passionate feelings for his airplane, the glorious view, and the almost transcendental solitude of the flight. If he could, he would rub the moment all over his entire body.

HE REENGAGED THE AUTOPILOT, put his headset back on and keyed the mike.

"New York Center, Cessna five-four-niner back with you, level at one-five thousand."

"Cessna five-four-niner, New York, contact Boston Center on one-two-four-point-eight-five," the reply came without delay and without reference to the chuckle that had been evident in Vince's voice when he called in. It was an early hand-off on a quiet evening. In addition to Vince's Cessna 421, the controller had been working only a USAir 727 southbound at 35,000 feet and a Mooney that had just entered his sector northbound along the coastline.

Vince acknowledged and checked in with Boston Center. Boston cleared him down to 7,000. Instead of reducing the engine power settings to lose altitude, Vince trimmed for a cruise descent and enjoyed letting the airspeed build up in the crystal clear and flawlessly smooth air.

His track over The Hamptons and Long Island Sound followed the same route he had taken dozens of times, in every season, in daylight and at night. The lights of Westerly lay ahead of him with the terrain beyond rendered in surrealistic charcoal by the twilight moon. Block Island, 10 miles off shore to his right, was clearly visible in the moonlit, satin-finished brilliance of the waters of Rhode Island Sound.

Before reaching Westerly, Vince canceled his IFR (Instrument Flight Rules) clearance and banked into a right turn to remain off-shore and take in the moonlit scenery of the shoreline route. Passing over the Harbor of Refuge with the Port of Galilee under his left wingtip, he banked to the left around the Point Judith Light to proceed up the west passage of Narragansett Bay with the island of Jamestown off his right wing. Soon the lights of North Kingstown, the Jamestown Bridge and the Quonset State Airport were distinct. Having been cleared for landing straight-in on runway 34, Vince drifted a little to the right to align himself with the runway. As he neared the northwest shoreline of Jamestown he thumbed his mike button and said, "Quonset five-four-niner, three mile final, runway three-four."

"Five-four-niner check wheels down, cleared to land."

TOMMY HEARD THE EXCHANGE on the handheld radio that lay on the glareshield of his dashboard. He looked to the right and saw the landing lights of the Cessna on final approach. Moments later, when it taxied off the runway toward the parking ramp, Tommy faced his car toward the plane and turned his headlights on and off twice. The Cessna answered in kind with its landing lights.

After all its lights went out and the props came to a stop, Tommy went around behind the left wing to the airstair door and lowered it into position. Seconds later, Vince emerged from the plane. The brothers greeted each other with a four-handed handshake, each taking the other's hand in both of his own. As always, their eyes met and held the other's with a warmth and love that required no words or ceremony to validate its bond or celebrate its meaning.

During the drive to Jeanne's house, Vince learned that Phil had gone to the Cathay Terrace, a fashionable Taiwanese restaurant, one of his regular lunch stops not far from his office. Instead of taking a table, he chose to sit at the bar. This struck Liu, the barman, as odd, since Phil, though not a teetotaler, rarely drinks at all and never takes a drink at lunch. Until today. After his third Jim Beam straight up, the effects were pronounced. Nonetheless, Phil ordered a fourth by repeatedly slamming his glass down on the bar.

Liu sidled up to Phil and asked him discreetly if he might prefer to order his lunch instead.

"I jus' ordered my lunch," Phil slurred, "Dintcha hear me? Jus' pour it right in here an' lea'me the hell alone."

One of the two businessmen seated across the horseshoe-shaped bar, both of whom were regulars and both of whom knew and respected Phil, said gently and solicitously to him, "Hey buddy, you want to take it easy with that stuff. It can put you away real sudden like."

"Who the hell asst ya, *buddy?*" Phil replied, unable to clearly focus his eyes on the man who spoke, "Whyncha stick t' your peanuts and beer and jus' butt out?!" His tone caught the attention of the nearby tables in the dining room. Liu reached under the bartop and pressed a button. Within seconds, Chen, the owner, appeared at the bar. After a brief, whispered conference with Liu, he approached

Phil and, with a friendly smile, said, "Mr. Peters how fine to see you again. How may I help you today?"

"You can tell this ape here t' fill up my freakin' glass." With that he began again to bang his glass on the bar. Chen shook his head at Liu and, turning to the two men at the bar, managed to convey an apology to them with nothing more than a slight, dignified bow of his head. Returning his gaze to Phil, he placed his hand over Phil's and started to say, "Please, Mr. Peters, if the glass breaks you can be seriously injured."

Before he could finish, Phil shouted, "Lea'me alone dammit!" rousing Tommy who was seated in the dining room enjoying an early lunch with his wife, Laura. Astonished to see that it was Phil who was creating the disturbance, Tommy excused himself and started toward the bar, arriving in time to see Phil yank his hand away from Chen in a wild, backhand sweep. In Phil's unbalanced condition, the momentum of his own sudden motion swept himself off his bar stool. In a grotesque, crumbling pirouette, he collapsed in a heap, but not before slamming against the live lobster aquarium, toppling it to the marble floor in a thunderous crash of shattering glass.

Unable to gain his footing on the wet floor, Phil thrashed about on all fours amid the live lobsters and shards of glass. Combining their efforts, Tommy and Chen were able to hoist Phil to his feet. Liu was still behind the bar and the two businessmen sat in open-mouthed wonder, transfixed by the scene before them. Tommy's attention was drawn to Laura who rushed in from the dining room at the sound of the crash and was openly relieved to see that her husband was all right.

With Phil safely on his feet, Chen turned from him and took Tommy's arm in a gesture of confidentiality. With their backs to Phil, he asked, "He seems to be all right, Lieutenant. Is there any reason for the Department to become involved in this?"

"Not unless you want to bring charges for the damages, Chen."

"I pay exorbitant sums for insurance. The aquarium and the lobsters are easily replaced," he answered, brushing off their importance with a backhanded wave of his hand. "I'm far more troubled about

Mr. Peters. He has always been the model of civility. I've never seen him like this bef… "

"No! Wait!" Laura shouted. Phil had decided it was time to leave.

Tommy and Chen spun to see Phil weaving through the foyer and out the front door onto the flagstone patio. They scrambled after him but there was no way they could reach him in time. Phil failed to negotiate the ninety-degree right turn to the walkway. Though his head and shoulders twisted to the right, his lower body missed the signal and churned straight ahead across the patio. The guard rail at the end of the patio caught Phil just below the belt. They watched helplessly as Phil somersaulted over the railing and disappeared into the shrubbery, five feet below.

"By the time Chen and I could get to him," Tommy went on, "Phil was in a daze, trying to extricate himself from the pyracantha. His face and neck and hands were pretty scratched-up. Lots of blood but nothing serious.

"After we got him up on his feet, I told Chen to go inside and take care of the mess Phil made in there. I assured him that there would be no reason for me to bring the Department in on it.

"About that time, this red Corvette swerves into the lot and comes screeching to a stop in front of us. The driver jumps out of the car almost before it stops and starts to run to us but she stops in her tracks when she gets a look at Phil. It looked like she was going to scream but she clapped her hands over her face to stifle it. She looked at Phil from between her fingers and her eyes flooded with tears.

"Well, you know my wife. Laura's a patsy for anyone in trouble. She rushes over and puts her arms around her and says, 'He's all right, Mrs. Peters. It's not as bad as it looks.' "

Vince listened silently as Tommy's account of the day's events neared its end. He told of how Jeanne had separated herself from Laura, taking Phil's scratched-up face in her hands with a tenderness that didn't escape Laura's notice.

"Oh, Philip, you poor, sweet boob," Jeanne had said through streaming tears. Then, without turning her eyes from Phil's, she said to the others, "I'm not Mrs. Peters. I'm Jeanne Aiello, Phil's … friend."

Laura noticed the hesitation. Tommy hadn't.

"I'll drive him home in his car, I told her," Tommy said, "and Laura can follow in ours, but Jeanne refused. She said something about Phil needing support and love and that Phil wouldn't get any of either at home.

"Then she jumped back into her car and said, 'My place isn't far from here. Follow me!' And here we are."

NINETEEN

"DIDN'T PARISI GIVE you a reason?" Vince asked during a lull in Jeanne's narrative as she served coffee.

"Not in words," she answered, "but, Vince, the way he handled it was weird."

"Weird is something Luco Parisi does well, but how do you mean it in this case?"

"Well first of all, regardless of whether the proposal was approved or rejected, why would he get personally involved by notifying the customer directly?" she asked. "It's always the responsibility of the originator of the proposal, in this case me, or the originator's immediate superior, in this case Howard, to inform the client."

"OK, he broke policy," Tommy joined in. "He's the president and CEO of the bank. He wrote the policy, I suppose he can break it if he wants. What's weird about that?"

"You'd have to know him, bro," said Vince. "Luco isn't one of the world's great standup guys. It would have been more in character for him to stay behind the lines and let Jeanne or Howard do the dirty work."

"Exactly. But there's even more to it than that," said Jeanne. "When I challenged him to give me a reason for the rejection, his entire appearance seemed to change. He became, how can I describe it … serene? … no, more like … fulfilled. Not fulfilled as in a condition of contentment. More as in a ... excuse me ... an après-sex context.

"That's when I lost it and turned into a ranting lunatic, but just before I did ... it was the strangest thing ... here's where the weird comes in. For a long, silent moment, his eyes burned right into me. For those few seconds, maybe I imagined it but it felt real, we could each read the essence of the other's thoughts."

Vince and Tommy looked askance at each other, earning a withering look from Laura.

"Can you be more specific for these two cretins, Jeanne?" asked Laura. "What else is there? I know there's more."

"Yeah, there's a lot more," the voice croaked. Waking to their voices, Phil walked unsteadily onto the veranda and took a seat next to Jeanne. He was barefoot but had pulled on his shirt, which hung unbuttoned outside his trousers. He made brief eye-contact with each of the others, smarting under the unmistakable look of reproach he got from Vince. Phil turned to Jeanne and said, "I made the mistake of looking in a mirror. Whatever I did, I'm sorry. Will someone tell me where we are and what everyone's doing here?"

Tommy spoke up. "Laura and I were having lunch at the Cathay when you decided to break the place up. Chen preferred not to have you arrested. We were about to drive you home. Jeanne arrived in time to head us off and convinced us to come here. This is her place. When she told us about the letter you got, I called Vince." His years in the Department had taught him to be concise and to the point.

"You said there's more," said Vince to Phil. "Let's have it. What's this all about?"

Phil felt the rebuke in Vince's voice. If the others noticed it, they gave no sign that they did. His tone was crisp and clipped. It was absent of any warmth. It was no ploy on Vince's part. Whatever had driven Phil to react to Luco's letter the way he did, Vince felt resentful and hurt that Phil had taken what he, Vince, considered to be a coward's way of dealing with it, and Phil realized it. At that moment, Phil felt worse about having diminished himself in Vince's eyes than about what he, himself, had suffered under Luco's actions.

Phil couldn't bring himself to make eye-contact with Vince while he related the history of Luco's running affair at Brown with Professor Handjob Hannah and of Luco's 'losing' Marla to Phil at one of Handjob's parties. He described how Luco had schemed to get Marla into a hotel room only to learn, too late, that it was Marla who had set Luco up and then had so unequivocally shot him down. Phil then told them how he had tracked Luco down and flattened him on the sixth tee at The Alpine.

"That's it, Phil!" said Jeanne, without realizing she had taken his hand in both of hers. The others noticed but said nothing. "I should have remembered! It was clear to me ... I mean absolutely clear ... that Luco's decision had nothing whatever to do with financial statements or cash flow projections or anything at all related to business. It was purely personal and purely vindictive. I could *feel* his hate for you."

"Are you saying your boss is taking revenge for something that happened in college over twenty years ago when he couldn't make any headway with Marla?" Laura joined in. "Excuse me, Jeanne, but I don't think so. No man burns with that kind of passion, present company excepted of course. They're just not made that way. To hear them tell it when they think we're not listening, there was never a shortage of women who were ready and willing to do the mating dance."

"That may be true, Laura, but it doesn't apply to Luco," said Phil. "To him, Marla was the one that got away and I'm the guy that got her. Add that to the bitter envy he's felt of me since we were kids and his ego couldn't handle it."

"No Phil, there has to be more to it than that," Vince said. "This isn't the first time you've borrowed from Greater Providence. Over the years, Luco has had plenty of opportunities to slam the door in your face but he didn't. We have to ask, why now? After all this time, why did he decide to do it now?"

"It was probably decided for him," Tommy said, slipping into detective mode. He got up, walked to the railing and leaned on it, looking out at the darkened shore. "Maybe he did recognize the past opportunities to stick it to Phil but, one, he didn't have the *coglione* to do it or, two, the passion wore off and he no longer cared enough to do it or, three, the timing was never right."

Turning to face the others, he continued, "Today, he blew reasons one and two out of the water by actually doing it. So we're left with reason number three, the timing. We have to conclude that something very recent has taken place that triggered his actions."

"You could be right, Tommy," said Vince. "Either something has already taken place, or something is about to take place, that gave his *coglione* a jump start." Turning to Jeanne, "Has anything happened recently? Maybe a new directive from the state or from the feds? A shakeup in the board of directors?"

"I wouldn't be one of the first to know of a new directive," Jeanne replied, "but as for the board, forget it. Luco Parisi *is* the board. Except for his nephew, Howard Pastore, no one has any say including me. We're nothing more than rubber stamps."

"Well *some*thing has changed," said Vince. "Jeanne, it's important, to Phil and to me personally, that I talk to Parisi. I was close to his father. Maybe I can reason with him. Can you arrange for me to see him in the morning?"

"I'm not sure I still have a job but I'll do my best. Where can I reach you?"

"He'll be staying with us," said Laura as she handed Jeanne a calling card. "Now I'd like to say good night. It's been a trying day. I wish we could have met under more pleasant circumstances, but I'm glad we did meet. If you need me for anything, even if only to talk, please call me."

Phil looked on in puzzlement as Jeanne and Laura hugged and kissed each other on the cheek in the manner of longtime friends. Clearly they had connected with each other. Jeanne's plaintive love affair with Phil had struck to the core of Laura's romantic soul. She was secretly glad she had never met Marla.

"It's been a long day for all of us," said Vince, "but, Phil, before we say goodnight, can we have a minute together? If you're up to it, can we walk on the beach?"

Phil went into the bedroom to retrieve his shoes. When he came out, his shirt was buttoned and it was tucked into his pants. Laura and Jeanne cleared the table as Phil and Vince walked to the water's edge, becoming silhouettes against the moonlit water.

Out of earshot, Phil started with, "Vince, I know what you're going to say. But I promise, whatever happens between the bank and me, somehow, no matter how long it takes me, I'll find a way to pay you ba … "

"No you do *not* know what I'm going to say, so just button it up and I'll say it for myself!" Vince's tone was like the sound of a freeze crack ripping across the frozen surface of a pond. He could not have stunned Phil more if he had delivered a resounding slap across Phil's face.

He continued, "Did you get a look at yourself?! You look like a sleazy reject from a skid-row bar. And today, that's what you acted like. A sleazy derelict, thrown out on his ass! But it wasn't a skid-row bar. It was the Cathay Terrace for crisake! You insulted Chen by using his place to make a total ass of yourself!

"And now you insult me! There's a lot more at stake here than the money you owe me. Have you lost sight of the fact that you have a plant full of people? That you have to face them tomorrow? Many of those people worked for me before they worked for you. By now they already know every bit of what happened today. They'll be looking for reassurance.

"You behaved like a sniveling coward. I know you're not. Hopefully, so do the people who work for you. But they deserve an explanation. You'd best spend the rest of tonight working out how and what you're going to say to them."

"You're right … and somehow, I'll handle it," Phil said. Then he turned to face Vince squarely. Choked with emotion, he continued, "But, Vince, about the other thing. I can't escape it. You gave me my start. I owe you far more than the mon … "

"Forget the money, Phil!" Vince interrupted. His tone remained intense but it became seasoned with compassion and friendship. "I'm not going to sneeze at $600,000 but I can get along without it. At least until you get things sorted out." He paused. For a long moment he looked right back into Phil's eyes. Then, putting an arm around Phil's shoulders, he guided him back toward the house.

"It's clear to me, and it should certainly be clear to you, that you're getting screwed for something that's unrelated to business. By definition, that makes this a personal matter between you and that …

that *aberration* … Luco Parisi." The word had been nagging at him since his father had first used it to describe Luco. "Since I, too, have a stake in this, it's now a personal matter between him … and me."

TWENTY

LUCO PARISI LIVED IN a huge estate home in the gentle hills of western Cranston. To say he and his wife, Celia, lived in it together would be to overstate the matter. Days would go by—weeks when he was in Nürnberg with Erika—during which Luco did not stay at home. Nonetheless, during those periods, he and Celia spoke regularly on the phone and were, if only on the surface, solicitous of each other's well-being. They maintained appearances by attending official functions and important social events together as husband and wife, but they slept in suites located at opposite ends of the house.

However, on those infrequent occasions when Celia's libido ran rampant, Luco was conscripted to provide his services on her behalf. At all other times, she didn't require his presence nor did she impose any limits on his activities beyond those implied by the admonition of her father regarding scandal or disgrace to his daughter. With Papa Cheech's sword of Damocles ever-poised to curtail the future of Luco's most cherished appendage, Luco assiduously avoided any situation that might in any way compromise security in his extramarital meanderings.

A week prior to the auction of Goyette's properties, all contact with Luco ended. He stopped calling home, he stopped going to or phoning the office, and he didn't return any of the many messages

Howard left on his answering machine and with his wife. Never before had he so totally broken off contact with the bank. Howard's discreet phone calls to The Alpine Country Club, to Luco's fitness center and to his other known haunts revealed that no one had seen or heard from him for more than a week.

HOWARD LOOKED AT THE papers he printed out when he first became suspicious of Mickey and his Uncle Luco. He had read them so many times that he had committed all the important data to his memory. He didn't have to study them. He simply looked at them, subconsciously wishing they would disappear from existence. Except for his in-your-face insistence on foreclosure at the board meeting, Howard had not again brought up the matter to his uncle. Nor had he mentioned it to Mickey. Unable to face him, Howard had been avoiding him.

Goyette's properties brought $400,000 less at auction than the unpaid balance of his loan. Howard knew without investigating that there would be no point in bringing suit against him for the shortfall. Goyette had no other known assets.

Howard had been clinging to a desperate hope that he had somehow misinterpreted what he discovered in the computer files. That the properties would somehow fetch prices commensurate with Mickey's appraisals. The results of the auction sale brutally restored Howard to reality.

He switched on his computer, entered a series of commands and watched the hourglass on the screen for several seconds as the computer whirred and clicked. When the screen came up, it scrolled a list of every mortgage loan that the bank had granted in the last twelve months. After a few more command entries, only those loans written by Luco Parisi remained on the screen. Each entry contained the loan amount, mortgagor's name and, along with other pertinent data, the name of the appraiser. Without exception, the appraiser was Michael K. Hoban. Howard stared for a long time at the screen.

He then expanded the search criteria to go all the way back to 1980, the year the bank started recording those types of records into the data base. For the first three years, there was nothing about Luco's loan applications to distinguish them from those of the other loan officers. However, midway in 1983 there was an abrupt change. From that point on, to the exclusion of all other appraisers, Mickey Hoban did the appraisal for every loan that Luco wrote for which real property was the major base of collateral.

Howard quickly revised the search criteria to begin with that date in 1983. Choosing several loans at random, he examined Mickey's appraisal reports. Focusing on the properties that formed the basis for Mickey's evaluations, Howard went into the tax records of the towns in which those properties were located. He pulled their official records up on his screen. As in the Goyette case, it became clear to Howard that Mickey had wantonly inflated the value of many of the properties that he had defined as comparables and that others were simply non-existent properties. He printed them out then returned to the Goyette file and printed that out as well. He inserted the printouts into a 9 x 12 manila envelope and put the envelope into the security pocket of his briefcase.

Whatever scheme Mickey and Luco had engineered began midway in 1983. There was another date in 1983 that was engraved in Howard's memory. July 18th. The day his beloved grandfather Giuseppe Parisi died and his son, Howard's uncle Luco, took over the reins of GPB&T.

"MR. BONETTA IS HERE to see you, Mr. Pastore," Mrs. Franklin spoke softly into the intercom.

Howard came out of his office to greet Vince. It was a ceremony of deference to his visitor. There are several ways a visitor may be greeted, each proffering a distinct level of honor and respect on a graduated scale. At the lowest level, the visitor is made to wait for a period of time that is long enough to be inconvenient, after which a terse announcement over the intercom says, "Send him in." At an intermediate level, he is politely asked to, "Please make yourself comfortable. Mr. Jones will be with you in just a few minutes," after which the announcement over the intercom is a polite, "Please show Mr. Smith in." It did not escape Vince's notice that he was being greeted at the summit of the protocol scale. The mountain had come to Mohammed.

"How good to meet you, Mr. Bonetta." Howard offered his hand, looking up into Vince's face with a friendly smile. He was several inches shorter than Vince and the slightness of his build was accented by Vince's broad, athletic frame.

"Thanks for seeing me on such short notice, Mr. Pastore," said Vince, concealing his surprise at the strength of Howard's grip.

Turning to his secretary, Howard said, "Mrs. Franklin, please hold my calls while Mr. Bonetta is here."

Howard closed the door behind them as they entered his office. The protocol dance continued, Vince observed, as they continued with small talk while standing in the middle of the room. Shortly, Howard motioned for Vince to take the leather couch while he, Howard, took one of the matching chairs directly opposite Vince with the coffee table between them.

Howard brought the small talk to a close by saying, "I'm happy, finally, to have met you in person. Though I haven't heard a lot about you, that which I *have* heard, both from Mr. Peters and from Miss Aiello, tells me all that I need to know. That, though you are still young, your values date back to a time when a man's word and his sense of honor were stronger and more binding than any written contract." His eyes bored unblinkingly into Vince's as he spoke.

Vince considered whether he was being manipulated. After a long moment, he concluded that the young man before him was incapable of guile. He said, "A lot of years ago, at a time when I was in dire need, I was deeply touched by a great man who did me the honor of likening me to my father. Because I was my father's son, he helped me. Today, I'm again touched, this time by the sentiments of that great man's grandson."

"Yes, he was indeed a great man, Mr. Bonetta," Howard said. "My own father died when I was a mere child. The only father I knew was my grandfather. He gave me all the love and attention and guidance any child could hope for. Your father and my grandfather were lifelong friends. Perhaps you and I are united in our heritage of values."

"I'll be honored to think of us in that light," said Vince. After a respectful pause, he continued, "I know you have a full schedule,

Mr. Pastore. Can you help me understand why I've been unable to see your uncle?"

Howard replied with a smile, "I neglected to mention that brevity and directness are other of your virtues that were confided to my attention." He waited a beat until all traces of his levity had disappeared, then continued, "Before we get to that, and we shall, can you tell me what you hope to accomplish when you do see him?"

"I assume you know I'm here about Phil Peters' loan." Howard nodded as Vince spoke. "I'm more clear on *what* I hope to accomplish than I am on the how. By any measure, Philip's loan should have gone through without a hitch."

"I agree. You are no doubt aware that I approved it."

"Yes. My purpose is to persuade your uncle to reconsider. To withdraw his demand for payment of the old loans and to approve the new loan as it was written. I want to restate the factors that weigh heavily in Philip's favor—his unblemished payment history with your bank; the exponential growth he has achieved in a few short years as owner of my old company; the solid equity in his business and in his commercial building."

Vince was grateful for the briefing Jeanne had given him. The way Howard listened, sitting motionless and looking without blinking into Vince's eyes, might otherwise have been disconcerting. Vince brushed away the distraction and continued, "Then, if I must, I'll go beyond that. I'll remind him about the personal relationships and how they are interwoven. His relationship with Phil since childhood. Mine with Phil since he was a teen and later when he was a key man in my company. My long relationship with Greater Providence Bank that dates back to when your uncle and Phil were still high-schoolers in the sixties."

"Yes, I see," Howard's perfectly timed interjection avoided the appearance of an interruption. "I'm afraid your appeal would have fallen on deaf ears, Mr. Bonetta. Both Miss Aiello and I, independently of each other, pointed out to him in forceful terms most of what you have just outlined. I'm now convinced that Mr. Parisi had a hidden agenda but I can only speculate as to its substance."

"Phil and I get the same sense of it, Mr. Pastore. We've done some speculating of our own and if we're right, your uncle is acting out some kind of vendetta against Phil. However, he seems to have overlooked an important fact.

"He's well aware of my friendship with Phil but he seems to have forgotten that Phil and I still have a strong business connection. A connection that involves a large financial consideration that could very well be impacted by the action he has taken against Phil. If your uncle Luco knows anything about me at all, he knows I will not take this lying down. It's important to Phil, and to me … and to your uncle … that I convince him … to … what did you say?"

"I don't know what you mean." Howard was puzzled.

"Would have fallen," said Vince. "You said, '*Would* have fallen on deaf ears! *Had* a hidden agenda!' Did I miss something? I think now is the time to address my original question. Why have I been unable to see your uncle?"

Howard rose and strode slowly to the window where he stood for a long minute in deep thought. Vince said nothing. It was apparent to him that Howard was grappling with something. After what seemed like another minute, without turning away from the window, he spoke, "I abhor duplicity so I will not attempt to contrive a fairy tale. I can tell you that … irregular events … have taken place but I am not at liberty to disclose their nature." He went back to where he had been sitting and lowered himself slowly into the chair. He continued, "Those events aside, it is my wish to be as forthright with you as I can, given the bounds of my position. It will require that I reveal information that might be termed sensitive. I will not do so without your promise to respect that confidentiality. On *your* solemn word," Howard's emphasis was not lost on Vince, "there will be no doubt in my mind that what I tell you will not leave this office."

Vince leaned forward, his elbows on his knees and his hands together with fingers tightly interlocked. He turned his face squarely to Howard's and locked onto his eyes for several seconds before saying, "If it's none of my business, I prefer not to know any of the bank's confidential information. On the other hand, if you feel it will help us get to the bottom of whatever the hell's happening here, I will, of course, respect your confidence. I give you my word."

"I accept it," said Howard. "In the event of the death of a principal officer of this bank, documents are in place that will execute the transfer of the duties and responsibilities of the deceased and will determine to whom they will be transferred. Similarly, those documents govern the temporary transfer of duties and responsibilities during a principal officer's authorized absence.

"Had my uncle passed away or had he been in some way incapacitated, and I hasten to add that neither is known to be the case, the powers now vested in the position he holds would have fallen to me with no lapse of time. In such event I would happily overturn the action taken by my uncle against Mr. Peters and, without delay, those documents would empower me to do so.

"Since, to our knowledge, my uncle did not die and has not been incapacitated, I am powerless in his absence to rescind his directive regarding Mr. Peters. The one eventuality the framers of the bylaws did not envision, it seems, is the one that now confronts us.

"The point of my convoluted preamble, Mr. Bonetta, is this. The reason you have been unsuccessful in your efforts to meet with my uncle is," Howard paused as he removed his glasses and intently polished them with a tissue, " … we don't know where he is. No one has seen him for more than a week," he put his glasses back on before concluding with, " … and we have no idea when, or if, he will return."

Vince was silent for a moment in disbelief. "What am I hearing?" he demanded. "Are you saying your uncle went over-the-damn-hill? Why?! You only do that if you're running away from something. And what about the bank? Are you telling me that because he didn't get run over by a truck in front of witnesses the bank is unable to do business?!"

"No. I'm not saying that at all. Our bylaws enable us to function quite normally in his absence. However, we are encumbered in one significant regard. A valid action, having been executed by an active principal officer, can be overturned only by a meeting of the board and only if that officer is physically present during the discussion and the vote. My uncle's rejection of Mr. Peters' loan is precisely the type of action the by-laws were crafted to protect. In the absence of such protection, the chicanery that could be unleashed would be limited only by the imagination.

"Ironically, had my uncle been officially absent at the time the loan came up for final approval, I would have had full authority to grant the loan. In such case, conversely, *he* would have been powerless to later rescind *my* action in *my* absence."

"Suppose we cut to the quick," Vince's voice took on a brittle edge. "Your uncle skipped town to parts unknown for reasons unknown and there's nothing the bank can do to help Phil. Does that cover it?"

"I'm afraid the picture I painted was incomplete. Please bear with me. I have called a meeting of the Board of Directors. I won't bore you with the details except to tell you that notice of a special meeting has been sent in accordance with the bylaws to all members of record. If my uncle fails to acknowledge said notice and/or fails to attend that meeting, the board will be legally empowered to act on all matters. It will then be within my purview to insist that the board revisit the Peters loan. Though I will do my best to convince them that my uncle's action be rescinded, I am mindful that, again with the exception of Miss Aiello, their loyalties rest not with me but with my uncle who appointed them to their seats."

"Hmm. I understand. And if he does return to appear at that meeting?" Vince asked.

"I'm afraid there will be little hope for any change. My uncle wields enormous influence over the board, Miss Aiello and myself again excepted. There is no doubt that the board will take whatever position he favors."

"How much of what you just told me, if anything, can I tell Peters?"

"You are free to tell him that a special board meeting has been called. You may tell him the purpose of that meeting will be to revisit the demand call of his loans as well as the loan package that Miss Aiello prepared and that I approved. That meeting is to take place on the fifteenth of next month."

"From Phil's standpoint, his only chance, however meager it may be, is for your uncle not to show up at that meeting."

"Agreed. But you cannot tell that to Mr. Peters without revealing the esoteric background I gave you in confidence about the bank's operational policies.

"Finally, my uncle's absence has, of course, been noticed by too many of our employees. I'm sure rumors have already begun to circulate. I'll not ask you to pretend ignorance of those rumors nor will I ask you to deny them. However, I would ask that you not lend credence to them by citing anything I have just told you."

"Of course," said Vince. They shook hands and Vince left.

SNIPPETS OF THEIR CONVERSATION resonated in Vince's thoughts during the elevator ride down to the garage. Something nagged at him. Howard had stated up front that he would hold certain elements back, so it followed that more was likely involved than what Howard had been free, or willing, to reveal. How much more might there be? What bearing might it have had on what Luco Parisi did to Phil? What bearing could it have on extricating Phil from the mess Luco created for him?

Something Howard said kept falling through the interstices of Vince's thoughts as he slipped into the southbound stream of traffic on I-95. He grappled with it as he drove to Production House Graphix where Phil was waiting to hear the results of Vince's meeting with Howard. Suddenly it hit him. Irregular events! That's what he said! Something about irregular events that Howard was not at liberty to disclose. Yet almost in his next breath he did reveal that Luco had gone AWOL. And he revealed all that *before* he swore Vince to confidentiality, Vince remembered. Thus, Howard's very mention of it clearly implied that Luco's disappearance, in and of itself, was not one of the irregular events to which he had referred.

Vince reasoned that Howard's discovery of those irregular events, whatever they might be, apparently coincided with and were somehow interrelated with Luco's disappearance. In a flash of unrestrained speculation, Vince reasoned further that it was likely one was the tripwire for the other. With everything his instincts told him about Luco's character, Vince concluded that Luco fled because he was involved in whatever it was that Howard had discovered, or was soon to discover.

He replayed in his thoughts the promise of confidentiality that he made to Howard. That he would scrupulously honor that promise was not even a question. On the other hand, he never promised nor had he implied to Howard that he would look no further for answers.

Phil Peters would have to wait a little longer.

From the left lane, Vince maneuvered across three lanes of traffic to take the Jefferson Boulevard exit ramp. At the end of the ramp he went left, crossed under the interstate, and took a quick left onto the access ramp to get back on I-95 headed north for the Branch Avenue exit. He would be at Cappie's Tap in a matter of minutes.

"IRREGULAR EVENTS?" RICO CALLED out as he stirred the simmering contents of two large sauce pans. He came out of the small kitchen off the back room of Cappie's Tap, took the stool next to Vince, and laid his cane on the bar. "What the hell did he mean by that?"

"Damned if I know, Rico, but those were his exact words. Then, in his next breath, he tells me that Luco's gone AWOL."

"And you figure there's gotta be a connection?"

"It makes some kind of sense, doesn't it? But what? And why?"

"Whatever it is, Cenzo, you can bet Parisi's in it up to his ass. Anyhow, I dunno about the 'what' but how's this for the 'why'? Whatever the 'what' is, Parisi's afraid Howard's gettin' close to figurin' it all out so he jumps ship."

While Vince pondered that possibility, Rico swung off the stool and went to the kitchen. He dipped a spoon into a pot and gingerly sampled it. Then he ladled some of the simmering mix of spicy Italian sausage, sweet peppers, cherry peppers, onions and mushrooms onto a plate. He cut the sausage into bite-size chunks and brought the plate back to the bar.

"Here. Try this out. It's for tonight's bocce crowd. Careful. It's hot."

Rico looked on expectantly as Vince sampled it.

"Oh, yeah," said Vince. His tone was almost erotic in its expression of pleasure. He took another sample and savored it slowly, with his eyes closed. "Made in heaven. Don't change a thing."

"This place has been called lots of things but heaven ain't been one of them," said Rico with a chuckle. "Anyhow, Cenzo. I guess you'll be flyin' back to Naples?"

"First I have to talk with Phil, then I'm gone."

"So, you want me to dig around a little? Find out what that asshole Parisi's up to?"

"Yeah, Rico. I'd really appreciate it if you would. It's important to Phil Peters, it's important to my old company—a lot of people can be hurt—and it's important to me. Call me with anything you find."

TWENTY-ONE

Naples, Florida

"TWIN CESSNA FIVE-FOUR-NINER, Naples, opposite-direction traffic now one mile at eleven o'clock, altitude unknown."

"Four-niner, roger, I have the traffic, altitude estimated two thousand," Vince replied. He had been keeping an eye on the small airplane below and off his nose to the left and had been expecting the call.

"Roger four-niner, maintain visual contact, descend your discretion, report entering left downwind runway four."

Click click.

In minutes, Vince was over Naples Bay on final to runway four with the Gordon River bridge and Tin City passing under his left wingtip.

TRAFFIC WAS LIGHT BUT as always on Airport Road, it was fast. Vince had no trouble accelerating into the flow, relishing the almost silent surge of power from under the hood of his big Buick Roadmaster. The baked pavement radiated in shimmering animation under the heavy sun as he turned east. Ahead of him, heaven had all its pots boiling. A line of bulbous thunderheads spread across the expanse of the sky. Their billowing tops, blinding white in the late afternoon sun, merged at their bases into a deep, menacing charcoal that blended into the surface of the horizon, rendering it indistinct and indeterminate as to distance.

Though absent of thunder, frequent but indistinct lightning pin-balled the breadth of what would have been the horizon, illuminating the clouds from deep within. Vince estimated the line of thunderstorms to be about twenty-five miles away, sucking up moisture from the Everglades. If they were coming this way, they could arrive in less than an hour. They wouldn't last long but they would disgorge prodigious amounts of rainfall.

Vince turned off the highway onto a short, winding road that leads to a concealed cul-de-sac with a gatehouse at the far end. He slowed to a crawl, allowing the gate time to open fully, and waved to the gatehouse attendant as he drove through.

He turned onto Osprey Lane which begins as a hundred-yard-long, vehicles-only, wooden trestle that crosses over a protected wetlands preserve. A steady but imperceptible flow of water from Lake Okeechobee, more than sixty miles to the north, drifts through the Everglades, flows under the nearby highway bridge, filters through the dense marsh grasses and cypress mounds of the preserve, passes under the roadway trestle, and empties into Osprey Pointe Lake.

On the other side of the preserve, Osprey Lane becomes a broad boulevard, divided by a wide median of precisely manicured grass, lush tropical plantings and several species of palms and pines. It traces the curved shoreline of a lake that is rimmed with large, widely separated, elegantly landscaped, estate homes. Osprey Lane circumscribes Osprey Pointe and is the only street in the entire community.

In counterpoint to the menacing weather that was brewing over the Everglades to the east, only a few, playful, cumulus, cotton-puffs decorated the blue, western sky over the Gulf, six miles distant.

The gold Jaguar XJ6 sedan that was parked under the portico at the end of Vince's long, crushed-shell driveway told him his guests had arrived early. Depositing his travel bag on the travertine floor of the spacious foyer, he passed through the living room and the great room, and headed for the breakfast room.

Gabriele had just emerged from the pool when she noticed her husband and broke into a smile. Through the glass wall of the great room, he could read her lips saying, "He's here!" as she motioned excitedly for the others to follow her in through the breakfast room door. The water ran freely off her, forming a puddle on the tile floor as she threw her arms around him, kissed him and endowed him with a playful but assertive pelvic thrust.

He was no longer surprised by Gabriele's sometimes overt sexual advances when in the presence of close friends. Though Günter and Margrit Lehmann simply accepted it matter-of-factly, as most Europeans would, Vince could never escape a tinge of embarrassment. He was seventeen years Gabriele's senior. His views on propriety had been influenced by the values that existed a generation before hers. Even so, he enjoyed every bit of it.

Vince and Günter man-hugged, clapping each other on the back while boisterously uttering the obligatory greetings.

"Wie geht's?!"

"Danke, gut! Und Dir?!"

"Ja danke, auch gut!"

"Schön Dich wieder zu sehen!"

"Dich auch!"

Vince's real self-consciousness surfaced when he was greeted by Margrit who, like Gabriele, was much younger than her husband. She was generously gifted, but unlike Gabriele who had left Germany twelve years earlier and had adjusted somewhat to American customs, Margrit was unencumbered by American notions of modesty in swimwear. She hugged Vince with exuberance and they kissed each other on both cheeks in European fashion. Vince groped aimlessly in the air behind her back, unable to find a region of her largely naked, anatomical geography on which he might possibly place his hands without risk of heightening his discomfiture.

In total, red-faced embarrassment, Vince made eye-contact with Günter and Gabriele over Margrit's shoulder. They shrugged to one another in helpless acknowledgment of her devastating naiveté.

When Vince awkwardly disentangled himself from her delectable grasp, Margrit was puzzled for a brief, passing moment by the smiling expressions of benevolent indulgence on the faces of the other three. Dismissing that thought, she proudly sought to demonstrate the progress she had made in her language skills by attempting to say to Vince in English, "I have so much happiness that I can see you again."

Betrayed by the convoluted word sequence of English as compared with German, and by the capriciousness of *Das Langenscheid-Wörtebuch*, the world-famous German/English word book, what she actually said was, "I am again pleased that you can see so much of me."

This time Margrit was doubly puzzled by their reactions. Gabriele and Günter burst into laughter. Vince's embarrassment was broken but he suppressed his own laughter to spare Margrit any further chagrin.

He abandoned caution. Hugging her gently, he let his hands fall wherever they chanced to land. Keeping one arm around her shoulders, he guided her out onto the lanai where Günter and Gabriele fought to regain their composure.

To assuage Margrit's confusion, Vince kissed her gently on one cheek, American-style, saying, "Vielen Dank. Du bist wirklich ein Schatz." *Thanks a lot. You're really a treasure.* Then, with a self-conscious grin, he said in English to Gabriele, "Maybe you should explain to Margrit what was so funny."

Turning to Günter, he said, "Fix me a drink, my friend. I'll slip into my trunks and be out in a minute."

TWENTY-TWO

MARGRIT WAS TALLER and slimmer than Gabriele. Her green eyes were featured by long, brunette hair that was loosely parted in the middle, flowing back naturally to terminate in a soft wave between her shoulders.

She was one of those fortunates who paid no heed to diet. She enjoyed eating and did so with gusto, devouring as much as she wanted of everything without fear of gaining an ounce. Though her figure appeared to be that of an athlete, she viewed exercise with horror. Beyond an occasional, playful romp in a swimming pool, Margrit avoided physical exertion of any kind.

Though shorter than Margrit, there was a statuesque quality to Gabriele's bearing that made her appear taller than she was. Except for a curly strand that hung at each temple, she wore her blond hair swept back and up into a loosely formed bun. Her gray-blue eyes appeared incandescent against her deep tan. Her figure was voluptuous and firm, but unlike Margrit, she maintained it only at the cost of regular workouts and unwavering dietary diligence.

AT THE OUTSET OF ANY new relationship, Vince's innate tendency was to be standoffish, to hold his instincts and judgments in reserve. Gabriele was the polar opposite. She was naturally outgoing and unaffected. Her genuine warmth and sincerity, never held in check, were immediately sensed by those who came into contact with her. New acquaintances fell into an instant closeness with Gabriele that otherwise would be found only in long-time friendships. As a result, women and men alike, whom she sometimes had met only minutes earlier, revealed to Gabriele outpourings of the most private and confidential nature.

Two years earlier, Günter Lehmann had contacted Gabriele in response to an ad she ran in a German newspaper. When he and Margrit arrived in the USA, Vince and Gabriele flew to Orlando to pick them up. Being met by a private plane, especially one as comfortable as Vince's, never failed to impress a prospective client. Air-conditioned and fully pressurized, the Cessna 421 Golden Eagle is capable of flying over the top of most rough weather, with its heavy insulation softening the sound of the twin engines to a comforting drone.

When they introduced themselves to the Lehmanns, Vince and Gabriele had no reason to suspect that Günter's haggard face and Margrit's glitzy veneer were not the real Günter and Margrit. On the flight back to Naples, Günter sat up front with Vince. Margrit took a seat in the cabin, stretching her legs out on the cushion of the seat facing her, with Gabriele across the aisle from her.

Though Vince's German was adequate, Günter spoke fluent English, with a mere trace of an accent, and he preferred to use English at every opportunity for the practice. Their conversation, interspersed with terse radio talk between Vince and the air traffic controllers, remained mostly on the airplane, its equipment, the flight, and the geography passing below. It was unstrained. Both men spoke in the same meter, eschewing meaningless chatter and feeling not at all compelled to say something when they had nothing to say. Each sensed the onset of a kinship with the other. Without voicing it, each knew that the other sensed it as well.

In the aft cabin it was another matter. Though she became a U.S. citizen more than ten years ago, after she and Vince married, Gabriele was born and raised in Nürnberg. She couldn't quite read Margrit whose eyes were hidden from view behind mirrored sunglasses. She thought Margrit's smile was, at times, a little too broad for the circumstances and that her tonal inflections seemed to be out of synch with the context of the words she spoke. It was as though she were going through the motions of polite conversation. Gabriele didn't dwell on it. She attributed it to the long transatlantic flight and the six-hour time difference.

Since the Lehmanns came from Nürnberg, Gabriele instinctively sought common ground with Margrit. Speaking in German, they talked about restaurants, shops, schools they attended, and parks and other landmarks they both enjoyed. Thinking they might possibly have mutual acquaintances, Gabriele asked, "Tell me Margrit, we are the same age, I'm sure we must know some of the same people. Who are your friends?"

Margrit became immobile. Her smile froze in place for a few seconds, then her face collapsed to a pathetic, mask of anguish. She sat up, retrieved her legs from the seat in front of her, and turned her face to the window.

"Margrit?" asked Gabriele. She was puzzled.

Still looking away, Margrit removed her glasses and dabbed at her eyes with a tissue. Finally, with her shoulders slumped in surrender to the demon memories that tormented her, she turned back to Gabriele, her eyes streaked with red.

"My God, Margrit," said Gabriele, "what is it?!" She moved quickly to the seat facing Margrit and took both of Margrit's hands in her own. Sympathy tears welled in her own eyes.

Margrit's floodgates burst. She looked pathetically at Gabriele whose eyes, by then, were running over with tears as profusely as Margrit's.

At first, Margrit had been hesitant about revealing the source of her sorrow to a complete stranger. However, once having begun to talk about it, her pain started to become bearable. By the very act of her listening, Gabriele seemed to extract some of Margrit's grief, absorbing it into herself. Margrit, until then, had never spoken to anyone about the depth of her loss. Except to Günter, who had his own scars to deal with.

Vince turned, looking back into the cabin to inquire as to the well-being of his passengers. He was stunned by the sight of Margrit and Gabriele hugging each other, sobbing, and clearly distraught.

"What the hell happ ... ," he began to say but stopped when he felt Günter's hand on his shoulder. Günter shook his head, nodding for Vince to return his gaze to the front. Then he reached behind them to silently close the sliding door that separates the cockpit from the cabin.

Günter said, "What happens back there could not be avoided. It *had* to happen. For Margrit's sake, I have *hoped* for it to happen."

He looked straight ahead as he spoke, with his pale blue eyes deep-set and shadowed under his thick, gray eyebrows. The hardness of his eyes was compromised by the pools of moisture that would surely spill over were he to make eye-contact with Vince.

"Your wife must be very special lady," he continued. "Until now, Margrit has been not willing, or not able, to talk about her grief. Let them have their privacy in this moment."

There was no question in Günter's mind as to what Margrit was relating to Gabriele. It was not in Günter's nature to reveal his innermost feelings to others. Moreover, in this case, he knew that if he did, he would be picking at the scabs of his own wounds. Yet, he knew that there was now no way to avoid it. He would tell Vince about it. But they were then approaching Naples airport. It would have to wait.

VINCE TAXIED UP TO THE HANGAR where his Roadmaster was waiting for them with its motor running and the air conditioner keeping the inside comfortably cool. Two line boys loaded the baggage while Vince secured the airplane.

During the short drive home, Vince learned that Günter had inherited great wealth along with control of his father's newspaper, *Die Nürnberger Nachrichten*. But he was a career policeman, not a newspaperman. Though he attended and participated in the newspaper's board meetings, he left the day-to-day operations of *Die Nürnberger Nachrichten* to those who had been running it when his father was alive. In his own career with *Die Kriminalpolizei*, the Criminal Investigations Department of the Nürnberg police, Günter had risen to the rank of *Kriminaldirektor*, Chief of Detectives.

His first marriage had been going through the motions for many years. It wasn't strong enough to ward off any outside threats. When he met Margrit, any last vestige of what once existed disappeared.

After their wedding, Günter's son, Friedrich, by his own choice, lived with them. He and Margrit, only three years apart in age, became best friends and as close as natural siblings. He became the brother she always wanted but never had. During the period when all three lived together, even the relationship between Friedrich and Günter blossomed under Margrit's influence, with father and son growing closer than they had been since Friedrich's childhood.

Suddenly, with no hint that it was coming, Friedrich disappeared without a trace. It was only after his disappearance, and during the search for him, that Günter learned Friedrich was gay. He held nothing back in the search for his son but even with his resources, they were unable to develop any good leads. As a policeman, Günter knew all too well that a person who did not wish to be found could remain "missing" indefinitely.

His relationship with his son had grown better than it had ever been before and it was clear that he, Friedrich, loved Margrit like a natural sister. Günter couldn't imagine a reason why Friedrich would not want to contact him, or if not him, then Margrit. Finally, after three years of agonizing over it, he resigned himself to the conclusion that Friedrich, for some unknown reason, perhaps a mugging-gone-wrong, was dead.

Margrit would hear none of that. She never gave up hope. When, out of the blue, the phone woke them at 3:00AM, she knew immediately. "It's Friedrich! It's Friedrich!" she screamed, reaching for the phone. Günter raced into the hallway to join in on the extension phone.

Friedrich told them of his ever-deepening remorse for having put them through such an ordeal. He had discovered and reached accommodation with his own homosexuality four years earlier but he was too ashamed to disclose it to his father. Yet, he lived in constant fear that his father would find out from someone else. No longer able to deal with the duplicity of it, he had fled without a word. He told himself that he would phone home in a day or two to explain. When days went by and he hadn't yet phoned, he revised his intentions, telling himself that he would write a letter instead. Time passed swiftly with each passing day adding to his burden, making it ever more difficult and painful to make the call.

When he learned that he was HIV positive, he made the commitment to himself, with the help of his volunteer counselor, that he would call that day. He stared at the phone for over twelve hours, finally picking it up and dialing at 3:00AM. He was glad it was Margrit who answered. They cried together, unable to speak through their sobs.

Günter fought back the bitterness and resentment he felt toward Friedrich for having disappeared without a word. For three years. For having brought upon his father the agony of resigning himself to his son's death.

Soon, he too was crying. Friedrich told them about his HIV and asked, tentatively, if there was any possibility that he could come home. Torn between the joy of having his son again and the tragic reality of what now faced them, Günter pressed his bitterness and resentment aside. With choked voice, he assured his son that he and Margrit wanted him at home with them. Günter wired an air ticket to him. The next day they were reunited. Nevertheless, even with the best of medical care, Friedrich failed quickly. Two years later, he died of AIDS.

During his son's absence, Günter had inured himself to accept the *death* of his son. Though Friedrich returned, Günter later confided to Margrit that he had nevertheless been unable to completely dispel the sense of loss he had suffered with his son's disappearance. It was as though, albeit against his will, he had held a small part of Friedrich's earlier *death* in reserve, as a down payment to be applied against the impact of the real event. Perhaps as its result, he weathered the real death of his son better than Margrit did, though both felt the need to reorder their life. They wanted especially to find a life far away from Nürnberg, a city that they loved but a city that would always be a breeding ground for tragic memories.

They responded to Gabriele's ad in the German newspaper, *Die Welt am Sonntag*, as a means of escaping from those memories, but it developed into something entirely unexpected. A special relationship grew between Gabriele and Margrit. They were almost the same age, both much younger than their husbands, and both were born and raised in Nürnberg. They felt like sisters. Soon, the Lehmanns and the Bonettas became fast friends.

BEFORE SHOWING THEM any properties, Gabriele escorted them on a tour that began at the chic Third Street South shopping district and continued onto Gordon Drive for a view of its imposing Gulf-front mansions. A stroll on the pier that juts into the Gulf at Twelfth Avenue South rewarded them with the spectacle of bottle-nosed dolphins frolicking and breaching almost within arms reach.

Over lunch at a sidewalk cafe on Fifth Avenue, the Lehmanns marveled at the range of clientele. Beach-bunnies in bikinis and flip-flops, taking a breather from the midday sun, mingled with bankers and investment counselors from the neighboring banks and brokerage firms. Gabriele wound up her tour with a showing of the model homes in several new communities. Later, Vince joined them for cocktails and dinner at an elegant dockside restaurant with a captivating view from its second floor dining room overlooking Venetian Bay.

Günter and Margrit soon fell in love with Naples. With his retirement only two years ahead, Günter set his sights on finding a going business that he could buy and operate, that would qualify him for permanent residency in the United States. What began as a half-hearted search for a modest vacation home escalated into full-scale plans to make Naples their home.

The following day, having saved the best for last, Gabriele showed them Silver Dunes. They crossed the brick-paved, arched bridge over a broad canal whose free-form shoreline meandered along a landscaped berm with neatly trimmed grass banks. The winding roadway led through lush and elegant tropical plantings that concealed the attended gate from the street. From that moment they knew where they would make their new home.

AFTER AN EARLY DINNER, mindful of the six-hour difference in the Lehmanns' circadian clocks, they returned home for espresso and Schnaps, Sambuca for Vince, at poolside. Vince and Günter drifted to the far side of the pool. They touched their glasses together to quietly toast each other in German, *"Zum Wohl!"* After a short sip, they repeated the procedure, toasting each other again, this time in Italian, *"Cent' anni!"* Whenever it was just the two of them, they never deviated from that ceremony. It had been created spontaneously the day they met, after Günter had described the loss of his son. Though intended as an offering of hope for a new beginning, it had become an icon of their friendship.

TWENTY-THREE

AFTER COMPLETING A FOUR-YEAR tour in the Air Force, Vince began Production House Graphix as a one-man design studio. By the time Phil Peters quit baseball and joined the firm, ten years later, Vince had expanded into lithographic printing and had established PHG as a leading presence in Rhode Island's burgeoning advertising and marketing industry. Five years later, Phil became PHG's first General Manager, answering only to Vince. His unique managerial talents came as naturally to him as his athletic skills. Taking full advantage of the regional fame he had achieved through college and professional baseball, he became a major factor in molding PHG into a position of preeminence in the field of graphic design and printing in southern New England.

In the meantime, technological upheaval had irrevocably changed the graphic arts industry. Computers had established a foothold in taking over many of the tasks that were formerly done by hand. Too often, though, the individuals who performed those computerized tasks either had talent but limited computer skills or had advanced computer skills but not much talent. Dozens of neophyte, computer-aided graphic design firms emerged from nowhere, rising rapidly to the surface. For many, their only hope to remain afloat was to shamelessly try to buy a piece of the market by charging prices that barely covered expenses. Many of them sank into oblivion just as rapidly as they had emerged.

Recognizing that computerization was here to stay and that it would be a force in the growth of the graphic arts industry in general and of PHG in particular, Phil viewed it with positive enthusiasm. Vince, on the other hand, was unwilling to accept it. In his view, the computer tail had begun to wag the graphics dog. For him, the business just wasn't the same anymore. The graphic arts business had made him a wealthy man, but it no longer motivated him.

When he suffered a mild heart attack, Vince knew he had to get out. He offered to sell the building and the business to Phil under terms that were so generous that Phil had difficulty believing the offer. Vince reassured him, telling him it was a reward for Phil's outstanding performance and devotion.

Vince signed the building over to him for the price of the remaining loan—about sixty percent of the building's value. All Phil had to do was continue the payments. As for PHG, Phil paid $100,000 up front with Vince taking a zero-interest note for monthly payments of $4,000 for fifteen years plus a balloon payment of $180,000. The grand total was a fraction of the book value of the business.

AFTER HIS HEART ATTACK, Vince set about sorting out his priorities. He went into physical fitness big time, and continued to fly and train regularly in his Cessna 421 under the critical eye of an instructor in the right seat. Vince easily passed a new FAA medical exam and Biennial Flight Review (BFR).

Vince and his wife, Gabriele, took up permanent residence in what had served as their winter home in Naples, Florida. Gabriele went with a vengeance into real estate, the business she had merely dabbled in while in Rhode Island. After a short period of idleness, Vince craved something to keep him busy. With nothing constructive to do, he busied himself by rearranging the furniture and the contents of the kitchen cupboards every few weeks, placing a strain on the limits of Gabriele's patience and understanding. With her blessing—more precisely, her urgent pleading—he bought a thirty-six foot Chris Craft sport fisherman and got his captain's license. In very short order, it became clear to Vince that running charters into the

Gulf, through the Keys and in the Stream off the other coast was not something he would find satisfying or fulfilling for very long.

Meanwhile, Gabriele's business had grown so much that she decided to open her own office. Though it proved to be a good move, it placed even greater demands on her time. She asked Vince if he would join her in the business since she could use the help and he could use the activity. Vince didn't need a lot of convincing.

TWENTY-FOUR

IN ADDITION TO BEING HIS personal pleasure aircraft, the 421 became a useful and impressive asset to their real estate business. Taking full advantage of Gabriele's background—she was from Nürnberg—they marketed heavily in Germany. They greeted their incoming German prospects at several ports of entry—Miami, Orlando, Tampa—and flew them to friendly Naples Airport where Vince's car would meet them at the plane as soon as the propellers came to a stop.

In the course of such activities, Vince and Gabriele developed solid and promising contacts in various parts of the state. Vince was in his element, doing a masterful job of setting up satellite offices that were soon operating productively in six cities. He devised operational procedures and he established standards by which performance, not only of each office but of each employee, could be reliably and equitably monitored and measured. He hired managerial and office staff of the highest caliber and paid them well. All the offices were computer-linked to the main office on Fifth Avenue South, as well as to Vince's office at home. As a result, his physical presence at any of his offices became less and less necessary. He had much more time to enjoy his "retirement."

Vince enjoyed what he was doing. After several years in Naples, he had learned a lot more about how to relax. With memberships at several country clubs, he played golf at every opportunity and he continued to work out daily at the gym as he had for years. When not golfing or working out, he could be found doing what he loved most—hanging out at the airport tinkering with his airplane. Or flying.

VINCE HAD JUST RETURNED from a short flight to check out one of his navigation receivers that had undergone repair. He was at home, engrossed in the weekly activity reports he had called up on his laptop. The voice that answered him on the lanai intercom speaker took him by surprise. When the doorbell rang, he had been expecting a representative from a shutter company to take measurements and draw up a proposal for rollup hurricane shutters. He didn't expect a woman's voice.

He went to the front door where a woman in her late thirties introduced herself as Elsie MacLarter and took his hand in a strong grip. She wore no makeup and Vince assessed that, even if she had, her features could not have been improved upon. Her hair was light brown, tinged with blonde and it fell to between her shoulder blades in a loose ponytail. She wore a short, white, cotton blouse with a soft collar and no sleeves, buttoned demurely almost all the way to the top. Its hem stopped short of the waistband of her beltless, faded blue jeans which, Vince was pleased to notice, did little to conceal her curves. White sneakers without socks completed her ensemble. Her left hand held a black, padded nylon bag about the size of a camera case. Vince marveled at her casual mode of dress. It was curiously in keeping with the phenomenon regarding dress code, or lack thereof, that had achieved growing acceptance in many business situations in Naples.

Her lightly tanned skin bore a loose smattering of the faintest freckles on the curves of her shoulders. Neatly shaped eyebrows were her only apparent concession to self-adornment. Beneath them, her hazel eyes held Vince's in a grip as strong as the grip of her right hand on his.

Vince, thrown slightly off-balance, couldn't think of anything to say.

Still holding his hand, she said, "Maybe if y'all asked me to come in we might get started." Her accent was soft and easy to take.

"Of course, Miss MacLarter," Vince said, having almost recovered. "Please come in."

Her lips parted ever-so-slightly in a mischievous grin as she continued to grip his hand for another beat. Only then did she release his hand and motion for him to lead the way.

As he led her through the house, Vince attempted to regain his footing by saying, "Please excuse me if I seemed distracted. I was doing some paperwork when you rang and I guess I couldn't quite switch gears."

"Not t' mention y'all were expectin' a man, not a woman," she replied with a smile in her voice. She broke *man* into two syllables as in *ma-yun*.

"Yeah, that too," he replied with a chuckle as they stepped onto the lanai. He motioned for her to take a chair opposite him across the glass-topped table at poolside. Egrets waded knee-deep at the edge of the lake about forty yards away. There was no sign of human activity at any of the houses within their view.

When Vince turned to face her, she avoided making eye-contact. Instead, she averted her eyes, examining the chair, the lake, the egrets, her bag—anything, it seemed—other than his face.

Vince, on the other hand, couldn't take his eyes away from the deep, inviting cleavage of her luxurious bosom. 'Wow!' he thought, almost saying the word aloud. As she turned slightly to swing into her chair, she leaned forward, affording Vince a partial view of one magnificently shaped breast and a full, unobstructed, albeit momentary view of the other. Vince flashed back to how her blouse was buttoned almost to the top when he answered the door and compared it with what he was looking at now.

'Well I'll be damned,' he thought. She had unbuttoned the three top buttons while she followed him from the front door to the lanai. He felt strangely flattered, reflecting that she had done so apparently after having appraised him. Reluctantly, he lifted his gaze. Finally, she met it head-on with hers. She wore that same mischievous grin while she coquettishly, and unhurriedly, drew her blouse together in a show of propriety, though pointedly neglecting to rebutton it.

She asked him a few questions related to the type of installation he might be interested in, though ten minutes later he would be unable to remember either her questions or his responses. She then rose from her chair, again bending forward so very effectively. However, this time she moved much more slowly and deliberately, bestowing on Vince a prolonged and sumptuous view as she busied herself with the contents of her bag. Sensing the onset of a budding physiological reaction to her performance, Vince chose to remain seated.

"Now y'all just keep on with what y'all were doin' while I take a few measurements. Then we can talk some about … what I might can do for you. OK?"

As Vince watched her leave the lanai with her tape measure and her clipboard, his gaze surveyed with ardent appreciation the form and motion presented to him by the rear view of her jeans. Vince was nonplussed. This wasn't the first time he had been on the receiving end of the advances of a pretty woman but it certainly qualified as one of the most flagrant. Elsie MacLarter had succeeded in awakening his appetite and he enjoyed every bit of it. However, although the appetizer had been so delectably presented, he knew he would leave the main course untouched.

After a short time, Elsie returned. Still unbuttoned, she performed the same erotic choreography as she leaned over her bag to set up her laptop computer. Recognizing the more pragmatic likelihood that this gorgeous creature might have another, more commercial agenda, albeit at the expense of his male ego, he simply sat back and enjoyed the entertainment, making no further attempt to be discreet with his eyes.

When it appeared to him that she was nearing completion of her work, Vince started to say, "Miss MacLarter, I w … ," but she cut him off.

"Elsie," she said, "please call me Elsie," as she reached out her hand and placed it on his.

"No … ," he said with what he hoped was a non-committal smile, "I think I'll stick with Miss MacLarter." He paused while he withdrew his hand from under hers. "You are a beautiful woman. I'd be a craven liar if I told you I didn't enjoy looking at your … ," her eyebrows rose as he caught himself, " … at you. But please, I would be grateful if you would button up your blouse."

Elsie looked away and said nothing as she self-consciously started to fasten her buttons.

Vince continued in a tone that he hoped would not sound like a lecture, "I already know all there is to know about your product. The owner of your company is one of my golfing buddies and I've been through your factory several times. When I asked him to send someone, I expected nothing like you.

"I admit I was flattered by your attention, at first. I would like to seduce myself by thinking it was only because you found me irresistible but we both know that's not the case. My point is this. You work for a fine company, they produce an excellent product and from what I've heard, your prices are competitive. Why did you feel it necessary to offer yourself as an added inducement?"

For a long moment, Elsie said nothing. Her eyes darted from direction to direction as though examining the scenery. Slowly, her facial expression sagged. Tears started down her cheeks. She began to cry as she spoke, unable to make eye-contact with Vince.

"I feel so … cheap … and dirty," she said between sobs. "I've never done anything like this before … it's been so long since my last sale … I've tried so hard … I need the money so bad … I didn't know what else to do … I thought if I found a good looking man, a real nice guy … like you … just once I'd … oh, I feel so terrible … " She covered her face with both hands and trailed off into silent sobs.

Vince was destroyed. He wanted to comfort her but didn't dare touch her for fear a neighbor might see something that could only be misunderstood. He went inside and returned quickly with a box of tissues and a glass of ice water. She used the tissues, took a tentative sip of the water and seemed to regain a little control.

"Miss MacLarter … Elsie," said Vince. His voice was soft with compassion. "Don't be so hard on yourself. When we're under enough pressure, we sometimes don't use our best judgment. No harm's been done." She was recovering nicely, he saw. With a smile and a light manner, he finished with, "Actually it worked out rather well. When all's said and done, your honor has remained intact, you did wonders for my day … and you made a sale to boot."

It took a moment to reach her, but when it did, she shrieked, "I what?! I made a sale?!" She gasped, "Oh! Thank you!" She leaped from her chair, grabbed Vince's face in her hands and planted a hot, moist, deep and unhurried kiss squarely on his mouth.

'That ought to set the neighbors' phones to ringing,' Vince mused to himself, 'but damn, it was worth it.' Nevertheless, after saying their goodbyes, he thought it prudent to remain conspicuously on the lanai as Elsie showed herself out.

TWENTY-FIVE

THE HOUSE AND the lanai were in darkness, with only a crescent moon and the pool's underwater light providing soft, subtle illumination. Still dripping, Vince wore only a towel, wrapped around his waist. He wrapped the mid-thigh-length terrycloth robe around her, concealing her nakedness from prying eyes as she emerged from the pool. He knew it was very likely that, diagonally across the small lake behind their house, Admiral Bristow sat behind his tripod-mounted, naval binoculars peering between the slats of his vertical blinds. Since the admiral's wife died eight months earlier, his rapid decline, a concern of his neighbors and friends, soon became a continuing annoyance.

Gabriele drew the front of her robe together leaving the belt undone as Vince poured the Chardonnay. She sank into a lounge chair and Vince sat at her feet. She lay back, running her toes up the inside of his towel, curling them against his thigh.

After taking a long sip of wine, cradling her glass in both hands, she laid her head back with a sigh of contentment.

EARLIER, OVER DINNER AT Pazzo's on 5th, Gabriele had told Vince about her day. She described her client, Kurt Stöpsel, a prominent banker from Switzerland, as a gold-plated jerk—she had made such purely American expressions part of her lexicon, finding them so utterly apropos—and his wife, who had written such endearing faxes and had sounded so charming on the phone, as a bitch. Frau Stöpsel, it soon became clear to Gabriele, was an insensitive and tasteless autocrat who derived her greatest pleasure from treating waiters, waitresses and other service providers with ill-disguised contempt.

Stöpsel was well known in banking circles in the city of Basel. Yet, he had somehow convinced himself that his true destiny was to achieve fame as a singer—a country-western singer—and that discovery of his talent was just around the corner.

He and his wife devoted all their free time in that pursuit. Dressing themselves in gaudy, dude-ranch cowboy costumes, they drove through the streets of Basel in a Jeep Cherokee with a hood ornament that consisted of a set of four-foot horns from a longhorn steer. Stöpsel had become a local curiosity, performing in nightclubs and concert halls in the Basel area. It became his passion to see his name up in lights in Nashville.

His touring company consisted of himself on voice and guitar, his wife on electric keyboard, and a drummer. Since their Swiss audiences largely spoke only rudimentary traditional English, and hardly any 'countrified' English, they happily accepted the banker's absurd renditions of country-western inflection and phrasing.

Gabriele had gone to the Edgewater Beach Hotel earlier that day to meet the Stöpsels for the first time in person. She was unprepared for the scene that greeted her. Standing in the middle of the lobby, Herr Stöpsel flailed incomprehensibly on his guitar while rendering his version of the ancient country-western classic, *Cool Water*. The country twang he tried to affect, combined with his convoluted Swiss-German accent to convince most of the curious onlookers that they were witnessing a comedic parody.

Their appreciative laughter inflamed Frau Stöpsel. She swept menacingly into the group to confront them nose-to-nose while scolding them heatedly, "Why laugh you?! My man is profetzional! On all of Svitzerland he make concert for much pay! Laugh you on Charlie Pride?! Laugh you on Villy Nelson?! Stop laugh you on my man!"

Believing her to be part of the act, they rewarded her with enthusiastic applause. The spectacle drew handfuls of hotel guests and employees from rooms and offices, much to the incredulous consternation of the management of the staid and dignified hotel.

Ultimately recognizing the reality of what was happening, Frau Stöpsel drifted to the sidelines where, with the thin line of her lips set in a strained caricature of a smile, she restrained herself, letting the show take its own course.

Stöpsel observed the lobby filling with people but was unable to hear their laughter over the sound of their encouraging applause and his own voice. He soared without interruption into another mournful chorus with his audience playfully joining in to intone the words *cool water* at the end of each refrain. Herr Stöpsel was in ecstasy.

Gabriele had shrunk imperceptibly to a far corner of the lobby where she remained, hopefully in inconspicuous anonymity, until the performance was over and the crowd had dispersed. The Stöpsels remained in the middle of the lobby looking around for her, finally making eye-contact with her as she approached. Gabriele quickly introduced herself and hustled them out to her waiting auto.

VINCE TURNED IN THE CHAIR, straddling it to face Gabriele, and took her feet in his hands. She gathered up the thread of her narrative that lingered from dinner, continuing as though there had been no interruption. Beginning to feel the wine, and in almost a hypnotic languor with Vince massaging her feet and her calf muscles, she finished with, "The man is such an arrogant, conceited ass. And his wife is a boring, overbearing snob. I'm not looking forward to another day with them tomorrow. Let's talk about something else. How was your day?"

Vince had been only half listening. Images from his meeting with Elsie MacLarter that morning mingled with the sense of his touch on his wife's body. Her unfastened robe had slipped partially open, revealing the mounds of her breasts in the eerie illumination. His mind flashed back to Elsie's open display of herself in the bright light of day. He was struck by how this view of his wife, in the faint, surreal lighting, was intensely more erotic.

Vince summed up his day simply. "I thought it was pretty good," he muttered, "but compared to this, it was dismal." There was no point at all in mentioning anything about Elsie MacLarter.

"Do we have to talk right now?" Gabriele asked. Her voice had become a hoarse whisper.

"Uh-uh, later's better," he mumbled.

Further words became unnecessary. Gabriele stretched her arm fully out to the side, placing her wine glass on a nearby end table, then did the same with her other arm. The motion caused her robe to fall completely open. As Vince continued to rub her feet and her legs, the touch of his hands became softer, no longer a massage, but a caress. She closed her eyes and gave herself to it, rolling her head back with a long, soft, "Mmmmmm."

Her legs were still drawn up and pressed together. Vince's hands traced a sensuous path from her toes upward. When they reached her knees, she parted them to grant passage to his exploration down the insides of her thighs. She extended her legs, reaching her feet to the insides of his spread-eagled thighs. Her toes conducted a sinuous exploration, drawing closer and closer together where they found hard evidence of his commitment.

At the same moment, his hands brushed lightly over her warm, moist apex. With an involuntary shudder, she exclaimed through clenched teeth, "Ach, ja! Aber bitte, noch nicht!" *Oh yes! But please, not yet!* Though Gabriele spoke perfect English, in times of heightened passion it was German that came naturally to her. She urgently drew his hands to her breasts. Her breathing grew labored.

Vince leaned forward, kissing her below the navel. Her voice came in a hoarse whisper, "Mein Gott, nein! Bitte, noch nicht!" The next kiss was lower. The one after that even lower. She pushed him away. Holding each other's hands with their fingers interlaced and their arms extended in front of them, her toes found him, caressed him, curled around him, over the tip of him.

Abruptly she drew up her legs, swung them over the side of the chair and sat up.

"Nicht hier. Ich will Dich im Bett. Sofort!" *Not here. I want you in bed. Right now!*

Her robe hit the floor the second they were inside. His towel would have hit the floor at the same time had it not hung up on him. She pulled the towel free of him, then pressed herself to him. They made their way unsteadily to the bedroom with their arms locked around each other and fell to the bed. In a half roll, Vince lay on top but before he could establish his territory, she executed another half roll. In an instant, she was sitting on his waist. She bent forward. His eager lips found her breasts and traced circles around first one nipple then the other.

She had been rubbing circles of her own on his belly when suddenly she rasped, "Ach Scheisse. Ich bin fast da! Bist du bereit, Baby?!" *Oh shit. I'm almost there! Are you ready, baby?!* She didn't wait for an answer. She slid down, engulfing him, with her breasts brushing softly against his chest in rhythm with her motion. Her half-open eyes were locked on his. She no longer had to instruct him. He knew that with his wife, anything goes when they make love. There is only one rule. You must look into each other's eyes in those moments leading up to and during climax.

Their contortions grew frenzied as they neared release. Though it became increasingly difficult, they continued to look deeply into each other's eyes, hungrily devouring each other's lips, even through the final, explosive moment.

They lay coupled for a long time. Nuzzling. Caressing. When finally she rolled off him, Vince rose to one elbow and kissed her cheek. With a short chuckle he said, "Good night, baby."

She looked at him askance and asked, "What's funny?"

"Admiral Bristow," he replied. His amusement was still apparent.

"What about him?" she asked suspiciously. "He couldn't see anything ... could he? ... It was dark."

Vince stifled his laughter. "Admiral? ... Navy? ... Those night-vision glasses he's so proud of?" He continued to study her from top to bottom while lightly caressing her still-heaving breasts. He then returned his gaze to her eyes but remained silent, still grinning, waiting for her to catch up.

When after several puzzled seconds it struck her, she bolted upright to a sitting position. In a reflexive, albeit futile reaction, she crossed her hands and arms in front of her to conceal her breasts, unconsciously drawing her knees up and pressing them together.

"Oh no!" she cried in helpless realization. "Do you suppose he was watching?"

"Well ... only the beginning. We came inside for the best part."

"Damn! I forgot all about him!"

"Thank you, Schatz." Vince was enjoying this. "I'm happy I was able to please you," he said, feigning misunderstanding. "It was good for me too."

"That's not what I meant and you know it," she said.

Vince flopped down on his back, laughing softly. Gabriele, getting caught up in the lightness of it, slapped him playfully and broke into a giggle. She stretched out beside Vince, draping a leg over him and resting her head on his chest.

"Well, if he *was* watching us, let's hope he didn't have a coronary," she said while she nibbled his chest.

Vince kissed her lightly on the forehead and said, "Good night, baby. Let's get some shut-eye."

She kissed him back. But she wasn't drowsy. Though Vince's little joke was over, it had the effect on her of dissipating her après-sex lethargy.

"Do we have to?" she asked.

Sensuously sliding her hand down from his chest to his lower regions, she took the matter in hand with a prolonged, assertive squeeze.

Vince's eyes popped open.

"You're about to talk me out of it."

TWENTY-SIX

"MR. BONETTA, LONG DISTANCE call for you on line three. Mr. Bonetta, line three." The PA system reverberated throughout the hangar. Its volume was set on max to be heard over the sounds of pneumatically driven tools and aircraft engines running-up on the tarmac just outside the hangar doors. Vince stepped out of the Cessna Citation Jet he had just flown on a demo flight. Excusing himself from the salesman, he went through the hangar to take the call in the quiet of the pilot's lounge. As he passed the receptionist, she said, "It's a Mr. Caputo calling from Rhode Island."

The lounge was empty. Vince muted the TV, picked up the phone and flopped into the sofa.

"Rico, my friend. What's happening?"

"Same old shit, Cenzo. I'm making the free 'eats' for tonight's bocce league. Chicken necks and cherry peppers in spicy marinara sauce."

"Free?! Who are you kidding, Rico?" said Vince with a hearty laugh. "When they start sucking the meat off those chicken necks and your hot sauce goes to work, you won't be able to draw the beer fast enough."

"You could be right, Cenzo," said Rico, joining in with the laugh, "that stuff works like a charm." Then, changing subjects without missing a beat, he continued.

"Listen, Cenzo. Since the last time you was up here, I been nosin' around the way you told me. Lemme tell you. Your guy Luco Parisi? He done one hell of a job of gettin' lost. I haven't got a clue where he went. Least not yet. Anyhow, I figured you'd want to know you're not the only one's looking for him."

Without waiting for Vince's question, Rico said, "You ready for this? Tubby Bagnatore."

"Tubby Bagnatore?!" Vince exclaimed, bolting upright. "What the hell's *his* stake in this?"

"Word I get is he's got personal money in Greater Providence. Big time money. Stashed in a buncha small accounts so's they don't attrack too much notice. Phony names on the accounts. Anyhow, word is that Greater Providence is steppin' in the shit and Tubby's gettin' antsy. Got his boys turnin' over stones lookin' for Parisi."

"What kind of problem is Greater Providence having?" Vince asked.

"Best I can make out is somethin' about a … wait a minute, I wrote it down … a huge 'deficit in collateralization,' what-the-hell-ever that means."

"It means the bank's borrowers owe the bank more money than what their collateral is worth."

"Yeah. Anyhow, word leaked out yesterday morning. By middle of the afternoon, the bank was doin' a bang-up business. People scramblin' to take out their money.

"They was waitin' this mornin' since before daylight at all the drive-thru windows. Cars standin' in line backed all the way up onto the main drags. Traffic jams like when the gas stations was havin' them price wars. Then they closed."

The syntax confused Vince. "Who?" he asked.

"Who what?" It was Rico's turn to be confused.

"Who closed, Rico?!" Vince failed to conceal his impatience.

"Geez, Cenzo, the drive-thru windows! Who else we talkin' about? Anyhow, about an hour after they opened, they closed."

"The drive-thru teller windows closed?" Vince was having a little trouble staying on the rails.

"Naw, Cenzo," said Rico in exasperation that his friend could be so dense, "the bank! The whole Greater freakin' Providence Bank closed!"

"For crisake, Rico," Vince struggled for control, "the bank closes and you hold that back until last? Didn't you think I'd be interested in that little fact? What else is there?!"

"Nothin' Cenzo," Rico remained unperturbed. "Anyhow, those state guys are over there lookin' into it."

"The state guys?" Vince gritted his teeth. "Do you mean RISDIC?! The Rhode Island Share & Deposit Indemnity Corporation? *They're* involved?!"

"Yeah, RISDIC," Rico said brightly. "That flashy broad with the big knockers on PROV-TV was just talkin' about it."

TWENTY-SEVEN

Providence

A THICK, FRIZZY MUSTACHE merged with his full-face beard. The blackness of his facial hair matched the blackness of his bulging eyes that glared, bug-eyed, from behind thick, steel-rimmed glasses.

The immense bulk of his midsection sagged to below the level of the seating surface of his hard, straight-backed chair, the only kind of chair capable of accommodating his girth. He sat with his hands on his thighs, his feet planted on the floor and his legs spread wide. In a sitting position, it was impossible for Tubby Bagnatore to bring his legs closer together.

"I ain't interested in what *you* done." His voice wheezed from deep in his chest. The heavy sounds of his breathing, laboring under the oppressive weight of his upper body, dictated the cadence of his speech. A raspy, audible gasp accompanied each inhalation. It was a sound much like a diver would make, sucking in his first, desperate breath of air after staying underwater too long. Though each breath drew in an enormous volume of air, it was sufficient only to utter a few words. To get as much as possible from each breath, he spoke until he completely exhausted his supply of air. Sometimes, when, in the heat of the moment he neglected to pace himself, he rendered his last two or three words as a breathless, almost unintelligible croak.

"I already know what you done. You wanna confess to somethin' go down the street to the Holy Ghost. Father Raimondo's always willin' to hear a juicy confession. I ast you where's Luco. I didn't ask for no song and dance. I don't wanna hear no song and dance."

They had persuaded Mickey Hoban to admit his part in the loan-boosting fraud Luco was running, though he had deftly underplayed the extent and importance of his own participation. Tubby Bagnatore looked on dispassionately while Mickey was being urged to cooperate by Rocco Giordano, aka Rocky Jordan, former light-heavy contender for whom the bell had indeed tolled one too many times.

Chetta Lograno, Rocky's concubine, aided him in the execution of his agenda. At five-foot-ten and slender of build, Ms. Lograno's broad, sloping shoulders and flat belly accentuated the well-defined musculature in her limbs and buttocks. She was textbook mesomorphic. Her former career as a physiotherapist-turned-masseuse had endowed her hands and long, powerful fingers with incredible, vice-like strength. It had also provided her with esoteric knowledge of the human body's pressure points both of pleasure and of paralyzing pain.

It was in her explorations of the former that she had won the love and devotion of Rocky. Regarding the latter, Chetta now applied the pressure of her thumb to one such point located directly aft of Mickey's scrotum. The pain she induced was sufficient to levitate him to his toes, rendering him helpless and unable to fend off the staggering blows delivered by her paramour.

On Tubby's signal, they took a short breather. Rocky eased Mickey onto a straight-backed chair, hung his own arms loosely at his sides and shook them out. Chetta went to the restroom and returned with a towel she had soaked under the cold water tap. She handed it to Rocky. With it, he gently dabbed at the blood that flowed from Mickey's nose and from the cuts that he had opened on Mickey's cheekbones and lips. Before beginning, Rocky had inserted a boxer's mouthpiece into Mickey's mouth. Now he removed it, spread Mickey's lips, examined his teeth and with an exuberant thumbs up sign, said, "Awright! Nice set o' teeth ya got there, pal. Didn't break none o' them."

"That's supposed to make me feel better?" Mickey gasped through his pain. "What about my ribs? I think you broke my ribs."

"Hey, asshole!" said Tubby. "These two ain't even started yet. You got a lot more things to break. I ain't gonna wait forever."

"I don't know where he is," said Mickey. The anger that had masked his fear retreated under Tubby's ominous stare. Fighting against the horror that tingled up his spine, he did his best to demonstrate a bravado he did not feel, but the certain realization of the danger that he faced constricted his throat. His voice became scratchy and his swollen lips deformed his words. "And what the hell difference does it make anyway? You don't need him. Your deposits are insured for crisake?!"

"Oh yeah, that's right! I forgot. They're insured! Geez, what a relief! Now I'm embarrassed I made Rocky knock you around for nuttin'. Rocky, you hear that? The asshole says I got nuttin' to worry about." Tubby's voice seemed playful. Mickey's eyes were swollen to mere slits so he couldn't see if Tubby was smiling. Mickey was confused. But not for long.

Tubby's next words radiated with rage. His body rocked with the force of his shouting, "Hey, asshole! What are you tellin' me? You sayin' I'm some kinda fuckin' retard?! I don't know the bank carries insurance?!"

Mickey's pretense at bravado deserted him. There was no mistaking the pleading in his tone as he replied, "I didn't mean it like that, Mr. Bagnatore, I ... "

"Shut up, asshole!" Tubby roared without giving Mickey time to respond. "You tellin' me I'm too ignorant to know the banks ante-up premiums every year? Like that money's turned over to RISDIC for protection? Like RISDIC puts all that money inta the pot? So when a bank gets a tit caught in the wringer, like with the scam you and that other asshole Parisi done to Greater Providence Bank, they can jump in like Tonto and the Lone fuckin' Ranger and save everybody's ass?!"

Tubby was getting exercised. His panting came in huge, sucking gasps. His face turned purple as he tried to squeeze out the final few, breathless words of sentences that ran too long. He was getting near the edge. Mickey's thoughts were in a maelstrom. He tried desperately but was unable to think of something ... anything ... he could say to calm this madman. His terror rose to a level he had never before imagined. Sweat ran down inside his collar. His entire body felt clammy. He fought to keep his senses.

"But guess who *runs* RISDIC?!" Tubby bellowed. "The same fuckin' banks they're supposed to insure! They got their own front men sittin' on the Board of fuckin' Directors of RISDIC. The foxes are protectin' the fuckin' chickens! They been sandbaggin' their premiums for years, takin' a free ride.

"So guess what else, asshole?! There ain't no fund. Never was! RISDIC's an empty suitcase. They got no money to bail anyone out. Greater Providence is gonna suck wind. And so am I! And soon as the Providence Journal finds out, so's everybody else who's got money in that bank," he croaked.

He remained silent for a long time, his enormous chest heaving, until his face regained its normal color and his breathing was again under control. It was as though it was a cue for Rocky and Chetta. Without a word or gesture from Tubby, each drew up a chair very close to Mickey. They sat in front of him, one on each side, facing him at forty-five degree angles. When Tubby continued, he was calm and all business.

"So now you listen to me, asshole. The bank's goin' down the toilet with my money. I know Parisi skimmed at least eight mill in that little scam you and him was runnin'. He skipped with it. I want it."

Mickey wondered if he heard right. 'Tubby's only after Luco,' he thought. 'He doesn't know how much I made or he'd be after me too. Thank God he … wait a minute … what did he say? Did he say eight million?! What eight million? Luco got eight million? And I got only a mil?! That lying, no-good son of a bitch! He told me we were equal partners!' In that instant, he wished he knew where Luco was so he could tell Tubby.

Mickey's reverie was abruptly shattered when a pile-driver right hook slammed into his solar plexus. His universe erupted in pulsating bursts of green, yellow and dayglo red, and a blinding explosion of searing pain. Mickey didn't see the eyeball gesture that Tubby had flashed to Rocky.

"I got your attention, asshole?"

Mickey was doubled over in his chair with his arms wrapped around his midsection. He tried to speak but could create only an unintelligible groan. At another eye gesture from Tubby, Chetta got up, pressed her fingers and the heels of her hands into several points on Mickey's hands, arms, upper chest, neck, temples and mastoids. His pain subsided to a tolerable throb. Then she grabbed his hair and yanked his head up.

"Now you tell me where he went." The menace was unmistakable in Tubby's tone.

"I don't know where he w … AAHNGHH!" Chetta's thumb burrowed under his trapezius muscle to press against the nerve. A second before he would have passed out from the pain, she released her grip.

The stark reality of what he faced overwhelmed Mickey. He was frozen with terror. Though sweating profusely, his entire body shivered with icy tremors. He felt a warm wetness fill his crotch and spread to his seat and the insides of his thighs as his bladder released in a sudden, uncontrolled gush.

"I don't wanna hear no more tap-dance from you."

"How can I tell y … ?"

"That's it. Do him, Rocky."

"NO! NO, WAIT!" Mickey screamed as Rocky rose deliberately from his chair. "I SWEAR I don't know. For the love of God don't you think I'd tell you where he is if I knew?"

Tubby lifted the fingers of one hand and Rocky lowered himself back into his chair to await further directions.

"So, Rocky," asked Tubby after studying Mickey for a long moment, "is he tellin' the truth?"

"I dunno, Mr. Bagnatore," Rocky replied while clinically studying Mickey, "I think so. I hurt him good. Busted a couple-a ribs an' all. But I can't be sure. He takes it pretty good."

"How about you, Chetta? Is he tellin' the truth?"

"I agree with Rocky, Mr. Bagnatore," she said, "I can't be sure. Maybe we ought to do a pinkie."

Mickey's eyes jerked to each speaker in sequence. He didn't like it that they weren't sure. And what the hell was that about a pinkie? Though they had stopped speaking, his eyes nonetheless continued to snap involuntarily from one to the other. He had to remind himself to breathe.

"Yeah, maybe so," said Tubby after thinking about it. Then, addressing Mickey, he asked, "You right-handed?"

"Right-handed?" asked Mickey, thoroughly confounded. "Yeah. I'm right-handed."

"The left one, then," said Tubby, "who wants to do it?"

"Oh, *I'll* do it!" Chetta answered brightly, "Please! Let *me* do it."

Having no idea what they were talking about, Mickey was a step or two behind them. Rocky locked Mickey's right hand in a captive handshake grip. Mickey simply observed with detached curiosity as Chetta took his left hand in hers. In her left hand, she gripped his thumb and first three fingers in a tight bunch. Then with one swift, twisting, lifting, spreading motion of her right hand, she snapped his little finger, breaking it in two places.

Rocky jammed the towel into Mickey's mouth before his agonized scream could reach full force. Mickey's eyes glazed-over and lost their focus. His head bobbed and rolled independently of his will. His scream plummeted in a groaning glissando to silence.

Chetta was entranced, almost hypnotized, by Mickey's tortured reaction to what she had done. Her eyelids drooped. Her tongue caressed her parted lips. She hugged herself, fondling her body with her hands. She became wet. Her hips writhed to the motion of her thighs rubbing sensuously against each other. Her head fell back and she moaned softly in carnal rapture.

After a long, fascinating minute of watching her, Tubby remembered why they were there.

"Now, you got somethin' you wanna tell me?" Tubby's tone was gentle. Almost concerned.

"Switzerland," Mickey mumbled when Rocky removed the towel from his mouth. Why didn't he think of Switzerland earlier? he asked himself.

"Switzerland? Where in Switzerland?"

"I don't know, goddammit!" Mickey snorted through his battered and swollen lips. His anger welled up in him, masking his pain. He stuck his throbbing hand out to the woman, locked his eyes on hers and snarled, "Go ahead. Break another one. I still won't know!"

Chetta broke eye-contact first. Only then did Mickey turn his gaze back to Tubby. His tone reflected a complete change of attitude. He had gone beyond terrified and defensive. He had reached the level of in-your-face-do-whatever-you-have-to-do-but-get-this-bullshit-over-with-and-go-fuck-yourself angry. Tubby recognized the transformation and regarded Mickey with admiration. He looked at him for a long time, then his face softened.

"Okay. Okay. So you don't know where. What else do you know?" Tubby asked with a friendly smile.

"Just Switzerland. And I'm not even sure he's there. I just remembered him telling me about this weird Swiss banker he knows."

"Weird? Weird how?"

Neither of them understood how or why, but it was no longer an interrogation. They had fallen into rapprochement. It had become almost like two acquaintances shooting the breeze.

"The guy's some kind of bank executive but he drives around in a funny car with cow's horns on the hood. Dresses like a cowboy. Whips out his guitar and sings at the drop of a hat."

"Yeah, that's weird."

"It came to me while Bluto here was pounding me. Maybe Luco made a connection with that Swiss banker. Maybe that's where he put his money. And if … "

" … and if that's where his *money* is," Tubby finished Mickey's thought, "maybe that's where *he* is."

Mickey tried to smile his agreement but winced at the pain from his swollen lips. Tubby noticed.

"Geez, sorry about that," Tubby said as he rose ponderously from his chair, "but what else could I do?" Turning to the others, he continued, "Fix him up. Get him whatever he needs … a drink … somethin' to eat … a broad … whatever. The guy's awright. He's got *coglione!*"

Then he went to the door but, before leaving, he turned to Mickey and said, "By the way. Nothin' personal, but any word of this leaks out, keep in mind you got nine more fingers."

TWENTY-EIGHT

VINCE WAS ALREADY ten minutes late. The traffic cop, in obsequious deference to the PROV-TV news van that was parked at an arrogant angle to the sidewalk, stopped Vince's lane of traffic with an upheld hand and a blast on his whistle. One of the TV crew, a pudgy, pasty-faced, unkempt gnome wearing mirrored sunglasses and a baseball cap with the visor backwards, leaped from the van. Waving his clipboard, he waddled quickly toward the cop. In a piercing, nasal, high-pitched wail, he commanded, "Hey! Hey, you! What the hell was that?! A whistle?! We're set to do a live, freakin' shoot and you make with the freakin' whistle?! No freakin' whistles! Just stick the whistle in your freakin' pocket, OK, pal?!"

"Oh, yes sir. I'm terribly sorry, sir." The cop actually bowed but his eyes were not on the gnome. He had them fastened on the talent, anchorwoman Laramie Duquette. She had observed the exchange and decided to soften the blow for the cop. While the gnome's attention was elsewhere, she gazed seductively into the cop's eyes while deliberately moistening her smiling lips with her tongue. Slowly, affecting reluctance, she turned back to her work.

Vince saw the whole thing. He tasted the bile of cynicism as it welled up in him. He couldn't decide if it resulted more from the news media's contempt for everyone outside the media or from the cop's lack of spine. Just then, the cop waved him through. As he swerved impatiently around the van, Vince stole another look at the talent. Rico was right. Flashy. Nice tits. She was talking into a boom-mike with the main entrance of Greater Providence Bank & Trust as her backdrop.

Vince turned right on Weybosset and swung into the GPB&T parking garage. Horace opened Vince's door and with a head motion toward the entrance, said glumly, "Been expectin' you, Mr. B. They told me to let you right in."

"Good morning, Horace," Vince replied. "Don't tell me your money's locked up in this mess Greater Providence got itself into and you can't get at it."

He started toward the brass-framed glass entrance door with Horace close on his heels.

"Shee-it!" Horace replied with a snort. "I don't have no money to get at, Mr. B. After feedin' five teenagers they ain't none left over to put in no bank." He hesitated, then continued. "It's my momma. She don't have much but everthin' she have is in this here bank."

Vince's distant objectivity deserted him. "What are you saying?" he asked, knowing the essence of the answer before asking.

"I'm sayin' my momma work like a dog her whole life doin' for me and my two sisters." Helpless frustration and anger generated ripples in the surface of Horace's deep, resonant voice. "An' now the time come for her to take it a little easy. But the bank tell her she can't have her money. Her own money! She don't know what she gonna do. Me and my sisters, we'll do what we can. But we ain't got nothin' left over and momma, she know that. It ain't right, Mr. B."

For the first time, Vince was struck by the reality and the magnitude of what Luco Parisi had set into motion. It's not just Phil Peters and Production House Graphix. There are real people involved. Hundreds, no, thousands maybe, of very real, very innocent people. The hardship that was about to be visited upon Horace's mother would be visited upon thousands of depositors. Many of them were elderly and entirely dependent on their savings.

And businesses. Hundreds of businesses. They would lose access to the millions of dollars they had deposited into their tax escrow accounts as required by law, to cover payroll taxes. Under the threat of crippling penalties and interest, they would be forced to make duplicate payments to comply with the IRS's rigid, no-excuses timetable. Many businesses, especially those with low cash reserves, would fail, forcing hundreds, perhaps thousands of employees out of work.

Vince suddenly felt a sense of shame for his narrow and selfish grasp of the matter, but it soon gave way to fury, and a consuming desire for revenge against Luco.

"No, Horace. It isn't right." The way he said it and the way he looked when he said it awakened a tiny spark of hope in Horace.

"You figure there's a way out of this, Mr. B?" Horace's face softened and he almost smiled as he held the door open for Vince.

"That's what I intend to find out, Horace."

VINCE FOLLOWED JEANNE into Howard Pastore's office where they found Howard and Phil watching Laramie Duquette who spoke earnestly from the TV.

> " ... that their deposits are insured by Rhode Island Share & Deposit Indemnity Corporation. Earlier today, the chairman of RISDIC, Herbert R. Steinwand, declined to answer this reporter's questions after he read a prepared statement."

The TV scene went to a head shot of a fiftyish, athletic-looking man with graying, wavy hair, and the capitol building in the background over his shoulder. Laramie Duquette was off-camera holding her mike in front him as he read a prepared statement.

> "In keeping with RISDIC's long-standing policy, we will not discuss the precise details of those factors that led to the temporary closing of Greater Providence Bank & Trust until we have completed our audit. Suffice it to say that we are proceeding with all possible haste so as to minimize any hardship that might be caused by the closure.
>
> "We have been asked by Howard Pastore of Greater Providence Bank to reassure its customers that the bank is in no danger. It is functioning. Deposits and other in-

vestment instruments will continue to accrue interest. On the other hand, so will loans. He urges their customers to make loan payments on a timely basis to avoid late charges and other penalties.

"We are confident that the closure is temporary. The doors of Greater Providence Bank will reopen as soon as we have determined the extent to which RISDIC's funds might be needed, if at all. At that time an appropriate announcement will be made to the press."

The TV scene changed to take in both Steinwand and Laramie.

" 'If at all?' Mr. Steinwand," asked Laramie, repeating that part of his comments. "Does that suggest the possibility that Greater Providence might not need RISDIC's help? That this was all a bizarre mistake?"

Steinwand remained silent as he looked at his watch, then turned to glance at the capitol building behind him as Laramie continued.

"Or does 'if at all' suggest that even with RISDIC's help, Greater Providence is doomed?" Laramie asked.

"I want to emphasize to the viewers that those were *your* words, not mine," said Steinwand, as he glared at Laramie. "Now if you'll excuse me." His voice was controlled but his anger was unmistakable. He spun and walked quickly away, retreating into the background toward the capitol building.

The TV returned to Laramie on Dorrance Street in front of the GPB&T building.

"Mr. Steinwand's reluctance to answer our questions is mirrored by Howard Pastore's refusal to take our calls. This does not bode well for thousands of Greater Providence banking customers, many of them elderly and infirm who, without ready access to their money, will be faced with indescribable privation.

"More at six. Updates as they develop," she concluded with a grim smile.

"Doom? Elderly and infirm? Privation?" Howard said through clenched teeth as he pressed the OFF button with a resounding snap. They gave silent greetings to one another with eye-contact and nods of their heads as he continued, "So much for reportorial ethics and objectivity. Of course I won't talk to her. What could I possible say to her that she won't turn inside out."

"You're probably right to keep your distance from her, Howard," said Vince. "Even though Herb Steinwand had a prepared statement, you saw what she did to him. But rhetoric aside, I have to tell you she isn't far off the mark. I was just talking with Horace down in the garage. His mother is already feeling the effects. People will be hurt by this."

"I was made painfully aware of that just last night, Vince," Howard replied. No one even noticed that they had slipped into using first names. "Whenever I work late, as I did last night, Mrs. Masters, that marvelous lady who cleans the offices, brings me a cup of coffee and we visit for a few minutes. It has become a ritual with us and is one of the bright spots of my day. Last night I learned that the meager amount she earns here supplements what she earns at her daytime employment as a housekeeper for an invalid couple. This beautiful old lady is sixty-eight years old and she's holding two jobs!

"I also learned that her entire savings are in this bank. That without access to that money, she will very soon be in default on several, time-sensitive obligations.

"She didn't volunteer this information. I had to draw it out of her. Even so, she didn't whine nor did she complain. When I pressed her, she reluctantly confided that she didn't want to say anything to me because of *my* problems. She was concerned for *me*. She didn't want to add to *my* burden."

In the quiet that followed, Howard left the group and walked to the corner windows. With his back to the others, he surreptitiously wiped the moisture from under his eyes with his fingers.

Still with his back to the others, he continued, "Mrs. Masters will not be hurt by this. I will see to that personally."

"I understand what you're feeling and I admire you for it," said Vince, "but, Howard, what about Horace's mother? Will you cover her obligations too? And the others, the thousands that you don't know personally. Do you also intend to pay all their bills?"

Howard turned slowly to face Vince as Vince continued, "You can't cure all their problems. There are too many of them. Besides, you cannot ... and you *should* not ... assume any guilt for what's happened. You're not responsible for causing whatever hardship they might have to face. And what about Phil, here? Doesn't he deserve som ... ?"

"Wait a second, Vince," Phil interrupted. "I intended to say this to you privately but, well, it seems we're all wrapped up in this in one way or another.

"First, I'm ashamed for the way I reacted when I got the letter and I apologize. On the other hand, that whole embarrassing episode woke me up to certain realities. As a result, I've taken the first steps toward getting my personal life on track."

Howard had been in the dark about Phil and Jeanne and about Phil's marital situation. However, he was able to surmise the essence of what Phil was saying by the tenderness in their gaze as Jeanne sidled up to Phil and took his hand.

Tearing his eyes from Jeanne's, Phil continued, "Beyond that, I have a broad and loyal client base, a good track record and a good reputation. If the worst happens and I lose my company, I'm sure I'll have no problem signing on with one of my present competitors. In time I'll start a new company and do it all over again. Whatever happens with PHG, I'll be able to deal with it.

"With one major exception," he said, turning to face Vince. "I have no idea how long it will take me to repay ... "

"Hold it!" Vince held up his hand like a traffic cop. "We've had this discussion before and nothing has changed. I can wait as long as it takes. Besides, no one's going to take your company or your building or your home or anything else."

"How can you make such an assertion, Vince?" Howard said through his astonishment. "Irrespective of the circumstances that led to it, the fact is that Philip is in default on $837,000. When he failed to retire his $480,000 line of credit, he triggered the actions that followed, however repugnant and vindictive my uncle's motivations might have been. The terms of the loan agreement were very specific, giving the bank the full right to demand payment of Philip's other loans as well. My hands are tied. I've explained to you that the scope of my authority is well-defined. I'm powerless to overturn the actions taken by my uncle."

"Suppose I were to give you my personal guarantee against the $837,000?" Vince said it evenly and matter-of-factly.

"What?!" Howard, Phil and Jeanne exclaimed in unison.

"You heard me. I would be willing to sign a personal guarantee if you would be willing to give me thirty days to find your uncle and convince him to rescind his actions. If after thirty days I have been unable to find him, I'll pay the $837,000. In either event, I'll require that Phil's credit standing remain unblemished."

"I'm sure we can work something out," Howard said. "Of course, a financial statement will be required."

Jeanne's and Phil's wide-eyed gaze switched back and forth between Vince and Howard as each spoke.

"Now hold it, Vince," Phil's mind was in a whirl, "slow down a minute and let's think ... "

"My accountant can fax one to you within the hour," Vince replied, totally ignoring Phil's comment. "I assure you my holdings are more than sufficient."

Howard considered it for a brief moment, then extended his hand. Vince took it and they both knew they had a contract that was stronger than any that they could put on paper.

Vince turned to Phil and placed a hand on his shoulder. "Phil, don't lose any sleep over this. PHG is as strong as ever, and as soon as the real estate market returns to normal around here, your building will again be worth far more than what you owe on it."

Phil started to respond, but before he could, Vince went on.

"The main issue is that worm, Luco. He brought all this on." Turning to Howard, Vince continued gently, with compassion evident in his voice, "I'm sorry Luco is your uncle. He's a miserable bastard. Your grandfather was a great man. He had a powerful influence on my life as he did on yours. But for some unfathomable reason, he was cursed with Luco for a son. An aberration, as my father once described him. An acorn that fell too far from the tree.

"I'm going to find him. I'm going to make him sorry for what he did to Mrs. Masters and to Horace's mother and to all the others. I'm going to make him sorry for what he tried to do to Phil … and to me. And most of all, I'm going to make him sorry for what he did to his father's memory. But I'm going to need all the help you can give me."

Howard turned from Vince and walked slowly to the windows. He didn't answer right away. When finally he spoke, his tone was subdued. "I can't fault you for your opinion of my uncle. There is no question that what he has done is deserving of contempt. But he's family. I don't know where he is but even if I knew, how could you expect me to betray family? You don't know what you're asking."

"Yes Howard I do, but listen carefully. I'm not the only one who is interested in finding him."

"What do you mean?"

"I've been told there's a large sum of money in your bank that has been earned illegally, almost certainly from drugs, prostitution, extortion and gambling. It has no doubt been thoroughly laundered and now resides in dozens of small accounts. Accounts that are now frozen by the closing of the bank. This money constitutes working capital for a wiseguy named Tubby Bagnatore. He is … "

Howard had half-turned to Vince as he spoke. Now he approached to face him. Jeanne, feeling a little weak from what Vince said, lowered herself to the couch, pulling Phil down to sit by her.

"I know who he is," Howard said in a challenging tone. "I hope you're not saying my uncle is tied up with him."

"I don't know anything about that. All I know is Tubby's looking for him and I wouldn't want Tubby looking for me … for any reason."

"Oh my God," Howard exclaimed softly, suddenly aware of the implications, "nor would I. You're right. We must find my uncle. Before Tubby does. But how can I help you? I really don't know where he is."

"Well you can be sure of one thing with Luco," said Phil. "There's a woman involved in some way. Luco's been unable to keep his zipper up since grade school. It's a trait he couldn't conceal if he wanted to and, believe me, he doesn't want to."

"Rochelle!" Jeanne leapt to her feet. "Howard, buzz for Rochelle. Tell her to come in here."

She said it so assertively that Howard didn't even question her. As he went to his desk, she told of her long-standing suspicions that Rochelle and Luco were having an affair. Suspicions that were confirmed beyond any doubt the day she stormed into Luco's office to find Rochelle and Luco on the couch.

"Howard, wait a second," said Vince before Howard picked up his phone. "Let me have a few minutes with her by myself. Tell her I'm coming to see her but don't tell her why. Jeanne can introduce me as an old friend of Luco's. I want to question her in Luco's office if I may."

Howard punched in a three-digit number. When Rochelle answered, he said, "This is Mr. Pastore. In a few minutes, Miss Aiello will escort a Mr. Bonetta to you. Please show him into Mr. Parisi's office. He's here to help us. Give him any information and assistance he asks for. With no restrictions."

ROCHELLE LED THEM INTO Luco's office and motioned for Vince to take the couch. With Jeanne's earlier recounting of the couch incident still fresh in his mind, Vince took the settee instead. Rochelle made a move for the side chair but was too late as Jeanne slipped into it just ahead of her. Rochelle had no choice but to take the couch. As she lowered herself into it, she awkwardly avoided eye-contact with Jeanne but was unable to avoid the embarrassing memory of their last encounter in this office.

"Rochelle," Jeanne began, "Mr. Bonetta has known Mr. Parisi for a long time and also knew his father. He has offered to help in any way he can to try to find Mr. Parisi and to get to the bottom of this. Mr. Pastore thought, and I agree, that it might be easier for you to speak freely if neither I nor Mr. Pastore were present. So, please excuse me." With that, Jeanne rose to leave. "Take as long as you like. I'll arrange for your calls to be taken by someone else until you're finished," she said before closing the door.

"Now what was that supposed to mean? Why wouldn't I speak freely?" Rochelle asked with ill-disguised annoyance, still looking at the closed door.

"I'm sure you're aware, Rochelle," Vince said, ignoring her question, "that much of the bank's present trouble stems from the disclosure of certain irregularities that have appeared in loan documents." She turned to face Vince at the sound of his voice.

"I don't have anything to do with loan documents," Rochelle said defensively, "and I certainly didn't have anything to do with irregularities."

"No, I'm sure you didn't but I'm also sure you're aware of the rumors. As with many rumors, there can be an element of truth. The element of truth in these rumors is very compelling."

"What element? What truth?" She asked while she again looked at the closed door, still disquieted by Jeanne's remarks.

"A bank fraud has been committed," said Vince. "That's a fact, not a rumor. It will reach into the millions. That is also a fact. The rumor part of it is that your boss did it. His disappearing at the precise moment the fraud was discovered is the compelling part. Wouldn't you agree?"

"No I wouldn't!" she snapped. She forgot about Jeanne and turned her full attention to Vince.

"What part don't you agree with?" Vince spoke in a soft, non-confrontational manner.

"I don't agree with any of it. Mr. Parisi would never do that."

"Your loyalty is admirable but we already know that someone in this bank did it. There is no doubt that fraud has been committed and there is little doubt as to its magnitude. That leaves only *who* did it open to speculation. Now, would you agree with that much?"

"What do you care what I agree with or don't agree with?" She tried to sound angry and impatient but Vince read it accurately as doubt and anxiety.

"I care because I do believe what you're telling me. I also believe what you have *not* told me, the parts that you don't want to tell yourself. Your boss left and he didn't tell you a thing. Not where he was going nor when you would hear from him. Has he ever done that before, Rochelle? Gone away without notice, leaving no way for you to reach him in an emergency?"

She didn't answer.

"I didn't think so." Vince waited a long time, just looking into her eyes. She couldn't hold his gaze and kept breaking away. Up to this point his manner had been low key and sensitive. When he resumed, he spoke in a firm, crisp, authoritative voice that momentarily startled her.

"I'm here because we're all concerned about Mr. Parisi. He's in grave physical danger. Unless we find him before certain others do, it is likely your boss will be tortured, perhaps killed."

"What?!" she shrieked. It was precisely the reaction Vince expected. "What are you saying?! Who would do that? Why?!"

"It doesn't matter who. It's the why that matters. The money. Face it. The people who are looking for him want it and only he knows where it is. He won't want to tell them where it is, but he will. They have effective methods of getting information from people who don't want to give it. And after they get what they want from him, no one will ever hear from him again. Unless we find him first."

"No. You're lying! How can you say such things?" Her eyes begged for comfort.

Vince hated what he was doing to this woman. He pushed aside the rage he felt toward Luco and abandoned the tough guy act. Whatever her life had been with Luco was none of his business. Still, he forced himself to continue.

"I'm sorry, Rochelle. He used you. He isn't going to send for you." Vince felt sorry for her. He softened his tone. "You have to try to help us. For his sake, and for yours."

"No, don't say that," Rochelle whimpered. She clasped her hands together in her lap, shaking her head slowly in denial of the undeniable. She closed her eyes but couldn't prevent the tears from cascading down her cheeks. She made no attempt to wipe them away. "He loves me. I know he'll call me. I know it! He's going to get a divorce. He told me he just needs a little more time. He wants to marry me. I know he loves me."

He continued, "I'm sorry, Rochelle. I'm truly sorry to hurt you but he doesn't love you. He never did. I've known him a lot longer than you have. He's never loved anyone and that includes his wife."

Vince fetched a box of tissues from the credenza behind Luco's desk and returned, placing the box next to her on the couch. Rochelle pulled several tissues from the box and worked on her face as Vince continued.

"Did you truly believe that he was faithful to you? That he was committed to you?" He didn't leave any space for a reply. "I don't think so, Rochelle. Somewhere deep inside, you had to know. You pushed it aside, but you knew, didn't you?" This time he gave her time to frame a response. When she didn't, he reached out and took her free hand gently in both of his. In a voice that was almost a whisper, he said, "I've known him long enough to be certain of one thing. Somehow, in some way, a woman, some *other* woman, is a part of this. And you know that, too, don't you?"

Rochelle balled up her other hand, the one holding the tissues, and beat her fist slowly and repeatedly on her thigh, with her eyes tightly closed, and her head nodding yes in the same deliberate rhythm. Abruptly, all motion stopped. Then, after a long moment of silent deliberation, her head began slowly to shake from side to side. Her face became contorted in a mask of fury.

Perplexed by her body language, Vince followed his instincts and said nothing.

"That snake! That miserable, lying snake!" she hissed. With her eyes still closed, she went on, "I tried to believe him. I wanted so much for it to be true."

"Wanted what to be true?"

"He told me she was just a secretary."

"Who are we talking about, Rochelle?"

"Erika."

"Erika? Erika who?"

"I don't know. Just Erika," she said, opening her eyes and slumping back in resignation.

"OK, then. Erika is someone's secretary. Whose secretary is she?"

"A banker in Europe. At least that's what he told me."

"That's what who told you?"

"Mr. Parisi. But he never took her calls."

"Why, Rochelle? Why wouldn't he take her calls?"

"I don't know. Maybe he thought I would listen in. He always called her back on his private line."

"How often did she call?"

"Almost every day. Sometimes more than once a day."

"Do you know her number?"

She shook her head.

"What's the banker's name? Or the name of the bank?"

"I don't know. He never told me."

"Did you ever talk with the banker directly?"

"No."

Vince waited. He wanted to be sure that every word they had spoken after Rochelle first mentioned Erika's name was burned into her consciousness before he asked the next question.

"How many times has Erika called since your boss disappeared?"

Rochelle hesitated. She looked directly into Vince's eyes. Then, shaking her head in resigned emphasis, she said, "Never. Not once." The sound of her own words brought the cold reality of their meaning home to her.

The passion that had sustained her anger abandoned her, taking a new direction as the specter of revenge wriggled into focus. Still holding her hand in both of his, Vince saw in her eyes a spark that he was unable to fathom except for the certain realization that she no longer needed his support. He gently released her hand and drew back from her, but he continued to look steadily, quizzically, into her eyes.

It was as though she had found a new source of strength and purpose. Her gaze didn't falter. It flicked back and forth several times, focusing first on one of his eyes then on the other. He perceived something in her bearing—how could he define it?—an awakening?—at the same time he noticed that the corners of her mouth had curled into the start of a humorless grin.

"What is it, Rochelle?"

"Would you like to have Erika's phone number?"

"Of course I would," Vince said, "but I don't understand. You said you don't know her number."

"I don't," she said as she abruptly got up and went to Luco's desk, "but I know someone who just might be able to get it for you." She picked up the phone and dialed three digits. A voice on the other end said, "Security. Sheila McCusker."

TWENTY-NINE

THE ONLY LIGHT IN SECURITY CENTRAL came from the bank of monitors whose cameras covered almost every square inch of Greater Providence Bank & Trust. Claude scanned the monitors as Vince peered over the shoulder of Sheila McCusker who sat at the center console, master control panel. She tapped the keyboard and columns of data scrolled up the screen of the full-color, large-screen monitor. After several lines of data appeared, she pressed the PAUSE key to bring the scrolling to a halt.

ANZEVINO, CHERYL X-797

JANUARY 1990

03	212-647-3500	0916	:08	HOLLOMAN IMPORTS
03	617-434-6930	0957	:12	BAYSTATE FLORAL
03	401-467-2541	1410	:05	PERSONAL
04	508-434-3058	1042	:06	FALL RIVER HOME BUI
04	212-644-7878	1322	:16	EMPIRE GEMOLOGISTS
04	401-467-2541	1407	:02	PERSONAL
04	401-467-2541	1644	:05	PERSONAL

"This sample shows the type of data that's automatically recorded for all outgoing toll calls," said Sheila. "Most of it is obvious … employee's name, month and year, and on the right-hand side, the extension number."

"How far back can you go?" Vince asked.

"The program boots to the first alphabetical employee and the first day of the current year," said Sheila, "but we can call up any period we want to look at. We can go all the way back to when the system was installed."

"And you have this kind of data on every employee?"

For the first time, Sheila looked away from the screen. She turned to her assistant and said, "It's about time for you to take your break, isn't it, Claude?"

"It ain't time yet, Miss McCusker," Claude replied, puzzled, looking at his watch.

"Yes, it is," Sheila insisted. "Besides, there isn't much going on with the public locked out. And Claude … no need to rush back. I'll call for you when I'm ready."

Claude got the message. He glanced back and forth from Sheila to Vince, then with an informal salute, he said, "I'll just fix up a cup of coffee for me an' Horace. I'll be downstairs in the garage when you need me."

After Claude left, Sheila picked up where they had left off.

"You asked if we keep phone records on every employee. The answer is yes."

"Including Luco Parisi?"

"I kind of figured that would be your next question." She turned away from him, swiveling slowly in her captain's chair to check each security monitor.

"And?"

She swiveled to face him again. "And, I need to know just where we're going with this."

"What do you mean?"

"Look, Mr. Bonetta. I like my job. I've got a good deal here. Lots of responsibility. Good pay. They leave me alone to do my job and I damn well do it."

"I'm listening," said Vince when her pause lasted a beat too long.

"Suppose there *is* such a data file on Mr. Parisi ... and suppose that file can tell you whatever it is you're looking for? But suppose that file was never authorized," she swiveled to face away from him, " ... and nobody knows it even exists ... except me?"

Vince muddled his way through the silence that followed. Suddenly it struck him.

"Well, I'll be damned," he burst out laughing. "You *do* have a file on him and no one else knows about it! How in the world did you manage that?!" Just as suddenly, he became serious again and he didn't wait for an answer.

"Sheila, listen to me. No one will ever learn it from me. First of all, there's no reason for anyone to ask me, but even if someone did, I swear to you I'll deny that I got the information from you."

Sheila studied Vince carefully. Without knowing why, she knew he could be trusted to keep his word. Finally, she nodded in assent.

"OK," he said, offering his hand. She shook it in a firm grip. "But wait a minute," he continued. "Rochelle told me this system was Luco Parisi's very own brainchild. That it was installed to help control costs. But he's the president of the bank?! Why would he subject himself to such controls?"

"He wouldn't," she said.

"You did it against his orders?!" Vince said with raised eyebrows.

"No, I didn't! It wasn't like that. When they told me to set up the system, they never told me they wanted to block out any phones so I did all of them. Later they gave me a list of phones to be excluded. By that time I had already completed the installation. I guess I did the job a lot faster than they thought it could be done."

"Would it have been difficult to delete those phones from the system?"

"No. Not at all. It's a lot more complicated loading them than deleting them. That's why I kept them in. I thought they might want to add them back in later, so instead of killing them, I bracketed them with macros that hide them in the background."

"Meaning?"

"Meaning, without the password that I buried in those macros, the screen display skips past those files as though they don't exist."

"And you're the only one who knows the password." He said it as a statement, not a question.

She nodded her head. "If I get run over by a truck, those files will be lost forever," she said with a self-conscious grin.

Vince couldn't suppress a chuckle as he said, "Well Sheila, before you go out and play in the traffic, suppose you tap in that password. Let's see who Mr. Parisi has been talking to."

He pulled another chair alongside hers and watched as she typed in a series of commands. When the question, "What is the current password?" appeared on the screen, she typed it in. He focused on her fingers but they were too fast for him to follow. The screen displayed a row of four asterisks. Though he had been unable to make out the password by watching her fingers as she typed, he smiled inwardly that the number of asterisks equaled the number of characters in Luco.

Sheila pressed ENTER then PAGE DOWN. The screen filled with data.

PARISI, LUCO X-PVT

JANUARY 1990

08	49-911-53-10-272	0916	:01	UNKNOWN NAME
08	49-911-53-10-272	0921	:19	UNKNOWN NAME
08	508-321-6930	1037	:12	COLUMBIA ELECTRONI
08	401-795-0303	1348	:44	GOYETTE, RENÉ
09	49-911-53-10-272	0928	:14	UNKNOWN NAME
09	212-536-5800	1407	:16	MERCANTILE BANK OF
10	41-61-302-95-11	1001	:31	UNKNOWN NAME
10	802-597-8543	1137	:27	LAKE FABRICATORS
10	49-911-53-10-272	1356	:02	UNKNOWN NAME
10	49-911-53-64-347	1400	:02	UNKNOWN NAME
10	49-911-53-64-347	1603	:34	UNKNOWN NAME

11	401-728-7000	0902	:02	GOYETTE PROPERTIES
11	401-795-0303	0905	:01	GOYETTE, RENÉ
11	41-61-302-95-11	0921	:31	UNKNOWN NAME
11	407-435-7600	1114	:28	FIRST NATIONAL BAN
11	401-728-7000	1356	:02	GOYETTE PROPERTIES
11	401-728-7000	1409	:21	GOYETTE PROPERTIES

Vince's attention focused immediately on the phone numbers with the 49 and 41 prefixes that he recognized as the country codes for Germany and Switzerland. He asked, "Does the system show 'unknown name' for all international calls?"

"In Mr. Parisi's data file it does," she replied. "For anyone else, whenever an unidentified number shows up, that caller has to furnish the ID for that number to his supervisor. The supervisor would determine if it was business related or not. If yes, the ID would be entered into the data base and would automatically show up on-screen whenever that number is called. If not, it would be displayed as a personal call. But as I said, Mr. Parisi didn't know about this file and I sure wasn't going to ask him to fill in any blanks."

"OK, Sheila, let's jump ahead to present date and work back from there."

She pressed CONTROL - END and, in an instant, a new screen appeared. He asked Sheila to search backwards. As she did, one screen at a time, a pattern began to emerge. Certain international numbers appeared regularly. One number in particular, a German number, appeared almost every day, often more than once each day and often around the same time of day.

The chirp of Sheila's telephone disrupted his concentration.

She answered, listened and returned it to its cradle. "That was Rochelle. There was a call for you. A Mr. Caputo? He wants you to call him."

Vince marveled at Rico's uncanny ability to track him down. He asked Sheila to print out the thirty days preceding Luco's last day in the office. After again reassuring her that he would not compromise her position, he thanked her and left.

"I'M ON MY WAY TO Martella's-On-the-Hill, Rico," Vince interrupted. "My father and Mr. Lanieri are meeting me for lunch. Why not join us? You can tell me the rest of it over the pasta-e-fagioli."

"Naw, Cenzo, I wish I could. Their pasta-e-fagioli's even better than mine's, but I gotta guy that's out and I gotta mind the place."

"Too bad. OK, so go ahead, when did it happen?"

"I dunno for sure. A week ago. Maybe a week-an'-a-half. Anyhow, he shows up for work one day lookin' like Max Schmelling after his second go with Louis."

"Maybe he was mugged."

"Mugged?!" Rico laughed. "Not a chance. I told you, Bagnatore's been all over the lot tryin' to get a lead on Parisi. Talkin' to everyone knows him. He's got these two specialists do his heavy work for him. An ex-pug named Rocky Jordan and his nutty girlfriend. What I hear she enjoys the work so much she'd do it for nuthin'. How many muggin's you heard of they bust a guy's ribs and then they snap his little finger?

"Anyhow, Mickey Hoban's the closest thing to a friend that Parisi has so I figure there's gotta be some kinda connection. But Hoban turned into a clam. He's not sayin' nuthin' to nobody. Tell you the truth, take one look at him you gotta understand why."

"OK. Thanks, Rico," said Vince as he waited for a break in the Atwells Avenue traffic to let him turn into the restaurant's parking lot, "Sure you won't join us?"

"Can't do it, old friend. Catch y' next time."

"SO WHAT ARE YOU getting worked up about?" Lorenzo asked. "You're not even sure it was Tubby Bagnatore that did it, but if it was, *figlio mi'*, you want to stay out of it."

"Lorenzo's right, Cenzo," said Pierino. He held his voice down and looked to both sides before continuing, "Tubby Bagnatore is an animal. He's dirt. A disgrace to our heritage. Whether or not he had cause to do this thing to Mickey Hoban, we may never know. But if he did it, you can be sure of this, he had what *he* thought was a reason. Cenzo, promise me you won't cross his path. I've seen his kind before. He is not a man to provoke." Pierino squeezed Vince's forearm. "Promise me, Cenzo."

Vince patted his father's hand, and making eye-contact first with Lorenzo then with his father, he said, "OK, pa, don't worry. I promise I won't make Tubby Bagnatore mad enough to hurt me."

"What the hell kind of a half-assed promise is that?" Lorenzo fired back. His words carried just enough heat to draw glances from neighboring tables. "How the hell will you know how much is enough for that madman? How will you know when just enough is in danger of becoming too much?"

"Take it easy, Mr. Lanieri," Vince said softly as he picked up the wine bottle. He topped-off Lorenzo's glass and his father's, slowly and deliberately, to restore calm and to recede from the attention of the other patrons.

"Why do you even care about what happened?" Pierino demanded. He spoke quietly but the tightness in his voice made it clear to Vince that his father was just as hot as Lorenzo was. "You hardly know that Hoban fellow. Did you ever go to his house for dinner? No. Did you play golf, or tennis, or anything else with him? No. Did your wives play cards together? Did they get their nails done together? Call each other on the phone? No. You bump into him at wakes and weddings and that's all. You don't count him as one of your friends."

"I can't dispute that, Pa, but I'm convinced there's a connection between Mickey Hoban and Luco Parisi and this whole situation with Greater Providence."

"So what if there is, Cenzo," this time Lorenzo spoke at a level that only Vince and Pierino could hear. "You're what … you just turned fifty-three? You're a rich man. You live where you can play golf in the sunshine all year. You got a great wife she makes big bucks on her own. You fly back and forth in your own airplane like Naples was in Narragansett. You made it through a heart attack and now you're in great shape. Enjoy your life! What the hell do you care about Greater Providence or where Luco is? That's their problem! Not yours."

"Our friend is right again, Cenzo," said Pierino, "and he gives you the advice of someone who loves you as his own son." He looked a long time at his son before continuing. "But, there's more, isn't there? Something more compelling than anything we can say to you."

"Yeah, pa, there's more. Greater Providence got its start in the back room of a barber shop. Your father's shop, Mr. Lanieri. It was on Giuseppe's honor and reputation that it grew to what it is. Now, Greater Providence might be forced to close its doors forever. Businesses will shut down. People will lose their jobs. Even if the bank reopens, it will be with a permanent stain on its reputation, the reputation that was built on Giuseppe's name. And it all stems from his own son. That … what did you call him, pa? … that aberration … Luco. I'm going to find him."

"And when you find him," said Pierino, "what will you do then? You have no legal power. You have no authority over him. What can you hope to accomplish?"

"Revenge!" said Vince. The word shot from his lips before he realized it, bringing a look of dismay from his father and their friend. "No, don't worry, pa. I'm not going to beat him up, though such an idea does appeal to me. I haven't sorted it out yet, but in some way, I'm going to make that miserable bastard sorry he did this."

There was no mistaking the finality in Vince's tone. Lorenzo and Pierino, recognizing the futility of saying anything further to try to dissuade Vince, said nothing.

From across the room, the owner, Mr. Martella, noticed the lull in their conversation. He took that opportunity to approach their table to refill their wine glasses. Vince placed his hand over his glass and in an attempt to lighten the mood, said, "Not for me, Mr. Martella, but I'll take an espresso when these two kids are ready for theirs."

Recognizing his son's signal, Pierino forced a measure of good humor into his words. "Well you can fill ours, Mr. Martella," he said, wagging his finger first at Lorenzo's glass then his own, "we don't have to fly anywhere."

How strangely elegant, Vince thought. His father and Lorenzo have been coming to Martella's-On-the-Hill for over thirty years and it's still Mister Bonetta, Mister Lanieri and Mister Martella.

"I take it you'll be heading back to Naples again, Mr. Bonetta?" Martella addressed Vince while pouring the wine.

"Right after the espresso, Mr. Martella," said Vince with a nod of his head. "And thanks for another perfect table. The veal steak was made in heaven, the pasta-e-fagioli was, as always, world-class, and tell Vito he should apply for a patent on his Caesar salad."

"Hear, hear!" Lorenzo and Pierino said in unison, bringing their glasses together. Their somber mood retreated into the shadows of their earlier conversation.

THIRTY

Naples

VINCE AND GÜNTER had drifted away unnoticed from the lanai where one of Gabriele's famous dinner party evenings was revving up over cocktails and hors d'oeuvres around the pool. Margrit and Günter would leave the following day to return to Germany. Gabriele and Vince had invited some close friends and a few professional and business people that they wanted to bring together with the Lehmanns.

In the privacy of Vince's second-floor study, behind closed doors, he and Günter clinked their glasses. *"Zum Wohl!—Cent' anni!"*

Earlier, before the first guests arrived, Günter had agreed to help Vince try to find Luco. With his newspaper's reporting staff, his own detective force in *Die Kripo*, and his contacts on *Das Landeskriminalamt*, the state police, his investigative resources were formidable. Günter assured Vince that he would use whatever resources were necessary, albeit in an unofficial capacity. If Luco Parisi were in Germany, his people would find him.

Vince handed Günter a recent photo of Luco. He had taken it from the credenza behind Luco's desk. He also gave him a copy of the printout of Luco's telephone activity that Sheila had given him. As they sipped their drinks, Günter listened without comment, looking at the photo of Luco while Vince described the long-standing relationship between Luco Parisi and Phil Peters. He told of Luco's bitter envy of Phil, how it began in their youth as promising baseball players and festered through their college years at Brown, ultimately to drive them apart. Vince told Günter of the episode between Luco Parisi and Marla and how Phil Peter's very direct handling of it had driven the final wedge between them.

"So OK, Vince," said Günter, "this man Luco Parisi ... we agree he is not a nice man. But can a bank be closed in your country only because its president is mean and vindictive?" His crooked grin made it clear he knew otherwise.

"No, of course not, Günter," Vince grinned back. "Luco committed bank fraud. I don't know the details of how he did it, but it was bank fraud. Big time. Big enough to bring the bank down. I just wanted you to have a feel for the kind of man you'll be looking for."

"Assuming, of course, you are correct that he is in Germany."

"I think after you've studied his telephone records you'll come to the same conclusion."

There was a polite knock. Before Vince could respond, the door opened briskly. Gabriele entered just as briskly, her form-fitting gold lamé cocktail dress highlighting her curves and accenting the sensuous motion of her hips. They rose as she approached. Though she wore a smile, Vince and Günter recognized the smoldering fire in her eyes, an unmistakable sign that they had been absent from the party too long.

She started to speak, but before she could utter a word, Vince said with mock solemnity, "Let me save you the trouble, my love. I know what you're thinking and you're right. We're a pair of selfish, ill-mannered, insensitive louts. We are unworthy of the love and devotion that you and Margrit so selflessly shower upon us. Honor leaves us no alternative."

He pointed a forefinger dramatically into the air and continued in a rising, theatrical tone, "Let us away to the garage, Günter, my friend! There's a container of gasoline! We must immolate ourselves without delay!"

Gabriele was unable to sustain her anger. With a sparkle in her gray-blue eyes, she playfully jabbed her elbow into Vince's ribs and said, "If you do, you big dope, let me be the one to strike the match." Then she pressed her hand gently against his cheek in a sign that all was forgiven.

"I'm sorry, baby," said Vince. He turned and kissed the palm of her hand. "I lost track of the time."

She leaned against him and kissed him back. On the lips. Briefly, softly. A friendly kiss, with her lips only slightly parted and her eyes looking directly into his. Something warm and personal passed between them. Günter cleared his throat, said quietly, "Perhaps I must excuse myself," and started for the door.

"No, Günter. Wait." Gabriele separated herself from Vince and slipped back into party mode. "I came up here to tell you that Trent Thomas has arrived."

"Thomas?" asked Günter looking from one to the other. "I didn't know he would be here. Could this mean he is still interested?"

"Oh I'm sure that dirty old man is interested in *something*, Günter," she said with a coquettish jiggle of her shoulders and breasts. "When I left him, he was drooling into the top of your wife's dress." Taking both their arms, she herded them back to the party.

TRENT THOMAS WAS SOLE OWNER and publisher of Golf-On-the-Gulf, a life-style magazine featuring golf course communities from Key West to Pensacola. Over cocktails after a round of golf several months ago, Thomas made his first mention of retirement. He was tired of business and had all the money he would ever need. He announced without preamble to Vince, "It would be first rate, don't you see, to occupy myself only with golfing, sailing and drinking rum Collinses." Then as an afterthought, with added emphasis, he finished with, "And for the rest of my days, enjoying the sexual ministrations each night of a different young maiden whose age must not be a day over twenty-two."

Thomas got married when he was nineteen. He soon learned that he couldn't bear the thought of going to bed with the same woman every night. It lasted three weeks. He never remarried. Vince didn't doubt for a minute that Thomas, though he was 62, was serious about his fantasy.

With each cocktail, his manner of speech became more British. That was odd, since Thomas was made in the USA and had never left its shores. Born in Bayonne, New Jersey, he grew up in Hackensack and went to high school, his highest level of education, in Hoboken. Though he had never held what could be called full-time employment, he was a born entrepreneur. He possessed unerring instincts to spot an opportunity to turn a profit and the invaluable ability to wangle himself into situations that would ultimately pay off. After each payoff, inevitably, he would lose interest and would again sniff the trails for the next opportunity.

Over the years, his deals grew ever larger and his wherewithal multiplied to substantial proportions. After buying Golf-On-the-Gulf for a song, he broke tradition by actually working at running the business. He had to. The previous owner had left him with a staff that was hobbled by incompetents. Now, nearly two years later, he had a magazine that could run very well without his help. But the long hours and the exhilaration of the challenge had worn off. Without realizing it, he was again sniffing the trails. Vince asked him if selling Golf-On-the-Gulf might interest him. When he answered that he might consider it, Vince put him together with Günter.

Margrit rolled her eyes at them over Thomas' shoulder as they approached. He didn't notice. He held his head bowed forward to gain an advantageous view into her delectable décolletage.

"Trent Thomas, how good to see you," said Günter, coming up behind him.

"Günter, old sock," said Thomas, tearing his eyes reluctantly from Margrit's impressive cleavage. He was on his third rum Collins. He turned to one side to greet Günter and Vince while, at the same time, moving closer to Margrit to enhance his vantage point in relation to her bust. "How could you have left this lovely thing unattended for so long?" he said. Though he turned to Margrit, his eyes were downcast to capture the view into her dress. He continued brightly, "But, not to worry, old man. I've been standing guard,"—he pronounced it *bean*, not *been*—"manning the ramparts. She's been in my capable hands. Oh dear, I say old sport, only in a manner of speaking of course!"

"Of course," Günter said. Then by prearrangement, Gabriele stepped between Thomas and Margrit, and taking her arm, said, "If you gentlemen will excuse us, Margrit and I must attend to something in the kitchen." Vince excused himself, leaving Günter and Thomas to talk in privacy.

AFTER SAYING GOODNIGHT TO the last departing guest, they turned off all the lights except the underwater light. Sitting on the lanai in the silent pleasure of one another's presence, they listened to the haunting sounds of the night creatures. After several minutes, Vince was first to speak.

"He's there, Günter." He said it softly, so as not to destroy the mood. "Everything points to it. The call sheets. The mysterious calls from that woman, Erika."

"If he is there, Vince, we will find him." Günter had been on the same wavelength. "But then what? If he breaks no German law, I cannot arrest him. What will you have me do when I find him?"

"I've given this some thought, Günter. Here's what I propose."

Vince laid out the essence of his scheme to the astonishment and occasional giggles of Gabriele and Margrit. Günter listened carefully. He saw stumbling blocks that only a policeman could see and he worked out steps to bypass them. He pointed out weak spots and suggested ways to strengthen them. Together they devised strategies to cover points that Vince had overlooked. When they were finished, they knew they had a plan.

THIRTY-ONE

Basel, Switzerland

IT WAS A DISMAL, GRAY DAY, with the kind of misting rain and stale air that often lasted days at a time. But, for Erika Böhringer, it was more than that. It was the people. Seldom cheerful and outgoing, as were the people in her native Nürnberg, she found that many Baslers on such a day seemed to absorb the dreariness of the weather into their personalities. They even dressed that way, wearing garments of uninspired design in barren blacks, ghastly grays and boring browns—even on the brightest days. It's as though, she thought, they were reluctant to wear something bright and colorful, fearful that doing so might dispel their gloom and strip them of their excuse to be humorless and impolite.

Especially as they were to Germans. And most especially as they were to a young German woman who married a handsome Basler, moved to Basel, and joyfully sought to make a new life there. Until her handsome Basler husband grew tired of her bed. When it became apparent that he was intent on making his way through the seemingly endless supply of waitresses, nurses, secretaries and neglected housewives, she left him and returned to Nürnberg. There was nothing, absolutely nothing about Basel that gave Erika a good feeling.

The big, black Mercedes glided to a stop with no hint of a lurch. Reiner, her driver for the last eight years, was totally solicitous of her comfort and safety. He reached for the umbrella on the front seat, went quickly around to open the right rear door and guided her under the umbrella to the main entrance. Engraved in the granite header over the door was the name SCHWEIZER NATIONAL BANK.

All eyes followed Erika as she walked briskly across the main lobby carrying a black leather briefcase. She went directly to the first unoccupied person she saw, a teller.

The thirtyish teller, bespectacled and prematurely balding, had been counting a stack of bills when Erika entered the bank but lost himself in mid-count at first sight of her. He couldn't take his eyes off her and looked on in ecstatic disbelief that she was approaching him. In a voice that was at once deep and velvet-smooth, she asked him for directions to Herrn Stöpsel's office.

"Herr Stöpsel?" the teller asked weakly, for all the world as though the name were unknown to him. Never in his life had a woman so elegant as this one looked so openly into his eyes. He shook his head in a feeble but unsuccessful attempt to wrest his eyes from hers. He murmured again, "Herr Stöpsel?" unable to fathom why such a simple request caused him such bewilderment. Finally, wrenching himself out of his trance, it came to him, "Ach, Ja! Herr Stöpsel! What have I been thinking? There!" he pointed to an archway leading to a corridor, "Go to the end on the right side."

She was amused, though pleased, as always. She had enjoyed such a reaction many times. Thanking the teller, she cast him a teasing glance then turned and walked away from him, employing greater-than-normal hip motion for him to savor. He pushed up on his toes and leaned over the counter with his head through the teller's window to gain an unobstructed view of her oscillating derriere. Even after it disappeared through the archway, he remained poised in that position, lost in his reverie.

Deep in the background of his mind, he became aware of a tapping sound. It grew louder. He turned to the front and in an instant, every trace of the vision of Erika vanished.

He found himself face-to-face with a customer. She had come unnoticed to his window as Erika walked away, and in time to witness the teller's reaction. She was gray-haired, dressed head-to-toe in faded black, and grossly overweight. Her chin and upper lip were covered with conspicuous facial hair and she was rapping her knuckles on his counter. Finally having gained his attention, she shoved her papers at him and snarled through tobacco-stained teeth, "You are a fool to gape at that one. You have no chance! Get back to business!"

LARGE, BLACK TYPE, ENGRAVED in a polished brass nameplate, spelled out KURT STÖPSEL with his title, *Generaldirektor*, under his name in smaller type. A smaller plate below that one bore the name ILSE BETZGER and her title, *Sekretärin*. The instant Erika entered through the ornately paneled door, a scratchy, high-pitched voice demanded, "Ja?" It came from the mirthless, chalk-white face of a woman with jet black hair that was pulled back into a tight bun, and high, wide cheekbones that cast shadows into the hollows of her cadaverous cheeks. She peered up at Erika with eyes that were grotesquely distorted through thick-lensed, black-rimmed glasses. She looked like a black and white line drawing, Erika mused.

With her head turned toward Erika and her hands poised motionless over the keyboard of her word processor, she repeated, this time with more force, "Ja?!"

Erika said, "I wish to see Herrn Stöpsel, please," as she extended her calling card.

Frau Betzger took the card, glanced at it without moving her head and ran a finger down the page of what was apparently an appointment book. She said, "You have no appointment."

"You are quite right, Frau Betzger." Erika forced herself to smile and to speak in a cordial tone. "Please tell him I wish to see him."

"What is the nature of your business with Herrn Stöpsel?"

"I will be happy to explain the nature of my business," Erika's smile tightened as did her voice, " ... to Herrn Stöpsel."

"Herr Stöpsel is very occupied," she started to hand the card back to Erika but the look of challenge on Erika's face changed her mind, " ... but, very well." She rose and stalked toward Stöpsel's office, coming to a halt at his door. She looked at it for a few seconds, then knocked tentatively. There was a muffled response. She entered but failed to close the door behind her. Erika was unable to hear what Betzger told him but Stöpsel's response was clear. His tone was coarse and rude.

"Böhringer? Böhringer?! I know no one by that name. Why do you disturb me with this? Have you no concept of priorities? Are you so inept that you cannot handle such a simple matter?! Do not bother me with such trivialities! Tell her to make an appointment."

He dismissed her with a condescending, backhanded wave of his hand.

Frau Betzger returned to the outer office red-faced and with downcast eyes. She was mortified. Her autocratic bearing crumbled. Erika felt embarrassed for her. "I'm so sorry, Frau Betzger," she said. "I didn't realize he was such a … that he was so … I couldn't avoid hearing."

Frau Betzger was touched. "Thank you, Frau Böhringer. You are very kind."

"Perhaps I should have given you this before you went in." Erika held out a small, white envelope? "I assure you, it is important. He will want to see this."

Concealed inside the envelope was half of a sheet of paper that had been torn in two. When mated with the other half, the handwritten message would read, "This will introduce Erika Böhringer of Nürnberg. She is authorized to act as my proxy in all matters regarding my account in Die Schweizer National Bank." The outside of the sealed envelope said in bold, red letters, "Privat—Kurt Stöpsel—Privat."

The note was dated two months earlier when Stöpsel last met with Parisi. They had agreed on the wording over cocktails at the beachfront tiki bar of the Naples Beach Club while waiting for the girlfriends they had hired for the evening. Luco had written it in his own hand, leaving a blank space in which he would later enter Erika's name, on a sheet of Beach Club courtesy stationery provided by a waiter. It was signed by Luco Parisi and witnessed by Kurt Stöpsel. Luco had torn it in two, retained the half that would bear the name of his proxy, and gave the other half to Stöpsel.

Frau Betzger took the envelope from Erika and looked at it for a long moment, weighing whether she should chance going in there again. Finally, she straightened, threw her shoulders back, and marched to Stöpsel's door. This time, she knocked assertively and entered without waiting for a response, again leaving the door open.

In a moment, Erika heard the tearing sound of the envelope being opened. A moment later, she heard him say in an annoyed tone, "Do people not make appointments in Germany? Have they no culture? I suppose I'll have to see her. Send her in."

Frau Betzger ushered her in and announced her. Stöpsel didn't look up. Instead, he acknowledged the announcement with a grunt as he busied himself with some papers on his desk. Betzger exchanged a glance with Erika, then left without another word, closing the door behind her.

"Ja, ja, please be seated," he said impatiently with a careless wave of his hand as he continued to study the papers before him. Erika made no move to take a seat. Instead, she remained standing just inside the door, one hand holding her briefcase, the other defiantly on her hip.

In a conspicuous display of idly tidying up his desk, Stöpsel said with pompous authority, "My schedule is full, but I suppose a few minutes won't … ," when at last he looked up. He was speechless. He had no idea Luco Parisi's proxy would be so ravishing. He drank in the vision in one gluttonous draft.

He rose unsteadily to his feet, his frenetic gaze sweeping her repeatedly from top to bottom and back. He careened around the corner of his desk and scurried to her.

"Frau Böhringer, how delightful to meet you!" He gushed. Bowing slightly, he grasped her free hand and brought it to his lips. "I'm so sorry Frau Betzger kept you waiting. She should have brought you right in."

"Really, Herr Stöpsel?" She held her head high and looked down her nose. Her tone was icily brittle as she withdrew her hand from his grasp. "Perhaps you should commend her. After all, she was merely shielding you from yet another … uncultured German?"

It took a moment to register. When it did, he said contritely, "My regrettable comment was not meant for your ears. It was unforgivable."

She looked at him coldly for several seconds, then simply nodded her head in tacit dismissal of the need for any further mention of it.

With a grand sweep of his arm, he ushered her to a seat in front of his desk. As she gracefully lowered herself into the chair, her skirt crept up to an enticing height. Reluctantly he returned to his chair behind the desk from which vantage point, he noted with chagrin, he would be unable to view her succulent thighs.

Erika glanced around the office and observed that the walls were curiously absent of paintings and other works of art. There were, of course, the obligatory, plainly-framed citations and credentials, but there was nothing that would conjure the solemn and dignified image of banking and high finance that one would expect in the office of a high-ranking Swiss bank executive.

Instead, the walls were festooned with photographs of a man with a guitar, wearing a gaudy American cowboy costume, performing before audiences in various settings. The man, whose features were partially obscured in the shadows cast by his broad-brimmed Stetson hat, was vaguely familiar. In several of the photos, the man was posed with an American station wagon that featured an absurd hood ornament.

Suddenly making the connection between the man in the photos and the man sitting across from her, she turned to Stöpsel to find him leering at her.

"My hobby," he said. "I have a loyal following. You must come to one of my concerts." His eyes slowly traced a path over her body as he continued with a leering grin, "I think you would find great pleasure in … my performance."

Erika bristled at the suggestive implications of his comment. She flashed him a withering glance.

"You have compared my half of the note with yours?" she asked in an icy tone that wiped the grin from his face.

He nodded. "It is in order."

Erika placed her briefcase on Stöpsel's desk, dialed the combination and popped the clasps with a loud snap. She removed a single sheet of paper that was encased in a clear vinyl cover and placed it on the desk in front of Stöpsel.

"For several years, you have facilitated the transfer of funds into Mr. Parisi's account in this bank. From time to time you may be asked to transfer funds from this account to another account in another bank. Only Mr. Parisi and I have the authority to make such a request. No one else.

"In the unlikely event that someone else, anyone else, claims to have such authority, that person will be lying. In such case, you are to inform me of the details at once by calling the telephone number shown on that paper. It is a private number, and in my absence, it is a private fax, for my eyes only, so there will be no need for circumspection. Have you any questions before I continue?"

"None, Frau Böhringer," Stöpsel said. "Nothing you have said will present any difficulty."

"An account has been established in Der Raiffeisenbank in Nürnberg," said Erika. "You will find the account number and the identification code on that paper. At present, that account is barren. We will need a small amount transferred immediately for ordinary conveniences. How soon can you transfer 200,000 Deutschmark?"

"That amount will be in the Raiffeisenbank account long before you return to Nürnberg, Frau Böhringer," he answered with a smug, condescending smirk.

"Very well, then," she said. As she started to get up, Stöpsel rose swiftly to his feet, partly out of courtesy but mostly so he would have a view as she uncrossed her legs. He was not disappointed.

He strutted with shameless ego as he proudly escorted her down the corridor and through the main lobby, pretending not to notice the heads that turned in admiring appraisal of Erika. He opened the door and held it for her, but he stood in the doorway, blocking her passage.

He said, "I regret my earlier indiscretion, Frau Böhringer. Perhaps I can make it up to you. It's almost time for lunch. I would be honored if you would join me. It would be an opportunity for us to get to know each other," he paused as he once again rubbed his gaze over the entire length of her body, letting it come to rest on her bosom, " ... personally."

Reiner, Erika's driver, had seen them come to the door and was making his way toward her with his umbrella when he saw them come to a sudden stop. He also saw the annoyed look on her face when she turned to the man who was with her. He reached them in time to hear her say, "I already know you, Herr Stöpsel. Better, perhaps, than you would like to think. Certainly better than I want to. Now, please step aside."

Her sharp tone filled in the blanks for Reiner, who sensed the essence of what had taken place. He towered over Stöpsel. With his eyes glaring menacingly at him, he said, "Is there something you would like me to do, Frau Böhringer? Anything?"

After a meditative pause, she slowly shook her head. Then she spun, took Reiner's arm and never looked back. As she slipped into the back seat of the Mercedes, Reiner turned in time to see Stöpsel fling the door open and storm back into the bank.

THIRTY-TWO

Naples

VINCE CAME IN from the lanai to answer the phone but a familiar voice from the TV stopped him in his tracks as he passed.

> " … has impounded its records and State Police have sealed off the premises. When reached only minutes ago, the Attorney General would neither confirm nor deny that further indictments of RISDIC officials are imminent."

Clutching the microphone with both hands, she wore big, woolly mittens in bright, Christmas colors with a matching wool cap pulled over her ears. Swirling snow accumulated quickly on the shoulders of her down-filled, nylon ski jacket. She wore it with its broad collar turned up around her neck and cheeks. Her breath made frosted puffs in the air as she signed off.

> "From the steps of the capitol building in Providence, Rhode Island, this is Laramie Duquette, PROV-TV News."

He picked up the ringing phone. Still fully distracted by what he had just heard, he answered absently, "Merry Christmas." He turned off the TV from the remote but remained transfixed with his gaze on the blank screen while he tried to sort out what Duquette had just reported. The early arrivals were on the lanai getting a quick start for the evening and their party noise drowned out the voice on the phone that repeated, louder this time, "*Buon Natal*, old friend!"

"Rico? Is that you?!" The smile was clear in Vince's voice. He pressed the phone hard against his ear and placed his hand over his other ear.

"Yeah, Cenzo, it's me," said Rico in wonderment at the background noise. "But it ain't even seven o'clock yet for crisake. What the hell time you guys start your parties down there in Naples?"

"Rico, hang on. I can't hear you. I'm going to put you on hold and take this upstairs in my office." Vince pressed the hold button and bounded up the staircase to his study.

It had become something of a tradition for Vince and Gabriele and their friends, many of them Germans who had bought vacation homes from Gabriele. They planned their winter vacations around the Christmas holidays and looked forward happily to her annual Christmas Eve party. Every year, she tells them eight o'clock and every year they begin to wander in at six-thirty. It doesn't matter. She's always so eager to get started herself that she's ready for them by five. They love it and Gabriele loves doing it, though Vince much prefers smaller, more intimate gatherings.

"OK, Rico, I'm back," Vince said, slouching down into his chair, grateful for these few minutes of peace and quiet.

"Yeah, Cenzo, that's better." With no further concession to pleasantries, Rico continued, "Anyhow, you know that Duquette broad on PROV-TV? Well she just went national. Would you believe it? She made the NBC Six O'Clock News. You seen it?"

"Just the tail end. Has someone been indicted?"

"Yeah. Guy named Steinwand."

"Herbert R. Steinwand?!" Vince sat upright in amazement.

"You know this guy?"

"Not personally. But I know who he is. He's the chairman of RISDIC for God's sake! What the hell's going on?"

"He's also president of Meshanticut Bank & Trust," said Rico. "Anyhow, the Attorney General claims he's been shaving Meshanticut's premium payments big time."

"Steinwand?!" Vince was incredulous.

"Yeah. Everybody figured him to be Mister freakin' Clean. And he ain't the only one. Anyhow, word on the street is some of the other esteemed members of RISDIC's board of directors are gonna be collared real soon. Jerry LaFollette, the top honcho at Lincoln Valley Credit Union, Eban Tulle at Westminster Trust, Barry Weiser at Puritan-Hope Bank ... and you ready for this? ... your old pal Luco Parisi of Greater Providence Bank & Trust. If they can find him."

Providence

LARAMIE DUQUETTE WAS NOTHING if not persistent. When Greater Providence closed its doors in August, she saw something more sinister in the unexplained disappearance of its president than the press was being led to believe. Refusing all interviews, Howard Pastore, the acting president, issued sporadic press releases that, when stripped of their expressions of concern for Parisi's well-being and of consolation and hope for his family, were void of substance.

Tracing a path through Parisi's family ties, Duquette sensed that she had struck paydirt when she stumbled upon Mickey Hoban. Fresh from his 'conference' with Tubby Bagnatore, Rocky Jordan and Chetta Lograno, his face was battered and stitched, his left hand wore a cast.

She was there when he emerged from his home and made his way toward the curb where a taxi waited for him. He moved slowly, with tentative steps, half-stooped over in obvious pain. She wondered why the woman, apparently his wife, who was standing in the open doorway wearing a shortie house robe, didn't help him to the cab. The woman gave Duquette an appraising top to bottom once over and a defiant scowl came over her face.

Duquette approached and met Mickey when he was halfway down the front walk, introducing herself in a tone loud enough for the woman to hear, "Good Morning, Mr. Hoban. I'm Laramie Duquette, PROV-TV News."

"Sure an' I know who you are, lass" he said softly. "Top o' the marnin' to y'," In spite of his pain, laugh wrinkles formed as his light blue eyes shone with a spark of mischief.

Duquette melted. She gently took one of his arms and said, "Here, let me help you." The woman in the doorway spun, went into the house and slammed the door. Duquette's eyes held his.

"Would you believe I stepped on a bar of soap?" he replied, in answer to her unspoken question.

"Of course not," she laughed.

"Then darlin,' if you don't ask the question, I won't have to lie to y', will I? Look, I don't have to be a genius to figure out why you're here but there's nothing I can say to you that I want to hear on the eleven o'clock news." He had abandoned his Irish lilt for the last of it but his tone remained polite and gentle.

"Look around, Mr. Hoban," she said with a sweep of her arm. "There's no camera crew. I'm here by myself. I swear to you, I will not reveal anything you tell me without your specific approval. Let me drive you to your office. Please."

Mickey hesitated and glanced at the cabby who was watching them with undisguised impatience.

"Wait right here," she said. Reaching into her shoulder bag, she scurried to the cab and handed the driver a bill through the right side window. It must have been a big one, Mickey thought, judging from the smile on the cabby's face as he pulled away.

The drive into the city was not a long one. To stretch it out, Duquette avoided the expressway, deliberately creeping along on the traffic-laden city streets. After a tentative moment, Mickey started it off by saying, "You probably know more about Greater Providence than I do, and before you ask, I don't have a clue as to where Luco Parisi is."

There was no way he was going to even hint at the scam he and Luco had been running. He was sure it would all come out soon enough but he wasn't going to make it easy by blabbing about it. Especially to a reporter.

On the other hand, he had nothing to do with the RISDIC scam that Tubby had ranted about. If he could send Duquette off in that direction, maybe she would focus on RISDIC and some of the heat might be taken off the closing of Greater Providence.

"This whole mess was as much RISDIC's fault as it was the banks'," he began. "RISDIC was supposed to be a state-run version of the FDIC, the Federal Deposit Insurance Corporation. They would collect premiums from the banks and credit unions and, in return, they would insure the bank customers' deposits. It was a good idea that had the misfortune of being created by politicians. By the time its final draft was approved by the General Assembly over twenty years ago, its major flaw had been carved in stone."

"Flaw?" she asked.

"Yeah," said Mickey, chuckling. "You ready for this? RISDIC's board of directors was to be comprised of top executives from its member banks and credit unions."

"What?! Isn't that like ... like ... ?"

"Like the foxes were protecting the chickens?" said Mickey, still amused.

"Yes! I don't believe this."

"Believe it, darlin'. Under its charter, they got to set their own premiums, establish their own rules for payment, conduct their own hearings and assess their own penalties. In short, they would answer to no one but themselves.

"Nothing I've said so far is confidential. Every bit of it is a matter of public record," said Mickey, "but before I get into the juicy part, let's be clear about one thing. I can't reveal how I learned about this and neither can you. Besides, *where* you heard it is meaningless. Unless you investigate it and develop it, it will remain meaningless. But if you do, it has the potential to launch your story into orbit."

"I give you my solemn word, Mr. Hoban. I'll reveal nothing that can in any possible way be traced to you. To eliminate any doubt or any possibility that I might do so inadvertently, I also promise that I'll report nothing before I clear it with you first. Deal?"

She extended her hand.

Mickey looked deeply into her eyes, not reaching for her hand, not even looking at it. She didn't waver. After a long moment, he took her hand.

"Deal," he said in dead seriousness. "OK. I don't have to give you the names of RISDIC's board of directors. It's a matter of public record. You can look it up. You'll find that they're all top officers of the banks they're supposed to be insuring. Here's the part that the public doesn't know. They've been underpaying their premiums since day one. Sometimes they didn't pay them at all. RISDIC has been underfunded for years. Any notion that RISDIC will come to the rescue of Greater Providence Bank & Trust is a pipe dream. As of this moment, RISDIC is incapable of doing what it was created to do, and that is to insure the deposits of the bank's customers."

"That's awful!" she cried. "It can be a financial catastrophe!"

"Yes, it can. But you can't report any of it without betraying my confidence so you'll have to develop the facts for yourself. I'm holding you to your promise not to attribute any of it in any way that can come back to me. I don't think I can handle slipping on another bar of soap. Now, if you don't mind, you can let me off here."

Laramie pulled to the curb and stopped. They were several doors away and around the corner from Mickey's office. She turned to face Mickey directly and said, "I gave my word, Mr. Hoban, and I'll stick by it."

Mickey again studied her eyes. After a moment, he nodded his head and opened the door. He had difficulty getting out of the car. Laramie quickly went around to his side and helped him get to his feet. He leaned heavily on his cane, feeling the pain caused by the exertion. She looked at him intently.

"Can I ask you just one question?" she asked.

"Still the same deal? Off the record?"

"Absolutely. Not long after your wife's uncle disappeared, the bank was vulnerable to a run on deposits. Howard Pastore saw it coming and he closed the bank before it could get started. But he can't keep the bank closed indefinitely. People are clamoring to get at their money. Clearly, Greater Providence is on shaky ground. If you're right and RISDIC truly is an empty shell, what is the likely scenario that will follow?"

Mickey hesitated, then answered with a friendly wink, "I can't answer that, Miss Duquette. I'm just a property appraiser. I don't know any more about the banking business than you do. But I'll make just two points and then I'll ask you to drive away before we're noticed talking together. First of all, though I won't tell you how I know it, I want to assure you that I haven't the slightest doubt about the accuracy of any part of what I just told you."

He hung the cane over his other arm and extended his hand to her. She took it and held on to it.

"You said two points?" she asked.

"If this turns out to be the story I think it can be, remember where you got it." He looked intently at her, squeezed her hand before releasing it, and finished with, "I might need a favor some day. Until then, forget we ever met."

Laramie Duquette then became the moving force behind the investigation into RISDIC. For months she battled against the forces of bureaucratic obstructionism and inertia that tried to keep her away from the records she sought to examine. When, finally, she won a court order giving her full access, she convinced the PROV-TV brass to send in their team of auditors.

By the time she broke her story on PROV-TV, she was too far ahead for the local competition to catch up. Her dogged persistence, combined with her on-screen presence, captured the attention of NBC News. Tonight's broadcast was her first national spot. It was the most exciting Christmas present she ever received.

"WHAT WAS THAT SHE said about the State Police?"

"Yeah, Cenzo. They showed up this morning before RISDIC opened. About a dozen troopers in full uniform. The RISDIC people was gonna work only half-a-day seein's how it's Christmas Eve an' all. Anyhow, except for a couple file clerks and the supervisor with the keys, the troopers sent everyone else home. About 10 o'clock, a whole freakin' army of accountants from Blinkhorn, Blinkhorn & Slattery. You know, that big CPA firm in the Turk's Head Building? They get ushered in by the troopers and they been there all day. On Christmas Eve! What a freakin' bill the State's gonna get for that!"

"Any word from the governor, Rico?"

"Same old double talk. The usual kinda bullshit about 'makin' a full investigation' and 'gettin' to the bottom of this,' " said Rico with a scornful laugh. "Anyhow, in seven days he's out of a job, Cenzo, don'tcha remember? Jeremy Sindauer's our new governor. He inherits this mess, the poor sap. He takes over on the first."

THIRTY-THREE

THE FINAL WEEK OF THE YEAR had been a week to remember. It began on Christmas Eve when Laramie Duquette's bombshell on national TV caught the local broadcast fraternity by surprise. The other stations had been giving only perfunctory coverage over the last few months to the plight of Greater Providence Bank & Trust. They virtually ignored the larger issue of RISDIC's role in the crisis, while Laramie was single-handedly investigating and developing what was destined to become a major story.

After her national exposure on the NBC Six O'Clock News, it became open season on bankers. No executive of any bank could step from his office without having a microphone jammed in his face and being pressed for his comments about the RISDIC indictments and their possible effect on the public. Like fire-ants, every anchorperson in southern New England, as well as one from Poughkeepsie and another from Puerto Rico, swarmed to attack the toe that had disturbed their mound.

Rhosewalla Ortega, news anchor of Channel 6, had fought her way out of the streets of New Bedford and clawed her way to her present position. She was going to make it to the top but she was going to do it her own way. And that way had become her trademark. She spent much of her investigative time studying the daily rituals and movements of her intended subjects so she might pounce on them without warning. Having cornered a subject, she wouldn't jab or feint. She would lead with a roundhouse punch and, in many cases, having been knocked off balance, the subject would counter with admissions that he would later most certainly regret having made.

Of course, Rhosewalla didn't win them all. One such event was when she found herself toe-to-toe with Lilli Siravo, Chief Loan Officer at the headquarters branch of Puritan-Hope Bank in Pawtucket.

Rhosewalla was bent on uncovering an angle on the RISDIC story that she could play off the new governor the minute he took office. He was certain to receive a glut of press coverage and she hoped to use it to her advantage. She knew that Governor Jeremy Sindauer would officially take office the following day and although rumors of further RISDIC indictments persisted, nothing along those lines had yet been uncovered to validate them.

Barry Weiser was Puritan-Hope Bank's top executive. He was also on the board of RISDIC and, according to the rumors, as yet unsubstantiated, he was next to be indicted. With her sights and her hopes focused on the likelihood of the indictments, Rhosewalla had shadowed him over the weekend to be sure he would be available.

It was the last day of the year. No serious business would be done. Coffee, cake, cookies and punch would be offered to customers. Weiser and his executive staff would augment their punch in the privacy of his office and a party atmosphere would prevail until the bank closed at noon. Weiser would be easy prey.

Rhosewalla knew he was in the building because she had followed him there. After he parked his car in his reserved space in the parking lot, locked it and headed for the front entrance, she called the news van from her cell phone to join up with her.

However, reflected in the glass door as he pulled it open, Weiser saw the Channel 6 News Van pull into the parking lot. He hurriedly paged his top officers and took refuge with them in the security office where they huddled around the closed-circuit TV monitors. Weiser turned up the volume as they watched anchorperson Rhosewalla Ortega sweep into the lobby with cameraman and sound-man in tow. They saw her eyes sweep the lobby, taking in the vacant side offices and coming to rest on Lilli, the only person in view who looked important enough to interview.

When Reiser and the others saw Rhosewalla zero in on Lilli, one of the VPs, stifling a laugh, said, "Oh shit, Barry, we couldn't have planned this any better. I almost feel sorry for that broad."

The VP of Marketing, a woman, also fighting down a laugh, said, "Normally I would take exception to your sexist terminology, but not in this case. If ever a broad deserved to be called a broad, it's that Ortega broad."

From a distance, Lilli Siravo looked as though she should be in a Norman Rockwell painting, happily mixing up a bowl of chocolate frosting for the cake that was in the oven, with a half dozen little kids waiting to rub their fingers in the bowl and begging to be the one who gets to lick the spoon. It wasn't until you got up close that you could see the glint of cold steel in her gray eyes and the lapel button she wore that read USMC RETIRED.

She had done thirty years in the Marines including two tours in Korea and two in Vietnam, rising through the enlisted ranks and retiring six years ago at the rank of bird colonel. Though she had adjusted well to civilian life, if there was one thing she wouldn't tolerate, it was incompetence. If you worked for Lilli and you had a job to do, you better damn well do it and do it well. Though she was a model of decorum with customers, when dealing with one of her staff who had run afoul of established procedure, the pungency of her language grew in direct proportion to her displeasure.

Lilli had been in the restroom, didn't hear Weiser's call to take cover, and was returning to her office when she was blindsided by Rhosewalla.

Rhosewalla rushed up to her and snapped in a challenging tone, "Rhosewalla Ortega, Channel 6. And you are?" as she jabbed the mike abruptly toward Lilli's face. The total effect startled Lilli. From her years of hand-to-hand combat training, Lilli's reaction was pure reflex. She spun to confront her adversary head-on. However, when she recognized the situation for what it was, her adrenaline rush turned swiftly to embarrassment. Then to fury!

Lilli retaliated with a swift, menacing finger-thrust that stopped a mere quarter-inch from the tip of Rhosewalla's nose. With lips drawn back, through clenched teeth, she growled a seething, scathing, "You TRY that AGAIN you dumb shit, I'll kick your sorry ass out onto Main Street!"

It was Rhosewalla's turn to be startled. She recoiled backwards half a step, losing her grip on her microphone when she slammed into her sound man whose attention at that moment was focused not on Rhosewalla but on his equipment. The microphone fell to the marble floor, setting up an excruciating feedback in the headset of the sound man.

"AAARRGH!" he yelled in pain, clutching at his headset while he twisted and lurched in a grotesque pirouette. His headset sprang free and his arm shot out, slamming a forearm chop across Rhosewalla's chest. She went down on her ass in a classic pratfall.

The sound man staggered around the lobby doubled over in pain with his hands pressed to his ears.

Rhosewalla sat with legs splayed. "Shit! Shit! Shit!" she hissed again and again.

The cameraman, not one of her biggest fans, couldn't resist the temptation. He held up his thumb to her in the universal symbol of triumph and called out, "Got it, Rhosie!"

The muffled sound of cheering and applause wafted across the lobby from the direction of the security office.

BUT CHRISTMAS WEEK HADN'T ended yet. Partygoers throughout the state of Rhode Island threw themselves with abandon into the spirit of New Year's Eve. The year had been a disaster for many and they were ready to put it out of their minds for a few hours.

For reasons that few people would be able to agree on, Rhode Island's real estate market had suffered a convulsion two years earlier that sent property values into a deep and prolonged decline. Ultimately this drew the attention of federal bank examiners who grew wary of the shortfall between the total debt owed to the banks and the total value of the properties that secured that debt.

Borrowers whose loans were secured by mortgages on their properties, soon found themselves with loan balances that exceeded the reduced value of their mortgaged properties. In banker parlance, such loans were labeled "bad loans."

The bank examiners insisted that the banks immediately improve their loan-to-assets ratios, even if it meant calling in all "bad loans." The banks resisted, reasoning that it was only by esoteric definition that such loans were termed "bad loans." In terms of performance, most borrowers made the payments on those loans, almost without exception, on a timely basis. The banks argued that those loans, therefore, were "good loans" and they should be allowed to stand. They reasoned further that soon, real estate values would recover and all this would be remembered merely as an academic exercise.

The feds turned deaf ears to the banks' argument and forced the banks to comply.

The results were foreseeable. Thousands of homeowners faced foreclosure. Many "good" business loans, secured by mortgages on the business owners' personal homes, went instantly into default when the banks called for immediate payment in full. Borrowers' attempts to pay off the loans by selling the mortgaged properties were futile, the resale value of the properties having been dramatically slashed by the failing real estate market. Dozens of businesses, some of them founded more than a hundred years earlier, closed their doors. Thousands lost their jobs.

It was at the height of all that, that Luco Parisi disappeared without a trace and his bank closed, trapping millions in depositors' funds in a deep-freeze. Now, a week after the media reported the indictment of Herbert R. Steinwand, chairman of RISDIC, no details have yet been made public.

So it was understandable that at bars, clubs, lounges, and private homes throughout the state, with just minutes to go until the year took its final gasp, Rhode Islanders sought release in the revelry of New Year's Eve. With their eyes glued to the TV broadcast of the countdown from New York's Times Square, they tried to shake off the ravages of 1990 and looked to 1991 eagerly, with hope.

They were woefully unprepared for 12:03AM.

In the midst of the bedlam that heralded the new year, hardly anyone noticed that the TV had gone silent and a printed message appeared across its screen. It read,

WE INTERRUPT THIS PROGRAM
FOR AN IMPORTANT ANNOUNCEMENT

A close-up image of the seal of the governor's office appeared with a voice-over that announced,

"Ladies and gentlemen, the governor of the State of Rhode Island, the honorable Jeremy Sindauer."

The scene cut to a shot of the new governor seated behind his desk, flanked by the flags of the United States and the State of Rhode Island. He faced the camera squarely with his arms before him on the desktop, his hands joined with fingers loosely interlaced.

> "My fellow Rhode Islanders. A few minutes ago, the oath of office of governor of our state was administered to me by the honorable Judge Michael J. Feeley. It is with regret that as part of my first official act as governor, I must interrupt your holiday festivities.
>
> "The voluntary closure in August of one of our leading banking institutions, Greater Providence Bank & Trust, was the first in a bizarre chain of events that have dominated the attention of the previous administration. I commend former Governor DiPaolo for his diligence and his timeliness in keeping me informed of every development as it occurred.
>
> "Only twelve hours ago, my closest advisors and I met with Governor DiPaolo and members of his staff to analyze a report that had been completed only minutes earlier. That report summarized the findings of an intensive audit that has been in process around the clock for an entire week. It analyzed its findings in juxtaposition with spot examinations performed since last August by federal banking examiners and how, combined, they bear upon the safety of the funds on deposit in all our banks and credit unions.
>
> "One of the conclusions reached by those findings cannot be contested. It has been determined that the Rhode Island Share & Deposit Indemnity Corporation,

RISDIC, is incapable of performing its chartered function. In plain language, RISDIC is broke. With hard work, sacrifice and a rededication of all our efforts, we confidently hope that this condition can be reversed.

"In the meantime, we are faced with a crisis that demands immediate action. Should a run on deposits take place, and indications over the last several days have shown such an event to be imminent, without a strong and healthy RISDIC, the potential for disaster cannot be ignored.

"Therefore, by executive order, effective immediately, every bank and credit union licensed to function in the State of Rhode Island is hereby closed until further notice. As each institution is examined and is shown to be sound, it will be allowed to reopen.

"Until then, many of you, through no fault of your own, will suffer inconvenience and hardship. This cannot be avoided, and for this I offer you my sincere compassion and my promise that we will work with all possible speed for a return to order and normalcy.

"Again I apologize for being the carrier of such news on New Year's Eve. In a strange way, perhaps these events attach a more meaningful measure of poignancy to my wish to all of you ... to all of us ... for a healthy and happy new year."

THIRTY-FOUR

Nürnberg, Germany

MAX MÜLLER WAS SURPRISED when Günter came personally to him and asked him for his help. He shouldn't have been. The bond that cemented their loyalty and friendship, developed when they partnered together as young detectives, remained unchanged. Though their professional lives drifted apart as Günter's rise to the top gained momentum, their personal relationship continued at the level they had enjoyed as partners. Their difference in rank wasn't a problem for either of them. Though they saw each other infrequently, they continued to enjoy each other's company as though nothing had changed. However, it had soon become apparent, long before Günter became Kriminaldirektor of Die Kripo, that their wives would be unable to deal with the disparity in their husbands stations. Inevitably, unable to mollify their wives' attitudes, he and Günter drifted apart.

Max was older than Günter Lehmann and was genuinely happy for his friend's success. As for himself, he always liked working the streets as a detective. He was good at it and he missed it. Even now, as squad commander, he looked for every opportunity to go out on a case. He made himself available as an eager replacement for any of his cops who had to be out on personal time.

This was the end of the line for Max and he couldn't have been happier about it. He was lacking in the social graces that are so essential to further advancement in these days of political correctness. He was pragmatically aware of that shortcoming and he had neither the inclination nor the desire to change.

This will be " ... an official 'unofficial' investigation," said Günter. "You remember those, Max. We ran a few when we rode together."

"Yeah, Günter, I remember," he answered with a chuckle. "That means we get to do some digging, maybe get our hands dirty, but we don't tell anyone in the department what we're digging for and who told us to start digging."

"I want you to understand, Max," Günter became dead serious, "Die Kripo has no official standing in this matter. The man we're looking for has not even been accused of a crime. If you would rather not do it, I swear to you I'll understand and nothing will change between us."

"Are you kidding, Günter?" Max said with enthusiasm. "I like it already. It'll be a kick working with you again. Sign me on. But what'll I tell that dumb, chicken-shit bastard I work for?"

"I'll talk to him. He won't ask you any questions." Günter knew Max's boss. He considered him an incompetent popinjay and a weak sister in his chain of command. Günter agreed with Max's accurate, if impolitic, assessment. Max's captain would do what he was told and he wouldn't have the balls to ask why.

Getting down to business, Günter continued, "You might need some help. Hand pick two or three people you can depend on. After you talk with them, give me their names. Then I'll talk with your captain."

Neither of them would have used first names and Max would not have referred to his captain in such a manner if anyone else were present. But here, alone together for the first time in years, in the privacy of Max's car, they were old partners again, working on a case. Günter hadn't taken notes when Vince briefed him but he had total recall and was able to repeat every word and every detail. Max interrupted Günter at will as questions popped into his mind. It didn't disturb Günter's flow at all. That's the way they had worked so well together as partners. Günter handed Max the list of calls

Luco had made, and the photo, and told him he was to report directly to him, Günter, day or night, and to nobody else.

After they finished with business, they sat for a few moments without saying a word, just grinning at each other and reading each other's thoughts. Then, with fervent 'let's-get-together' promises that both sadly expected would not be kept, they said their goodbyes.

THIRTY-FIVE

FINDING ERIKA'S SHOP WAS easy. Max had selected several numbers that appeared repeatedly on the printout of Luco's phone calls and faxed them to his contact at the phone company. In minutes, he received a return fax. Some of those numbers were assigned to banks and some to brokerage offices, the types of establishments, Max recognized, that a man in Luco's position would be expected to call in the course of his business. However, the number that appeared with the greatest frequency on Luco's call list was assigned to an entirely different type of establishment. An exclusive, high-fashion, women's boutique.

Max's eyebrows rose expectantly when he read that the name of that shop was Mode-Erika. The tax records at city hall revealed that Mode-Erika was solely owned by one Erika Böhringer, who listed her home address as Kohlbuckweg in Erlenstegen, a fashionable suburb east of the city of Nürnberg.

There was another number that appeared frequently on the list but was not identified by Max's contact at the phone company. Max dialed that number. A male voice answered, "Böhringer."

Max replied, "Sorry. Wrong number," and hung up.

That was enough for Max. He was satisfied. He knew that Luco Parisi, the man in the photo, had placed calls to someone at Mode-Erika though, admittedly, he didn't know to whom. However, he knew that Parisi had also made calls to the unpublished number at Böhringer's home. By all odds, Max thought, Erika Böhringer, the owner of Mode-Erika, had to be the same Erika who repeatedly called Luco Parisi's office in America.

He considered questioning her directly but abandoned that idea after only a moment's reflection. If she was, in fact, the right Erika, and she was, in fact, in contact with Parisi, and did, in fact, know of his whereabouts, so what? To Max's knowledge, she had broken no laws, nor had Parisi. Max held no leverage over her that would compel her to cooperate. He could try to fake her out, but if she wanted to, she could simply tell Max to kiss off and not tell him anything. And if her connection with Parisi was something more than strictly business, social perhaps, or even romantic, any attempt to question her would be certain to sound an alarm to Parisi. There was too little to gain from questioning her, and too much to risk.

Finding Mode-Erika was one thing. Finding Luco Parisi was turning out to be another matter entirely.

MAX HAD RECRUITED TWO bright, young rookies who showed a lot of promise. They were happy to get a chance to work in street clothes and an unmarked car. They had watched Mode-Erika and her house for the last two weeks, but were unable to report anything out of the ordinary. There had been no sign of Luco Parisi. Reiner, Erika's driver, delivered her to her shop every day, arriving precisely at ten, and he fetched her every day precisely at seven.

Today was Max's day off. He was working on his own time. He didn't mind. Ever since that morning when he got home after an all-night stakeout and found a note from his wife that said, "Goodbye—I've had enough," he had nothing better to do. He chuckled as he thought about it now, admitting to himself that, in reality, he likes it better this way.

Max had just devoured several Nürnberger Bratwürste smeared with sinus-clearing horseradish, plus a generous portion of sauerkraut, and was enjoying a Warsteiner beer on the front terrace of the Bratwursthäusle. Across the street, a young man was taking a photo of his wife and two small children. They posed stiffly in front of the Schöne-Brunnen, an ornate bronze fountain that's surrounded by an eight-foot-high, wrought-iron fence. One section of the fence contains a four-inch, solid-gold ring that, according to legend, has the power to grant a wish to any person who rotates it three times in its precisely-grooved tracks.

From his outdoor table on the second-floor terrace, Max looked down at Schöne-Brunnen, standing in the near corner of the Hauptmarkt, a broad, cobble-stoned plaza. A massive cathedral, the Frauen-Kirche, stands two hundred meters distant at the far end of the Hauptmarkt. The huge clock in the soaring steeple of the church told Max that Mode-Erika would close in fifteen minutes.

He refocused his attention on the matter at hand. The reports told him there had been no change of routine during the last two weeks. Every day, Erika's black Mercedes came up Rathausplatz from the right of Max's present position, rolling to a stop in front of Mode-Erika, directly across the street. Every day, Reiner stood by the right rear door of the Mercedes, waiting for Erika to come out of her shop.

Max had sent his two rookies out to Erlenstegen to keep an eye on Erika's house while he watched the shop. He glanced repeatedly at the clock on the church steeple but kept his main focus down the street to the right. When he saw the car slow down as it passed the Hauptmarkt, he knew this day would be different. As was his routine, Reiner came to a stop at Mode-Erika's door, but this time, he wasn't driving a black Mercedes. It was a cream-colored Rolls-Royce. Reiner got out but didn't take up his normal position at the rear door. Instead, he walked directly into the shop.

A gray BMW drove past the Rolls and pulled into a no-parking zone four car-lengths ahead. A young, pretty woman stepped from the right front passenger seat and threaded her way through the traffic, crossing to Max's side of the street. She wore dirty white running shoes, snug-fitting designer jeans, and a blue T-shirt that was unequal to the task of concealing the bounce in her step. Uschi Braun raced up the outside stairs of the Bratwursthäusle two at a time with her long, blond ponytail streaming behind her. When she got to the level where Max sat, she breezed right past him with a tight frown on her face and a tiny, nervous wave of her fingers, and disappeared through the front door.

Max laughed involuntarily, drawing the curious attention of nearby diners. As a young cop, he had done stakeouts with female partners and it all came back to him now. In a very short while, she came out looking far more pleasant and relaxed. When she slid into a seat at Max's table, he was wearing a gleeful smile. She lit a cigarette, took a long drag and said in exasperation, "Do you have any idea, Lieutenant, what it's like to be trapped inside a car with a man who has cast-iron kidneys? God, I had to pee so bad I could taste it. Not only that, he's a goddamm non-smoker."

"Sounds like true love," Max kept his eyes on the Rolls but he was still grinning. "When's the wedding?"

"Oh God no!" she moaned in mock agony. "I'd have to give up smoking and my lungs couldn't stand that kind of shock."

"Look, you want me to talk to him? You shouldn't have to ... "

"NO!" She didn't mean for it to come out so loud. She looked apologetically to the nearby tables. "No, Lieutenant, please don't. It's not that way at all. I'm just having a little fun with you. Gerd is a nice guy and he's a good cop. It's just that I really did have to go so bad and he hasn't taken a leak all damn day! How do men do that?" She didn't really expect an answer to that. She didn't get one.

"You didn't say much on the phone. Bring me up to date," said Max, easing back into business.

"OK. Just when Gerd and I are about ready to give up on the Böhringer house, the Rolls pulls up. It's filthy with road grime. We can't get a clear look at the driver's face through the dirty windows. He rolls his window down and says something to the speakerphone next to the gate.

"Gerd starts to roll but before we get close enough to identify the driver, the gate swings open and he drives inside. He pulls up under the portico and with the shrubbery and all, we still can't get a clear look at the driver.

"The big guy? Frau Böhringer's driver, Reiner? He comes out of the house. The driver of the Rolls gets out and goes into the house. Reiner drives the Rolls around behind the house where it's out of our view. That's when Gerd called you and told you we thought Luco Parisi had just arrived but we couldn't be absolutely certain."

"And we still can't be certain," said Max. "I can't see a thing through those damned smoked-glass windows."

"I know, Lieutenant, but Gerd and I figured the odds were with us. After a couple of hours of no activity, the Rolls comes out from behind the house. It's sparkling clean. The gate swings open and the Rolls pulls out. It's time for Reiner to pick up Frau Böhringer. He's driving and there's a back seat passenger, even if he's only a shadow through that dark glass. That's when I called and said they were heading into the city."

IT HAD BEEN GERD'S TURN at the wheel of the BMW. Every day for the last two weeks, they had followed Frau Böhringer's black Mercedes on the same route into the city. They took Sulzbacherstrasse to Bartholomäusstrasse, following along the north shore of Wöhrder See, a two-mile long lake fed by the Pegnitz River. Crossing on the Adenauer Brücke, the bridge where the Wöhrder See meets the Pegnitz, a sweeping curve to the right put them on Bahnhofstrasse. There they angled off to the right on Marienstrasse and right again on Peter Vischenstrasse. Two more bridges, Hen Brücke and Spital Brücke, took them over the Pegnitz. Then they turned a sharp left around the Heilig Geist Spital, once the Holy Ghost Hospital, now a popular restaurant. A few zigzags later, around the edges of a large area of Old Nürnberg that was open only to foot traffic, they turned right on Rathausplatz at the Hauptmarkt.

WITH HIS ATTENTION RIVETED on the front door of Mode-Erika, Luco Parisi didn't see Uschi get out of the BMW. He first caught sight of her as she made her way through the traffic to cross the street. In an instant, he surveyed every inch of her body. He observed with special approval the ripple of her thigh muscles through her skin-tight jeans as she pranced across the street on the balls of her feet between the passing cars. He caught only a glimpse of her face when she reached the Bratwursthäusle.

As she bounded up its steps, he stared with licentious craving at the marvelous orbs that shaped the seat of her jeans. He wanted her.

When she disappeared inside, he fought off the impulse to go after her. He forced himself to focus on greeting Erika.

Uschi told Max that though they felt confident the subject was Luco Parisi, she and Gerd never got a look at his face. Even as they spoke, she and Max couldn't be sure whom they were looking at through the smoked-glass windows of the Rolls. As they continued to watch, Uschi took a playful, and refreshing, sip from Max's beer just as the lights inside Mode-Erika went out and the front door opened.

Uschi jumped to her feet, wiping the back of her hand across her lips. With a quick, "See ya," to Max, she flew down the stairs and made her way inconspicuously back to the BMW to rejoin Gerd.

Across the street, Reiner opened the rear door of the Rolls and positioned himself to one side. Erika did not get into the car. Instead, the man in the back seat got out. He and Erika fell into an embrace that surprised Erika with its passionate urgency, she being unaware that Luco's appetite had been ignited by his lustful appraisal of Uschi a moment earlier.

However, Erika disliked being the center of attention. She considered it gauche to put oneself on public display. With some embarrassment, she put both hands on Luco's chest and pushed herself gently away. The setting sun shone directly into Luco's face. Max pulled out the photo and compared the face in the photo with the face across the street. They were one and the same.

Still sipping his Warsteiner on the terrace of the Bratwursthäusle, he glanced up the street and caught Uschi's eye. She too had gotten a good look and gave Max a thumbs-up. He returned it. Looking back across the street, he saw the three in some discussion. Luco was doing most of the talking while pointing up the street toward the Burg, the Kaiserburg Castle on the hill, as though giving directions. Though Max couldn't make out what they were saying, the essence of their discussion soon became clear. Luco and Erika had decided to walk to wherever they were going.

Uschi rejoined Gerd in the BMW. They remained in place and watched as Luco and Erika walked up Rathausplatz with the Rolls creeping along behind and Max following on foot. Max was astounded. Parisi was behaving like a normal guy taking a leisurely stroll with his girlfriend. He was making no attempt at concealment. Max motioned for the BMW to lag behind.

Just below the castle, after Rathausplatz becomes Burgstrasse, Luco and Erika turned left followed by the Rolls. As they fell out of sight on Schmiedgasse, the BMW accelerated quickly up Rathausplatz toward the Burg.

Max was waiting for Uschi and Gerd at the corner of Burgstrasse and Schmiedgasse where he flagged them to a stop.

"They went into the Waffenschmied," said Max without preamble as he slid into the back seat of the BMW. "Reiner waited until they were inside then he took off. I suppose he'll come back later to pick them up. You two go in and have a nice dinner. Try to get a feel for what they're up to. Call me at home later. No matter what time."

"I'M SORRY, SIR, WE HAVE nothing available," said the maitre d' as he scanned Gerd and Uschi from top to bottom. "Perhaps you can come back at another time when you are ... more appropriately dressed."

Gerd and Uschi simultaneously pulled out their badges and Gerd said in a prissy tone that mimicked the maitre d's, "Perhaps another time might be better, don't you think, Uschi? We can come back appropriately dressed ... in full uniform."

"Oh yes, Gerd!" Uschi fell right into step. "And won't we look chic in our riot helmets as we question the waiters and some of the distinguished guests about a gay prostitution ring while they're enjoying their soup?"

The picture that formed in the maitre d's mind made him feel woozy. With one hand, he braced himself against his podium, while with the other, he whipped his handkerchief from his breast pocket and patted his brow. "Perhaps I can find a place for you," he said weakly.

"That table would be lovely," said Uschi, pointing to the table next to the one occupied by Luco and Erika, "wouldn't it, Gerd?"

"I would have selected that very table myself," Gerd replied with a grin.

"Please follow me," the maitre d' murmured as he turned and walked unsteadily to the table they had selected. After seating them, he made his way across the dining room where he conferred heatedly with the headwaiter who glowered at Gerd and Uschi.

Luco Parisi strained to keep a straight face. Looking past Erika's shoulder, he saw approaching his table the same, exciting, jeans-clad thighs that had captured his fantasy only a short while earlier. As she lowered herself into her seat with a sensuous swing of her hips, Uschi glanced from beneath lowered lids to see Luco's eyes trace a slow path upward from her thighs. Their eyes met for a brief moment, then she turned away.

If Erika noticed the wandering scope of Luco's attention, she gave no indication of it. At the sound of her voice, he forced himself to recapture the thread of their conversation as she said, "Some of the most important and powerful business leaders in all of Nürnberg have accepted my invitation. How can you even think about inviting that … that … " She groped for but was unable to find a word that would adequately describe Kurt Stöpsel.

"No! I will *not* invite him," she continued. "I'm afraid that's simply out of the question."

Before Luco became distracted by Uschi's appearance, Erika had been talking about a dinner party she had planned for a select handful of her customers. They were powerful, influential and enormously wealthy. It would be difficult to identify a successful business venture in not only Nürnberg but in all of Bavaria in which they were not heavily invested. Luco had set his sights on them. His goal was to become a part of their social activities and then to become a player in their circle of operations. He had better than ten million salted away in Stöpsel's bank and he wanted to put it where it would make a lot more.

These people were the heavy hitters, the movers and shakers that made it possible for business and industry to flourish. Luco knew it wouldn't be easy to gain their acceptance and confidence. To them, he was an unknown quantity. He thought at the outset he might win some stature with these people by bringing Kurt Stöpsel into contact with them and introducing Stöpsel as his personal banker.

When he suggested that to Erika, she blanched. Her reaction dampened his enthusiasm.

"OK. OK. I admit it. He's a jerk, but he's a high level executive in a Swiss bank for crisake and I can introduce him to your friends as my personal banker. Do you really despise him that much?"

"Yes, Schatz, I'm sorry, but I do despise him," she softened her tone. She had surprised even herself with her earlier reaction. "He is conceited, crude and arrogant. Oh yes, he made an attempt to be charming ... after he noticed I had legs. Your friend, Kurt Stöpsel, is a disgusting, insufferable ass."

"Look. He's not my friend," said Luco. "He's a VIP at a Swiss bank. That's gotta mean something to your rich friends even if he *is* a pompous, self-centered jerk."

"No, Schatz. My friends will see *only* that Stöpsel is, as you said, a pompous, self-centered jerk. To them, that will be *all* that matters." She spoke gently but Luco could see that on this, she would be unyielding as she added with finality, "Now, please ... let's order the wine."

GÜNTER LEHMANN PICKED UP the phone on the first ring and quietly murmured, "Yes?" before turning to check on Margrit. She squirmed for a moment, burrowed her face deeper into her pillow and continued to breathe evenly in deep slumber. He listened in silence to Max's report. When it was done, he whispered, "Thanks, old friend," and lowered the phone gently into its cradle.

Günter looked at his bedside clock. It was 2:00AM. Max and his rookies had a long day. In Naples it was only 8:00PM yesterday evening. He slithered gently out of bed, padded into the hallway and down the stairs to his study and punched in Vince's number. He gave Vince the high spots of Max's report. When he got to the part about Luco's arrival at Erika's Erlenstegen estate home in his Rolls, Vince interrupted.

"His Rolls!" Vince exclaimed. "Damn! I forgot all about his beloved Rolls. I should have known he wouldn't leave home without it."

"That's the strange part, Vince. He knows that such an auto will draw attention wherever it goes. He strolls openly on our streets.

This evening he had dinner in one of our finer restaurants and instead of asking for a secluded table, he took one that was in plain view of the entire restaurant. He is not acting like a man who is in hiding. I don't understand."

"I do, Günter," said Vince. "So far, he hasn't been charged with anything in Rhode Island and he must know that."

"How can that be? Surely, Greater Providence Bank must know by now what he did."

"Yeah, but maybe they don't know for sure *how* he did it and how *much* he skimmed. My sources tell me the bank's auditors are having trouble finding proof that any money changed hands ... "

" ... and without that proof," said Günter, completing Vince's thought, "maybe he feels beyond their reach."

"Right," said Vince. "Besides, with the state investigators focusing mainly on the collapse of RISDIC, maybe Luco's nephew, Howard, is keeping a lid on his findings. He worshipped his grandfather and would do anything—short of actually breaking the law—to conceal the scandal and to salvage the bank."

"It would appear, then, that the authorities feel that they have insufficient proof to make a case against him."

"Seems that way," said Vince. "That could explain why Luco's so relaxed."

"Does he know you're looking for him?"

"Maybe he does and maybe he doesn't. Either way, it wouldn't matter to him. He knows I have no official power over him."

"On the other hand," said Günter, "since he's being so out in the open, he can't have any idea that Tubby Bagnatore is looking for him, either."

"Of course! You're right!" Vince brightened. "If he did, he'd go limp with fear. Any sane person would. It's clear he doesn't suspect anything. But Günter, if *we* were able to find Luco, Tubby can't be far behind. We'd better reel him in before Tubby gets to him."

"I agree, Vince, but there is a complication. Parisi is staying at the home of the Böhringer woman, not at a hotel where we might more easily arrange access to him."

"That won't be a big problem. Luco won't stay alone for long while his girlfriend is at her shop. I promise you, at the first opportunity, he'll go out on the prowl. You can count on it. And when he does, do you have someone in mind, Günter?"

"We had some luck in that regard. During dinner, Parisi was quite taken with one of my officers, a rather fetching young woman named Uschi Braun. She and her partner arranged to be seated at the table next to Parisi's during dinner. She reported that he had, how do you Americans say it, given her the eye, several times during dinner when Erika Böhringer was not watching. Braun played along with it, making seductive eye-contact with him. She's confident he will remember her if they meet again."

"I'm sure he will. Your young officer has good instincts. Put our plan into motion, Günter. There's no time to waste."

THIRTY-SIX

GÜNTER SIPPED HIS WINE and glanced at his watch. He had arrived early so he might order the wine and see that it was properly chilled before his guest joined him. Though the Steigerle restaurant was, as always, filled to capacity with luncheon customers, they assured him there would be a table for him when he told them his guest would be Wolfgang Badorrek. Badorrek was the founder and CEO of a company with department stores in every major city in Germany.

Günter stood up when Badorrek entered the dining room. As always, he was awestruck by the appearance of this eighty-three-year-old man. He was broad-shouldered, he stood straight and tall, and his meticulously shaped, handlebar mustache and goatee complimented a full head of silver hair. His step was sure-footed and agile and his jaunty manner was accented by the carefree swing of his walking baton.

The maitre d' ushered him to the table and stood to one side as they exchanged greetings.

"How good of you to join me on such short notice," said Günter, taking Badorrek's extended hand.

"Nonsense, Günter. You are the only son of my dearest friend. We don't see each other often enough."

After seating Badorrek, the maitre d' gestured toward the wine that lay napkin-draped in the ice-filled Wein-Kühler.

"May I pour, Herr Badorrek?" he asked.

Badorrek raised one eyebrow and said with a good-natured grin, "That would depend, Siegfried, on what it is you intend to pour."

His attempt at light banter failed. Siegfried became flustered. He hastily removed the napkin from the wine bottle and displayed the label to Badorrek.

"I assure you, Herr Badorrek," said Siegfried, "Herr Lehmann has made an excellent selection. A three-year-old Chablis. Fourchaume, 1987."

Badorrek nodded his approval and glanced at Günter who was trying to suppress a grin. The maitre d' poured, then excused himself.

"To your father's memory," said Badorrek with raised glass.

"My father," said Günter in return.

They clinked their glasses and drank. After a respectful moment, with a motion of his head in the general direction of the maitre d', Badorrek said, "For eighteen years I have been trying, without success I would add, to get a smile out of that Siegfried, but the man is completely humorless."

Badorrek set his glass down gently. A shadow of sadness crossed his clear, blue eyes as they studied Günter.

"What is it, Wolfgang?" asked Günter, though he already knew. They had done this before.

"It's as though he were here, sitting across the table from me," said Badorrek, his voice almost a whisper in wonderment. "You look so much like him. But it's more than that. When you speak, I hear your father's voice. Your gestures, your mannerisms, they are uniquely yours, yet, when he was alive, they were uniquely his. It's uncanny ... and I know this is uncomfortable for you so I'll stop. Please forgive me."

"There's no need to apologize, Wolfgang," said Günter. "You were his dearest friend. Being with you, in some strange way, brings him back to me for these few minutes."

They again toasted the memory of the elder, departed Lehmann.

"Siegfried was correct, Günter. You chose a superb wine." He paused briefly, glancing around the room. "The Steigerle was his favorite restaurant. We took lunch here almost every day."

He and Günter's father were business associates as well as friends. Badorrek's company, with head offices in Nürnberg, was the largest retailer in Germany. They advertised heavily each day in newspapers throughout Germany. One of those newspapers was Die Nürnberger Nachrichten, Günter's father's, and now, Günter's newspaper.

"And now, Herr Kriminaldirektor," Badorrek was proud of his best friend's son and bowed his head ceremoniously as he used Günter's official title, "tell me. How can I help you?"

After a marvelous dinner at Waffenschmied the previous evening, Max's rookies reported that they were able to hear most of the conversation from the neighboring table. Erika Böhringer and Luco Parisi had talked about arrangements for a dinner party they planned to host at Erika's house in Erlenstegen. In the course of their conversation, Erika mentioned the names of some of their invitees, all of whom were prominent industrialists and entrepreneurs.

When Max relayed their report to Günter at 2:00AM, Günter had recognized the names of all the invitees. An idea came to him at the mention of one name in particular, Wolfgang Badorrek. Günter called Badorrek, told him he could use his help on a matter of some sensitivity and asked if they could talk about it over lunch.

"I have been told by one of my officers who is on a special assignment that you have been invited to a dinner party at the home of Frau Erika Böhringer. Can you confirm that?"

"Yes."

"Has the date been set?"

"Yes. In five days. This coming Saturday."

"Have you accepted the invitation?"

"No. I thought I would send regrets instead. I met her gentleman several months ago and didn't like him at all. The man is, to say the least, shallow."

"You're quite right, Wolfgang, but it goes beyond that. He has brought a great deal of financial pain to a great many people. I'm not at liberty to divulge all that I know. I simply caution you that it would be a mistake to become involved with him in any business enterprise or even to associate with him on a social level."

"What of Frau Böhringer, Günter?" asked Badorrek. "What is her position in whatever is going on?"

"We're not sure. We know only that she and Parisi have been ... shall we say, friends ... for many months, perhaps years. So far, we are not interested in her."

"Mmmm," Badorrek stroked his goatee. He had more questions to ask but knew they would have to wait. "You have not yet told me how I can be of assistance."

"If you were to accept Frau Böhringer's invitation, could you arrange to have the invitation extended to a young female companion? I have someone in mind who, I assure you, is quite up to your standards."

Badorrek was a lifelong bachelor and for most of his life has been the most sought after, and most elusive, catch in all of Germany. He enjoyed an active social life and appeared always with one and frequently with two gorgeous young women on his arms. It has been reputed, and never refuted, that Badorrek's sexual appetite and his performance in its fulfillment continued undiminished by his years.

"But of course!" he replied with a hint of indignation. "It would indeed be expected of me to arrive with a beautiful young woman on my arm. To do otherwise would most certainly raise eyebrows."

"Please forgive me, Wolfgang," said Günter with a slight bow of his head. He paused before continuing, "Then I want you to accept the invitation."

"But, you just told me it would be ill-advised to socialize with that Parisi fellow."

"That I did. But if what I have in mind works out, you will never again have to be in his company."

THIRTY-SEVEN

"HERR BADORREK and his guest," Reiner announced. He had been pressed into service as head butler for the evening.

Wolfgang Badorrek introduced her as Frau Braun. Luco recognized her immediately and couldn't believe the luck that brought her to him. She gave no sign of recognition as she took first Erika's hand then Luco's.

Those magnificent thighs that had rippled inside skin-tight blue jeans the last time Luco saw them were now calling to him through the sheen of her form-fitting, black satin, cocktail dress. Supported by spaghetti straps, it was tantalizingly décolleté, but its back plunged daringly to the fourth lumbar vertebra.

He feasted on the brazen and conspicuous view she presented of her smooth-muscled back when she turned from him to hand her wrap to Reiner. The marvelous orbs that had shaped the seat of her jeans as she bounced up the stairs of the Bratwursthäusle, their image permanently burned into the retina of his memory, were now the mounds that defined the cleavage of her buttocks.

A small combo played in the great room that adjoined the dining room. As instructed by Luco, they played only the old standards of the forties and fifties. They rendered them well, with sensitivity, and softly so as not to intrude on the dinner conversation.

After dinner, the party adjourned to the great room where they acknowledged the band with a polite round of applause. Some guests dispersed into small groups while others took to the floor for dancing. Erika and Luco strolled slowly, nodding and smiling to each group. When they reached a spot where they were out of earshot of the others, she pulled Luco to a stop and turned to face him. Dinner conversation had been strained. With all the money and power seated at the table, Luco had been like a hyena on the scent. He had made a shambles of protocol and etiquette. Erika's tone was anything but warm as she spoke through a strained smile.

"What - could - you - possibly have been thinking?" she asked.

"What do you mean?" he asked. "What did I do?" He really didn't know.

"What did you do?! You asked Herrn Volkmann where he has invested his money. To be courteous, he answered in general terms, but you pressed him for specific names. I can't believe you did that. Look around you. He is no longer here. His wife was overcome with a sudden headache and they have gone home.

"You told Herrn Brandl what your net worth is, a matter in which I am sure he has not the slightest interest. Thankfully, before you could ask him his, he excused himself from us."

Luco was unabashed.

"What's the big deal? That's how we do it in the States. We don't jerk around with small talk. We talk business. That *is* the small talk."

"Please, Luco! These are very important people," said Erika. She spoke quietly but a brittle edge was evident in her tone. "They have been very helpful in the success of Mode-Erika."

"No shit! Have they?!" he replied sharply. His words spewed out in a rapid-fire burst. "Well let's not forget, lady, who bought out the lease in that crummy storefront you used to operate in when you were dying and you could hardly pay the rent, and who set you up where you are now ... to the tune of half-a-million US dollars."

Nearby groups of guests turned at the sound of his voice. Erika didn't know if they had understood Luco's actual words—he had spoken so rapidly, and in English—but she was certain that they had heard his tone and seen the anger on his face.

She drew him close, put her arms around him, and pressed her face to his chest.

"Oh, darling, I am sorry. I do owe it all to you," she said through her smile while making eye-contact with the nearby guests. "It's just that these people are important. To both of us. They are my friends and I want them to become your friends."

They didn't notice Uschi and Badorrek approach until Badorrek tapped Luco on the shoulder. Luco and Erika instinctively pushed aside the effects of their conversation and turned to them wearing smiles.

"With your permission … ," said Badorrek to Luco, then turning to Erika, "may I have the honor of this dance?"

"On the condition, Herr Badorrek," Luco turned with a slight bow to Uschi, "that Frau Braun gives me the same honor."

"NOT MANY WOMEN CAN BE so alluring as you, whether in jeans or in evening dress." The touch of her naked back under his hand as they danced made his tongue thick and unwieldy. As a result, though he was very capable in German, some of his words were awkwardly distorted.

"Perhaps English might be more comfortable for you. I'm quite fluent, you know," she said with the slight Oxford accent that was typical of so many Germans who learned English in school. "And thank you for your compliment, but what did you mean about jeans?"

"You mean, you don't recognize me?" He feigned a look of despair. "I'm crushed."

"You do look somewhat familiar, actually," she said blithely. "Have we met?"

"Not actually met. No."

"What, then?"

"You were wearing jeans … very tight jeans … sneakers and a dark T-shirt. You took the table next to mine at Waffenschmied's."

"And what was so memorable about me?" she asked. "That is, besides my … very tight … jeans." She accented 'very tight' by pressing herself against him for a brief moment that was indiscernible to the other dancers, but unmistakable to Luco.

Luco felt himself responding. He fought it off. How would he possibly explain a bulging fly if someone noticed? What if Erika were to notice? His forehead and his upper lip became clammy with perspiration.

"Are you all right? You seem to be rather warm. Perhaps we shouldn't be dancing so close," she said coyly as she pushed away to put some space between them. "By the way, I've been toying with you, actually. I really do remember you."

"You do?"

"Of course. You were so obvious. The way you looked at me all evening, whenever you thought she wasn't looking at you. The message in your eyes was quite clear."

"And what message are they sending to you now?" he asked. He was beginning to regain his control.

"Oh, there's no mistaking their message, Mr. Parisi," she spoke through a smile with her gaze drifting about the room. Anyone watching might assume they were making polite party chatter. "But it's as pointless now as it was the other evening. After all, you were quite occupied then," she said, still smiling, with a nod of her head in Erika's direction, "and it's clear you're quite occupied now, isn't that so?"

"As I remember it, you were tied up too."

"Yes. I was with a business associate. It was quite hopeless for us don't you think?"

She wasn't turning him off. She was going along with his play. Right here, in bright light, shoulder to shoulder with other people and Erika not ten feet away. He could sense it.

Just then, Erika and Badorrek spun by close to them, Uschi smiled at Erika and blew a kiss to Badorrek.

"What about the old guy you came with?" said Luco, almost trembling with anticipation.

"He's just an old friend. He has no claim on me. But what about you. If I thought you could say the same about her ... but you can't, can you?"

He glanced quickly about the room to find Erika still dancing, safely out of earshot. He caught her eye and they smiled at each other. He ignored Uschi's question and said with urgency, "The music will stop soon. We've been given this chance, let's make it work. Where are you staying?"

"What? No! It's not possible," she gasped, "I'm afraid you've misunderstood."

Luco felt it slipping away and he was gripped by frustration.

"No, I haven't," he hissed through a forced smile. "Tell me. Quickly!"

"It isn't what you think," Uschi feigned innocence, stalling, keeping one ear attuned to the music. "It was just a harmless flirtation." She looked at him longingly, saying, "I was just playing with … oh, damn … " and just before the last note died, she squeezed his arm and said, "all right … the Grand Hotel."

THIRTY-EIGHT

"DO YOU REALLY THINK I'm such a fool, Luco?" Erika spoke softly. If she felt any anger, there was no hint of it in her tone. "Can your opinion of me be that low that you imagine me to be so stupid?" She looked at him in the three-paneled mirror of her dressing table where she sat removing her jewelry. She had removed her shoes and her dress but still wore her slip. It was black, with a clinging lace bodice and a lace hem that fell to mid-thigh. She removed the various pins and other devices that held her hair in place and, with a shake of her head, her hair tumbled softly to spill over her shoulders.

She had just confronted Luco about the way he had reacted to Frau Braun. She saw Luco sweep his eyes over every inch of Uschi the moment she arrived. Throughout the evening, Erika pretended not to be paying attention. She saw the way Luco looked at Uschi during dinner and the way they looked at each other when they danced.

"How can you think that, sugar? Awright, she's pretty, but I was just being a good host." Luco still felt some of the arousal that Uschi had stirred in him. "Now what do you say we enjoy what's left of the evening?" He came up behind her, kissed her on the neck and cupped her breasts in his hands.

She didn't remove his hands but she didn't respond in any way. She didn't squirm, she didn't make a sound, she didn't move, she didn't even close her eyes. When finally he looked up and met her eyes in the mirror, she said in the tone that Luco had come to recognize as trouble, "We have much more to talk about, Luco."

"Like what, sugar? There's only one thing I want to talk about right now." He continued to knead her breasts. She remained immobile and unresponding.

"Why did you, both of you, pretend not to know each other? Your reaction to seeing her when she arrived was so obvious."

He removed his hands and stood up straight. Still looking at her in the mirror, he said, "I don't know her. I never saw her before tonight. What are you talking about?"

"Oh come now, child," she said with a measure of scorn coloring her level tone, "perhaps your memory will improve if you picture her in skin-tight jeans and a blue T-shirt."

Luco was put off-balance. How could she be this close to the actual facts? He skipped a beat. By instinct, he realized he'd better cut his losses.

"Wait a minute. The other night. At Waffenschmied's! Yes! That could have been her at the next table couldn't it? I'll be damned. I never would have made the connection."

Erika looked at him blankly.

"So I didn't recognize her and she didn't recognize me," he continued. "What's the big deal?"

"Don't lie to me, Luco. I can deal with most anything but I cannot deal with lies." Her voice remained quiet but emphatic. "You cannot undress each other with your eyes, not more than two meters apart, for an entire evening, and not recognize each other a few days later."

Luco's puzzlement was so pronounced on his face that he didn't have to ask the question.

"The mirror, Luco," she continued as she rose to her feet and turned to face him. "There was a mirror on the wall behind you. I saw everything. It began with the wink of your eye. A detestable American mannerism. Please don't wink at women any more, Luco. It degrades you.

"As the evening progressed, you pretended to hang on my every word ... while you massaged each other with your eyes. She even went so far as to express her rapture by moistening her lips with her tongue while gaping at you from beneath lowered lids."

Luco thought frantically for a way out. There was none. His little-boy-caught-with-his-hand-in-the-cookie-jar approach was his only hope.

"Aw come on, sugar. I was just having a little fun at Waffenschmied's the other night. OK, I admit it, it's a kick for a guy my age to have a young chick like that come on to him. But she was there with her young stud, for crisake. What the hell was I going to accomplish? Sure, I recognized her tonight when she came in, but she played it like we never saw each other before. I figured it had something to do with the old geezer she was with so I went along. Then after a while, it became awkward for me to mention it to you so I decided to just let it pass."

Erika studied him for a long time. She didn't buy it. She had seen too much on the dance floor tonight but she decided she had gone far enough with it for one evening. Still, she felt the need to impress on him that she was not to be trifled with.

"All right, Luco." She allowed a slight, forgiving grin to shape her lips as she continued, "I'm not angry but you have hurt me and I need to think it through."

He went to her, put his arms around her and kissed the crooks of her shoulders and her neck and her ears. He slid his hands down and pulled her to him. Forcing her awakened desire to the background, she placed her hands against his chest to push herself away, and as she leaned back, she pressed herself unmistakably, if only for a brief instant, against him.

He interpreted her move, as she knew he would, to be a sign of encouragement for him to continue. He tore at his clothes and was down to his undershorts when she stopped him.

"I'm sorry, Luco," she said, casting a glance at his lower regions, "but that will have to wait for another time. I'll try to accept what you have just told me, but these last few days, since the way you behaved at Waffenschmied, have been difficult for me. I'll need some time to adjust." She kissed him gently on the cheek and said, "Now, if you'll excuse me, I want to undress for bed."

"Damn!" he exclaimed. So that's it. When they got home from Waffenschmied's that evening, she had relented and granted him a ceremonial, welcome-back quickie in deference to his arrival that very day. He hadn't gotten laid since then and now he knew why.

"I'm sorry, Luco," she repeated. "Please try to understand."

HER HUSBAND, her first love, had strayed from her bed because she had been so naive about sex. He had been her first lover. How could she have known that holding his sexual interest would require such thought and planning? That it could be like nurturing a delicate flower. That, given too much nourishment, it might grow sick and die. Too late she learned that a man's desires and needs can best be heightened by the thrill of a sexual adventure that carries with it the risk of rejection.

Erika had been so giving of herself, so compliant, so willing to submit to his every sexual whim. Soon, when he no longer felt the adventurous thrill with her, he found it outside their marriage. In abundance. She would not let that happen again.

LUCO UNBUTTONED his shorts, shoved them to the floor, and started toward her. Though her heart was pounding furiously, Erika forced herself to remain aloof and remote, giving Luco no hint of her raging passion.

"I said no, Schatz! Now please leave. I want to go to bed."

The look on her face told him not to come any closer.

THIRTY-NINE

"MARTINI ON THE ROCKS, extra dry, extra olives," the barman said proudly in unaccented English. He set the drink in front of Luco who, at the moment, was the only customer in the entire lounge of the Grand Hotel. Luco took a sip and said, "Amazing. It's perfect! You wouldn't believe what I've been served in this town. You must have worked in the States."

"Four years in Chicago. Great town!" said the barman with a friendly smile. "Enjoy your dri... wow!" He jerked his head in the direction of the gorgeous creature that had just entered the lounge.

Luco swiveled on his stool. One look at her fluid, seductive motion and all his senses scrambled to full alert. Her eyes were hidden behind dark glasses that merged with the blackness of her pixie-cut hair. Her simple, green dress was buttoned high, revealing a mere hint of cleavage. White buttons down the front held the dress together. The provocative sway of her hips, given emphasis by her three-inch heels, was further accented by a broad belt of matching fabric around her tiny waist. The opening below the lowest button revealed most of each thigh with every dazzling stride.

She slithered onto a stool one stool removed from Luco, swiveled toward him and languorously crossed one leg over the other. Her dress fell open up to the first button. Luco couldn't see her eyes through the dark glasses but he was certain she was looking directly into his own.

"You're just in time," he said in German, with a nod toward his drink. "I thought I might have to drink alone. May I offer you something?"

She skipped a beat or two then said, "Campari-Orange," without turning to the barman.

"The lady would like a Campari-Orange," Luco repeated to the barman who reluctantly turned his attention to the business of preparing her drink.

After a few surreptitious glances, Luco abandoned discretion and looked long and directly into her thighs. When finally he looked back up, she had removed her glasses and was wearing a playful grin.

"Are you pleased with what you see?" she said. Her voice was deep and soft. Shaped lashes and a delicate touch of mascara gave the illusion of hypnotic luminescence to her green eyes.

"Yeah. Yeah, I'm real pleased."

She examined him inch by inch, tracing a path from his eyes to the region below his belt where she held her view steadily for a long moment before looking back up. "So am I," she said, still grinning.

Luco, already titillated by her beautiful legs, and still on short rations from Erika, flamed into arousal.

The barman returned and placed the Campari-Orange on the bar. She lifted it, raised it to Luco and said, "Call me Andrea." She pronounced it "ahn-*dray*-uh."

Luco raised his glass in return and grunted, "Luco." They sipped their drinks in unison.

"I find directness to be a virtue, Luco," said Andrea. She took another sip while peering at him over the rim of her glass, and continued, "I hope you agree." She hesitated, then said, "Can you find space for me in your plans for this afternoon?"

Luco was astounded. He made a show of looking at his watch, then said, "Andrea, I never thought I would hear myself say this to a woman as beautiful ... and as desirable ... as you. But I can't. I'm waiting for someone. She'll be here in just a few minutes." He glanced at the barman who had been taking it all in, pretending to be busy. The barman rolled his eyes and shrugged in an expression that clearly said, 'Tough break, Pal. I wish I had that problem.'

"Oh, what a pity," she sulked playfully, "and I have the entire day to myself."

"Well then, there's always tomorrow, isn't there?"

"I'm afraid not. I have a long drive ahead of me tomorrow. I'll be checking out in the morning."

"Checking out?" Luco asked. "You mean, you're staying here? In The Grand?"

The bar phone rang. The barman looked wistfully over his shoulder at Andrea as he walked to the far end to answer it.

"Yes, I am." She slipped from her stool and moved to the one next to Luco's. In the process, she performed a symphony of erotica with her legs. "It's a quite lovely suite. Wouldn't you like to see it?"

As Luco glanced nervously toward the main entrance, looking for Uschi, he noticed the barman looking at him and nodding his head as he talked on the phone. But he didn't dwell on it. His attention was held by this totally exciting woman, with her long legs wantonly brushing against his.

"Oh, how I wish I could, Andrea, believe me," he said, stealing another look at his watch.

Just then, the barman returned and asked, "Excuse me. Is your name Luco?"

"Yeah, that's me," Luco answered.

"The party on the phone described you perfectly," he said, handing Luco a slip of paper, folded in two.

The note read, "Trapped in Hannover. Flight cancelled. No replacement airplane until tomorrow. Have to rush. Mad scramble for a car and a room. Can't tell you how sorry. Call me again. Please ! ! ! Uschi."

Andrea studied him closely as he read the note. When he finished it and looked up, he wore a grin that defined lust. Methodically ripping the note into ever smaller fractions of the sheet, he said, "You were saying about your lovely suite."

She read his expression accurately.

"Oh, how completely marvelous!" she breathed. She took his hand and placed it on her thigh. "Let's finish our drinks. Hurry!"

The barman seemed to be feeling their heat just by being there. He said with a leer, "Take it easy, you two. You turn the temperature up one more degree and I'm going to have to douse you with cold water."

They downed their drinks eagerly. Luco threw a handful of bills on the bar and winked at the barman. As they got up from their stools, Andrea glanced at the bulge in Luco's pants and smiled. She took his arm and they hurried to the elevator.

When they were out of earshot, the barman lifted the phone. A voice at the other end said, "Yes?"

The barman answered, "They're on their way up."

FORTY

"WHAT IF HE DECIDES to turn off the lights?" asked Max. "Will there be enough light?" He spoke quietly, without looking up, keeping his gaze fixed on the tableau in the adjoining room.

"Yes, we're using low-light lenses," Uschi answered in almost a stage-whisper, "but it won't come to that. Most men like to have the lights on during sex."

Both Max and Gerd turned and looked at her in wide-eyed wonder.

"I've been told!" she added hastily, skipped a beat, then continued, "But even if he breaks the pattern, Andrea will insist that some lights remain on."

Gerd was running a tripod-mounted video camera and Uschi was taking stills with a Polaroid.

On the other side of the one-way glass, Andrea had both hands behind Luco's head and her fingers intertwined with his thick, black hair, while she explored the inner recesses of his mouth with her tongue. She pulled his shirt up out of his trousers and fumbled with the buttons. He scrambled for her belt buckle to start to undress her.

"No, Luco," she said. She reached up under his shirt and rubbed her palms over the bare flesh of his back.

"I want to *see* you first. *All* of you." She pressed herself against him. A soft moan escaped her. "I must see that you truly want me, as I want you. Then I will undress for you."

Andrea reached down, released his waistband and lowered his zipper. As his trousers fell to the floor, she again grabbed his head in both her hands and pulled it to her, pressing her lips hard against his. Low, growling sounds came from deep inside him as she sucked his tongue into her mouth while she ground her pelvis against him.

"Wait!" she said breathlessly, suddenly breaking away from him.

She spun him to face the mirror and embraced him from behind. Reaching around him, she unbuttoned his shorts and let them fall. "I like to look at us in the mirror," she said in a tight, dry voice. She caressed his chest with one hand while her other hand went south.

"Oh God, I'm so hot!" she gasped, with her head peeking from around his shoulder.

Luco was in ecstasy. He emitted a long, unbridled groan as his head rolled back then fell to one side. He took her hand to his lips, and as he kissed her fingers, she worked them between his lips. He took them into his mouth and licked them with abandon while she fondled him.

GERD HAD HIS EYE GLUED to the eyepiece of the video camera. Not so much because he was enjoying the show, but because, with Uschi standing there right next to him, he was mortified with embarrassment. Though they had been partners for many months, Gerd had avoided making a single physical or verbal advance that would betray the strong attraction he felt toward her. In moments of solitary reflection, he wondered if he was in love with her. At the right time, if she ever gave him the slightest hint that she, too, harbored similar affection for him, he would bare his feelings to her.

With what was taking place on the other side of the glass, he couldn't bear the thought of making eye-contact with her. He wanted to hide.

Max felt even worse. He was much older. When he was growing up, things like this happened only in tattered, dog-eared, black-market books that passed from wide-eyed kid to wide-eyed kid. Though he had witnessed a lot since then, he was, nonetheless, painfully uncomfortable viewing it in the flesh in the presence of a woman who was young enough to be his daughter.

Without looking at her, Max said, "Listen, Uschi … uh … if you'd like to step outside for a smoke … I mean … I can work that camera if you'd rather not be here."

"Oh, that's precious!" she said. The laughter in her own voice didn't register on her until she saw that Max was dead serious. When it did, she, too, became serious and said with affection, "That was nice of you, Max. Really nice. And thank you. But I can handle this. I'm a big girl. I wouldn't miss that creep's reaction when the final curtain comes down on this show."

"UNNHH … STOP!" LUCO REACHED down and pulled Andrea's hand away. Through labored breaths he said, "OK, I want you! Can't you see I want you?! Take your clothes off. I want to see you!"

As he spun to look at her, she pressed herself against him, shoving him backwards. His legs bumped against the bed and he fell to a sitting position.

"Take your clothes off!" His throat was constricted. His tongue unwieldy. His German became difficult, almost unintelligible.

"C'mon, dammit, I wanna see. Lemme see!" Without thinking, he had switched to English. She undid the buckle of her belt and let it slip to the floor, then she brought his hands to the top button of her dress. "Yes, undress me!" she pleaded. "Now!" Her voice was shaky and apprehensive.

With fumbling fingers, he undid the top button and worked his way down. When he got to the last button, before he could undo it, she pushed his hands aside.

"Awright, goddammit! Enough is enough," he said through a string of grunts. "I want to see you!"

She reached up under her dress, wildly tore off her panties and tossed them away. Then she moved close to him, standing between his spread legs.

"Now I want to show you!" she gasped. "It makes me so hot to show myself. But please, we must do it my way!"

Luco was no longer capable of formulating words. Whatever it was that he attempted to say was unintelligible. He made a scrambling reach for her bra but she captured his hands, brought them to her lips and licked them as she exclaimed, "No, don't touch them!" Her words rushed out in an explosive burst of breath. "Not yet! My breasts are very small but they are so sensitive." Her breathing grew erratic. "Take them at the very last!" She could barely speak. "When we are ready to finish!"

She undid the last button but held the front of her dress together with one hand. With the other hand, she grabbed his hair and pulled his head back, forcing his face to look up at her.

"You must look only into my eyes until I tell you!" Her voice was low but intense. She shrugged the dress from her shoulders and let it fall to the floor.

"Now, Luco! Now!" she commanded. Standing before him wearing nothing but her bra, she held onto his hair, looking down into his eyes. A low, raspy groan came from her mouth as she took his face in her hands, bent over and kissed him. He made primordial sounds as she sucked his tongue into her mouth. Abruptly she broke the kiss and she straightened, still holding his face firmly in her hands, tilted up, looking into her eyes.

He reached behind her, cupped her firm roundness in his hands and drew her to him with their eyes still locked together. His Neanderthal grunts were incoherent except for the sense of out-of-control urgency that they conveyed. She undid the front clasp of her bra. With a powerful thrust of her pelvis, she loudly moaned in her deep voice, "Yes! Luco! Yes!" as she whipped off her bra and flung it aside.

At long last! Luco snapped his head down to feast his eyes on her.

For a long moment, he was unable to comprehend what he saw. He found himself face-to-face with a turgid penis that was scant inches from his face. Paralyzed first with puzzlement, then with shock, his eyes and mouth opened wide in horror, he could do nothing more than stare at it. When he began to understand what was happening, he whipped his hands from behind Andrea and shoved her away in revulsion.

"GERD, YOU BETTER GET on in there quick," Max ordered. "We don't want that Parisi guy to go berserk and hurt that young boy."

Gerd rushed into the other room. Luco's confusion was still evident and it was heightened by Gerd's sudden appearance. Luco had risen to his feet and was in a state of retreating tumescence. Andrea, glancing warily at him, had almost finished getting dressed.

Gerd handed Andea—Andrew—an envelope and hustled him out with his thanks and congratulations for a job well done. Gerd stood facing the door, with his back to Luco. After a long moment, he went to Luco, looked at him with disgust, and with a mighty shove, sent Luco sprawling onto the bed. Then he went to the door between the rooms, hesitated, and turned.

"Put some clothes on, you maggot, and come in here," said Gerd. "The show's about to begin!"

FORTY-ONE

LUCO STEPPED TENTATIVELY into the room. What he saw stopped him in his tracks. A tripod-mounted video camera still pointed through a window that he immediately realized was a mirror in the other room. The very mirror in which, minutes earlier, he had lustfully viewed his own naked image with Andrea's arms and hands encircling him from behind. He looked at the rumpled bed from this viewing angle and knew at once that nothing had been concealed from the camera. His thoughts blurred as he tried to reconstruct from memory the images that he now knew had been captured on film.

Turning from the window, Luco saw Uschi across the room. She wore the same jeans, dark T-shirt and scruffy white sneakers she wore the first time he saw her. She sat in a sofa with her legs tucked under her. Gerd was next to her, sitting on the arm of the sofa with his arms folded across his chest. His short-sleeved polo shirt revealed his well-developed biceps and forearms. Luco remembered him as the guy Uschi was with at the restaurant.

He didn't recognize the other man who stood with his fists on his hips, behind an empty chair that faced the television. Max was older, and tough looking, and he wore a menacing expression on his lined and creased face. A shiver of apprehension ran up Luco's spine when their eyes met.

Max motioned for Luco to sit in the chair. Uschi tossed a handful of Polaroids onto the coffee table next to him. Reflexively, Luco picked them up. He blanched and made a choking sound as he riffled through them. Max then nodded to Gerd who pointed the remote at the TV and pressed the PLAY button.

Luco's grunts filled the room as the final moments of the video came to life on the TV. When it reached the part where Andrea's deep voice moaned, "Yes! Luco! Yes!", Gerd froze the picture. The screen was filled with a close-up of Luco's face, gaping wide-eyed and open-mouthed, mere inches from the incriminating evidence.

"What the fuck?! Whoa! Wait a minute!" Luco shouted and started to get up. Max pushed him back down into the chair. With another nod from Max, Gerd pressed the STOP button and handed the remote to Max. Then Gerd and Uschi went into Andrea's room and closed the door.

Luco's eyes followed Max as he went to the bedroom door, knocked on it and returned. On the way back, Max placed another chair alongside the TV, facing Luco, then resumed his standing position behind Luco. The bedroom door opened, Günter entered the room and eased himself without a word into the chair that Max had set up for him. Luco looked uneasily over his shoulder at Max, then at Günter, both of whom remained silent as Luco's anxiety level escalated.

Without preamble, and in a level, quiet tone, Günter recited a detailed synopsis of the failure of the Goyette loan. He described with accuracy the foreclosure and unsuccessful auction of Goyette's properties and how that had triggered the investigation into Luco's complicity. He followed with details of Luco's loan-boosting scam, including Mickey Hoban's part in it.

Günter's description of their scam was, in part, educated speculation that was developed by Vince and Howard, largely based on Howard's research into the computer files of Luco's loan history. Nevertheless, it left no doubt in Luco's mind that this stranger sitting before him had been very thoroughly briefed.

Luco tried to affect a show of bravado despite the question that nagged at him. How could these people, on another continent, know so much?

"Awright. So what is this? A shakedown?" he asked.

Günter ignored his question. "You went to great lengths to betray a man that you have known all your life. A man who was guilty of nothing more than being a better athlete than you … "

"Phil Peters," Luco interrupted with a derisive snort.

" … and having a wife who preferred not to open her legs for you," Günter went on with no change of tone.

With that, a dark look came over Luco. He growled, "You can kiss my ass!"

Günter continued as though Luco had said nothing. "Mr. Peters is in debt for a substantial sum of money to a gentleman of your acquaintance. Because of the despicable action you have taken against Mr. Peters, he will be unable to repay that debt. As a result, that gentleman has taken your actions as a personal matter between you and him."

"Yeah? Now who would that be? And how is this any of your business?"

"That gentleman is a dear friend of mine. And it became my business when he asked me to convince you to make matters right with Mr. Peters. Without delay. Not the next time you are in the states, not next month, not next week. Not even tomorrow. But now!"

"What the hell are you talk … ?"

"Silence!" Günter snapped. His tone startled Luco. "A father's greatest blessing is the love of his children. You denied your father that joy. He died knowing that his only son is an empty shell. You are a wretched snake. You have destroyed everything that your father achieved. You are *less* than a snake. You are a cockroach!"

"Go fuck yoursel … "

With a look from Günter, Max grabbed a handful of Luco's hair and yanked his head back sharply. With a roundhouse swing, Max delivered a resounding slap across the face and ear, snapping Luco's head sideways and leaving a loud, high-pitched ringing in his ear.

"Moreover, you are a fool!" Günter hissed. "It was so easy to find you, and there are others, not so congenial as us, who are looking for you."

"What do you mean?" Luco's smartass attitude lost some of its edge.

"Think a moment, you imbecile! There is a man who has a great sum of money in your bank. Money that he needs to conduct his day-to-day transactions. Because of you, the bank is now closed. He no longer has access to his money. You have made it difficult for him to conduct business. Alphonse Bagnatore is not amused."

"Tubby Bagnatore?!" he said with alarm.

"One and the same. And he has sent the two psychopaths who work for him to find you. I'm sure you know of Rocky Jordan and Chetta Lograno and their exploits. They are presently in Switzerland, looking for your friend, the banker who hopes to be Nashville's next great sensation. The one whose auto sports a hood ornament of cattle horns. As I said, you were not difficult to find.

"Oh, I almost forgot. Your niece's husband, Mickey Hoban? He appears to be recuperating, though slowly and painfully."

Luco's eyes asked the silent question.

"Yes, Mr. Parisi. You see, Mr. Bagnatore, Rocky Jordan and his devoted companion, Chetta Lograno, recently paid Mr. Hoban a lengthy, and most painful, visit."

Oh my God, Luco thought. No trace of his bravado remained.

"According to this letter," Günter said as he handed over a copy of Luco's letter to Phil, "Mr. Peters' total debt to Greater Providence Bank is $837,000."

"Max, may I borrow your notebook please?" As he wrote in it, Günter said to Luco, "It is now nine-fifteen a.m. in Naples, Florida. The banks are open and doing business. You will instruct your Swiss banker friend to wire transfer that amount to this account in Naples using these routing and transit numbers. I suggest you start right now."

"Are you fucking crazy?! 837 thous … "

"In addition," Günter interrupted as he continued to look directly into Luco's eyes, "you will call Mode-Erika. You will instruct Frau Böhringer to withdraw 15,000 Deutschmark in cash from your account in Raiffeisenbank here in Nürnberg. You will tell her to deliver it to you here. Immediately. This cash will be used to cover our out-of-pocket expenses—the hotel rooms, the chic cocktail dress worn by Frau Braun at Frau Böhringer's dinner party. Oh yes, and a generous fee to Andrew, the aspiring young actor who delivered such a stimulating performance. I'm sure you understand." His voice remained controlled and calm.

"Understand my ass!" Faced with the prospect of giving up that much money, Luco momentarily forgot the circumstances of his position. "There's no way I'm … "

Another look from Günter. Another yank of the hair. Another crashing blow from Max. More ringing in Luco's ear.

"You are a fool! You are wasting time that you do not have. Max, please dial that number I gave you."

Max dialed a single digit, then after a moment, a 13-digit number. Luco spun in his chair when he heard Max say into the phone, in English, "Mr. Bonetta? This is Max in Nürnberg … Yes, thank you, it went very well. One moment please." He nodded to Günter who picked up the other phone.

"Good morning, Vince. I just want to say hello before putting him on the phone … and to say you were right. He is incredibly stupid. Max, please give your phone to Mr. Parisi."

"Bonetta? Vince Bonetta? What the f… ?" Luco was confused.

"Shut up and listen, you moron! How stupid can you be? You got Tubby Bagnatore pissed at you. He wants you bad. For now, he thinks you're in Switzerland with your money. How hard do you think it's going to be for those two lunatics of his to find that dizzy, guitar-whacking, banker friend of yours? I'd be sticking to the shadows and looking over my shoulder if I were you, so listen up. These are your two options and they're all you've got.

"Option one. You refuse to do exactly what I say and here's what happens. By this time tomorrow morning, those photos will be on the bulletin board in the men's locker room at The Alpine Country Club where they'll be on display for the amusement of all your old golfing buddies.

"They'll also be seen by your father-in-law, Papa Cheech, but he won't be amused, will he, Luco? Remember the promise he made? What he said he'd do to you, if you ever brought shame to his daughter? Something about separating you from your dick? He'll have no trouble finding you, especially when I tell him where to start looking. And he will. Papa Cheech has the money and the connections, and these photos will provide all the motivation he needs.

"In addition, the photos and video in which you performed with such enthusiasm will be published on the Internet. By the end of the week, you'll be starring on computer screens all over the world. If you had any hopes of rubbing elbows with the heavy hitters of Nürnberg—or anyplace else for that matter—you can forget about it. They're going to avoid you as though you had the plague.

"And there's more. The gentleman who's on the other phone with us controls one of the largest newspapers in Germany and has worldwide connections in the publishing business. To cover all the bases, he'll see to it that your photos appear in tabloid newspapers worldwide. You'll be on display at checkout counters in every supermarket and convenience store in the free world. Some of the seamier tabloids won't even use those little black boxes to obscure the private parts of you and your lover."

"What lover?! It was a setup and you know it!" While there was anger in Luco's voice, it was overshadowed by resigned pleading.

"I wasn't finished with option one. Here's the best part. I pick up the phone and place a call to one Alphonse Bagnatore. I'll gleefully give him your precise location. I'll also assure him that you'll be under continuous surveillance until his loyal servants arrive to take you into their less-than-benevolent custody. You'll find yourself pulling for Papa Cheech to get his hands on you before they do."

After a long pause, with all pretense gone and a large measure of trepidation in his voice, Luco asked, "You said two options?"

"Option two, on the other hand, is very simple," Vince said brightly. "You do what my friend told you to do and do it right now. I'll stand by this phone until I hear from the bank that the money has been wired to the account that my friend has designated. Then I'll phone Max, who, along with his two young friends in the other room, will have entertained you until that time. When I give him the word, he'll give you custody of the video and the Polaroids, and will provide you with safe escort to the home of Erika Böhringer in Erlenstegen, after which, you'll be on your own."

"But $837,000!" Luco whined. "For crisake, Bonetta!"

"Plus expenses," Vince replied.

"Shit!"

"Just consider it vigorish, Parisi. Word is you skimmed over eight mill. Tax-free! What we're talking here is less than 11 percent one-time vig. Where can you get a better deal than that?"

"Awright!" Luco blurted. "Awright! But I'm not gonna make the call from here where your guys can trace my call and record everything I say."

"However you want to do it. So long as you do it immediately. Günter, you still there?"

"I'm here, Vince."

"As soon as he makes the arrangements, call me back. If I don't hear from you in thirty minutes, I'll place a call to Bagnatore. Talk to you later, my friend."

"Until later, my friend."

Max walked Günter to the door. "Call me the minute the transfer has been arranged, Max," said Günter. "You know where to reach me." He waved goodbye and started to close the door, then hesitated as he thought of something.

"By the way. The Grand Hotel has a superb kitchen. After I'm gone, bring in your two fine young rookies and order a very expensive lunch." He chuckled as he added, "Mr. Parisi is buying."

LUCO DIALED A LOCAL number from a phone booth in the lobby with Gerd and Uschi watching from a few yards away, beyond hearing distance. The voice on the other end answered, "Mode-Erika."

Luco said, "Frau Böhringer, please. This is Mr. Parisi."

When she came on the line, Luco said hurriedly, "Listen carefully, sugar. Get a pencil and write this down. There's something you've got to do right away."

Recognizing the urgency in his voice, Erika didn't say a word as Luco told her what she had to do. When he finished, she said, "You want *me* to call Herrn Stöpsel?! You know how I despise him."

"Erika, sugar, forget about that!" He fought to hold his control. "I'm not asking you to sleep with him for crisake. Just call him up and tell him what I just told you. And tell him I want him to handle it personally. There can't be any delays. As soon as he faxes you proof of the transfer, bring it to me here with the 15,000 Deutschmark in cash. Leave it for me in a sealed envelope at the concierge desk of the Grand Hotel."

"The Grand Hotel?" she asked. Her suspicion was conspicuous. "What are you doing at th… "

"Not now, goddammit!" He said sharply. Regrouping, he softened his tone and continued, "Please, sugar! Later. I'll explain later." He hung up without another word.

Erika did as she was asked. In less than thirty minutes following Luco's urgent phone call, she had phoned Herrn Stöpsel at Die Schweizer National Bank, given him his wiring instructions, and received his confirming fax. On the way to the Grand Hotel, she stopped at the Raiffeisenbank, withdrew 15,000 Deutschmark and delivered the package to the concierge. In spite of her burning curiosity, she left at once to return to Mode-Erika.

FORTY-TWO

Luco's thoughts skittered wildly, barely in control, during the drive back to Erlenstegen with Gerd and Uschi following closely in their car. He struggled to force behind him the images of Andrea, Uschi and Gerd, Max, that other guy with the ice-cold eyes, and that holier-than-thou son-of-a-bitch, Vince Bonetta, as he concocted a cover story for the events of the day.

Later that evening, sitting around the kitchen table with the blinds closed and the lights low, Luco told Erika and Reiner that before leaving Rhode Island, he had received several phone calls, each more ominous than the previous one. When he arrived in Nürnberg, he told them, he hired a private investigator with offices both in Germany and in the USA.

According to Luco's story, they had met with at the Grand Hotel earlier in the day. The detective reported that a 'client' whose money Luco had been laundering had suffered dramatic reverses. Though, for Reiner's ears, Luco referred to the laundering as 'customized banking services', Erika readily made the connection with the cash-filled suitcases.

The detective also reported that the 'client' places the blame for those reverses directly on Luco and demands that Luco return the 'commissions' he received for those services, a sum reaching into the millions. The report concluded with the warning that the 'client' has hired two notorious thugs to find Luco and force him to turn over the money.

While Luco had been convincing enough in his telling of the first part, when he got to the part about Rocky and Chetta, though he didn't mention them by name, his fear was genuine and it became vividly apparent.

"I know of these people. I've heard of things they've done. If they find me ... "

Erika took Luco's hand in both of hers and pressed it to her cheek, looking helplessly from Luco to Reiner. "This can't be happening. What can we do, Reiner?" she pleaded. Her eyes were wide with alarm.

Reiner stared at his hands. After several, long, silent moments, he glanced at Erika then looked steadily at Luco.

"You cannot escape them. I have known men like that in this country. On the other side of the wall. Before it came down. There is no place you can go that they cannot find you, and when they do, you will plead with them to stop so you can tell them everything you know and do anything they ask. And when you have given them what they want, then they will ... "

The sound of Erika's gasp stopped him. He looked down at his hands, paused in thought, before continuing.

"The only escape from them is ... death!" he concluded with a sidewise glance at Luco and the onset of a grin that was out of phase with his words.

"Ach! Mein Gott im Himmel!" she cried in desperation. "What are you saying?!"

Erika was too distraught to have picked up on it but the look in Reiner's eyes and the set of his lips were not lost on Luco.

"Easy, baby," he said soothingly, reaching over to caress her hair. "Let's hear what Reiner has in mind."

LUCO LOOKED AGAIN at the grandfather clock as he crept to the other side of the living room. With his back to the wall, Luco inched his way to the side window. Carefully, so as not to cause any movement that might be seen from outside, he held his breath and peered out with one eye through a tiny slit between the curtains. He scanned as much as he could see from that vantage point, then quickly, he scurried to the next window and did the same.

In a semi-crouch, like a foot soldier darting for cover from doorway to doorway, he crossed the room to the other side. Hesitating again in front of the grandfather clock, he looked in desperation from the clock to his wristwatch, unable to grasp that it was only two minutes later.

His almost-affair with the boy actor seven days earlier, the meeting with Günter and Max, being extorted out of 837 thousand dollars by Vince Bonetta—it was all a blur. They were all out-of-focus glimpses of a fuzzy memory.

But not Rocky Jordan and Chetta Lograno. There was nothing fuzzy about them. It didn't matter that they had not yet been seen in Nürnberg. They dominated his imaginings with microscopic clarity.

He remembered how it was when he met them. They had been sitting across the room, passively watching a TV with the volume turned down so that only they could hear it, while Luco played gin with Tubby and the rest of his "staff." Tubby's boys laughed raucously, regaling one another with tales of assignments that the two maniacs had carried out. Their stories included gleeful and finely detailed descriptions of the brutality that they had administered. Luco remembered being chilled by the emotionless reaction of Rocky and Chetta as they listened. He couldn't shake the apparition of them from his mind.

As he duck-walked into the kitchen to check on the rear of the property, he saw that the curtains and blinds were fully open. He flung himself flat against a wall and slithered to the floor.

"The blinds!" he yelled in English. "Close the goddamm blinds!" Reiner stood with knife in hand at the island work center, cleaning and cutting vegetables for the dinner salad. This was not the first of Luco's outbursts. Lazily, Reiner ambled to the window, looked out in all directions, making no attempt at concealment, and returned to his vegetables.

"No. I will not close the blinds," Reiner replied in German. At first his tone was quiet. "No one is out there. The wall that surrounds the garden is almost three meters high and is at least thirty meters from the house at its closest point. Over open ground! The only way in is through the front gate. But the gate is locked! And we can see through it!"

As he went on, waving the chef's knife for emphasis, his voice began to rise. "Are your friends so brave, or so stupid, that they would try to come over the fence?! In broad daylight?!"

Luco cowered on the floor. "You don't know those two," he croaked. "Especially that woman! She's a psychopath. She loves to inflict pain. Really loves it! Suppose they come at night?!"

"At night?" Reiner bellowed. "At night?! Because of you, we are lighted even more brightly than the Frankfurt airport!" For added emphasis, with a swift and powerful downward plunge, he buried the tip of the blade deep into the cutting bench.

The wall-mounted phone rang at that very instant.

Reiner and Luco both looked up at the kitchen clock. It was exactly four o'clock. Following Luco's instructions, Erika called every hour, on the hour.

The phone rang again. Reiner, glancing repeatedly at the phone, went tentatively back to preparing the vegetables.

On the third ring, Luco scrambled to his feet, motioned for Reiner to be still, took the receiver off the hook and put it to his ear. He and Reiner froze in place, looking into each other's eyes, saying nothing. Luco held his breath, listening to the silence at the other end. After several seconds that seemed like minutes, a soft, tentative voice from the other end asked, "Is it you?"

His shoulders sagged as he let out his breath. Reiner relaxed, put the knife down, stepped to the fridge, removed the cap from a bottle of beer and drank deeply.

"Yeah, sugar," Luco said with relief, "it's me." He sank onto a bar stool and continued, "Talk to me."

"There has been nothing, Luco," said Erika in the manner of a mother comforting a child who wakes from a bad dream, reassuring him that there are no ghosts lurking under the bed. "There has been nothing out of the ordinary. Just as there was nothing one hour ago, or this morning, or all week. Please, try to relax, Schatz."

"Relax? How can I relax with those two hyenas out there looking for me?" The tension in his voice was seasoned with fear. "I'm not gonna relax until this is over."

"But when, Schatz?" she pleaded, "Reiner thought it would be only a day or two but it has been more than a week. Has there been nothing available?"

"Not the right kind, sugar," Luco replied.

He looked at Reiner whose eyes said he understood what Erika had asked, without having heard her voice. With a helpless shrug of his shoulders, he told Luco, "I cannot tell you when. But it will be soon. That much I know."

"Reiner said he … ," Luco began.

"Yes Luco, I know," Erika interrupted. "I heard Reiner. I'll call again at five. Now I must go."

The phone rang the instant Luco hung up. He picked it up by reflex, thinking it was Erika calling back with something she had forgotten to tell him.

"Yes, sugar?" he said.

"How sweet," the man's voice said. "I get all misty when you call me that."

"Bonetta!" Luco soared into instant rage. "How'd you get this number?!"

"Come on, Luco. Get real," Vince answered with a scornful chuckle. "I called to bring you up to date on a couple of items. First, about our mutual friend, Phil Peters. He was overjoyed to learn that an anonymous benefactor—that's you, asshole—has paid off all his debt. He's now free and clear."

"Yeah? So what?!" said Luco bitterly.

"The second item also might be of interest to you," said Vince, giving no indication that he heard Luco's comment. "It's about your banker friend in Switzerland. He was doing a concert when he failed to return to the stage after the intermission. They found him in his car behind the theater."

"No, that's not right," Vince continued. "They found him *on* his car. He was spread-eagled, face down on the hood with his hands tied behind his back and his feet tied to the sideview mirrors. His neck was tied to what remained of a ridiculous hood ornament. He was naked from the waist down. The pointy, curled-up end of the other half of the hood ornament was stuck up hi… "

"Awright! What're you getting at?!"

"There was quite a bit of blood. Your friend was awake and screaming, but of course, with his Jockey shorts stuffed in his mouth, who could hear him? It brings new definition to the term 'stuck on the horns of a dilemma' don't you think?"

Reiner put the knife down and stopped what he was doing. He leaned heavily on both hands and listened intently, watching Luco's eyes grow wider with each passing moment as Vince spoke.

"What's your point, Bonetta?" Some of Luco's anger was displaced by wariness.

Again, Vince ignored Luco. He went on with exaggerated calm.

"How well do you know your Swiss banker friend? How much will he take just to protect you? You figure he can outlast the kind of pain Rocky Jordan and Chetta Lograno like to dish out?"

Luco remained silent. His forehead became beaded with perspiration.

Vince continued, "But what am I saying? We're only guessing that it was those two that worked him over. Yeah, it was probably just a routine mugging."

"You enjoying this, you miserable bastard?" Luco seethed.

"Oh, yeah, I am. But not nearly as much as what comes next," Vince replied with relish. "As soon as we're finished with this delightful little chat, I'm going to place another call. In about ten minutes, Tubby Bagnatore is going to know exactly where you are. His two nut-case goons will be all over you before you have a chance to go underground."

"Wait a minute!" Luco yelled. "We had a deal! I did what you told me to do. Didn't I bail out Phil Peters the way you said?"

"So I lied," said Vince. "Sue me."

"What're you trying to pull?" Luco screamed. "You said … "

"I know what I said!" Vince said sharply. He lowered his voice. His tone became brittle and frigid. "Now here's what I'm saying, you creep. You brought down the bank that it took your father a lifetime to build. You've violated every virtue that guided his life. If I thought it could erase any of the shame you've brought to his memory, I would personally strangle you without giving it a second thought. You've hurt a lot of people. Ordinary, hard-working people. Like the mother of Horace, your garage attendant. And Mrs. Masters, the lady who cleans your offices. These people have no way to get back at you. But I do, you slimy bastard."

"Yeah? Well, you said you wouldn't turn me in if I made it right for Phil Peters. And I did! Now you're gonna go back on your promise?! What does that make you?"

"An avenging angel?! A man with a mission?!" Vince snapped back harshly. His bitter rage bubbled through the surface. He forced himself to regain control before continuing. "Call it anything you like. I made a higher promise. To Phil Peters. To myself. To my father. But most of all, to the memory of my father's dearest friend, *your* father. I promised I'd make you sorry ... and I'm just getting started."

Luco skipped a beat. "What are you saying?"

"Take a peek out your front door. See the gray BMW parked across the street just outside your gate? Go on. Open your door and give them a wave."

Luco started to protest.

"No, go ahead. It's perfectly safe. They're Nürnberg cops. Matter of fact, it's Uschi Braun and her partner with the muscles. It's their day off so they thought they'd just drive by to say hello. Go ahead. Wave at them."

Luco opened the door slowly. Tentatively. Immediately, a door of the BMW flew open. Uschi stepped out and gave Luco an enthusiastic wave, bouncing on tiptoe with one arm outstretched high overhead. Luco stepped into the opening, looked furtively both ways and gave a half-hearted wave in return before stepping back inside and closing the door.

"OK. So I waved at them. Now what?"

"Tomorrow morning, they'll appear at your gate. They'll deliver you to the Nürnberg airport where a first-class ticket, with my compliments, will be waiting for you."

"What makes you think I'm going anywhere?"

"First stop will be Frankfurt." Vince totally ignored his question. "A member of the security police at the Frankfurt airport will escort you from the plane. He'll see to your comfort during your layover, after which he'll escort you to your seat for your flight to Boston."

"Boston?! No way I'm going to Boston!"

"Upon your arrival in Boston, an official from the Rhode Island Attorney General's office will greet you. That official will then escort y... "

"Awright, enough of this bullshit!" Luco forgot for the moment how frightened he was and was now livid with anger. "Get to the fuckin' point!"

"Oh. I'm sorry, Luco," pleasure permeated Vince's tone. "I thought I had made my point. I'll try to be clear. If you reject my offer, by this time tomorrow you'll be in the hands, literally speaking, of Rocky Jordan and Chetta Lograno. They can be very convincing. The cattle-horn hood ornament that your Swiss banker pal found so unpleasant was a stroke of genius, don't you agree? Try to imagine the creative delights they'll have in store for you.

"On the other hand, if you agree with the wisdom of my suggestion and accept my hospitality, you'll be safely out of their reach. Before they know what's happening, you'll be winging over the Atlantic enroute to the welcoming bosom of justice." Vince didn't even try to conceal his gleeful satisfaction.

Luco was trapped and he knew it. His mind churned out of control. He grew pale and sank heavily into a chair. Reiner raced into the kitchen and returned with a glass of water. Luco drank eagerly from it, spilling some down the front of his shirt. He handed it back to Reiner and wiped the back of his hand across his mouth. Breathing deeply, his eyes regained their focus, settling on Reiner whose look of concern seemed to have a calming effect on Luco. Luco wagged one hand in a gesture of assurance to Reiner that he was all right again.

With his eyes locked on Reiner's as though receiving a transfusion of strength and determination, Luco said, "The choice I'm left with, Bonetta, is no choice at all." There was no trace of anger, or fear, or anxiety in his voice. "I accept your offer. To do otherwise would be to express a death wish."

"A good decision," said Vince, though he was perplexed by the abrupt turnaround in Luco's demeanor.

"Actually, it'll be a relief to put this all behind me. But, I have to ask you for a little leeway."

"Spell it out, Parisi, and you better make it good."

Luco's eyes continued to hold Reiner's steadily as he continued, "Not for me. It's *my* mess. I made it on my own and I'll take whatever's coming to me. But others are involved and they had nothing at all to do with what I did. I've entered business deals with them. Can you give me a few days, a week at the most, to get myself out of their lives? Some of them have put up big money and I don't want what I did to come down on them. All I need is some time to get the lawyers to write me out of their deals. You and I both know, once I turn myself in, I won't be coming back here for a long time.

"In the meantime, you know I can't go anywhere. With your connections in this town, like your two friends out there in the BMW, you'll know where I am every minute of the day. Besides, there's no way in hell that I want to take the chance of running into Rocky Jordan and Chetta Lograno. What do you say?"

Reiner and Luco remained motionless and unbreathing with their eyes holding unblinkingly on each other's, waiting for Vince's response. There was a long pause. Then, it came.

"Seven days." Vince's voice was like ice. "One week from tomorrow morning, expect Uschi at your front door."

Vince hung up without another word.

For a long time, Luco said nothing. He punched the hang-up button without taking his eyes from Reiner's. Slowly, a grin took shape on both their faces.

FORTY-THREE

HE WAS GRATEFUL for the rain. It began without preliminaries in late afternoon just before the traffic hour, slanting down in drenching torrents that raced ahead of an angry wind. About two hours later, the wind quieted to a capricious zephyr and the rain throttled back to a steady, relentless pace.

There will be no one standing outside taking a cigarette break, he thought. Nevertheless, he kept to the far side of the employees' parking lot where he had a clear view of the receiving dock. For a long time he sat motionless, with the engine running, without lights. He never took his eyes away from the steel double doors with their small, wire-reinforced windows. Cascades of rain traced random courses down the windshield, distorting his view. It was only for a brief moment, with each pass of the wiper blades, that he was able to make out the sign above the doors that read, *Städtisches-Krankenhaus.* Nürnberg City Hospital.

One of the double doors opened. A figure appeared, silhouetted against the light that spilled out. The driver flashed his headlights on and off three times. The figure reached back inside and the lights under the shed-roof over the dock area flashed three times in return. The driver inched ahead without headlights, turned, and maneuvered the big Mercedes into position with its trunk at the base of the stairs that led up to the dock.

Neither the car's interior lights nor its trunk compartment light came on when the driver popped the trunk lid, got out and hurried up the stairs to the platform, leaving the engine running. He had thought to remove the light bulbs earlier.

One of the doors swung open as the driver approached. However, as he attempted to go inside, he ran into the man who had signaled with the lights. He was a large man, almost as large as the driver, wearing smudged, hospital whites. With a shake of his head, he pressed his hand against the driver's chest, holding him back. The driver murmured an apology and pulled an envelope from his inside pocket. The man took it, swiftly concealed it under his tunic and motioned for the driver to follow.

Minutes later, the lights over the dock area and in the inside hallway went out. The doors opened. The man stepped out, looked in every direction, then signaled the OK. Carrying a large bundle, the driver went down the stairs, quickly dumped the bundle into the trunk and firmly, but quietly, closed the lid. He got into the driver's seat and eased the door closed. When he turned to bid goodnight to the man, the dock was deserted.

FORTY-FOUR

THE CAR WENT AIRBORNE, rolled spectacularly in midair, landed on its roof and bounced nose-over-tail several times with one of its headlights still ablaze, tracing cartwheels in the low-hanging mist. It came to rest at the base of the hill.

Four hundred feet above, a large man and a woman, both dressed in black, stood at the ridge of the slope. They scanned both directions on the roadway. Seeing no headlights in either direction, the man hurled an object into the air. It came to rest halfway down the slope. The woman pointed a small, black device toward the car below and pressed a button. A flash of light illuminated the entire hillside as the car erupted into flames.

The two looked again in each direction before springing into motion. The man opened the rear door and the woman leaped quickly into the back seat. He hurried around the back of the car to the driver's door, lunged in and sped away. Without headlights.

GÜNTER'S COVER LETTER ASKED Vince to call back after reading his fax but Vince needed a little more time for the essence of it to sink in. It was a cut-and-paste of a story from the late edition of Die Nürnberger Nachrichten that began its tease below the fold on page one and jumped to page nine for photos and story.

Page nine opened with a three-column photo of the wreck scene taken after daybreak. Either the rescue team had extinguished the blaze or it had burned itself out in the steady rain, but smoke still drifted from the charred and twisted hulk and the surrounding brush. The heat from the fire had been so intense as to have transformed the car's chassis and superstructure into a surreal *objet d'art*. Without prior knowledge, it would be near impossible for an untrained observer to identify the remains as having once been an automobile.

Halfway to the top of the hill, in the background of the photo, two men struggled up the rocky, muddy slope, toward a waiting ambulance, wrestling with a litter that carried a strapped-in body bag.

In the foreground, two uniformed police, one of them a woman, both wearing rain-slickers, used a tape to measure from the wreck to an unidentified point up the slope. If he had met her in person, Vince would have recognized Uschi Braun as the officer nearest the camera.

An in-column photo of Luco Parisi, a recent one furnished by Erika Böhringer, appeared under the 24-point, two-column lead that read, in German, "American bank executive loses control of auto. Dies in fiery plunge!"

Vince read the entire story for the fifth time. It gave only the high spots of Luco's Rhode Island background that the grieving Erika and her faithful driver and man-servant Reiner had no doubt furnished. The story focused more on Luco's presence in Nürnberg. It defined his relationship with Erika only in oblique and delicate references to their living together. It named some of the more important social events at which he had appeared and it speculated on his likely connections with the prominent business leaders who had also attended those functions.

It speculated further that the cause of the crash might be linked to lack of experience, common to many Americans, in high-speed travel on the Autobahn. For emphasis, it pointed an accusatory finger at the road surface, made slick by the misting rain that had fallen all day and through the night.

Alongside, under a one-column file photo of Erika, a sidebar began by briefly defining Erika's connection with the main story. The rest of the sidebar devoted itself to Erika, her prominence in the Nürnberg social whirl, and a large measure of complimentary editorial about Mode-Erika.

"My God, Günter!" The news had shaken Vince. "I never anticipated anything like this."

"Of course not, Vince. No one could." Günter's voice from the phone was quiet and somber.

"From the photo, it's hard to believe you were able to identify the body."

"Actually, we could not identify the body. The fire burned most of it down to the skeleton. It appears that the tank ruptured and gushed into the passenger compartment, soaking the driver in gasoline an instant before the explosion and fire. The heat must have been incredible. With God's mercy, he was already dead or at least unconscious when that happened."

Vince didn't interrupt. He knew Günter would fill in the blanks in his own time.

"Vince, do you remember those two young rookies who worked so well with Max?"

"Yes I do, Günter. Uschi Braun and Gerd Weber."

"Since their special assignment ended, they have resumed normal patrol duty." Günter paused for a beat to sort it out in his mind before continuing. "They were pulling a graveyard shift last night and were first on the scene after the call came in. When the fire was extinguished and the body removed, they searched the surrounding area for possible other victims that might have been thrown from the car. They found no other bodies. But several meters up the slope from the wreck they did find something else. A wheel-cover."

"A wheel-cover?" Vince asked. "With the Autobahn running by that spot, couldn't a loose hubcap easily fly off a speeding car and find its way to that slope?"

"This wheel-cover was from a Rolls-Royce, Vince."

"That does narrow the scope of coincidence, Günter. Go on."

"As you know, those officers had recently been tailing a Rolls, so they became curious. They went back down to the wreck and examined it closely. Every centimeter of it. They could find nothing that might be used to identify the wreckage.

"Suddenly, one of them, or both of them, it doesn't matter, noticed that one end of the wreckage was partially buried in the soft, water-soaked earth. Using a loose piece of the wreckage as a spade, they dug the earth away. They found that the parts of the car that had been buried were still intact. Though the earth cover was unable to prevent the paint from burning off, apparently it had provided sufficient insulation to preserve the metal.

"Digging further, they found the license plate. The paint was gone but the raised letters were clearly readable. It was a USA plate. From Rhode Island. The same plate that they had followed from Erlenstegen to Mode-Erika. When they delivered the wheel-cover and the license plate to Max, he immediately called me."

"What about notification of next of kin?"

Günter skipped a beat. "I'm hoping you can do that for me."

"Of course, Günter."

"Frau Böhringer wants to take custody of the body and conduct a proper funeral service, but legally, she has no standing. That is, unless Mrs. Parisi is willing to sign a release. By all means, Vince, give them my name and tell them how to reach me if they want to, but I feel they might prefer to deal through you."

"I'll do it right away and I'll fax you the details of how they want you to handle it. But just one more thing."

"Yes?"

"For the sake of whatever remains of the Parisi family name, can you leave mention of his involvement with Erika out of any communication you will have with them?"

"I can. And I shall. Goodbye for now, Vince."

"Until later, Günter."

FORTY-FIVE

Providence

THE OLD GUY WEARING a battered Ben Hogan cap sent plumes of vile, blue smoke from a Parodi stogy into the night. He was standing along the sidelines with the other spectators watching the bocce matches at Cappie's Tap. He pretended not to be paying attention to the conversation that was taking place between the two men standing in front of him.

"Luco Parisi?! You gotta be kiddin' me!"

"What! I'm gonna kid about somethin' like that?"

"Come on, Willy! You tellin' me he rolled a seven?! Wha' th' fuck's he doin' over there?"

"How th' fuck do I know? All I know's what I heard. I'm deliverin' a load of laundry at The Alpine. I walk inta the office to get the receipt signed and I hear the manager talkin' to a couple a guys. He's tellin' them he just got word that Parisi croaked in a car wreck in Germany."

The old guy with the stogy quietly left the crowd and went inside to the pay phone. When the old man was finished, Tubby Bagnatore thanked him, pressed the hangup button and dialed a fourteen-digit number.

It was four in the morning Switzerland time. In a hushed whisper that was filled with sleep, Chetta answered, "Oh, hi Mr. Bagnatore," successfully concealing her annoyance.

"What the hell you whisperin' for?" The six-hour time difference never entered his mind.

"It's Rocky, Mr. Bagnatore," she continued to whisper. "He's sleeping so nice, I don't want to wake him up unless I have to."

At the mention of his name, Rocky stirred. Chetta leaned over to him, brushed his hair lightly with her hand, adjusted his bed cover and cooed softly, "Shhhh, I'm right here, sweet baby. Go back to sleep. Your babylove is right here." She had held the phone out, facing away, but Tubby was able to hear it all.

The image materialized of its own will in his mind. He could see her half-naked, hard body, stretched out next to Rocky's, her body touching his. 'No, wait,' he imagined, 'maybe she's not half-naked. Maybe she goes to bed totally bare-ass. Yeah. Yeah! I bet she goes to bed bare-ass! But what about Rocky? Was he bare-ass too? What's that she's lookin' at? His dick? Yeah! Looka' the way she's lookin' at it. Unghhhh!' He reached down between his legs for confirmation that the stirrings he felt were more than imagined.

Not since he was thirteen had he been able to see his own erection without the aid of a mirror. Nonetheless, with his hormones and chromosomes having been arranged in a straight line at birth, Tubby regularly required female assistance in satisfying his prurient needs. Bimbos to be rented for such purposes were never more than a phone call away. Having long ago come to grips with the brutal truth that women found his appearance repugnant, he no longer indulged in fantasies that included any trace of romance.

Except when they involved Chetta. His wistful yearnings for Chetta transcended reality. It wasn't a matter of being in love. He didn't love her. He wanted to *make* love to her, with all the hugging and touching and exploring and caressing and kissing that in his entire life he had never experienced. But as always, at some point in his Chetta-fantasies, he found himself face-to-face with a conundrum. When it came time to enter her, he wanted to have her, but not in the way he had his rent-a-bimbos who would, with feigned ecstasy, mount him and service him from any direction. For them, he had only to be present and flat on his back. As for his bimbos, it didn't matter to him what they thought, if, in fact, they thought at all. They made a deal. They did their job. They got paid. They got the hell out.

But Tubby grew up believing that it was the role of a real man to elevate his woman to ever-higher plateaus of pleasure. That, to do so, at some appropriate point, he should be on top, dominating and commanding the action. He *ached* to be on top. And he knew that it was not possible. Inevitably his Chetta-fantasies, flights of glorious delight, fell from the sky to crash and burn.

"Naw, that's awright, Chetta, let him sleep." Tubby took strange pleasure in talking with her 'privately' while Rocky slept. It was as close as he would ever get to pillow talk with Chetta. "First thing in the mornin' I want you and him to go to Germany."

"Germany?" she asked in a way that sounded as though she thought Germany was on another continent.

"Yeah, Nürnberg." He resisted the impulse to inform her that the border with Germany was less than five miles from her hotel. He didn't want to come off as a smart-ass and run the risk of spoiling their 'intimate' moment. "There's noise goin' around here that Luco got his ass fried in a car wreck over there."

"Awww gee, Mr. Bagnatore," she said. "And we were just starting to get somewhere with that banker clown, until someone called the cops and we had to make tracks. One more visit, though, and he'll give us what we need."

"Forget about him, honey." Tubby took the liberty of using a pet name. "You and Rocky get over there. Call me after you find out for sure what happened."

Nürnberg, Germany

ROCKY AND CHETTA HELD THEMSELVES apart from the crowd. Hundreds attended the church services. Most of them were curiosity-seekers, drawn by Erika's social status and lured by the possibility of getting a glimpse of her famous and powerful friends. When Mass was over, they had formed into small groups in the church foyer and on the steps that led down to the street while the pallbearers loaded the casket into the hearse. Rocky and Chetta paid no heed to the onlookers, focusing instead only on the casket. The moment it was inside the hearse, they made their way quickly to their rented Audi.

A small group of invited friends and relatives of Erika left the church early to avoid the crowd that they knew would gather outside. They had already made their way to the Heintke & Busch Bestattungsinstitut, a crematorium, where they waited in the small chapel. Erika had arranged a private, intimate service for them following the Mass of Christian Burial. In accordance with the wishes of Celia, Luco's widow, Heintke & Busch would FedEx the urn containing Luco's ashes to her in Cranston, Rhode Island.

The limo carrying Erika curved through the parking lot and eased to a stop under the Heintke & Busch portico with the hearse and the small procession close behind. The Audi peeled off from the procession and pulled into a parking space. Erika stepped from the limo and entered the chapel through the double glass doors. Rocky and Chetta got out of the Audi and quickly walked to a position from which they could see the casket as the pallbearers removed it from the hearse and carried it into the chapel.

Chetta then walked to the limo, opened the rear door and poked her head inside, looking around to be sure it was empty. Having observed her from inside the chapel, the limo driver pushed through the glass doors saying something aggressive to her in German. She spun on him, stuck a finger in his face and said, "Back off, dickhead!" He didn't understand a word of what she said but he did understand the look on her face.

"Ja! Ja! OK!" he said, with a strained attempt at a smile.

She turned from him and walked to the rear where Rocky had made a similar inspection of the hearse. "Nothing in the limo sweet baby," she said in a sugar-coated, sing-song lilt. "How about in there?"

"All clear in the hearse, babylove," he answered. His voice, too, was dipped in syrup.

In a few minutes, the limo and the hearse drove away. Rocky and Chetta returned to the Audi and repositioned it so they could observe the doors of the crematorium through the windshield without craning their necks. They waited.

Twenty minutes later, a black Mercedes turned into the parking lot and made its way to a stop under the portico. Reiner stepped out from the driver's seat and stood beside the car with his arms folded across his chest. Several minutes later, ushers swung the doors open. Erika took a position just inside where she took the hand of each of the mourners and exchanged a few words with them as they left. When they were all gone, Reiner opened the rear door of the Mercedes and she got in. They waited until after the last of the guests' cars had departed. Only then did the Mercedes drive away.

In the Audi, Rocky looked at his wristwatch and asked, "What time is it in Providence, babylove? I can never get it straight."

"Oh, it's so easy, sweet baby," Chetta sang as she leaned over to him. She took his wrist in one hand, and with the other, she pointed her fingernail at the hour hand of his watch. "It's quarter-to-three over here right now. So-o-o-o, pretend that the dial is the Atlantic Ocean and you wanna cross over it back to Providence. So-o-o-o, just imagine that the hour hand crosses over the ocean, like thi-i-s, to the other side of the dial, to the nine. Like magic, it's quarter-to-nine over there. See-e-e-e? It's easy."

Rocky grinned happily, like a little boy who has successfully tied his own shoelaces. Chetta couldn't resist the impulse to kiss him on the cheek.

"It might be a little early," he said, looking again at his watch. "Wudd'ya say we get a cup of coffee and kill an hour before we call him."

"Fuck the coffee. Wudd'ya say we go back to the room." The sing-song lilt had vanished and her voice took on a husky timbre. "There's better ways to kill an hour."

FORTY-SIX

Providence

"I KNOW IT'S TEN O'CLOCK but I told ya. He ain't here yet. So wha'd ya find out?"

"C'mon, Dolfo, what's the point me tellin' you when I gotta tell him all over again? Jus' call me back when he com… "

"Hey! Hold on, Rocky. Lemme put ya on hold," Dolfo cut in. "His wagon jus' pulled up out front."

GETTING INTO AND OUT of a conventional auto had grown too difficult for Tubby Bagnatore. His custom Ford van was specially fitted-out with an over-sized captain's chair on a swivel base. It was through-bolted to the floor directly opposite the sliding door. To provide easy access to it with a minimum of hunching over, the roof was raised twelve inches. At the rear, a comfortable settee faced the front with a fold-out conference table and wet bar between the settee and the captain's chair. The van heaved a sigh of relief when Tubby stepped out through the wide, sliding door.

Thumbing his lapels, he stood for a moment surveying his kingdom. To his right, the space that adjoined his office was occupied by a laundromat. It was spotlessly clean and had an enclosed kiddie area that was abundantly furnished with toys. It was unique in more than one respect. The machines always worked, there has never been an incident of vandalism, and no one has ever stolen a toy. The name painted colorfully on the window read, TUBS & BUBBLES. Though it would require a scrupulous search of the records of corporations in the Secretary of State's Office to reveal that the sole stockholder of Tubs & Bubbles is one Alphonse Bagnatore, it was a matter of common knowledge to residents of Federal Hill.

His own storefront window looked out over Atwells Avenue and was mirrored to make casual gawking difficult. Gold-leaf, serif lettering curved in a gentle arc across the window, reading, ALPHONSE BAGNATORE PUBLIC ACCOUNTANT.

Dolfo went to the door to hold it open.

"It's Rocky, Mr. Bagnatore," said Dolfo with a head motion toward the phone with its blinking line button, "from Germany."

Dolfo had been sitting at a gray steel desk with matching swivel-chair, both of which, if turned upside down, would reveal the stenciled words, CITY OF PROVIDENCE DPW. To his right was a brown, steel folding chair. It was the type used to convert a Boys' Club gymnasium into a banquet hall for a Local 57 Beer & Pasta Night. It stood next to an end table that could only be defined as neo-noncommittal. Lighting was provided by recessed, overhead fluorescent fixtures whose frosted plastic panels served as the final resting place for dozens of dead bugs.

There were no file cabinets. Tubby's services generated no paperwork.

"I'll take it in back o' the office," Tubby answered. "Gimme a minute."

A door leading to the rear was located next to Dolfo's desk. The only way into the rear quarters from the street was through that door. The only way to get to that door was to get past Dolfo.

Entering the rear office, the contrast between its exquisite comfort and the dreary dinginess of the front office was breathtaking. But it was the absence of sound that was first apparent. All the walls, including the wall and door that separated the back from the front, were fully sound-proofed. Muted, indirect lighting highlighted elegant, floor-length, Siamese tapestries that alternated with panels of hand-carved travertine marble.

Rich, plush, deep-pile carpeting covered the entire floor. Except for a twelve-by-twelve-foot section near the restroom. That area was used for conducting interviews. The type of interview that was suffered by Mickey Hoban at the hands of Rocky Jordan and Chetta Lograno. In deference to the stubborn nature of any blood that might likely be spilled, ceramic tile covered that area of the floor to facilitate janitorial services.

With an agility that was incongruous to his massive girth, Tubby made his way to his richly carved and polished oak desk. Nevertheless, the exertion left him wheezing for breath. He sank into his custom-made executive chair and surveyed the room, waiting for his breath to come back before reaching for the phone.

"So awright, Rocky, what're you got?"

"We been with Parisi every minute since we got here, Mr. Bagnatore," said Rocky. His manner of delivering a report carried no fluff. "Chetta and me went to his requiem Mass this morning. His girlfriend's a real looker. Must be some kinda important broad. Lotta big shot friends was there. Lotta gawkers too, eye-balling the big shots. There wasn't no wake. Just the Mass. Casket was closed. We hear he was burned up pretty bad in the crash. Then they took him to another place and left the casket there. Gonna cremate what's left of him. That's it, Mr. Bagnatore."

"Awright. So that's it." For Tubby, Rocky's closing sentence carried dual meaning. It meant Rocky was finished with his report. It also meant Tubby's hopes of getting at Luco's stash of money were finished as well. "You and Chetta can come on back now."

FORTY-SEVEN

Nürnberg, Germany

THE NOON LUNCH CROWD WAS at full throttle when Günter jogged up the outdoor staircase of the Bratwursthäusle. He scanned the terrace that looked out over Mode-Erika and the Schöne-Brunnen on the Hauptmarkt across the street. Only two seats were available and those were at occupied tables. Though it was a commonly accepted practice to take a vacant seat at an otherwise occupied table, those two seats were at widely separated tables. Maybe Max was already inside.

Passing through the heavy timber doors, the noise level was nerve-rattling. He had to make his way through the waiting standees who crowded the foyer. They didn't make it easy for him. Man and woman alike, they glowered and muttered epithets at him, grudgingly giving way to him only after he was left with no alternative than to elbow and shoulder his way through.

Günter reflected on how he had never before noticed the surly and aggressive attitude of his fellow Germans when they are waiting for something. Like boarding a tram. Or waiting for the next teller in a bank. Or making their way into a checkout line at the market. After several visits to Naples, Florida, the difference between how his fellow Germans handled themselves in such situations was in stark contrast to the way he found it in America. In similar situations in Naples, most Americans he encountered would engage him in friendly chatter. About anything. The weather. Their kids. Where they are from. Where you are from. Anything. Amazingly, they will step aside and hold the door for you to pass through first. He found older people being kind to young and young being kind to old. It was clear that age had nothing to do with being nice. And the cashiers actually smiled and joked with you.

Having made his way through the crowd to the main dining room with its centrally located, flaming grill, he saw in the far left corner a man waving vigorously to him. It was Max. He had been holding the last vacant seat at his table for Günter, warding off hostile glares from waiting patrons who wanted it.

Taking the seat, Günter looked back at the waiting crowd before turning to Max and saying, "My God, Max. I think they were forming up to attack." He was only half kidding. "How did you manage to hold them off?"

"Like this," Max said with a grin. He rose halfway from the seat and unbuttoned his jacket, letting it fall open to expose the holstered gun that he wore on his belt. He laughed and Günter joined in.

The others at their table completely ignored them. Incongruous as it may seem, in spite of the close proximity of their table partners and the loud, frenetic ambiance, it was possible to have a private conversation. They each ordered Bratwürste, Meerrettich, Sauerkraut, and Warsteiner beer. For a minute or two they didn't say anything of any more substance than, "How have you been?" or "Good to see you again," giving their tablemates space in which to return to where they had left off in their own conversations.

A hand clutching two huge mugs of beer with white, foamy heads reached over Günter's shoulder and placed them on the wooden table with a loud thunk. They picked them up, touched them together, said, "Prost," and took a long pull.

"OK, Max. What is it you thought would be so interesting?"

Max turned deadly serious. "It's about that Parisi fellow. The one you 'interviewed' at the Grand Hotel? You know about the accident, of course."

"Of course," Günter replied. "You reported it to me."

"His car went off the road? Rolled down a hill and burst into flames? We are absolutely certain that it was Luco Parisi's Rolls. Remember?"

"Yes, Max. I do remember. It was only four weeks ago, you know. I'm not that old and feeble yet." Günter said it with a smile, trying to lighten up Max's strangely somber mood. It didn't work.

"The driver was killed? Burned beyond recognition?"

"Max, I already know all that," Günter's mood also became serious. "It was in your report. What is this *really* about?"

Max nodded and raised his hand slightly in a gesture that asked Günter to be patient. After a moment, he went on, "The night before the accident, at Das Städtische-Krankenhaus? There was a theft."

"Someone stole something from the hospital? My God, Max. It must be a crime wave." Günter's attempt at humor fell flat on its face. He continued on a more serious note, "What possible connection can there be between that and the death of Luco Parisi?" He regretted the annoyance that had crept into his tone and was glad that Max didn't seem to notice it.

"A body," Max said simply.

It took a moment for Günter to sort that out. "A body? As in a human body?"

Max nodded.

"A human body was stolen?!"

"The night before Parisi's accident," said Max with another affirming nod of his head. "A seventy-year-old wino. He was found dead in an alley. No ID, and as of this moment, no one has yet tried to claim him. Last time anyone saw him he was laid out on a gurney in the hospital corridor." His serious act was over. He broke into a broad, gotcha smile.

"What are you saying, Max?" Günter asked. Then, after a short moment, a grin began to form when he realized where Max was going with this.

"Just considering the possibilities, old friend," said Max. He, too, was enjoying this. "An unidentifiable stiff disappears the night before an accident? An accident in which the only victim is ... an unidentifiable stiff?"

FORTY-EIGHT

Naples, Florida
Eleven months later

THEY WERE COMING TO THE END of an idyllic weekend. The last two days, spent in utter indolence, were a rare treat for them and it would be the last one for a long while.

It had been months since Günter and Margrit's last stay in their magnificent new home in Silver Dunes. They would arrive again in a few days, and if their coming visit turned out to be anything like their last one, the Bonettas and the Lehmanns were looking into the teeth of six frenetic weeks of social whirling. Gabriele and Margrit thrived on it. Their husbands stoically endured it.

Having given themselves over to sloth for the weekend, Vince and Gabriele had summarily discarded any idea that could in any way be considered useful or constructive. For two days, they did nothing and went no place that required anything more elegant than shorts, tank-tops and scruffy sneakers. They had turned off the world and shrunk its horizons to the very space they occupied at any given moment, focusing only on each other.

Vince and Gabriele enjoyed each other's company. At times they chattered like teenagers. At times they communicated in eloquent silence, their thoughts joined by the punctuation of a passing touch, a hug from nowhere, a glance that recited poetry about love and devotion.

AFTER THEIR LONG, LAZY walk down the beach to Gordon Pass and back, they stopped at the tiki bar of a beachfront hotel. They had hoped to watch the sunset over a quiet cocktail. Before long though, the Sunday evening crowd of sunset-watchers grew in size. The volume of their chatter and the music from the small jazz combo intruded on their mellow mood. Vince and Gabriele abandoned their drinks and went down to the water's edge for a more intimate view of the approaching sunset.

It promised to be spectacular. The horizon remained brilliantly defined as the sun passed behind uneven layers of gold-trimmed stratus. As it increased its rate of descent before sinking into the Gulf, it radiated shimmering bands of red, yellow and orange to ignite the spaces between the clouds.

The electronic chirp of a cell phone was so foreign to the moment that it startled them.

"Oh, damn!" she cried with a tiny whimper.

"You brought your phone?" Vince asked incredulously.

"I didn't mean to, Schatz. Honest. I forgot to switch it to my other bag." Her eyes and her tone gave the apology as the phone chirped again.

"You don't *have* to answer it," Vince said helplessly but they both knew that Gabriele was pathologically incapable of leaving a ringing telephone unanswered. She shrugged in resignation as she reached into her tote bag and pulled out the phone.

"Hello." She touched her hand tenderly to Vince's cheek and looked into his eyes for understanding.

"Good evening, Mrs. Bonetta." It was a man. She couldn't recognize the pleasant and friendly voice. "Can you put Vince on please?"

Her hesitation asked the question.

"I'm just a friend from the old neighborhood in Providence and I want to surprise him." His voice and his manner were ingratiating. "It's for you." She handed the phone to Vince.

Vince put the phone to his ear but before he could say a word, the caller spoke.

"That's a great body Gabi's got under that pink bikini. Not too many broads her age could pull that off. You're a lucky man, Bonetta."

There was no threat in the man's voice. He seemed simply to be making an admiring assessment.

The voice was one that Vince felt he should recognize. Though he couldn't place it, something about it made his animus rise. His senses went on alert. They were being watched. How else could the caller have known when to begin talking? And how else could the caller know what Gabriele was wearing?

"Is that what you called me for? To tell me something I already know?" Vince measured his tone, keeping it light and non-confrontational. He wanted to hear more of the voice. Nonetheless, the look in his eyes and the way he slowly turned and scanned the crowd at the tiki bar made Gabriele mouth the question, "Who is it?" Vince silently shushed her with a finger to his lips and a shake of his head.

The sun had fallen below the horizon, leaving a star-filled but moonless sky. Yet, Vince and Gabriele were still dimly illuminated by the light that spilled from the tiki bar and the hotel's pool area onto the darkened beach.

The caller ignored Vince's question. "You didn't finish your drinks. And after such a long walk down the beach. My ass is still dragging. I was right there behind you all the way. Only thing made it worthwhile was the great view I had of your wife's ass in that bikini. Nothing personal, Bonetta, but you gotta admit, your wife's got world class buns. She puts 'em in a bikini, a guy's got to be in a coma not to look."

Vince was even more convinced that the voice was familiar. The caller spoke in a street dialect that would be familiar to anyone who grew up on The Hill. Old friends—*good* friends—growing up together on Federal Hill could talk to each other appreciatively about each other's girl friend or wife. If done with respect and within the bounds of proper street protocol, it was harmless and often complimentary.

Instinctively, Vince sensed that the caller intended no overt disrespect. Nevertheless, since Vince had been away from Federal Hill for much of his adult life, he could think of no one who should assume to have the right to open a conversation with him in that way.

"So you enjoyed your walk on the beach. Is there more to this?" Vince's annoyance rose to the top.

"Oh, yeeeah, Bonetta," said the caller with a dirty chuckle, "there's lots more."

The voice clicked. It was the dirty chuckle that did it. In his mind, Vince could see the contorted smile that went with it. Suddenly, everything that Günter had described to him a year earlier fell into place: the absence of skid marks where the car left the road, the Rolls wheel cover that turned up unscathed, the abnormally intense heat of the fire that burned the victim's body almost to the bone, the theft of the wino's body the night before the accident, no witnesses to anything.

Instinctively, determined not to register the astonishment he felt, Vince remained silent while he sorted it all out.

"Ah-ha! Looks like I've got your attention." The caller was feeling smug.

"What kind of a scam are you running this time, asshole?" Vince said it with uninflected blandness. Gabriele turned to Vince in wide-eyed wonder. He didn't notice. His focus was on Luco Parisi. He wasn't going to give him the satisfaction of hearing any shock or surprise in his reaction.

"A fine way to greet an old friend. I just called to thank you, Bonetta." Some condescension crept into his tone.

"Right. I tracked you down on another continent, forced you to pony up 837 thousand dollars to a guy you hate, and sic'd Tubby Bagnatore on you." Icicles had formed in Vince's voice. "Thank me my ass! What the hell are you talking about?"

"I read where half the banks in the State of Rhode Island have gone down for the count, including Greater Providence. Their remains are being force-fed to the big guys, banks like Fleet, Hospital Trust, People's, Citizen's, a few others.

"It took almost a year but I see the new governor's got a plan. Looks like every poor sap with money in Greater Providence Bank will get back every penny. That includes that fat tub of shit, Alphonse Bagnatore. They say it'll be paid out over a three-year period, no interest, but hey, nobody will lose a dime."

"I can read the papers, Parisi. Get to the point."

Parisi ignored Vince and continued, "Among other things for which he is better known, Tubby's an accountant. He'll do OK in this. Sure, he'd still like to turn Rocky and Chetta loose on me but he's out of luck. Luco Parisi is dead. That's the breaks."

Vince was put off balance by Parisi's manner. He couldn't detect any anger in it.

"What's so great about Luco Parisi being 'dead?' "

"Glad you asked. I wasn't making any headway with my girlfriend's powerful buddies. The local movers and shakers crowd. My fault, I learned too late. I came on to them like I was Donald Trump and I was gonna show the local yokels a thing or two about dealing. What a jerk. I'm chump change compared to those guys. I was an asshole."

"Hey, Luco. Who's better at it than you? After all, you've had a lifetime of practice."

"Fuck you, Bonetta!" Parisi responded too quickly and with more heat than he had intended. He immediately regretted that he let Vince go one up on him.

Vince spun quickly to see several heads at the tiki bar swivel simultaneously toward a single focal point and wondered if those people were near enough to Parisi to have overheard him. He scanned the crowd but couldn't see anyone holding a phone.

Luco collected himself then continued. "By the time I wised up, it was too late. They had me pegged. They tolerated me out of respect for my girlfriend, Erika, but they made it clear they weren't going to let me into their circle. Then you ran your sting on me with that faggot in the hotel. I gotta tell you, Bonetta, I was pissed." He said it lightly, with a smile evident in his voice.

"*Was* pissed?! I still don't get it." Vince had done everything he could to hurt Luco. To make him feel the pain for what he had done. He couldn't understand why Parisi was speaking of his anger in past tense. Vince felt that without Luco's continuing anger, his revenge would be unconsummated.

"My whole angle was going down the toilet. I kept trying to move in on those high rollers. Get them to take my money in with theirs. I mean, Bonetta, those guys are into top drawer stuff. But like I said, they froze me out.

"At that point, things didn't look too bright for my plans. Then you came along and told me Tubby's two psychotics were breathing down my neck and you were gonna tell them how to find me. I was scared. I mean, *really* scared."

"Oh, now I get it. Yeah. I can see you'd really want to thank me for that. What was I thinking?" Vince masked his confusion with sarcasm.

"What. I'm gonna carry a grudge?!"

"Are you forgetting it was your twenty-year-old grudge against Phil Peters that started all this, you idiot?" Vince was incredulous.

"What is it with you, Bonetta?" Parisi barked as he flared up. "You just like pushing my buttons?" He waited to get back down before going on. "I'm trying to tell you. This is different. You forced me to take evasive action. When Reiner came up with this scam," Luco continued without missing a beat, "I jumped at it. It worked like a charm and nobody got hurt. After a couple of months in Vienna in one of them swanky private hospitals I'm even better-looking than I was before. And now, as far as her big shot pals are concerned, Erika has a brand new boy friend. Me! I learned how to come on real quiet and polite-like and throw in a lot of that 'aw shucks' bullshit and they think I'm the best goddamm thing since Gary Cooper. Life is beautiful, Bonetta. And you made it all happen."

"Don't thank me yet, asshole," Vince was seething.

Gabriele didn't like what she saw in Vince's eyes. The simmering determination to go after Parisi again. To bring him down hard.

She took his face in her hands and kissed him gently on the lips. Pressing herself to him, she murmured in his ear, "No, Schatz. Please. Not again. It no longer matters. Don't you see? Luco has money, yet he has nothing. He doesn't even know who he is. Luco Parisi died in a car wreck. Now he must spend the rest of his life being dead. He has no family, no friends, no love. We have all of those. And we have each other."

Vince held her close. She tilted her face up to read his eyes. She nuzzled her face into the crook of his neck. Vince melted. He felt totally in love with his wife. His rage, his need for revenge, his contempt for Luco, slowly drained away. They clung to each other, oblivious to the music and the party sounds from the tiki bar and the shallow waves that lapped at their ankles.

They became aware of Luco's voice on the phone. "Bonetta?" he called. "You still there, Bonetta?"

Vince's tone was strangely calm as he brought the phone to his ear and said, "You may be wrapped in a new package, Parisi, but you're the same pile of slime you always were. Someone will recognize you or … "

"Not a chance, Bonetta," Luco interrupted, making no attempt to conceal his gloating. "You and your wife had a drink right here at the tiki bar, two stools away from me. I looked you right in the eye and you didn't have a clue."

" … more likely, you'll revert to character," Vince continued as though Luco had said nothing, "and you'll unzip your fly with someone else's woman. I'll bet you've already singled one out. You ready to put a move on her yet?"

"Yeah, awright, Bonetta!" Luco retorted. All pretenses of cordial familiarity vanished and were replaced with hateful anger. "Maybe I have. Yeah! And maybe I will!"

"Oh, there's no maybe about it, but I'd think twice before tipping my hand if I were you. Of course, you've already figured that out, haven't you? Why else would you be here in Naples? You could have made this call from Germany."

It had simply come to Vince with no conscious effort on his part and it became clearer as he spoke.

"But Germany isn't the same, is it? You're finding out Nürnberg isn't Federal Hill. You've got no local network over there. Erika spends her days in her shop, leaving you on the loose with all those women, the wives and girlfriends of the power hitters you keep talking about, ready to be plucked from the vine, but you don't dare because you don't know who's connected and who isn't. So you traveled 4,000 miles to get laid where it's safe.

"You'll soon get tired of that and then you won't be able to resist the easy pickings in Nürnberg. You'll slither into some woman's bed. Problem is, it just might be the wrong bed. And when you do, you'll find out just how much clout those heavy hitters carry. They didn't get where they are without squishing a few insects like you along the way. They've got the money and the power and they've got the connections. You could become the main ingredient in a shipment of Bratwürste. And it'll be condemned for containing putrid meat."

"Fuck you, Bonetta, you son-of-a-bitch!" Luco yelled. "Fuck you!" The party chatter at the tiki bar fell silent and all heads swiveled toward one direction.

Smiling broadly, Vince said, "Luco ... or whatever name you're using now ... you'll never know how much I appreciate your sentiments. It's been real nice."

Vince pressed the power-off button and dropped the phone into Gabriele's tote bag. He took her face in his hands and kissed her eyes and her cheeks, and just before he kissed her lips, she said softly, "How about we go home and see if we can steam up Admiral Bristow's binoculars?"

THE END

THE THIRD WIRE

This exciting new novel
by Al Giannini
is soon to be released.
Look for it online
or in your favorite bookstore.
Its opening chapter appears
on the following pages.

Chapter One

She wasn't sure if it was the hot sun combining with the gimlet she sipped that made her eyelids droop, or if it was the afterglow of having just had sex with her friend's husband. Not that she cared one way or the other. She felt radiant.

Sitting up on a cushioned chaise lounge beside her pool, hugging her legs, she took another long pull from her gimlet. The spirited meanderings of Corelli's *Concerto Grosso in D Major* wafted from the outdoor speakers on her lanai. Softly. She would never play her music so loud as to be an intrusion upon the serenity of her neighbors. On the other hand, she didn't give a passing thought to getting in some afternoon nooky with one of their husbands. After all, she reasoned, who's to know?

She refilled the glass and dangled it languorously over the side of her chaise as she lay back to soak up the sun. Surrendering to the drowsiness that overtook her, she aimlessly scanned the lake that lapped gently ashore not more than forty feet away. Feeling something brush against her hand, she recoiled in surprise. Attila, her dark gray Lhasa apso, had taken refuge under the chaise to get out of the mid-afternoon, South Florida sun. He deftly stole a few quick, lapping slurps from the gimlet she dangled in her hand before she could pull it away.

Roslyn said, "Oh, what the hell," and with a giggle, placed the glass on the floor next to him. As Attila slurped happily, she cooed, "Go ahead, Attila honey. Drink up. Mommy's gonna have to find you a nice little bimbo and get you laid, poor baby." She rested her head back and finished with a dreamy sigh, "Then you can feel as fabulous as I do." Finished with his drink, Attila yawned widely, stretched out and went to sleep.

After a few moments, Roslyn reached again for her glass to take another sip but suddenly remembered who had been drinking from it. She loved Attila dearly but drinking from his glass would be going across the line, she thought. She reached instead for the pitcher and drank from it, draining the small amount that remained. Droplets of condensation fell from the pitcher and traced a cool path down the valley between her breasts.

The flow of air across the surface of the small lake rustled the fronds of the palm trees that separated her house from her neighbors' on both sides. Barely qualified to be called a breeze, it was, nonetheless, sufficient to provide some cooling to her flesh, still damp with perspiration from the exertion of having sex only minutes earlier.

The ever-present mockingbirds engaged themselves in a spirited and melodic colloquy. While they carried their discussion from tree to tree, Roslyn's eyes fell closed and she sank toward the dark-gray murkiness that hangs in suspension between wakefulness and sleep. She loves the sights and sounds of nature's creatures and wanted to stay awake but it became impossible to keep her eyes open. It was only the insistent call of a loggerhead shrike that prevented her from falling into a dead sleep.

With each piercing screech of the tiny bird, Roslyn's eyelids flickered half open, just long enough to take a snapshot of the pastoral scene before her. She caught a glimpse of the anhinga, ten yards offshore. It paddled slowly with its body fully submerged, only its long neck and head above water. Roslyn's eyes fell closed again. She didn't see the anhinga when it dived, remained under for a long time, and reappeared with a fish impaled on its beak, fifteen yards from where it went under.

At another shrill call of the shrike, her eyelids parted to glimpse a freeze-frame view of two Muscovy ducks wading at water's edge directly in front of her. She stopped fighting it, and with a languid sigh, allowed herself to drift toward sleep.

Suddenly, Attila wakened with a start. Scrambling to his feet, with his hair on end, he ran to the screen, alternately growling and barking wildly, prancing back and forth on his forelegs. His uproar brought Roslyn out of her stupor. At that instant, there was a sudden splash, a thrashing of wings and a frenzied, squawking clamor from the Muscovy ducks.

Roslyn bolted upright, startled and wide-awake. With its four-foot wings flapping frantically, one of the ducks hurtled across the water in emergency takeoff mode, shrieking in panic. There was no sign of the other duck. In its place, a large, dark, glistening apparition retreated and disappeared below the disturbed surface of the water. Roslyn shivered involuntarily. She hugged herself. Goosebumps covered her flesh.

Attila witnessed the whole thing. Suffering an abrupt reversal in self-confidence, he streaked back to her and leaped into the chaise. Cowering and whimpering, he burrowed his muzzle into Roslyn's lap.

She scooped up her towel. Hugging Attila tightly to her bosom, she stumbled backwards into the house, unable to pull her eyes from that spot in the water.

To contact the author...

giannini@exit18.com

JAMES PAUL PUBLISHING COMPANY
4888 Davis Boulevard Box 110
Naples, Florida 34104